MICHIGAN BRIDES

THREE-IN-ONE COLLECTION

AMBER STOCKTON

BARBOUR
PUBLISHING

Scripture quotations are taken from the King James Version of the Bible.

This book is a work of fiction. Names, characters, places, and incidents are either products of the author's imagination or used fictitiously. Any similarity to actual people, organizations, and/or events is purely coincidental.

Cover Design: Kirk DouPonce, DogEared Design

Published by Barbour Publishing, Inc., P.O. Box 719, Uhrichsville, Ohio 44683, www.barbourbooks.com

Our mission is to publish and distribute inspirational products offering exceptional value and biblical encouragement to the masses.

 Member of the
Evangelical Christian
Publishers Association

Printed in the United States of America.

Dear Readers,

I am excited to share this collection with you. Making history come alive by showcasing the people who lived it is a passion of mine. To pen stories set at a time when the United States was changing during the Industrial Revolution is rewarding in and of itself.

Since my first book, you have sent encouraging and heartwarming letters, postcards, and e-mails telling me how much you enjoy my characters, the historical detail, and the stories I've written. I am truly touched by each note I read. Without readers like you, my career would be short-lived, so I thank each and every one of you from the bottom of my heart. You are the reason I write.

My career relies heavily on hearing from you, so please keep in touch. Share what you like or don't like about my books, and tell me if there's a setting or story you'd like to read in the future. I love to meet my readers through e-mail, letters, or online venues such as Facebook, Twitter, or my blog.

- Facebook: www.facebook.com/tiffanyamberstockton

- Amber Stockton Readers Group: www.facebook.com/group.php?gid=117209102310

- Twitter: www.twitter.com/amberstockton

- Blog: amberstockton.blogspot.com

- Web site: www.amberstockton.com

Looking forward to hearing from you.

Sincerely,
Amber Stockton

COPPER
AND CANDLES

Dedication

My top appreciation goes to my husband and my family on both sides for their unfailing support. Thanks also to my editors, JoAnne Simmons, Rachel Overton, and April Stier Frazier. I'd be lost without all of you! Supreme gratitude to my heavenly Father for the gift and joy of writing. It's a blessing to reach so many readers and touch lives through this creative outlet.

Chapter 1

Detroit, Michigan, April 1875
Near the business district

Felicity Chambers brushed sweat-soaked tendrils off Lucy Gibson's forehead. "Make sure you get some rest today, Mrs. Gibson. I don't want to return after work and find that you have overtaxed yourself."

The woman offered a weak smile, not even bothering to open her eyes. "I will."

The strain of a recent fever had taken its toll on the woman's frail body. Felicity's charity work involved delivering meals to the Gibson home. When complications developed from Lucy's pregnancy at just four months, the woman was forced to quit work at the candle factory. How could Felicity turn a blind eye to the need?

To her left another girl a couple of years younger than her nineteen years managed to corral the youngest boy of five children and get him settled in his high chair for breakfast.

"Marianne," Felicity said over her shoulder, "Timothy has been told that if you should need anything at all today, you are to send him to the factory to find me." She smiled at the thought of Lucy's oldest, the scrappy, quick-witted lad who had secured a place in her heart at her first visit to this home.

"Yes, ma'am." The young girl bobbed her head then turned her attention back to the toddler in her care.

Marianne lived two doors down and came to care for the home and children. With Lucy bedridden at the doctor's orders, Marianne was needed now more than ever. The other four children, ranging in age from three to eleven, scampered around the small house. Soft giggles and exclamations followed them. At least they showed respect for their mother's condition. Their shoes had holes and their clothes were a bit ragged, but they had a warm house and food in their bellies. With their mother unable to work, all of that would be taken away. Felicity couldn't let that happen.

On impulse she had sought employment at the factory and promised to give Lucy her wages. Felicity had grown tired of the constraints of her life of luxury. Working at the factory afforded her the chance at adventure without Mother dictating what charity work to do and overseeing her every move. For the first time in her life, she had a feeling of independence. She had chosen this work, and it felt good. It had seemed like the perfect solution. But now she wasn't so sure.

Grabbing her lunch pail and shawl for warmth against the cool spring morning, Felicity stepped outside and pulled the creaky, splintering door closed behind her. She smoothed a hand down the coarse fabric of her borrowed clothes. So different from the fine silks and linens she normally wore.

Am I ready for this?

Taking a deep breath and offering a silent prayer, Felicity stepped through the whitewashed gate with the chipped paint and hooked the latch. No sense prolonging the inevitable. And despite her reservations, she actually looked forward to this change of pace. Her charity work allowed her to see how less fortunate and struggling individuals lived.

But this! Working in a factory as a commoner, side by side with other girls nearing twenty or younger? It was almost more than she ever could have imagined. She'd wanted a change of pace from the never-ending parade of teas, invitations to come calling, and other social functions. And now she had it.

As she walked east toward the business district, Felicity took note of her surroundings. Small homes, some on the brink of collapse, lined both sides of the street. They were so close together it was hard to imagine the residents having any privacy. She thought about her own town house on the northwest side of the city. Healthy, green lawns and impressive gardening at the front and rear accented the brick three-story house with black shutters. A wrought-iron railing flanked both sides of the seven marble steps leading to the front door. Quite a difference from the overgrown cement and sometimes dirt paths that led to the fronts of these homes.

Felicity left the residential area and entered the business district. Only this part of the district wasn't anything like where she'd been with her father on more than one occasion. She quickened her pace to a brisk walk. It wasn't the first time she'd been in areas similar to this, but she still needed to be on her guard.

Garbage littered the ground at almost every turn. The disgusting odor forced Felicity to breathe through her mouth instead of her nose. She would have held a handkerchief over her face, but she'd left it at the Gibsons' with her personal belongings.

Her eyes watered at the acrid stench of decay. If she wasn't overcome by the smell, she might make it far enough to escape this part of the city. Felicity averted a mangy cat that looked like he hadn't eaten in weeks. Barking dogs and the screech of another cat from a nearby alley joined with the shouts of some of the street vendors hawking their wares.

"Customerrrr, come he-re!" called the singsong voice of a traveling vendor who walked beside his cart, laden with items of every shape and size imaginable.

Never in her life had Felicity seen so many different types of people clustered together in one place, nor so many faces reflecting despair and sad acceptance.

Did her efforts even make a difference? She had so much, and they had so little, yet they seemed to work hard despite their circumstances. The sooner she moved past this area, the better. Felicity didn't know how much longer she could endure the cacophonous sounds and heartbreaking sights.

She turned right at the next intersection, relieved she had almost reached the area near the factories, when raised and heated voices just ahead of her drew her attention. Stopping in her tracks, she took note of five men facing off in the middle of the street. Three of them stood face-to-face against the other two, and by the looks on their faces, the words they spoke were anything but friendly.

An inner voice told her to keep moving, but the prospect of a possible fight drew her like a child reaching out to touch a hot stove. She'd heard of brawls from her older brother, but she'd never witnessed one firsthand. And the thrill of danger was too tempting to ignore.

"I said I'd teach you a lesson with my fists if I caught you on my turf again."

This came from the shortest of the five men, but what he lacked in height, he made up for in bravado.

"And I told you we wasn't on your turf. Your man here"—the one on the defense pointed at a brawny man beside the first one who spoke—"he told you we was. But he should get his eyes checked."

The big man referenced swore loudly and took a step forward, but the shorter one held him back. Felicity gasped at the profanity.

"It's my word against yours," the first man countered. "And I say you *was* on my turf."

"I say we settle this right here and now."

More expletives came from both sides. Felicity had only heard *of* these words. She'd never been present to hear them spoken. No wonder Mother kept her sheltered.

Felicity held her breath. She looked around to see only a handful of kids and a few spectators who had gathered. Everyone else went about their business as usual. Why didn't someone stop this? Did they not care? But instead of stepping away, she edged closer, drawn into the small crowd.

No sooner had she settled in place than the shortest man threw the first punch with a sickening thud. Felicity gasped and covered her mouth. It was three on two, unfair odds in her estimation, but the two seemed to handle themselves fairly well. The crack of fist on flesh and bone made her cringe and close her eyes. She peered through one eye and then the other, almost not wanting to know how the fight progressed.

As one man tackled another and rammed them both into the ground, Felicity jumped back. The violence had begun in a small area, and it now expanded as the men swung at and dodged each other. Well-placed blows knocked them down and widened the circle of their dispute.

All right. She had seen enough. Why any man would lower himself and engage in this type of atrocious, animalistic behavior was beyond her. Felicity stepped back and turned away from the ghastly sight. She had almost made it to a vacant lot when the thump of one body hitting another caused her to look over her shoulder—just in time to see a man flying in her direction.

☙

Brandt Lawson ran down the garbage-littered street, the thud of his scuffed leather shoes on dirt keeping time with the frantic beat of his heart. He'd be late if he didn't hurry. He turned the corner only to have the wind knocked out of him as his forward motion suddenly changed direction. His lunch pail flew from his grasp. Sailing through the air for what felt like an eternity, Brandt hit the ground—hard.

It took him a few moments to catch his breath and clear his head. Vague awareness filtered through his mind as the shock wore off. Movement on top of him made him open his eyes. He propped himself on his elbows. Pain shot through his shoulder. As he tried to inch backward, he saw the mass of dark tresses splayed out on his chest, some pinned in a haphazard fashion on top of the woman's head while others tumbled free from their confinement.

"Mmmm."

The mumble came from somewhere within the tangle of hair, and the female form on top of him shifted. His senses took over, and he placed his hands around her as he attempted to move into a sitting position. Unable to do so with the weight of the other person, Brandt instead slid out from under her and knelt beside her.

The young woman's head rolled to the left and right, but she didn't open her eyes. At least she looked all right. Then again, Brandt had absorbed the majority of the impact. He glanced around to see what had caused her fall and saw the unruly bunch of men fighting not ten yards from where he and the young woman now rested.

Great. Just what he didn't need. He was already running late for his meeting before work, and now he had to be interrupted by a street fight. All attention from the crowd was focused on the men. Except for one young boy. The lad stood halfway between them and the group of spectators, his eyes wide and his mouth open.

Brandt turned his attention again to the young woman and smoothed back the hair from her face.

"Miss?" He patted her cheek a few times. "Miss, are you hurt?"

She stirred beneath his touch. Her eyelids fluttered then opened. She blinked several times, as if trying to gauge her surroundings. As soon as she focused on him, she sat up with a start and placed one hand on her chest.

"Dear me! I must apologize. Are you the person who broke my fall?"

Brandt opened his mouth to reply, but the lyrical, polished sound of her voice left him speechless. It stood in direct opposition to the fashion of clothing she wore. The young woman didn't seem to notice, though, as she continued with her ramble.

"It happened so suddenly." She swept one arm outward in an arc around her body. "One moment I was minding my own business and walking to work. The next I stopped to observe a shocking display of immature behavior." Her gaze stretched toward the ongoing fight. "Before I knew it, one of the men came flying toward me. I tried to escape, but to no avail." She looked back at him, her hazel eyes soft and apologetic. "If it hadn't been for your opportune presence, I might have suffered a more serious injury."

Opportune? Brandt wasn't sure he'd call it that. In fact, it couldn't have happened at a more *in*opportune time. He would have told her that if it hadn't been for the way her head tilted to one side as she regarded him. A dimple in her cheek appeared just to the right of her mouth, and she scrunched her eyebrows together in a most appealing manner. With a glance downward, Brandt realized she still sat in a heap on the ground. He silently scolded himself as he stood and extended both hands to her.

"Forgive me for neglecting my manners. Can I help you up?"

One corner of her mouth tugged upward, and amusement danced in her eyes. She offered her hand to him and accepted his assistance. When they were both on their feet facing each other, Brandt almost took a step back. Her head fell a few inches shy of his own. He stood just over six feet. He'd never encountered a young woman only four inches shorter than him.

But as much as he would have liked to stay and get to know more about her, duty called.

"I'm sorry to rush off, but I was already late when we ran into each other. And now unless I run I have no hope of getting to my meeting on time."

"There is no need for an apology. It's my fault for choosing you as my cushion instead of the street." She glanced again to the group of men who were the real cause of the delay and grimaced. "If it hadn't been for my curiosity, neither of us would be in this predicament."

And what a predicament it was. Under other circumstances, Brandt might have been more upset. But he didn't mind such a charming young woman being the additional reason for his tardiness.

He regarded her with a curious eye. "Well, as long as you're all right."

She dusted off her skirts, tugged down the edge of her blouse, and reached up a hand to touch her hair. A grimace crossed her delicate features, followed by a resigned shrug as she no doubt realized the tangled mess was a lost cause.

"I'm fine. I assure you. Now off with you before the number of minutes you're late is beyond excuse."

Brandt bent to retrieve his cap from the street and slapped it on his head. When he turned, he kicked the pail at his feet. How could he forget his lunch? He grasped the handle and looked up. The young lad who had been watching them raised his arm, another bucket dangling from the boy's fingers. Thrusting the one he held toward the young woman, Brandt nodded his thanks to the boy and took the other pail.

As he started to dash off, he turned his head and called over his shoulder. "I hope your day ends up being better than it started."

The echo of her giggle reached his ears and made Brandt smile for the first time that morning. When he left the house after breakfast, his father had reminded him for what felt like the thousandth time that he was expected to do his best at the refinery. He had dismissed the admonition with an absentminded wave, but he'd obey his father's demands. Like he always did.

As he ran toward the grouping of factories along the river, Brandt reflected on his life. Focusing on that kept his mind off the reprimand he was bound to receive when he arrived late. He would soon assume his father's place and take charge of the family investments. But first he had to learn what it was like to work at all levels, not just in management. Despite the inconvenience, the edict was a sound one. How else could he truly understand those who worked for him when he had never been where they were?

Brandt slowed as he reached the outer gate. Once past the entrance, he jogged toward the refinery, eager to begin his day and hoping the bumpy start this morning wasn't a sign of things to come.

His father's foresight in setting up this meeting and seeing to every aspect necessary continued to impress him. He hoped he'd be able to fill those shoes well when the time came. Approaching the manager's entrance to the refinery, he pushed open the door and stepped inside. Brandt was supposed to meet with one of the supervisors this morning before work to go over some of the details of his new job. He had a difficult balance to strike ahead of him. While performing as an average refinery worker, he also had to continue increasing his knowledge about the management end. He needed to make a good impression on both counts. And now he was fifteen minutes late.

If only he hadn't stopped by that music shop on his way to work. He might have been able to get the young woman's name or at least find out where she was headed. But then again, if he had taken the original path he'd planned, he wouldn't have been at that corner at that precise moment. And they never would have met.

The chords of the guitar mixed with the tonal sounds of the accordion had called to him. He couldn't ignore it. His love of music had made him take the detour. But he could only stop for a few moments. So he had taken the calling card of the shop and decided to return again when he wasn't so pressed for time.

After two flights of stairs, he reached the supervisor's office and knocked. At least he still had the card to remind him where the shop was located. As the door to the office opened, Brandt reached into his lunch pail for the card and found someone else's lunch.

"Brandt," his new supervisor greeted. "How nice of you to be on time."

The sarcasm wasn't lost on Brandt, but he had bigger problems than his punctuality. He was holding someone else's lunch! There had been only two interruptions to his walk to work that morning. The pail he held had to belong to the young woman who had knocked him down.

He stepped inside the office and tried to focus on the immediate details of his job. But it was no use. Visions of a dark-haired angel filled his mind. How was he going to return the pail to her? He didn't even know her name.

Chapter 2

Felicity looked down in dismay at the contents of the lunch pail on her lap. Two strawberry tarts, three dumplings, an apple, a handful of cookies, and several strands of licorice. The items reminded her more of a dessert table at one of her mother's social events than a healthy lunch. A tin cup with a balled-up napkin stuffed inside also rested at the bottom of the pail. She distinctly remembered packing a cucumber and butter sandwich, an orange, and a cup for water. She pressed her lips together, one corner turning downward as she regarded the pail again.

At least she still had the tin cup for water. And the apple would suffice in place of the orange. But the other components of this strange lunch? Well, she might enjoy one of the tarts after she finished the apple. She raised the fruit to her lips and took a bite.

"Hi, Felicity. Mind if we join you?"

"Why the long face?"

Felicity looked up as Laura and Brianna came to stand in front of her. With her mouth full, she could only nod and scoot over on the concrete wall to give them room.

Once seated, Brianna leaned close. "So I'll ask again. Why the long face?"

Felicity reached into the pail and pulled out the three dumplings, holding them up for the other two girls to see. "I bumped into someone this morning on the way to work, and somehow in the confusion our pails got mixed up. I must have ended up with his lunch."

"His?" Laura bent forward and peered around Brianna. "Did you say you bumped into a 'him'?"

She should have known. Upon their introduction that morning, the young woman with freckles spattered across her nose had made it clear she was enamored with anything that had to do with the male species. Felicity tried to think of a way to share what had happened without identifying the young man, but it was no use.

"So come on," Laura pressed. "Don't hold back with all the details. We want to know everything!"

"Correction." Brianna poked Laura with her index finger. "*You* want to know everything. I would only be interested in the basics."

"Oh, all right, Miss Priss." Laura leveled a haughty glare at Brianna. "*You* might not want to hear about this fascinating story, but *I* do." She stood and moved to the other side of Felicity, barely able to maintain her seat with the way she bounced on the wall, her eyes holding a decided gleam. Laura bit into her sandwich, then swallowed and bounced again. "Now do tell. How did it all happen?"

Felicity shook her head and laughed at the two girls who had become fast friends since that morning. It helped that she had been assigned a station nearby so they could also chat during work hours.

"You don't have to share anything with her that you don't want to share, Felicity." Brianna narrowed her eyes at Laura, who glared right back.

"Girls, please don't quarrel on my behalf." Felicity held out her hands as if to separate Brianna and Laura. "I'll be more than happy to share everything and answer any questions. Although there really isn't much to tell."

Laura folded her arms across her chest and sat back with a triumphant grin on her face. Brianna rolled her eyes and returned her attention to her own lunch, silently taking small bites of her sandwich. Felicity chuckled then took another bite of her apple, savoring the sweet juices. After swallowing, she shifted on the wall and settled back to retell her adventurous walk to work that morning.

"I was enjoying a leisurely stroll through the neighborhood until I entered the business district. About four blocks from this factory, I turned the corner and came upon five men about to start a fight."

Brianna gasped, and Laura leaned forward in anticipation.

"No one else seemed to be paying these men any mind. Only a handful of children and perhaps two or three onlookers stopped to watch."

"That's because fights happen all the time down here by the river." Brianna gave Felicity a curious look but waved her hand in dismissal. "We're lucky to have the secure fence and gate around this factory, or those fights might end up too close for comfort."

Felicity couldn't imagine living such a life on an everyday basis. But she was forced to do just that in this recent turn of events. If she let on that she was anything less than accustomed to behavior like that, her new friends might see right through her. As it was, she had to take special care with her speech and spend time studying their word choices. Her formal vernacular would be a sure sign. And she couldn't risk that.

"I agree." Felicity nodded. "I wouldn't want to encounter men like those after dark." She suppressed a shudder at the mere thought and tried to focus on something else.

"All right, so what happened after you saw the men?" Laura asked.

Felicity scrunched her eyebrows together. "It all happened so quickly; I find it difficult to recall specific details."

"Just tell us what you remember," Brianna said.

"Well, as the fight began, I couldn't tear myself away from the sight. So I remained where I stood to watch, but stayed back so I wouldn't get caught in the middle. I had just decided to leave when one of the fighters came flying in my direction and knocked me down."

"And is that when Prince Charming came to the rescue?" Laura folded her hands under her chin and batted her eyelashes.

Felicity smiled. "Not quite. When I was struck, I stumbled back a few feet from the shock and lost my footing. 'Prince Charming' as you call him is the one who broke my fall."

Laura sighed and closed her eyes. "How romantic."

Brianna reached across Felicity to poke Laura's leg, causing Laura to open her eyes.

"It's not *my* fault if you want nothing to do with the young men in town. For all we know, Felicity could have met the man of her dreams." Laura turned her attention to Felicity. "So what happened next?"

"Well, the man smacked my cheek a little and asked if I was all right. Then a few seconds later he was rushing off, saying something about being late. A young boy nearby handed a lunch pail to him, and he handed me the one he had retrieved from the ground."

"What did he look like? Was he tall? Handsome? Strong? Did he smile at you or give you his name?"

"No, no, and no." Felicity laughed at Laura's enthusiasm. If only she had taken the time to pay attention to such details. "I don't remember too much about his physical description, but as he helped me to my feet, I did have to look up at him. And since he was able to survive the impact without too much injury, I would guess he's strong."

"Oh, you're just like Brianna. You don't get the important stuff first." Laura pouted and slid off the wall to slouch against it.

Brianna exchanged an amused grin with Felicity, and they both shook their heads at Laura's antics.

"So is there any chance you'll see him again?" Brianna lifted the handle of the pail Felicity held. "I mean, you do have his lunch. You no doubt will have to figure out how to get it back to him and exchange it for yours."

Felicity hadn't really thought about that. There wasn't time to exchange names or personal information. She didn't even know where he worked. How was she going to find him again?

"Have you checked the pail?" Laura asked, as if reading her mind. "Maybe he left something in there that could identify him or help you find out where he lives."

Felicity peered inside and fished around between the tarts, dumplings, and licorice. A piece of what felt like cardboard fell between the items and against her hand. She looked closer and reached in for the card and pulled it out to read the words printed on it.

"Sam's Music," she read aloud. "Waterloo and Baldwin."

"That's what you found in his pail?" Laura peered into the pail herself then plucked the card from Felicity's hand. "Doesn't give you much to go on. But at least it's something."

The whistle sounded the end of their lunch break, and all three of them sighed.

Laura waved the card in front of Felicity's face. "So are you going to visit this music shop and see if you can find him?" She tossed it back in the pail.

"I don't know. I suppose I should, if for no other reason than I need to return his pail and get mine back."

"Right—don't even think about the possibility that he might be the prince of your dreams or anything, Miss Practical." Laura waved her hand in dismissal as she gathered her belongings and started to walk away. "Do me a favor, though. If you make a mess of things with this guy, don't tell me about it. I only want to hear about your meeting if things go well."

Brianna stood up next to Felicity and leaned close. "Don't pay any attention to her. You do what you feel you have to do." She placed a reassuring hand on Felicity's arm. "And even if Laura doesn't want to hear about your quest to find this stranger, you can come find me."

Felicity gave Brianna an appreciative smile. "Thank you. I will be sure to tell you both what happens." She glanced at the large clock on the wall. "Now we had best get back to our stations before the supervisor marks a demerit on our time cards."

Once back at work, Felicity couldn't get her mind off the man she'd met that morning. She had managed to push him somewhat to the back of her mind up to that point, but thanks to Laura's romantic fantasies, he now occupied her thoughts full-time. What was she going to do? She had promised both Brianna and Laura that she'd do something. But the only lead she had was the card with the music shop's address on it. She couldn't exactly go waltzing up to it, hoping to find him there.

Then again, why couldn't she?

&

The same three men who had been sitting outside Sam's Music Shop were there again the next day. Brandt breathed a sigh of relief that he remembered how to get here. Without the card in the pail the young woman had, he didn't know for certain. He still remembered the nicely wrapped sandwich and orange from her lunch. Hardly enough food to serve as a snack, let alone a full meal. But he had made do and eaten a healthy portion at supper that evening. His mother had questioned his appetite and asked how he could eat everything in his pail and still be so hungry. Brandt shrugged it off, unwilling to share anything about his encounter that morning.

The next day, standing outside the music shop on a Saturday morning, the guitar and accordion melodies called to him once more.

He tipped his hat to the three men, who all nodded at him as they continued to play. For several moments he stood there and soaked in the music, allowing it to wash over him and calm his spirit. If only his father could understand the importance of music and how Brandt would love to bring it to the factories. It might help the workers' attitude if they could hear live performances like this every once in a while.

After five minutes of listening, Brandt slipped inside the store to look around. Several rows of sheet music were on display, and a handful of instruments lay in their cases. A counter separated him from the clerk, who bent over what looked like a ledger book, and behind him was a large assortment of instrument parts such as guitar strings and picks.

"Can I help you with something, sir?"

Brandt turned to see the clerk looking at him over wire-rimmed spectacles. His hair was combed to the side, and he wore an apron over his clothing.

"No, thank you," Brandt replied. "I only have a few moments before I must be off to work. So for now I'll take a look around if you don't mind."

"Not at all. My name is Matthew if you need anything."

"Thank you."

Brandt thumbed his way through several pieces of sheet music, seeing only a handful of tunes he recognized. Oh, to have the time to browse to his heart's content. But duty called, and he had to be on his way. It wouldn't be wise to be late two days in a row. At least today he had gotten an early start.

"I will have to come back another time when I can look at everything more closely." Brandt nodded to the clerk.

"You are welcome anytime." The clerk turned his attention back to the guitar he was repairing, and Brandt slipped outside once more.

The three men sat and played a more upbeat tune, so Brandt tapped his foot to the rhythm and bobbed his shoulders in time with the beat. He turned his head to visualize the music, and from the corner of his eye he saw a young woman standing not fifteen feet away. When he pivoted to get a full glimpse of her, he almost coughed on his quick intake of breath.

It was the woman from yesterday!

Memories of their encounter and the desire to hear her polished voice once more compelled him to take a few steps in her direction. She didn't seem to notice him. Her attention was focused down the street.

Perhaps she was waiting for someone—maybe him. But she wasn't looking at the shop. So much for wishful thinking. Well, he couldn't exactly leave without at least saying something. He cleared his throat and pushed his best grin to his lips.

"So we meet again, only this time it is under more favorable circumstances."

The young woman pivoted so quickly that strands of her hair followed a second later. Her eyes widened when she saw him.

"Gracious!"

Chapter 3

There it was again. That polished quality to her voice. It didn't line up with her outward appearance at all. Dressed as she was, Brandt expected a bit more brass and a bit less culture. But her choice of words, her mannerisms, and her proper posture all led him to believe there was more to her than she was allowing him to see.

He bent in a stiff and quick bow. "I am sorry for surprising you yet again. I promise it isn't how I normally introduce myself."

She tucked a few strands of her dark curls behind one ear and offered a shy smile. "There is no. . .I mean. . .it's all right. I guess I'm a little skittish."

"Don't worry about it. I'm actually glad I ran into you." He gave her a lopsided grin. "At least this time it wasn't literally."

She ducked her head and looked down at the sidewalk where they stood. Her tongue darted out to lick her lips, and then she pulled her lower lip between her teeth.

He was about to continue when she looked at him. The light green and brown of her eyes sent any coherent thought straight from his mind.

She rescued him from the awkward silence. "I know I apologized yesterday, but I want to do so again. Not only did it make you arrive even later for work, but you were forced to sacrifice your nutritious lunch and have it replaced by a cucumber and butter sandwich."

The corner of her mouth twitched, and her eyes took on a teasing light.

"Yes, but thankfully I was able to have a rather large helping at supper last night to offset my hunger." He shrugged. "At least the orange was juicy."

"The same for the apple, which, I must admit, I was surprised to find amidst the tarts, dumplings, and cookies." She gave him a penitent look. "And I'm ashamed to say I forgot to bring your pail with me. I'm told that today the food is actually brought to the workers."

She must have a job at one of the factories. How else would she know about the deal his father had made with a local vendor? "Don't worry about the pail. We can arrange the exchange another day. As for my food of choice"—Brandt held out his hands in a helpless gesture—"what can I say? I have a healthy appetite, and I need to make sure I have enough strength to do my job."

She gasped. "Oh yes, your job. Did you have any problems with being late?"

"Other than a glare from my supervisor and a brief reprimand about how

19

many other men would love to have my job and gladly take my place, no."

He left off the part about Mr. Hathaway reminding him of the need to be professional and remain aboveboard in all aspects of his work. His supervisor was required to report on Brandt's performance to his father each week. The last thing Brandt needed was a report that cast him in a negative light. It could delay the unspecified timetable his father had established before allowing him to take over the refinery. And he was more than ready to get on with his life.

"I'm relieved to hear that. I would hate to find out that I had somehow caused you any additional issues after being the reason your day began so horribly."

"On the contrary," he countered. "Running into you was without a doubt the best thing that happened to me yesterday."

"You cannot be serious."

"But I am." He took a step to the right and pressed his shoulder against the cracked siding of the music shop's front. "I told you that I was already running late, and I just barely made it to work on time, but throughout the rest of the day I couldn't stop thinking about how we met." He winked. "Especially when I was enjoying that delicious lunch you had prepared."

A giggle escaped her lips, and she quickly covered her mouth with her hand. "At least you were able to eat your lunch in peace. I had two friends join me and spend the entire thirty minutes interrogating me about our little accident. I barely had time to eat between all the questions and answers."

"And what did you tell them?"

She pressed her lips together for a brief second. "That I had been knocked over by a young man running to work and that it took him a few minutes before he offered to help me back to my feet."

His jaw fell as his mouth opened. There was no way she had said that. Or had she? He didn't know her well enough to determine if she was joking or not, and her face didn't give away anything that would answer the question for him.

"Don't fret," she continued before he had a chance at a rebuttal. "I didn't say that. When they asked, I told them the truth." Her head tilted to the right, and she stared over his shoulder. "Of course, when I did that, it released a never-ending list of questions about you and our meeting."

Brandt crossed his arms. "The same happened to me when I told a few men at work about you."

She raised her eyebrows. "Oh really? You spoke of me with other men who work with you?"

"Only to explain why I had such an interesting lunch that day."

She giggled. "Ah, so you were forced to endure a similar situation to what I experienced."

"Yes, and it wasn't easy explaining what happened without giving the men details I couldn't provide."

A smile graced her lips. "It makes me feel better about my interrogation knowing that you had to answer questions as well."

"And I think I did a pretty good job, since I only had a vague physical description of you. I didn't even know where you were headed or how you came to be there that early in the morning."

"There wasn't exactly time for introductions."

Time. He mentally scolded himself for letting it get away from him yet again. Brandt pushed off the wall and pulled out a pocket watch from his vest. "No, and there won't be much more if we don't at least start walking." He held out his pocket watch for her to see.

She gasped and nodded. "Yes, I was almost late yesterday as well. And it was my first day. I wouldn't want to do that again. This job is too important."

"I agree." She had no idea just how important this job was for him. Everything in his life was hedging on the outcome of his performance at the factory. Then again, he had no idea what circumstances were forcing her to work, either. For all he knew, she could be in dire straits.

"So," he began as they walked side by side toward the factories. "Am I correct in assuming that you work along the river?"

"Yes. I work at the candle and soap factory."

"That isn't too far from the copper refinery where I work." In fact, it wouldn't be out of his way at all to escort her and make sure she arrived safely. This wasn't exactly a secure part of town. "We could walk together every day, if you like. Do you live nearby?"

She stumbled and nearly lost her footing. Brandt instinctively reached out to steady her.

"Are you all right?"

"Yes," she answered, sounding out of breath. "Yes, I'm fine. There must have been a crack in the sidewalk."

"All right."

"Now you asked if I live nearby." She paused and seemed to consider her words. "It isn't far away, but the woman who owns the house from where I walk is quite ill. It wouldn't be a good idea for you to come. It might do more harm than good to upset the routine."

If it wasn't good for him to come, how could it be all right for her to be there? And she didn't say she lived there, just that she walked from there. That sounded a bit odd. Brandt looked at the way she avoided his gaze and stared straight ahead. She also didn't seem willing to offer much more in the way of an explanation, so for now he'd let it be.

"Well, would you like to meet somewhere partway? I don't live too far away, either." He jerked his thumb over his shoulder. "We could meet at the music shop and go from there."

She nodded. "That would be fine."

At least she agreed to that. He didn't want to scare her off after just two meetings.

"In that case, I think it would be a good idea if we knew each other's names. If we're going to walk together, it'd be better for conversation."

She smiled and turned to look at him. "I agree."

He stopped, and she paused beside him. He extended a hand. "Brandt Dalton," he said, using his mother's maiden name, which he'd assumed for work to disguise his true identity.

She returned his handshake. "Felicity Chambers. I'm pleased to finally meet you."

⁂

The trolley bells jingled on Monday morning, and a handful of passengers exchanged places on the horse-drawn conveyance at the corner of Champlain and Field. Some stepped from the platform as others climbed aboard to catch a ride. Felicity raised her hand to shield her eyes as she peered down the street in search of Brandt. He'd suggested this corner for them to meet this morning.

Had he forgotten?

She covered her mouth as a yawn escaped and blinked several times, scrunching her eyes tight to clear the sleep from them. After the blessing of sleeping later yesterday before church services, dragging herself from bed at sunrise had been nigh onto impossible. Thank goodness for Cook's strong tea. Otherwise her driver wouldn't have had the time to get her to Mrs. Gibson's early enough for her to change clothes and rush out to meet Brandt. She only swapped outfits to avoid suspicion from anyone in the Grosse Pointe district who might see her in those early morning hours. Charity work didn't normally require such common apparel. And having to change today on top of already being late made her wonder if she'd missed Brandt.

It had only been two days since they had officially introduced themselves to each other and agreed to walk together to work. On Saturday, when she had noticed the copper refinery was actually on the farthest east edge of the assembled factories, she'd protested.

"You don't have to escort me all the way to the factory, Mr. Dalton. It isn't the first time I've walked here alone."

"Nonsense," he countered. "It will be my pleasure. What kind of a friend would I be if I didn't at least make sure you arrived safely? After all, we wouldn't want you falling into another unfortunate passerby and knocking *him* off his feet."

She started to reply with the same measure of teasing but held her retort in check. Mother had reprimanded her on more than one occasion about her penchant for speaking before thinking. And she was often too forward with her remarks. Especially where men were concerned. Brandt was a new friend. She didn't need to ruin that with her untoward behavior. So she chose to dip her head in response.

"Very well. If you insist."

"I do."

"Then it appears to be settled."

After a farewell and a brief touch of his hand to his cap, they had parted ways. Brandt headed for the refinery, and she turned toward the candle and soap factory. Knowing they would walk together each morning somehow made the thought of yet another exhausting day where she came home with dried wax on her clothes and sometimes in her hair seem less daunting.

Now Monday morning had arrived, and she stood waiting for Brandt. Felicity glanced down the street again, stretching up on her tiptoes to see farther.

"Are you looking for me?"

Felicity pivoted on her heel and found Brandt standing there with his hands in his pockets and wearing a rather mischievous look on his face.

"Yes. I thought you would be coming from the other direction."

"I took a shortcut."

"By the music shop would be my guess."

He winked and sent a devilish grin her way. "You discovered my weakness. Now we don't have a choice. We must remain friends lest you spill my secret to someone else."

Felicity grinned. He sounded so much like her older brother with his quick wit and easygoing charm. But that was where the resemblance stopped.

His baggy pants were held with suspenders that hooked over his wide shoulders and pressed his cotton shirt against his chest. Scuffed and worn shoes peeked out from below the cuffs of his pants. Top that off with a cap sitting on his sandy-colored hair at a crooked angle, and he looked every bit the picture of trouble.

In fact, he reminded her of a grown-up version of little Timothy, the scrappy street urchin of Mrs. Gibson's. And just as Timothy had promised to watch out for her, Brandt did the same with his offer to walk with her to work. She couldn't imagine any two better guardians. At least if Mother inquired, she could truthfully say she wasn't walking alone.

"Is this a good meeting place for you?" Brandt asked, breaking her from her silent observation.

"It works fine."

"What direction are you coming from?"

She extended her arm to the east. "Over there."

Brandt drew his eyebrows together and frowned. "Near the Grosse Pointe district?"

Oh no! She hadn't taken the time to get her bearings before responding. She just automatically pointed toward home. She had to think of something. Quick.

"What? No. I must have gotten turned around. I meant that way." She changed from her right to her left arm and pointed to the west this time. "I come from Maple on the other side of the cemetery."

"The Elmwood or Mt. Elliott?"

"Elmwood."

Brandt seemed to accept her response as he placed his hand at her back and encouraged her to start walking toward the factory. "That's a better part of town than some, but not quite like Grosse Pointe."

She couldn't argue with him on that. The area around Maple was far different from where she really lived, but at least she hadn't chosen the poorest section of Detroit for her false address. Felicity fell in step with him and breathed a silent sigh of relief. That was close. He obviously knew the town well. She'd better be careful from now on and take a moment to make sure she didn't repeat that mistake.

"My great-grandfather is buried in Elmwood." His breath caught, and he quickly added, "Just a little wooden cross marks the grave in an out-of-the-way spot."

She couldn't be sure, but she thought she detected a trace of agitation in the latter part of his statement. But why would he sound nervous sharing about his family? Unless he was ashamed they couldn't afford more in the way of a gravestone. Felicity turned to see him swallow several times before continuing.

"He fought in the War of 1812. From the stories my father and grandfather have shared, his valiant efforts helped his unit defend the areas east of the lake region. With the New England states refusing to lend troops or financial assistance, the soldiers needed everyone they could find. So he gave it all he had."

"I have heard similar stories from my family, although I don't know too many specifics."

"After the war, he decided to move farther west with his family. My grandfather had been born while my great-grandfather was fighting. That was when they moved here to Detroit and settled. My family has been here ever since."

"Sounds like quite a legacy."

Brandt reached up and slid his thumbs under his suspenders, drawing them away from his shirt, then letting go with a snap. "Yes, we might not have many things to talk about, but we're proud of what we *have* done."

She giggled at his antics and stepped with him across Sheridan. "That's just like my family. The only story I hear repeated over and over again is how my great-grandfather was at Fort McHenry when Sir Francis Scott Key wrote 'The Star-Spangled Banner.'"

He regarded her with a tilt of his head as they walked. "Your great-grandfather fought down in Maryland? That's quite a ways from Detroit."

Felicity almost said he had been in Washington when the White House had been burned, negotiating shipping supplies for his company. But that might give her away. "Like your great-grandfather, mine didn't always live here. He was actually born in Philadelphia."

"So how did he come this far west and north?"

She shrugged as they continued on Champlain, trying to make the relocation sound less important. "He wanted a change from the life he had known as a young boy."

Leaving off the fact that he had come by way of the river in one of his company's vessels helped simplify the story. It appeared as nothing more than a vagabond young man setting off for bigger and better things. She wasn't even going to broach the topic of legacies with the connections her family had to the presidential line and other influential members of the government. No, those stories would give her away for sure.

"Detroit is a great choice, especially now that the War Between the States is over. We've seen so much improvement in industry and development, and right here in this city we have one of the best collections of factories outside of Boston. When the Sault Locks opened in the Upper Peninsula twenty years ago, they brought opportunities for everyone. It's an exciting time to live here."

The enthusiasm in his voice matched the joy on his face. He looked like a little boy who had just been given his first piece of candy from the corner mercantile.

"I have to agree with you. Although working in the factory isn't glamorous, it provides a steady wage and gives me a sense of accomplishment."

"It's the same for me." He nodded. "Working at the refinery is hard, but I feel good at the end of the day."

He almost seemed surprised by that, but she brushed it off when he didn't say anything further.

They turned south toward Jefferson, near the river. Only a few more blocks and they would have to part ways. What could end up being a long, solitary walk would pass in no time at all. They continued in companionable silence almost to the fence surrounding the factories. Brandt paused just outside the gate.

"Do you have plans to share lunch with your friends again today?"

Now that was a question she hadn't expected to hear. "Yes, why?"

He held up her lunch pail with a sheepish grin. "Because I did my best to bring something I thought you would eat."

Laughter bubbled up from within. "Oh, gracious, I almost forgot." She dangled his pail from her fingertips. "I did the same, fresh-baked cookies and everything."

The hungry gleam in his eyes was thanks enough. She was sure Brandt would love the meal she'd brought for him. Handing him his lunch, she took hers with her other hand. Although she wanted to peek inside the folded cloth to see what he had placed in the pail, she resisted. Just in case she didn't like it, she didn't want to insult him by her expression or reaction.

"Thank you," he said with an appreciative sniff as he ran the pail under his nose. "I'm sure it'll be the best lunch I've had in a long time."

"I look forward to hearing about it tomorrow."

A crestfallen look replaced the one of anticipation on his face. "Do you not want to walk together this evening?"

She needed to get to Mrs. Gibson's as quickly as possible so she could return home in time for supper. And that meant she had to almost run to make it. She'd told Mother and Father that her work for Mrs. Gibson would require staying until five o'clock, but didn't specify it involved factory work. Mother seemed to allow for the delay and had agreed to push back the mealtime to accommodate the later arrival, but Brandt couldn't know that. "I. . .um. . .I actually take a different way home, and I wouldn't want to impose on you."

"Oh. All right." He didn't seem happy about that, but he accepted it anyway. "Then shall we meet at the corner again tomorrow?"

"Same time, same place."

"Good." He flicked the corner of his cap with his forefinger and stepped through the gate. She followed and offered a quick wave before heading for the factory. When she looked over her shoulder to see his departure, she caught him watching her, and a blush stole across her cheeks. Ducking her head, she slipped inside and out of view.

Brandt was far too charming for his own good. And if Mother knew she was keeping company with a young man of his social status? Oh my! She would forbid Felicity from continuing with this charity work. Father wouldn't be pleased, either. She only prayed she could keep it a secret.

Chapter 4

Brandt took a bite of his apple then licked the juice from his lips. He walked alongside Felicity and listened as she shared about the continued illness of Mrs. Gibson. Her sacrifice for the woman was admirable. He still wondered about the specifics of her circumstances, such as what she had done before she started helping Mrs. Gibson. For now, though, he let his curiosity rest.

Felicity sighed. "I simply can't understand why her condition isn't improving. For some reason this pregnancy is taking a greater toll on her than all five of her previous ones." Frustration and pain laced her words, and a frown marred her countenance. "I am making certain to follow all the doctor's instructions, administering the proper amount of medication and seeing that she gets as much rest as possible." She sighed, brushing wisps of hair out of her eyes. "But with each passing day, there doesn't seem to be much improvement."

Brandt took another bite and pointed the apple in her direction. "At least she isn't getting worse."

Felicity cast a quick glance his way and attempted a smile. "You're right. I only wish there was something more I could do for her."

He chewed for a moment, and she fell silent beside him. "But you are no doubt helping a lot by working at the factory. The money you share is keeping her children fed. That has to be a relief to her in this time of need."

She tilted her head and pressed her lips into a thin line. A breeze stirred the loose wisps of hair at the crown of her head, and she tucked the strands she could grab behind her ear. "I suppose you're right about that. If she had to worry about food and clothing while she's sick, she would likely be far worse than she is now."

"Exactly. So don't doubt your contribution, even if her health doesn't seem to be improving." He bit the final piece of apple then tossed the core into a waste bucket outside Hardwell's Meat Market. "I have a question for you."

"Yes?"

"How did you come to know Mrs. Gibson and take a job at the factory to help her when she could no longer work?"

Felicity stumbled, and he extended a hand to steady her. The handle of her pail made a creaking sound as it swung back and forth. She regained her footing and licked her lips several times. He hoped it was a crack in the sidewalk and not his question that unsettled her. After all, he'd only asked her to share her story. Why would that cause a problem?

"Are you all right?" He kept his hand on her elbow until she'd regained her balance.

"Yes, yes." Heavy breathing accompanied her reply, but she smiled in spite of it, and he released her arm. "I'm sorry. There must have been a bit of uneven sidewalk back there."

He motioned with his head over his shoulder and chuckled. "Yeah, the sidewalk sometimes has a way of coming up to trip you when you least expect it."

A full-fledged smile accompanied his joke, and he once again felt at ease. They'd been walking together for two weeks. He wanted to see their friendship improve with each passing day—not give her a reason to withdraw.

"Back to your previous question," she said. "You asked how I came to know Mrs. Gibson."

He nodded and placed his hand at her back as they crossed Sheridan. Not a lot of activity this early in the morning, but the manners ingrained in him from childhood couldn't be ignored.

"I met her through other work I had been doing, and we struck up a fast friendship. Her little ones are quite precious, and I loved spending time with them every chance I could get."

When she didn't continue, Brandt took the opportunity to watch her. She looked away and chewed on her lower lip. He thought he saw a flash of worry cross her face, but just as quickly it was gone. He must have imagined it. A few seconds later, she resumed talking.

"When Mrs. Gibson's pregnancy forced her to give up her job at the factory, I worried about her and her family. Her husband died not long before Christmas last year from a boating accident, and she has been the one to provide for them all in his absence."

Brandt looked across the street to the left at the small grassy area the local residents considered a park. The immaculate lawns near his home made this area seem ramshackle and scraggly, but the young mother with her two playing children didn't seem to mind.

"Does she not have any other family who can help?"

"None." Felicity shook her head and frowned. "Her family didn't approve of her choice for a husband, and they disowned her." Her voice choked, but she swallowed past it. "So she was left with nothing, and when her husband died, life got even worse."

"It's hard to imagine a family being so uncaring that they'd rather leave a mother destitute than help her in her time of need."

"Not all families can bring themselves to support one of their own marrying into a lower class."

It took a moment for Felicity's words to register, but when they did, he directed his full attention on her. She avoided his eyes and increased her gait to just a little faster than his own. As he altered his pace to match hers once more, her silence gave him pause.

He wanted to believe that his own family would understand if he should choose to marry a woman who didn't abide within the same social circles. Then again, when his younger brother had almost done just that, there had been quite the uprising. And after hearing Felicity's story, there would without a doubt be problems.

His parents had yet to start arranging pairings for him, but they weren't above manipulating the circumstances to bring him together with a woman of their choosing. At a handful of events during the past few years, he had managed to avoid their attempts to force his hand. But he was twenty-three already. Mother and Father wouldn't allow his games to continue for long.

As he and Felicity turned south and headed for the river, Brandt searched for something—anything—that might get the conversation going again.

"You sound as if you speak from experience," he said. "Has someone in your family been affected by a similar circumstance as Mrs. Gibson?"

Felicity covered her sharp intake of breath with her hand and continued to avoid his gaze. "I. . .um. . . ," she stammered as her eyes darted from left to right. "I have heard stories just like Mrs. Gibson's," she finally managed. She seemed to gain confidence from that statement and continued. "In an area like this where the lives of people from different social circles can easily cross paths, it makes sense that others would find themselves facing a similar fate."

"That's a good point. We have men at the refinery from all different parts of the city. And yet they all manage to work together toward a common goal."

"You sound surprised."

Finally, she looked at him again, but this time crossness appeared in the look she gave him.

He held up his hands in mock surrender and took a step away. "I didn't mean any harm by what I said. I only meant to point out how impressed I am to see that social status doesn't seem to matter to the men who work with me. We're all there for the same reason, and we find other things in common despite where we live."

Her expression softened, and she offered a sweet smile. "I'm sorry. This situation with Mrs. Gibson hasn't been easy for me. I don't like seeing people treat others badly just because they don't live in the right place or have the right amount of money or dress a certain way."

Brandt placed a reassuring hand on her shoulder. "It's all right. I feel the same way. I run into others who don't agree, and it makes me sick to see how they treat people they believe to be inferior."

"Yes. I see how much it hurts Mrs. Gibson, and I don't want to do that to anyone."

He'd have to store that statement and pursue it at a later date. A time when he felt comfortable sharing more details about his life. For now he wanted to learn more about her.

"So what about your work at the factory? What are the other girls like who work with you?"

❧

Felicity wasn't ready to talk about the girls she'd met, but since Brandt had shared about the refinery, it was only fair that she tell him something, too.

"It's a lot like what you describe. Do you remember the two girls I mentioned when we first met?"

He winked. "The ones who teased you about running into me in the middle of the street?"

A grin tugged at her lips. "Yes." She took his arm as they crossed Jefferson. "Brianna lives about four streets away from Mrs. Gibson's, and Laura's family is not too far from the railroad. But despite the fact that Laura doesn't have as much, they became fast friends the moment they started working together. Fortunately, they allowed me to join their little circle as well." She looked up at the cloudless blue sky and caught two sparrows engaged in a playful dance as they flew between the trees on each side of the street. "The days pass by much faster with their ongoing laughter and banter. Even the most mundane tasks seem easier with them working beside me."

Brandt grabbed a coin from his pocket and flicked it into the air before catching it again in his hand. "Sounds like you have a couple of great friends. They can be hard to find, but when you do, you don't want to lose them."

The melancholic quality to his voice momentarily distracted Felicity. But Brandt didn't seem to want to share anything more about his remark, so she let it go.

"I never imagined I would enjoy working at the factory as much as I do. The supervisors keep us moving at a grueling pace, but we all manage to make it through a day. It's not only a blessing to know that I am helping Mrs. Gibson, but it gives me confidence in my own abilities as well."

Brandt furrowed his brow for a moment, and she returned his questioning gaze. He waved his hands and dismissed what he had obviously been about to say, and Felicity shrugged. Perhaps it wasn't important or he was going to ask her later.

She sighed. "But it always surprises me to see how young some of the girls are who work in a factory."

"We have young boys in the refinery, too. Some of them are needed because of their small hands and ability to get in between the machines. Of course, this also means there is a higher risk of them losing a finger or suffering a greater injury as a result."

Felicity closed her eyes at that thought. Little Timothy came to mind, and she cringed at the idea of telling Lucy her son had been hurt on a machine similar to the ones Brandt described simply to keep the refinery running with smooth precision. Then again, Timothy didn't work at the refinery or anywhere near the river district. He ran errands for the local grocer and delivered food to those who couldn't get out on their own. For now he was safe.

"We have an area that uses machines like that," she continued. "But most of the work I do involves the shaping of candles and carving of soap after the other girls make the wax molds and combine the lye with the oils."

Felicity stopped in front of a window where the merchant inside replaced several wooden toys with newer ones. Brandt paused with her as they looked through the window to see a train with seven cars attached. A red rubber ball sat next to jacks that shimmered in the early morning sunlight, and she noticed what looked like a cup on a stick with a ball attached to a string. She wasn't sure what a child would do with that toy, but the merchant seemed proud to have it on display. He acknowledged them with a nod and a wave; then he disappeared farther into the store. Felicity turned and continued walking.

"There is a little girl, though, who isn't much more than eleven or twelve. Her name is Julia, and I met her last week. When I asked her about how she came to work at the factory, she said her family needed the money. With her father injured and her mother having to take care of three younger children, she was the logical choice."

Brandt sighed. "That happens a lot, I'm afraid. Several boys at the refinery are in the same situation."

Felicity placed a hand on Brandt's arm and turned to face him. "But that's not all. Julia went on to tell me how grateful she is that God blessed her with strong arms and legs so that she *can* go to work for her family." She pivoted and started walking again. "I was amazed at the faith she had at such a young age. You would think she might blame God for letting her father get injured or making it so that she was the oldest and didn't have a brother old enough to work in her place."

"It seems as if she's accepted her duty and found a way to be happy in spite of it."

"I could learn a lot from her."

"It's sad that she is forced to work at a young age, but you're not too different."

She scrunched her eyebrows together. "What do you mean?"

"Well, you didn't *have* to share your wages with Mrs. Gibson, but you chose to help her. I daresay little Julia wasn't given that option. She's helping her family, just like you. Still she smiles. And despite Mrs. Gibson's illness, you focus on the good things about your work for her rather than dwelling on the problems."

"When you put it that way, I can see what you mean." She hadn't even thought to compare herself to Julia, but Brandt was able to make a solid parallel. "I at least have my older brother to help, so I'm not solely responsible like Julia."

Brandt again flipped the coin he held into the air. "God has an uncanny way of helping us turn what we don't think we want into something we do."

Brandt must have some measure of faith as well. His self-assured delivery told Felicity as much. She believed her own to be steady, but at times she struggled with doubt. Knowing Brandt shared that faith and seeing how little Julia lived out her own each day made Felicity happy to be in such good company.

She tilted her head. "And if we stop protesting, we might be able to see the good."

"Right." Brandt pushed open the gate to the factories and held it as Felicity walked in front of him.

"It seems the time has come for us to part ways again. But I'll see you tomorrow?"

Brandt nodded. "Same time. Same place. I'll be there."

She headed to work, pleased to know she could count on him to walk with her. If only her future were so clear and certain.

Chapter 5

Brandt ascended the front steps of his home after work and reached for the brass latch just as the wide oak door swung open before him. The composed and dispassionate face of his butler, Jeffrey, welcomed him from the doorway. Every hair was in place, and every crease in his uniform ironed sharply. How Jeffrey managed to maintain such a crisp appearance all day never ceased to amaze him, especially when Brandt would wrinkle his clothing before even setting one foot outside.

"Good evening, sir." The stalwart man dipped his head in his customary greeting, never once breaking his rigid stance. "Your father has requested to speak with you as soon as you are settled."

Brandt stepped into the entryway. The polished wooden floors gleamed in the waning evening sun. He closed his eyes for a brief moment. Just what he didn't want the second he walked in the door. Perhaps he could stall for a bit.

He opened his eyes and looked at the butler. "Thank you, Jeffrey. Shall I find him in his study?"

"Yes, sir." The man didn't flinch. "And Cook has asked me to inform you that supper is to be served on schedule."

Brandt raised his eyebrow at Jeffrey. "On schedule? Is Cook in a good mood this evening?"

The barest hint of a grin tugging at Jeffrey's lips caused an answering one to pull at Brandt's.

"Never mind that, Jeffrey. I suppose I should be grateful and not jest. Otherwise I might find myself going without food entirely the next time."

"That seems to be the wise choice, sir."

No matter how hard he tried, Brandt had never been able to break Jeffrey of his unemotional state. Tonight obviously wouldn't be any different. So he handed his lunch pail and cap to the butler. With a shake of his head, he turned toward the broad staircase. It rose from the expansive entryway and curved around to the right as it connected to the second floor. His father could wait a few moments.

As he took the stairs two at a time, he turned to look over his shoulder to where Jeffrey walked toward the kitchen, head held high and lips pressed into a firm line. There had been times when the butler had allowed a brief smile or glint in his eyes to slip almost unnoticed. But Brandt always caught it. Somewhere deep down was a man with a diabolical sense of humor waiting to get out. He wondered if he'd be there to see it when Jeffrey let loose.

"Good evening, Sarah." Brandt dipped his chin and acknowledged one of the newer maids his mother had hired as she passed him in the wide hallway.

She bobbed a quick curtsy midstride and continued on her way without a word.

Brandt walked toward his private room. The carpet on the floor absorbed the sounds of his footsteps as he turned the polished knob and stepped inside. The scent of cinnamon and cloves greeted him, no doubt from the potpourri set out by Sarah not long ago. A pleasant breeze stirred the gauzy curtains on the far side of the room.

For a brief moment he entertained the thought of flopping across the soft mattress of his four-poster bed. But he might fall asleep, and that would anger his father. So instead he headed toward the window and brushed back the flimsy material. Leaning against the frame, he placed a fist on his hip and looked down at the street below.

Well-dressed men and women, young ladies and gentlemen, all ventured to and fro on their way to their respective destinations. He contrasted their polished appearances with the men who worked side by side with him and the young ladies Felicity described from the factory.

Uncomplicated and simple.

They no doubt never worried about how they would dress for supper or how to bow properly when addressing certain members of society or which form of address was required at social functions when greeting their hosts. No, they went about their days unhindered by the confines of social customs. Just once Brandt wished he could be that free.

For the time being, he had a glimpse of that life while working at the refinery. Beneath it all remained the truth that he would one day assume control of the place where he worked. And when that time came, his adventures among the common classes would be over.

A knock on his door made Brandt turn to see Sarah standing in the hall, her head down.

"Yes? What is it, Sarah?"

"Your father has sent me to fetch you, sir," she answered in a low tone, her words barely distinguishable.

Brandt released a heavy sigh and crossed the width of his room. "I do suppose I have kept him waiting long enough." He started to follow Sarah then looked down at his attire. "Uh, do allow me a moment to change first. Our talk will no doubt take us right up to supper, and I don't wish to appear at the table dressed as I am."

A tinge of pink stained Sarah's cheeks, but she continued to avoid his gaze.

She only dipped another curtsy and nodded, stepping back to allow him to close the door.

Her youthful innocence brought Felicity's face to mind. Perhaps he could recommend that his mother hire her as a maid in place of her work at the factory. No. That would no doubt cause them both discomfort. Not only that, but she'd find out the type of life he led. That wouldn't work at all.

Brandt kicked off his shoes and quickly swapped the rough work shirt, suspenders, and pants with a crisp cotton top and pressed slacks from his cherry-wood wardrobe. He donned freshly shined shoes and a dinner jacket to please Mother, and he once again moved toward the door.

When he opened it, Sarah stood waiting on the other side. Father had no doubt left explicit instructions for her to personally escort him downstairs. Far be it from him to cause one of their servants to disobey orders. With a nod at the young girl, he clicked his door shut and followed her until she left him standing at the doorway to his father's study.

"I was wondering when you would get around to joining me, son. I thought perhaps you had gotten lost again."

The poor attempt at a joke wasn't lost on Brandt.

"No, sir, I merely wanted to change out of the clothes I wore to the factory."

Every time he was late for a meeting or delayed his response to come when called, Father made some remark about getting lost. Brushing it aside, Brandt stepped into the darkened room.

Every bit of it fairly shouted his father's affluence. From the dusted bookshelves teeming with old and new books, to the oversize mahogany desk that sat in the middle of the room, to the oriental carpet that covered most of the floor. The imposing yet simple decorations fit the patriarch of the Lawson family, Devon Montgomery Lawson, to a *T*. Not a thing was out of place. Not a paper out of order.

"I applaud your foresight, son." He leaned down and struck a match on the hardwood floor and lit his pipe, then inserted the wooden piece into his mouth. Gesturing toward the Queen Anne chair opposite, he invited Brandt to sit.

"Was there something of import you wished to discuss, sir?" Brandt flipped up the edge of his jacket as he took his seat.

"Hmm?" His father mumbled around the pipe then removed it from his lips to hold it aloft. "Oh yes. It has been at least a week since we have spoken about your progress at the refinery. I wanted to inquire about your work there and your thoughts on how the entire operation is run."

"Well, sir, Mr. Sanderson runs a fairly tight order of operations. There isn't a lot that happens where he isn't aware of it."

"Ah yes. Bartholomew. He is one of the best men I have among the supervisors and management staff."

Brandt started to settle back into his chair, but at the disapproving glance from his father, he straightened. "His meticulous attention to detail can be both a benefit and a hindrance."

"How so?"

"Take the operating of the machines, powered by the water from the river. When something breaks or gets lodged somewhere inside, it can shut down that part of the refinery until it gets fixed, which can interrupt the production schedule."

"Go on." Father took another puff of the pipe.

"Since Mr. Sanderson seems to be everywhere at once, when a problem arises, he immediately has someone on hand to perform the repairs."

"As well he should. So tell me how it can be a hindrance."

Brandt leaned forward and placed his palms on the edge of the desk. "His presence can be intimidating to some of the workers, sir. They sometimes spend more time worrying about where Mr. Sanderson is than they do on their productivity levels."

His father pounded a fist on the desk, rattling the glass inkwell with a pen inside. "Then perhaps those men should find other means of employment. If they can't keep their minds on their work, they might not be the best men for the job."

He extended one hand toward his father, palm upward. "But that's not what I meant, sir."

"Then pray tell, do explain, for I am not following your line of reasoning."

"The men who work beside me are good men. Hardworking and devoted to their jobs. But I'm sure you can see how disconcerting it can be to have your supervisor seemingly looking over your shoulder at every turn. You can't help but wonder if you're doing a satisfactory job or if he is finding fault with your performance and you might soon be told you're no longer needed."

The truth of Brandt's assessment seemed to dawn on his father. The man took a few puffs of his pipe and stared over Brandt's shoulder at the paneled wall behind him. Several long moments passed in silence. Brandt didn't want to report anything that might jeopardize anyone's job. But Father had asked him to be honest about the working conditions and assess them from the perspective of a common worker, not a supervisor. That's exactly what he was doing.

"So," his father began, "you feel that the productivity levels will increase if Bart were to become a little less conspicuous and only appear when his presence is required?"

Brandt nodded. "I do believe that will help the workers to relax and allow them to breathe easier, sir. Yes."

"Allow me a day or two to mull over this further, and I'll speak with you again two days hence."

"Fair enough, sir."

"Now what of the young lady you encountered at the beginning of your work assignment?"

Brandt's eyes widened. How did Father know about Felicity? He hadn't said a word to anyone here at the house, other than Cook when he had asked her to prepare that special lunch last week. And she had promised not to tell a soul.

"Don't act so surprised, son. I am not without my own network of information, provided the need arises."

The smug expression on his father's face didn't help matters any. He had hoped to avoid this conversation for a little while longer. Just until he was more certain about Felicity. But he couldn't get out of this now. He had to give his father some kind of answer.

"She works in the soap and candle factory at the other end of the yard. We had an unfortunate encounter on our respective first days of work, and to apologize for my haste, I offered to walk with her and see her safely to work."

All right, so he had minimized the significance of their friendship. At least he hadn't lied.

"And does this young lady have a name?"

Brandt hesitated. Should he give his father that type of information? The man had just told him about the extensive resources he had at his disposal. Then again, what harm could come of providing a name?

"Felicity Chambers, sir."

"And you walk with her to work?"

"When our paths cross. Yes, sir." His father didn't need to know that they purposefully planned for their paths to meet every morning.

"Based upon the care you took in preparing lunch for her that one morning when you had to return her lunch pail, I suspect she has become more than an acquaintance you happened to meet on the road."

Brandt didn't say a word. He might reveal the truth of his feelings and convey to his father more than he wanted the man to know. He already seemed to know more than enough. No sense in adding to what he had discovered through other means.

"Your silence says more than words, my son. If she works at the factory, her status is not equal to yours, and I caution you to remember that. We cannot afford another situation like what happened with your younger brother when he attempted to steal away for a rendezvous with that waif he met near the park."

Now why did Father have to go and bring up that story? Brandt rolled his eyes. It had happened more than two years ago, and it had only lasted long enough for tongues to wag for a few days before everyone forgot about it and went about their business. His time spent with Felicity was nothing like that. She had more refinement than dozens of other ladies he knew. And to see her compared to the girl his brother had met made his ire rise.

"I assure you, Father," he began, keeping his temper in check, "you will not see a repeat of those circumstances. Felicity and I merely enjoy a conversation to break up the silence of the walk. When we cross paths, it helps pass the time on the way to the river."

"Conversation? That is all?" His father quirked an eyebrow and regarded Brandt with a wary expression.

"Nothing more, sir. I assure you."

His father inhaled deeply and stood. "Very well. I shall take you at your word, for now. But should anything change, be aware that I will find out about it."

Of course he would. His father kept a close eye on everything Brandt did. At times he felt like the workers under Mr. Sanderson's watch. Then he remembered that everything his father did, he did to prepare him for the responsibility of managing and owning the refinery and other factories. Once he assumed that position, his life would be under even tighter scrutiny. He couldn't afford any mistakes now, let alone after he was placed in charge.

"I understand, sir." Brandt placed his hands on the arms of his chair and pushed himself to his feet. "And I assure you, you have no reason for concern."

"All right. Now let's make our way to the dining room. From the smells coming down the hall, I believe we're having a roast this evening."

Brandt chuckled a little and relaxed. Despite his overbearing and somewhat intrusive nature, his father wasn't all bad. He handled things the only way he knew how. With direct bluntness. Better that than deception. At least Brandt always knew where he stood.

Now if only he could figure out Felicity.

❧

"What do you have for lunch today?"

Felicity peered around Brandt's shoulder and tried to sneak a peek at his lunch pail, but he held it away from her, out of arm's reach.

"Much of the same. Why?"

Well, the contents of his lunch seemed to speak of a different social class, but she didn't want to share those concerns with him. So she shrugged. "No reason. I merely wondered if you had decided to actually assemble a small measure of substance rather than the substantial amount of sweets you normally include."

Brandt quirked one eyebrow and leveled a smirk in her direction. "Are you saying you believe I'm less than the image of perfect health?" He stopped in the middle of the sidewalk then struck a pose with his chin held high, sticking out his chest in an abnormal fashion.

Felicity covered her mouth and giggled. "Well, you do have to admit the lunches I've seen have weighed rather heavily on the cookies and sweets side. It's difficult to imagine how you remain uninfluenced by the sheer levels of sugared items you consume."

Brandt tilted his head and regarded her with a puzzled expression. He relaxed his stance. The look on his face was a mixture of curiosity and uncertainty, as if he weighed her against some unknown standard. Felicity wasn't sure if she would wind up on the positive end of the scale or the negative.

"Is something the matter?" she asked.

"What?" He shook his head as if pulling himself from a trance.

"I asked if something was the matter. You're staring at me in an unusual manner."

"Oh, it's nothing." Brandt waved his hands in front of him in scissorlike fashion. "For a moment, I thought. . ."

"What?"

"No. It's not important."

She had a hard time believing that. If it wasn't important, why would it cause him to stare? And why would he be regarding her in such an odd way? But she couldn't force him to answer. If he wanted to tell her, he would.

The only thing that came to mind was her choice of words. He hadn't seemed to be bothered by that before. Even so, she should be more careful.

"You mentioned the other day that you had been late getting home after work. Did you make anyone else in your family upset because they had to wait for you?"

"No." He started walking again. "In fact, last night I was early. And I ended up having a talk with my father."

"Oh? About what?"

He stared straight ahead as they continued toward the river. Normally he would glance in her direction a few times as he spoke. Today he didn't. Perhaps that conversation was the reason for his behavior shift.

"Work, the refinery, how I'm liking my job, the men who work with me. Typical conversation topics where my father is concerned."

"At least he sounds like he supports you."

"He does do that. But he can try my patience, too."

"How so?"

"In some of his expectations and how he thinks there's only one way to do things. Once in a while he'll warn me about something when I know there's no reason for concern."

Brandt seemed to be rather vague this morning. Like he was dancing around the specifics instead of coming right out and saying what was on his mind. His father must have said something to bring about this change. And the difference she noticed wasn't just in what he said. It was in the way he looked at her and how distant he acted compared to the camaraderie they'd shared up to this point.

"Did you talk about a specific situation where he felt you needed to be careful?"

"Uh, no."

His answer came just a second after her question. And he again avoided her gaze. Something was definitely different.

"I'm sure he's only looking out for you. Like all fathers do."

"I suppose."

He fell into silence and didn't seem too interested in continuing the conversation. Felicity regarded him with a sideways glance as she matched her stride to his. He remained introspective and not forthcoming with much detail. Every man deserved to keep his thoughts close, but this didn't feel right. Something kept him distant, and she didn't like this side of him. She hoped this phase wouldn't last long.

Chapter 6

Felicity, dear, would you be so kind as to slip into the kitchen and see where Rebecca stands on preparations for the party?"

"Yes, Mother."

This task normally fell on Mother's shoulders, as she had a way with Rebecca. But this time it was Felicity's turn. Mother and Rebecca were a lot alike. Somehow they managed to maintain their civility and respect for one another, despite their equal penchant for perfection. Felicity knew everything would be in order. It was pointless to go check on Rebecca. She tried to keep her shoulders from slumping, but Mother noticed.

"Felicity." The warning tone made Felicity stop in her tracks.

"Yes, Mother?" She turned. *Here it comes.*

"We've had this conversation many times. It is high time you learn how to run a household. It won't be long until you marry and take charge of your own staff and servants. You need to be assertive and authoritative, showing confidence, not uncertainty or hesitation."

Felicity had heard the speech so often she had almost committed it to memory. Mother was many things, and repetitive held the top spot on the list. But Rebecca didn't need a watchdog. This task was pointless.

"I only remind you because I wish for both my daughters to receive the proper instruction and education in all areas of womanhood. It would simply not do if I sent you off on your own without adequately preparing you for what may come. And I don't wish to fail you as a mother."

On the contrary, it was more likely the desire to maintain control over everyone in her home that drove her. But Felicity wouldn't dare verbalize that thought.

"I know, Mother, and we thank you for your attention to detail." She lowered her chin a little. "I apologize for my poor behavior. Please forgive me."

"Apology is accepted. Now off with you. We have less than two hours before the garden party. Everything must be perfect."

Felicity headed for the kitchen, pushing open the swinging door and slipping inside before it had a chance to spring back and smack her.

Rebecca clenched a wooden spoon in her left fist and shoved her right hand against her slender hip as she spoke.

"Now how many times do I have to tell you? I'm working hard to get this menu finished for Mrs. Chambers, and—" She paused. Immediate remorse crossed her face, and she relaxed her reprimanding pose. "Oh, Miss Felicity. I didn't know it was you. I thought it was Martin again asking when the noontime meal would be ready."

That sounded just like their butler. Always thinking about food, no matter how recently he'd eaten. It could be thirty minutes after breakfast, and his mind would be on the midday meal. But Rebecca was another matter. Most women who worked in the kitchens of the families living nearby boasted a girth to match their obvious love of food. Not so with their cook. Her shapely form was the envy of all the other cooks on the avenue.

Felicity smiled. "It's all right, Rebecca. It's only me. Mother is otherwise occupied with matters pertaining to the garden party. She asked me to come and inquire about the progress you're making." With a reassuring hand on Rebecca's arm, she added a light squeeze. "As if I even need to check."

Rebecca relaxed and returned the smile. "Child, you are going to go quite far with an attitude like that. It's a real pleasure working here, knowing that I get to see your shining face." She wagged her index finger at Felicity. "I don't let too many people in my kitchen. But you are always the exception."

Felicity leaned in close, peering in both directions before meeting Rebecca's eyes. "Don't worry. I promise not to tell anyone. It'll be our little secret."

The woman straightened with a nod. "Good. See that it stays that way." She winked then pivoted toward the sideboards along the east wall. "Now let me show you what I've finished so far from your mother's menu." She grinned and winked again. "Because you and I both know she'll expect a detailed report. Here." She handed several pieces of paper to Felicity. "As I name each item, you can cross it off on the list."

Felicity stepped with Rebecca down the line of delectable items that had been prepared, drawing a line through each name as it was called. The cook had always been her favorite staff member. She had embraced Felicity's interest in cooking with enthusiasm, touting the little girl as a prodigy in the culinary arts. The cook and her husband had no children of their own, but Rebecca said Felicity brought her enough joy to make up for a dozen children.

But enough living in the past. Mother had a garden party to host. If Felicity dallied too long with Rebecca, Mother would grow suspicious and come investigate. Better to assemble the facts for a report and beat a hasty retreat from the kitchen.

"It seems you have everything under control. . .as usual." She winked at Rebecca. "I believe Mother is now outside. I'll venture out to the veranda and provide the update. Perhaps then she'll stop fretting over the food being ready in time."

"Oh, it will be," Rebecca vowed. "This isn't the first garden party your mother has hosted."

"Nor will it be the last, I'm certain." With a final brush of Rebecca's arm, Felicity slipped outside.

ɜ๑.

"So did you hear that Aimee Parker has been seen on the arm of Jonathan Hancock for nearly three weeks straight?"

"Really?" Angela's voice raised an octave. "How exciting! Who told you this?" She sat perched on the edge of her seat.

Rachel ticked off the path the news had taken, spread from one woman to the next. "Widow Callahan told Mrs. Wipple, who in turn told my mother, who then told me."

"Do you think this means we'll be hearing a betrothal announcement soon? I have the perfect idea for staging a celebration for Aimee if that's the case."

Betrothals, engagements, romantic entanglements. One of these days, it might be Felicity's turn to have one. Her mind drifted to thoughts of Brandt. In all their conversations he had never once mentioned a young lady's name. That didn't necessarily mean he didn't have a special person in his life. It also didn't mean he did. Sure, he'd been a bit distant the last time they spoke, and he seemed to avoid answering her questions with direct answers. Up to that point, though, he'd been attentive and quite the gentleman, expressing interest in her and what she had to say. If she didn't know better, she might think he was interested in her. But that was impossible.

Felicity sipped her tea and listened to the banter volley back and forth between her two friends. They reminded her of Brianna and Laura from the factory. Amazing how the two sets of girls seemed so similar, despite their respective social standings. Even more remarkable that she had found friends at the factory to help ease the loss of her best friends here in her familiar world.

"What about you, Felicity?"

"Yes, is there a young man who has caught your eye recently?"

Felicity blinked and started. She placed her teacup on the saucer and looked back and forth between Rachel and Angela. She had been trying to pay attention. How could she have lost track of the conversation that fast?

"I'm sorry. Would you mind repeating the question?"

The two exchanged a knowing look, grins turning their lips upward at the corners. Rachel spoke first.

"We want to know if any of the young gentlemen have caught your eye."

Angela ran her tongue over her teeth. The ever-present twinkle in her eyes brightened. "By the way we caught you daydreaming, it's clear what the answer will be."

The image of Brandt again popped into Felicity's mind, and she tried to dislodge it. There was no way she was going to tell these two about him. They wouldn't allow her a moment's peace until every morsel of information was revealed. There might come a day when that disclosure would be unavoidable, but for now she'd do everything she could to keep it at bay.

"As you both well know, there are several handsome and eligible men who have caught the eye of nearly every young woman we know."

"That isn't what we asked, Felicity, and you know it." Rachel pressed her lips into a thin line. "Now answer the question, or I'll have Angela devise an alternative method of getting what we want."

Rachel wasn't one to jest, so Felicity knew she'd better think fast. She sighed. Forcing nonchalance, she raised her shoulders about an inch and shook her head. "As of right now, there are no young men we know who have captured my attention." Her friends were about to protest, but she cut them off before they had a chance to form any words. "However, there may be one who has displayed a great deal of potential in the field of suitors."

They didn't need to know that the man to whom she referred was Brandt.

"Aha!" Rachel nearly upset her teacup when she sat up straighter. A handful of matrons cast disparaging looks in their direction, so she ducked her head and lowered her voice. "I knew you weren't withdrawing from the race."

"Race?" Angela asked.

"Yes, Angela," Rachel answered with a touch of impatience. "The race in finding a young man worthy of our affections so that he might become so enamored he will offer a proposal of marriage in an instant."

Felicity and Angela covered their mouths and laughed behind their hands. Rachel had just attracted the attention of the dowager women. They didn't need to do it again. And Mother had made remarks about Rachel's influence not being the best for Felicity. If word got back to her that they were being less than appropriate at this little garden party, Mother might forbid all association. That would be the worst thing that could happen.

"I'm surprised that your mother hasn't already been speaking with some of her friends about arranging a match for you, Rachel." Felicity tucked her chin a little toward her chest and leveled a glance at her friend. If she had been wearing eyeglasses, she would have been staring over the top of the rims. "Didn't she mention at one point that she didn't trust your judgment when it came to selecting the proper husband?"

Angela gasped. "Did your mother truly say that?"

Rachel rolled her eyes and raised her teacup with calm assurance. "The only reason Mother made that statement was because she happened to see me making eyes at Benjamin Bradford one time. She doesn't understand that despite his mischievous nature, he's a fine gentleman when the situation warrants it."

Felicity exchanged a knowing look with Angela, who smiled and nodded. "And I suppose you've been in such a situation with Benjamin where you've had the opportunity to witness this upstanding behavior?"

Pink stained Rachel's cheeks, and the young woman averted her gaze. She was normally unaffected by good-natured jabs. That telltale reaction said more than any words might.

"I thought this conversation was supposed to be about potential suitors *you* have in mind, Felicity. How did we get around to discussing my preferences?"

No matter what, Rachel always managed to steer the topic of discussion back where she wanted it.

"Isn't anyone interested in inquiring about *my* standing where beaux are concerned?"

Rachel waved off Angela's question with a simultaneous blend of indifference and yearning. "Oh, everyone knows you'll end up marrying Nicholas Kennedy. You two have been paired since birth. There's no way you're going to get out of that arranged match."

"And not likely either of you will protest." Felicity winked, and Angela grinned.

"It's true." Angela placed one hand on her chest and struck a dramatic pose, her facial features softening into a daydreaming state. "Nicholas and I have come to an understanding where our parents are concerned."

"Don't you mean, neither one of you is able to defy their edicts over your lives?" Rachel interjected.

"No." Angela straightened, indignation replacing the softness from a moment ago. "We simply have no desire to go against their wishes." Her chin thrust upward, and her eyes formed mere slits. "Nicholas and I are perfectly happy to continue with the plans that have been laid. Were we not in agreement, the circumstances would be quite different. But neither Nicholas nor I have any reason to challenge what we believe is a good match."

"Well, I think it's wonderful that the two of you have developed a fondness for each other in spite of the matchmaking schemes." Felicity caught Rachel's eye and silently advised her to let that particular topic rest. "Mother hasn't ventured into that territory in recent weeks, but I know it's on her mind. After all, we *are* approaching our twentieth year. Most other young ladies we know are married or engaged already. It won't be long before we're all married and starting families of our own."

"Yes," Rachel agreed with a nod, "but that time isn't here yet. So for now let's enjoy our time together while we have it."

Felicity allowed her friends to shift back into talk of other young women they knew or the latest faux pas committed at a garden party or cotillion. Brandt had popped into her mind at the mere mention of a beau. True, they'd been walking together for a month now and he'd been in her thoughts a lot lately, but that didn't mean anything. Did it?

Somehow, despite every attempt Felicity made to avoid it, Brandt had managed to sneak his way into the mental image she created each time she pondered her future. Where the picture she envisioned used to include two or three young men from fine, upstanding families, now it featured Brandt standing side by side with the other gentlemen. And when each one was compared against the other, Brandt always came out on the winning end.

That both concerned and excited her at the same time. To think that a common man like Brandt might be able to compete with the men who traveled in her social circles and come out the champion. It was too much to even imagine possible. So for now that prospect would remain in her dreams.

Chapter 7

Felicity ran a cool, damp cloth over Lucy's face.

"Now, Mrs. Gibson, you make certain you don't overtax yourself."

"I promise," came the weak response.

A hint of color had returned yesterday, and this evening the light in Lucy's eyes brightened the dull expression she'd been wearing of late. Felicity had worried that Mrs. Gibson's health had only continued to decline the past three months. But for the first time in weeks she showed signs of improvement. That alone gave Felicity hope and confidence in her service.

"I've put some chicken broth on the stove, and Marianne has the rest of your supper under control." Felicity reached for the handles of her carpetbag and turned toward the small room off the main one. "I must say," she continued as she glanced over her shoulder, "it is truly wonderful to see the spark back in your eyes."

Lucy offered a wan smile. "It is all thanks to you, my dear. And Marianne." Her voice lacked volume, but it was clear and strong. "You both have been true angels. I know God will reward you for your selfless help." She caressed her swollen abdomen. "I pray this little one will have the pleasure of meeting you and knowing such a beautiful young woman."

Felicity paused a moment. She hadn't thought about what she'd be doing once Lucy was back on her feet again. Mother would likely help her find another family in need of assistance, but it would be nice to be able to come back and visit. Lucy was just now reaching her eighth month, so she still had several weeks before that time came. For now, Lucy needed reassurance.

"That child of yours will be strong and healthy, as long as you continue to follow the doctor's instructions. Just wait and see." She placed her hand on the knob and opened the door to the other room. "Now I must change, lest I be late getting home this evening. Mother and Father already eat later than normal. I don't need to give them further concern."

Felicity swapped the coarse clothing for her fine silk walking dress in record time. The material almost felt foreign to her. These days she spent more time in the plain outfits than the tailored fabrics from her seamstress. She was a completely different person when dressed in such a simple fashion. If Mother ever saw her, the proud matriarch would suffer from a case of the vapors.

Mother! Felicity ceased her ruminations and shoved the working clothes into her carpetbag. With a hasty farewell she rushed from the Gibson home and headed toward the corner where she met her driver to take her to her family's town house on Belvidere in the Grosse Pointe district.

Sneaking in the rear door through the room next to the kitchen, Felicity peered around the corner to see Rebecca turned away from her. She tiptoed toward the back stairs and cringed when the bottom step creaked.

"If you insist upon attempting to slip into this house unnoticed, you might consider hanging a rope from your bedchamber window or using the tree branches to the rear of the house."

With her lower lip between her teeth, Felicity turned to face her cook. The woman's flaxen hair was wound into a tight bun with a few flyaway strands framing her face. A raised eyebrow mixed with the scolding tone made Felicity feel like a little girl instead of a nineteen-year-old young woman.

"I am sorry, Rebecca. But I don't wish Mother to take notice that I am late yet again. And if I used the front door, Martin would announce my tardiness." She pleaded with her eyes. "Promise you won't breathe a word to anyone?"

Rebecca pursed her lips and mimicked a chastising expression Felicity's mother often used. "All right. But there will come a time when I will no longer be able to conceal your activities. And be forewarned." The cook wagged her index finger in Felicity's direction. "I overheard your mother and father mentioning your charity work earlier this afternoon. They will no doubt wish to speak with you before supper."

Felicity's heart stopped for a second, and the blood drained from her face. Talk about her charity work? If Mother and Father together had discussed this, the result of that conversation wouldn't be good. Rebecca didn't need to see her worry, though, so Felicity forced a smile to her face.

"Thank you, Rebecca. You're a true kindred spirit."

The cook cleared her throat with a grunt and returned to her duties. Felicity spun around toward the stairs again and hastened to the second level. With a glance to the left and right, she verified the absence of any other household members then slipped toward the east wing and her private room. Just as she stowed the carpetbag behind some of her gowns in the wardrobe, a knock sounded on her door.

"Come in!"

The knob turned, and the door opened just a few inches. Her fourteen-year-old sister, Cecily, peered around the edge then bounded into the room and plopped on Felicity's bed, her carefully styled blond curls bouncing with the action.

"It's about time you came home. Father just arrived, and Mother sent me to fetch you. They're waiting in the parlor." She gave Felicity a mischievous grin. "Did you do something to upset them again?"

Felicity placed her hands on her hips and pursed her lips. "I'm sure I have no idea what you're talking about. Rebecca informed me that Mother and Father simply wish to discuss my charity work." And she prayed the end result of the conversation wouldn't put an end to that work. She wagged a playful finger at Cecily. "I'm sorry to disappoint you, but I doubt you'll find any fodder for your incessant torment." She forced a sweet smile to hide her inner turmoil. "Thank you for coming to notify me, though."

"Well, you'd better come tell me the moment you're done talking. I want to hear all the details."

Felicity shook her head. "I'm sure you'll find out everything one way or another. Whether it be from me or Father." She turned toward her dressing table. "Now I'm going to take just a moment to powder my nose and then report to the parlor immediately."

Cecily climbed off the bed. "Very well. I know when I'm not wanted." She headed back toward the door to the hall. "I will tell Mother and Father you will be down straightaway."

As soon as the door closed, Felicity breathed a sigh of relief. From the moment she heard the knock, her heart had been in her throat. That was too close. Just one minute longer and she might have crossed paths with Father. She normally made it home a full thirty minutes before him. There would have been no end to the questions had they arrived at the same time.

After a quick glance in the looking glass, she left her room and headed downstairs. If Mother didn't even want to wait for Father to relax after arriving home, Felicity had better not delay her appearance.

The soft murmur of voices traveled into the entryway as soon as Felicity stepped off the stairs. She sent a silent prayer heavenward that whatever her parents had to say, it wouldn't put an end to her daily work. Before she moved into the doorway, she took a deep breath and willed her heart to beat at a normal rhythm.

"Do stop dawdling in the hallway, Felicity dear, and please join us."

Her mother's voice carried across the room and beckoned Felicity to obey. At least she didn't sound upset. A trifle impatient, perhaps, but cordial overall.

Felicity walked toward her parents and attempted to gauge their thoughts by the expressions they wore. Mother perched on the settee with her hands folded in her lap and her long legs tucked underneath, her lips pressed into a nondescript line. Father towered behind one of the wingback chairs, his fingers curled around the wood frame above the cushioned back. His face held no indication of his thoughts. When neither of them spoke, she swallowed and wet her lips.

"Cecily came up to say you wished to see me?"

"Yes."

Mother's curt reply set Felicity's heart racing yet again. If that didn't give away her nervousness, her erratic breathing would.

"Please come and take a seat, Felicity." Father extended an arm toward the other wingback chair next to where he stood. "There is a matter we need to discuss with you."

A matter? Felicity took small steps toward the chair but didn't dawdle. Her parents would see right through her purposeful hesitation, and that might make the situation worse. Once seated, she smoothed her hands on the two pieces of custom-made, matching fabric covering the arms. They helped absorb the dampness of her palms as she awaited the start of this discussion.

She looked back and forth between the two before her. Father darted a quick glance at Mother, who cleared her throat with a dainty cough.

"Felicity, dear, it has come to the attention of your father and me that your charity work has been leading you into areas that possess a certain risk for someone of your position." Mother shifted and leveled a direct look at Felicity. "Specifically, the knowledge that you have recently been working at a factory near the river."

Felicity gasped. How had they found out? She'd been extra careful to cover her tracks and eliminate all evidence of her daytime activities. Everyone knew she spent the time helping Mrs. Gibson, but they didn't know about the factory. Felicity knew she'd dishonored her parents by lying. It was inevitable that she'd be discovered. She just didn't expect that day to come so soon. She started to open her mouth, but a wave of Mother's hand silenced the words on her lips.

"Your father and I have supported you for several years in the many endeavors in which you have been involved. We have permitted you to pay visits to undesirable areas of town with only a driver as your chaperone, and we have looked the other way when reports have come back to us of you taking your work a little too far when it comes to your generosity."

Remorse descended as Mother reminded her of the unwise choices she'd made in the past. Felicity wished those mistakes could remain unmentioned. She might have been naive enough to fail to recognize the dangerous attention of that father of the one family or to be so taken with the two young boys that one time that she didn't see they were taking advantage of her. But the current work she did was nothing like those experiences. Convincing Mother and Father, though, wouldn't be easy.

"Thankfully, those errors in judgment have been minor," Mother continued. "And they haven't caused our family any harm in regard to wagging tongues or social standing. But this"—she waved one of her hands in a wispy motion—"this factory work has caused several matrons among my acquaintances to question our position of authority where you're concerned."

Felicity wanted to speak out on her own behalf and defend her actions. But she knew her place. Mother would allow her rebuttal when the time came. For now she was expected to sit quietly and listen.

"Now as I said, your father and I support your endeavors to assist those less fortunate. But I cannot abide the idea of my daughter interacting with the surly sorts and others of questionable standing who reside by that area of the river. After all, it's not only your safety that concerns us. We also have our reputation at stake."

Reputation. As if this small affair with which she occupied herself would cause any lasting harm to the years her parents—and grandparents before them—had spent establishing themselves among the upper echelon of Detroit.

Father shifted and leaned forward, and Felicity turned to look at him while he spoke.

"What your mother means is that we don't wish to see you doing anything that might bring you harm. Our social standing *is* important." He cast a reproving look in Mother's direction and returned his attention to Felicity. "We know you have a strong desire to help those in need, and your service brings glory and honor to God. But your safety is of prime concern. We cannot guarantee that you won't meet with undesirable circumstances if you insist upon spending time in certain areas without a chaperone or without telling us where you've been."

Father slid his left hand along the back of the chair as he moved around it to take a seat, angling his body toward Felicity.

"Now why don't you tell us more about this current project of yours? Help us fill in the holes of what we're hearing."

Felicity paused before speaking. She'd worked out an explanation in her mind as her parents talked, but Father's words about honoring God made her rethink her planned speech. Mimicking her mother's posture, she took a deep breath and released it quietly as she sent a prayer heavenward for help. She meant well, and her motives were pure. However, more than a pure heart would be needed here. She'd lied, and she had to face the consequences. Hopefully her parents would understand. This had to work. Otherwise Father might forbid her from continuing. And she didn't want that. She smoothed her clammy hands on the material of her skirt and swallowed past the tightness in her throat.

"Yes, it's true that I have taken a job at the soap and candle factory along the river."

Mother gasped, but Father stayed her verbal outcry with his hand and nodded at Felicity to continue.

"But I assure you I am in no danger in the position where I've been assigned. And I don't intend to remain there long. When Mrs. Gibson delivers her baby and is given permission to end the doctor's orders, she'll seek work again at the factory, and my assistance will no longer be needed in that regard."

She made sure to include Mother but spent more time looking at Father. He would likely be more lenient and understanding. However, she still had to be careful or he'd issue an edict, and it would mean the end to her work.

"My supervisor has placed me alongside two other girls who come from modest families. I have come to enjoy the work I do very much. It's rare to see any altercations or threat to our safety, and a supervisor is in constant motion, circulating throughout the work areas. We also submit regular status reports. If evidence of a problem arises, it's handled immediately."

Father leaned back in his chair. "It does relieve me to hear of such a tightly run operation."

Mother's eyes filled with worry. "But what about the walk through that part of town? It is the business district, if I'm not mistaken."

"Oh, I don't walk alone, Mother. Brandt makes sure that I arrive at the gate safely."

Oh no! Had she just let Brandt's name slip from her tongue? She'd been so careful up to this point. And now this. She'd better make the best of it.

"Brandt?" Mother's voice raised half an octave. "Do you mean to tell us that you are keeping company with a young man who also works in the factories?" Reproach spilled over into every facet of Mother's features and body language. "Felicity Chambers, have we not taught you better than that?"

"But, Mother, Brandt isn't anything like some of those men. We meet along the way and share enjoyable conversation to make the time pass more quickly. His manners are impeccable, and he treats me with a great deal of respect."

Father regarded her through slightly narrowed eyes. "Does this young man have a last name?"

"I believe he said it's Dalton. We only introduced ourselves the one time, but I'm fairly certain I'm recalling it correctly."

Mother leaned forward. "What else do you know about him? Where does he live? Who are his parents? What type of lifestyle does he lead when he's not at work? Why has he singled you out to escort from the obvious dozens of other young ladies who work there?"

"Davinia, please." Father's low voice rumbled as he muttered the soft reprimand. "Let's give our daughter the benefit of the doubt before assuming too much."

Felicity shot him silent thanks for interceding. He might not support Mother's style of interrogation, but he still had questions in his eyes. She knew she'd disappointed them both. But she had been so sure she'd done the right thing. Now, despite Father's apparent patience, he quietly demanded answers. He wasn't satisfied yet.

"We appreciate your honesty, Felicity," Father began. "You could have denied everything and forced us to take other measures. But you didn't. However, without knowing more about this young man you've mentioned, we must caution you against developing a rapport with him."

"But, Father, it isn't like that at all." She unclasped her hands and rested them on the arms of the chair. "He is only a friend. Nothing more." At least that much was true in reality. Her thoughts were another matter. "We met on my first day of work. He was starting his first day at the refinery. It didn't take us long to realize that merging our respective paths wouldn't add any time. And it provides us both with a companion for the walk."

Father pressed his lips into a thin line. "And you say he is always respectful?"

"I have never found a single fault with his manners."

"Hmm." Father inhaled and released his breath in a loud sigh. He was about to make a judgment. She prayed it would be in her favor. "Very well. You have always provided clear explanations in the past, despite initial misgivings. And because of that we will trust you now. But be careful where this young man is concerned. Use wisdom and exercise caution. Otherwise, your mother and I will put a stop to your work." He turned toward Mother. "Davinia? Is that agreeable to you?"

Mother nodded and pursed her lips. "I do not see any cause to end your charity work, Felicity dear. But I agree with your father's word of caution. This young man might be respectful and possess manners that make you trust him, but I do not want to see you develop a relationship beyond friendship with him. There are more than enough young men right here in the Grosse Pointe district who would be happy to receive your affections. Guard your heart, and remember your place."

There it was again. That constant reminder of her social standing and the distinctive line drawn that separated her from everyone else who wasn't like them. Just once she'd like to see people judged according to their character. Not just by their financial holdings.

"Thank you, Mother. Father." She regarded them each in turn and dipped her head in acknowledgment. "I will take what you've said this evening to heart and not forget. It means a great deal to me that you trust me to make the right decisions. And I promise that you have no reason to worry. Should any risk develop, you have my word that I will cease all involvement."

Felicity prayed that day would never come as long as she was helping Mrs. Gibson. Her work and the time spent with Brandt meant more to her than anything else she'd done. Brianna and Laura made up for the daily absence of her childhood friends, and the skills she was learning gave her a feeling of accomplishment. A rather substantial void would exist if she had to give up everything—especially Brandt.

Father stood and extended his right hand toward Mother to help her rise before tucking her hand into the crook of his arm. "Now that we have that settled, let's adjourn to the dining room. I believe Rebecca has supper ready to serve." He looked at Felicity with a twinkle in his eyes. "Your brother has invited his fiancée to join us. They and your sister are no doubt anxiously awaiting our arrival so they can eat."

Felicity stood as her parents stepped past her. Just as she moved to follow, Father reached out and ran the backs of his fingers down her cheek. He gave her a loving smile, and she returned it with one of her own.

As they exited the parlor, Felicity stared at their backs. That conversation had gone better than she'd hoped. It could have been much worse. At least she was allowed to continue her work and her friendship with Brandt. If she wanted things to stay that way, though, she must be careful. And where Brandt was concerned, that became more and more difficult with each passing day.

Chapter 8

Brandt plopped down on the grass beside Felicity, and she jumped in response.

"Sorry. I didn't mean to scare you."

She waved him off. "It's all right. I must have been daydreaming."

Her voice trembled a little. She wasn't comfortable. That much was clear. He held a tin cup full of water in one hand and his lunch pail in the other as he assessed the secluded spot. A handful of people walked in the distance. The rear walls of the buildings kept them hidden from view of the streets, and the river to the south afforded a natural barrier. None of Father's employees would find him here. But now he wondered if this meeting was a wise one. She didn't need to see his hesitation, though. Felicity was already nervous.

"See? What did I tell you?" Brandt announced with forced pride. "This is the perfect spot."

Felicity looked around them with a guarded expression. "It is out of the way. That's for certain." She hesitated a moment then nodded. "But it does appear to be a good choice. We can eat our lunches quickly and not worry about anyone from the refinery or factory interrupting or delaying us. We don't have long for our lunch break."

Brandt snapped his fingers and pointed at her. "Exactly."

She took a bite of an apple but still looked to the left and right, as if trying to determine if anyone was watching them. He was the one who had to be concerned about a manager or supervisor spotting him in this non-business-related situation. They would report back to Father for certain. She had nothing to worry about. So why was she so jumpy?

"How did you find this place?"

Brandt jerked his gaze back to hers and stuttered. "Oh, um, I was out walking one day and stumbled upon it. Seemed like it would be a good place for an impromptu picnic." At least that wasn't a lie. She didn't need to know he had found it during one of his routine checks of his father's business holdings.

Felicity shifted her focus and regarded her apple as if it held some special secret. "It does seem lovely."

Her voice was so soft he had to strain to hear her above the lapping of the water against the shoreline and the noise from the nearby factories. It was time for a change of subject.

"How has your morning at work been?"

Felicity looked at him and smiled. "Quite well. And yours?"

He shrugged. "There haven't been any surprises or problems."

"We had a small issue when one of the churns for the soap stopped working. But Laura figured out there were some pieces of wax that had managed to get into the space between the teeth of the crank, causing it to skip and eventually jam."

Finally. A subject she seemed to embrace. At least the only problems they had were cranks breaking and wax melting wrong. The machines at the refinery were far more dangerous. "That didn't set you back by much in productivity, did it?"

"Not much, no." Felicity took a bite of her sandwich and chewed slowly then swallowed. "Laura wasn't too happy with the dirt stains on her clothing, though." She giggled. "She forgot to tie on her apron this morning, so when she had to reach in between the teeth, the dust and grime transferred from the crank to her."

Brandt chuckled at the mental image he formed from her description. The ladies he normally found among his acquaintance would never set foot in a place like the factory, let alone reach their hands inside a piece of machinery to fix a broken crank. The mere idea of dirt usually sent them running off to change clothes.

"Well, at least she fixed the problem. And working at the factory, she likely gets oil and wax on her often."

"Not in the least. I believe she was upset because she's supposed to meet a young gentleman after the final whistle blows. Rumor has it he'll be walking her home." Felicity smiled and took a drink from her tin cup.

Brandt waggled his eyebrows. "Aha. That explains it. She's besotted."

Her lips tightened, preventing the water she'd just drunk from escaping.

He laughed and placed his hands in his lap as he attempted to school his expression into one of nonchalance. It was no use. "I'm sorry," he said through barely contained chuckles. "I do thank you, though, for sparing me the spray of your drink."

With a swallow and dainty clearing of her throat, Felicity once again regained her composure. "You are most welcome," she replied, raising her cup again to her lips. "But I cannot guarantee that should a repeat occurrence take place, you will remain free from harm."

It took Brandt a moment to process what she'd just said. He narrowed his eyes at the playful threat laced between her words. She spoke with such calm, her expression devoid of any mischief. He couldn't tell if she was flirting or serious. And she likely preferred it that way. Such a unique blend of sophistication and affability.

He reached into his pail and retrieved a sandwich wrapped in a red-and-white-checkered cloth. Holding it up for her perusal, he raised his eyebrows and grinned. "Well? What do you think?"

"About your sense of humor or the fact that you finally brought a sandwich for lunch?" She took a final bite of her apple, the corners of her lips turning up slightly as she chewed.

"My—" He paused. Wait a minute. Had she just given him a taste of his own medicine? He clenched his jaw and raised his chin a fraction of an inch. "The sandwich, of course."

She swallowed and tossed the core into her pail. "In that case, I approve. You simply do not know what you're missing eating all those cookies and cakes."

He leaned back on his elbows and regarded her through half-lidded eyes. "Well, I thought it might be wise to give your suggestion a try." Taking a bite of the ham and mustard between the bread, he released an overexaggerated groan. "Mmm. It's the best sandwich I've ever had."

Felicity covered her mouth and giggled. "And probably the first."

Brandt shook a finger in her direction. "That's not true. I seem to recall my mother making some when I was a boy."

She reached for her own sandwich and daintily set about unfolding a checkered cloth that matched his. When she looked up at him again, she grinned. "And since then you've likely taken your fill of whatever was convenient."

He propped himself on one elbow. "I'll have you know our cook prepares delicious meals and makes sure each one of us eats some of everything she's made."

Felicity paused with her sandwich midway to her mouth and stared, her lips parted. "You have a cook?" she managed, her voice thick.

Oh no! How was he going to get out of this one?

"In a manner of speaking. She lives with us and is part of the family. Cooking is how she earns her keep and pays for her room."

She cocked her head and remained silent for several moments. Brandt could feel the heat warm his neck and creep toward his cheeks. If she figured out he had a butler and maidservants as well, there'd be no end to the long line of questions she'd ask.

"I can understand that," she finally said with a nod. "Mrs. Gibson has a girl working in her home to take care of the children and the house. She doesn't live with Mrs. Gibson, but she just as easily could."

Brandt didn't dare offer anything more. He might give away the address of his family's three-story town house or some other critical piece of information that would reveal his charade. Time to get the focus off of him.

"What about you?" He took a small bite of ham and swallowed. "Does this girl working for Mrs. Gibson make your meals, too?"

"Oh no! I don't live with Mrs. Gibson."

He drew his eyebrows together. "But I thought you walked to work from there every morning."

She finished her sandwich and shook out the crumbs from the cloth before putting it back in her pail. Then she dusted off her hands and placed them in her lap. "I do, but I walk there from home before that."

"And where is home?"

"Um, not too many blocks from there."

Now *she* was the one being evasive with a nondescript answer. Perhaps there was something she didn't want to tell him. Or she might be ashamed of where she lived.

"So you found out Mrs. Gibson had to quit, and you offered to share your wages until she recovers?"

"Yes."

"Don't your own folks need your wages, too?"

Felicity yanked the stem of a dandelion weed from the ground and twirled it between her fingers. "Well, they have my older brother, Zach, to help."

He pushed himself to a sitting position and leaned forward. Softening his voice, he tried to coax out a little more about her home life. Maybe it would give him more insight into her background.

"But I get the feeling they don't exactly approve of this."

A pained expression flitted across her face before she had the chance to hide it. "They would definitely prefer it if my work were not the factory, but they don't mind the temporary help I'm offering."

If only he could take away the hurt she was feeling and replace it with the carefree nonchalance she'd always shown. Then again, if he did that, he might not find out anything more about this young woman who'd become such an important part of his life.

"Have you told them you're not exactly in any danger working where you are?"

"Yes." She inhaled then puffed out her cheeks and blew on the white seeds of the weed. "And I even told them that I had you to walk with me."

Brandt reached out and covered the hand in her lap with his own, offering her a slight grin. "Well, if they care about you, as it seems they do, telling them you're keeping company with me might not reassure them in the way you had hoped."

❧

Felicity looked down at the hand covering hers, his tanned skin a stark contrast to her pale peach shade. She gave him a wary look. "Mother did mention her concerns about that."

Actually, if truth be told, Mother had overreacted in her interrogation regarding Brandt. Father hadn't been too pleased, either, but at least he had maintained a cool head about it all.

"And what about your father?" Brandt continued, as if he'd read her thoughts. "I'd think he'd want to keep his daughter safe, too."

"Yes. But he was more willing to trust me when I told him there was no cause for concern." She toyed with the idea of removing her hand from underneath his, but it felt so good to have his touch and reassurance.

"I take it this conversation happened rather recently."

She inhaled a sharp breath. "Why do you say that?"

Brandt leaned back and rested his forearms on his knees. She immediately felt the loss of warmth from his withdrawn hand, but his nearness still offered a great deal of comfort in its place.

"I noticed when I first sat down that you seemed a bit distracted. And you weren't yourself. That easygoing manner of yours was missing."

Felicity ducked her chin. "Oh." And she had hoped her teasing remarks and smiles might cover up the inner turmoil. Obviously they hadn't. Brandt had seen right through her unsuccessful attempts. And now he wanted to know more.

She saw his hand before his fingers touched her chin as he raised her head to meet his gaze. "Hey," he said softly. "You can't be expected to be blithe all the time. Life isn't that perfect."

He moved his index finger back and forth on the underside of her chin. She quelled the shiver that started somewhere near the base of her spine. Instead, she got lost in the coffee-colored depths of his caring eyes.

As if he had read her mind, he jerked his hand back and put some distance between them.

"Sorry about that." He averted his gaze for a brief second then released a short sigh. "So what was the outcome of this conversation?"

Felicity blinked a few times. Conversation? Oh, right. The one with her parents about her work and Brandt. She'd better get a handle on her emotions. And fast.

"It was good."

A dimple in his right cheek appeared, accompanying his grin. "Just good?"

She shrugged. "Well, as I mentioned, Father was more willing to trust me to make the right decisions. Mother wasn't quite so sure, but she eventually agreed as well." She broke off a few blades of grass and played with them. "Of course, this came with the obligatory reminder that I need to be careful at all times and not let down my guard where anyone is concerned."

"Especially not with strange young men who offer to escort you safely to the factory."

"Yes. That's almost exactly what they said, although it was more inferred than spoken."

He resumed his former position with arms on his knees. "At least they seem understanding."

"For now." Felicity nodded. "But I still have to be careful."

His hand touched hers again. "I promise not to give them any reason to worry more than they already are. And if it helps, I'll even tell them so myself."

She straightened. "Oh no! That won't be necessary."

Gracious. If they were to meet Brandt, there would be no way she'd be permitted to continue her association with him. Her parents would judge him based upon his clothing, no matter how clean he kept himself or how mannerly he was. No, it was best he remain nothing more than a name to them.

"All right. All right." He chuckled and patted her hand. "I'll stay a faceless escort if you wish."

"Thank you."

Oh how she wished he could become something more than that. His concern for her warmed her heart. And the softness in his eyes all but wore down her resolve to keep those parts of her life a secret. No. She dared not risk it. She walked on thin ice as it was.

If she didn't control the circumstances as much as possible, that thin layer would crack and she'd be pulled beneath the safe surface into the turbulent waters below. If the crashing jolt of reality coming face-to-face with the day-to-day world she'd created didn't ruin her, her parents' reactions to the truth would.

The whistles at the factories blew loud and strong, releasing clouds of steam high into the air and signaling the end to their lunch break.

"Looks like it's time to get back to work." Brandt stood and dusted off his pants, then retrieved his cap and slapped it on his head. He held out a hand to assist her. "You ready?"

She placed her hand in his and smiled. "Not exactly, but what other choice do we have?" Standing, she fluffed out the folds of her skirts.

Brandt bent to pick up her pail and grabbed his as well.

"Not a lot. But just think. Only a few more hours and we'll be done for the day. I'm sure the time will fly."

"Yes, and then we have our one day of rest and Sunday services before starting all over again."

He handed her pail to her and mumbled something that sounded like, "Don't remind me."

"What was that?"

Brandt cleared his throat. "Uh, nothing. We do have one day of reprieve, and it's a much-needed one." He started walking, and she had to almost jog to keep up with him. "We'd better get back. Don't want to be late and receive a demerit for tardiness."

Well, the least she could do was show her appreciation for the enjoyable thirty minutes they'd shared.

"Thank you for joining me for lunch. And for finding this little spot."

He stopped and turned toward her. "You're welcome. We should do it again."

"Perhaps."

"Well, off I go." He touched two fingers to the brim of his cap and saluted. "Until next week."

Felicity rushed toward the factory and stepped inside with two minutes to spare. She had such a good time with him today. In fact, every time they were together, he managed to lift her spirits and make her forget her troubles. . .even if only for a little while. But that was where she had to watch out. If she wasn't careful, the sincerity in those deep brown eyes of his would be her undoing. No. Forgetting simply wasn't an option.

Chapter 9

"Felicity!" Laura ran toward her from across the courtyard later that day, waving a slip of paper high above her head. She stumbled but caught herself before a fall and continued her advancement.

Felicity paused. What scheme did Laura have in mind now? Felicity had hoped to step out for a breath of fresh air. They only had fifteen minutes. Laura had better make this fast.

The young woman halted in front of Felicity and doubled over, breathing hard. "I'm sorry," she said in a whoosh. "I didn't. . .mean to. . .interrupt. . .your break." Laura took several deep breaths and stood straight. "But this notice was just posted on the bulletin board near the front entrance."

"What does it say?" Felicity tried to catch sight of some of the words, but Laura wouldn't hold the paper still. "If you'd stop waving it, I might be able to read it."

Laura bit her lower lip and offered a sheepish grin. "Oh, sorry." She extended her hand with the note. "Here. Read it for yourself. But be quick about it. I have to put it back when we're done."

Felicity took the paper from Laura and scanned the brief missive. When she finished, she lifted her eyes over the top of the paper, quirked one corner of her mouth, and raised her eyebrows. "You came running all the way across the courtyard for this?"

Laura's shoulders slumped. "What do you mean, 'for this'?" she mimicked. "It's a picnic! In a park by the river!"

"Yes." Felicity nodded. "I read that."

"But aren't you excited?" She spun in circles, her arms straight out to the sides, making her look like one of those seeds from a maple tree twirling to the ground. "Just imagine. They're closing the factories on a Saturday for this. That's big news! And everyone's been invited." She paused and gave Felicity a smug look. "That means the young men from the refinery, too."

"Ah, so now I know why you're anticipating this auspicious event."

Laura tilted her head. "Aus-what event?"

She did it again. Felicity closed her eyes a second then opened them. She had to be more careful about her word choices. But sometimes they just slipped out. "Auspicious. It means fortunate or promising."

Laura straightened with a quick jerk of her head, a wide smile transforming her face. "Oh, then yes. It will be very promising, maybe for you and Brianna, too, if you don't botch it."

"What are we going to botch?"

They both turned to face Brianna, who joined them.

Felicity held out the paper. "Laura here is exclaiming over the great opportunities we'll all have at the upcoming picnic hosted by the management of the factories here along the river."

Brianna snatched it and held it up to read. She gave Felicity an amused look. "Oh, she is? And why do you think there will be 'great opportunities,' Laura?"

Laura stamped her foot and shoved her fists against her hips. "Oh, you two are such spoilsports. It's a wonder you manage to have any fun at all."

"Just because we don't have your type of fun, Laura, doesn't mean we don't have any." Felicity gave her friend a light shove in the shoulder. "Besides, why are you so interested in other men from the refinery? What happened to that young gentleman who was supposed to walk you home the other day?"

Brianna leaned forward and tapped one finger against her lips. "Yes. You never said a thing about him afterward. So let's have it."

The young woman shrugged and dropped her arms as if the meeting she'd anticipated for days meant nothing at all. "He walked me home, we said good night, and that was the end of it."

Brianna crossed her arms and smirked. "Not your type, or are you looking to increase your options a bit more?"

"I'll have you know," Laura replied, turning to bring her face within inches of Brianna's, "that I am in no hurry to marry the first man who crosses my path." She stuck her nose in the air and closed her eyes. "I have standards, thank you."

Brianna gave Laura a little shove and laughed. "You are such an easy target when it comes to men."

"That's because I have them in my life," Laura said, her pointed words succinct.

"And who says I don't?" Brianna replied.

Laura stopped her verbal onslaught with a quick halt. Her entire demeanor changed from puffed-up self-confidence to supreme interest in Brianna's last remark. Felicity stood in silence watching the verbal volley. There was no way she dared interject, or they might turn everything around on her and start the interrogation about Brandt. With her feelings for him so uncertain, questions from her friends were the last thing she needed.

Laura clasped her hands in front of her and stared wide-eyed at Brianna like a little girl in front of the candy jars at the mercantile. "Do you mean you've been keeping company with a young man and you haven't said anything to us?"

Brianna shrugged it off with a nonchalant air. "I didn't say that."

"Then why did you say what you did?"

"To see you react the way you are right now," Brianna replied with a wink and a grin.

Laura huffed. "Well, I never!"

"Like I said. You make an easy target." She reached for Laura's hands and gave them a quick squeeze. "But that's why we love you."

Laura pretended offense at the good-natured teasing, but she relaxed her shoulders and cast a quick glance from the corner of her eye at Brianna. Everything was fine again. The two were still best friends.

"So what about this picnic?"

Leave it to Laura to get the conversation back on track to where she wanted to steer it.

Felicity took the paper back from Brianna and read it again. "I believe it sounds like a truly splendid idea. It will be a delight to escape the cavernous surroundings of the factory and bask in the warm sunshine for a change."

When no response came from either of the two girls, Felicity looked up. They stood staring, their mouths hanging slightly open.

"What? Did I say something wrong?"

"'Truly splendid?'" Laura echoed.

"'Cavernous surroundings?'" Brianna added.

"Honestly." Laura expelled a sigh and brushed her bangs out of her face. "If we didn't know better, we might mistake you for one of those hoity-toity gems from the Pointe."

If only they knew. Felicity chuckled, the hollow sound and her pounding heart making her palms sweat. She brushed them against her skirt but made it look like she was removing pieces of dirt instead.

"I'm sorry. I guess it's all the books I read. Sometimes those words just spill out." Felicity hunched her shoulders and splayed her hands, palms up. "If it happens again, just smack my arm and let me know."

"Oh, you can count on that!" Brianna said with a twinkle in her eye.

"Perfect." Laura draped her arms around the shoulders of Felicity and Brianna and steered them toward the west entrance. "Now can we get back to talking about our plans for the picnic?"

☙

One week later Felicity stood at the edge of the park and stared. What a sight to behold! There had to be hundreds of people gathered on the grassy areas, and that didn't include the number in small dinghies or rowboats on the water, or even those brave enough to risk the frigid river. It might be August, but she'd stepped in that river on the hottest day of the year. And nothing would make her repeat that experience.

"Well, don't just stand there! Come on!" Laura turned her face to the wind and sniffed. "I can smell popcorn and fried chicken. And the music is so lively. Let's go!" She ran ahead of them, almost bouncing along the way.

Brianna turned toward Felicity. "Some days I wonder if she'll ever be less excitable."

"If she did that, she wouldn't be Laura," Felicity countered with a grin.

Brianna sighed. "True."

Felicity tucked the handles of their picnic basket with a few extra treats into the crook of her right elbow and grabbed Brianna's arm with her left as they followed in Laura's wake. "You have to admit, though, there is never a dull moment with her."

Brianna tilted back her head and laughed. "No. You're right about that. Still, I wonder what it will take for her to settle down."

"Are you saying you envy her exuberance?"

"Me?" Brianna slapped her free hand against her chest, her top lip curling a little. "No, but I look forward to when we meet the man who will tame her."

A giggle escaped Felicity's lips at the thought of a man being able to tame Laura's wild ways. "Now *that* would be a sight to see."

"All right. Let's find a good place to set out our blanket and food. Then we can go see who else is here."

Felicity spied an area a little off to the side and out of the way. Perfect. Just the right amount of shade and seclusion, but still at the edge of those gathered on the ground nearby. Brianna was looking in the opposite direction, but Felicity gave her a tug.

"Why do you want to go way over here?" Brianna jerked her thumb over their shoulders toward the men onstage performing a spirited number with their instruments. "The center of activity is over there."

Exactly where she didn't want to be. What if someone who knew her recognized her? She would never be able to explain her presence or her acquaintance with them to Brianna and Laura. And what about Brandt? He was sure to be here. It was only a matter of time until he spotted her, too. She hoped to be alone when that happened, and she wouldn't be if they were in the middle of the crowd.

"I know, but I thought it might be better to have a little peace and quiet." She stepped into the clear space and set down the basket, lifting the lid to retrieve the cloth on which they'd sit.

Brianna grabbed one end and stepped away to help Felicity spread out the cloth. "All right. We'll probably want the quiet after being here a few hours."

Thankfully they were in a part of town that her friends didn't frequent. But that didn't mean she was safe. She couldn't let down her guard even for a minute.

"I'm going to find Laura and see what kind of trouble she's gotten herself into."

Brianna walked around Felicity then turned to look over her shoulder. "You going to be all right here?" She grinned. "I'm sure it won't be long before Laura finds us again."

Felicity waved her away. "I'll be fine. Don't worry about me. Go and take a look at everything. There will be plenty of time for me to do the same later."

"Bye."

She watched as Brianna disappeared into the crowd. Truth be told, sitting alone was exactly what she preferred. The less she wandered around, the less chance of being discovered. How would she ever explain her clothing and association with girls like Brianna and Laura if someone from the Pointe district were to appear? It might not be likely in this area, but anything was possible. Of course, if Brandt were with her, perhaps they might think she was someone else and keep on walking.

"Excuse me, but is anyone sitting here?"

Brandt!

Felicity raised a hand to shade her eyes and stared up at the shadowed figure standing before her. It was as though her thoughts had conjured him into appearing.

"No." She lowered her head and extended her hand toward the space in front of her. "Please. Sit down."

"Don't mind if I do," he said, snapping his suspenders against his chest.

As soon as he was settled, he swiped off his cap and dropped it beside him. Shocks of unruly hair shot out in all directions. It reminded her of when they first met. Felicity giggled. He couldn't be more endearing.

"What?" He raised his hands to his head and offered a rueful smile. "All right, so I forgot to brush my hair this morning." Grabbing his cap in his fist, he held it out in front of him. "That's why I have this," he said and let the cap fall once more.

Felicity covered her mouth and spoke through her fingers. "If you don't mind, I don't mind."

Brandt slapped his hands together as if ridding them of dirt or crumbs, then plunked them down on his crossed legs. "Good. Now that we have that settled." He rose up just a bit on his knees and sniffed in the general direction of the picnic basket. "What are we having for dessert?"

Felicity tugged the basket a little closer to her. Her friends would tar and feather her if she gave up any of their sweets. "That is for Brianna and Laura."

He chuckled and splayed his hands in defense. "I was only teasing." Patting his stomach, he sighed, the sound full of contentment. "Besides, I already had my fill from a few of the vendors on the other side of the park. The barbecued beef was delicious. Decided to take a walk and ended up finding you."

She smoothed out the folds of her dress and placed her hands in her lap. "We arrived not long ago. Laura ran off as soon as she smelled the food and heard the music, so Brianna went to find her."

"And left you alone?"

Felicity pointed to the basket. "Someone had to stay and look out for our belongings."

"Good point."

&

Brandt leaned back on his elbows and regarded Felicity for a moment. He'd seen the trio the moment they arrived, but he waited for the opportune moment to approach. At least he didn't have to wait long. And since he'd already eaten, he had no reason not to spend the rest of the time with Felicity. Or at least as long as she would allow.

The place she'd chosen was perfect. He'd already dodged one of the supervisors once. He didn't want to do it again. Some of them knew of his "assignment" from Father, but his friends from the refinery didn't. And they'd invited him. It was best to save face and not risk anything more. Why she preferred to be away from the center of activity, though, he didn't know.

"So," he said by way of continuing the conversation. "Is there anything you wish to see here at the park today? You've already mentioned the music. But would you like to see some of the entertainment on the other side?"

She pursed her lips and tilted her head, the long braid she'd fashioned falling over her shoulder. A few wisps framed her face, giving her a cute and appealing image.

"Well, I heard they were going to have mimes performing. That might be interesting to see."

He nodded. "The mimes are here, and in the part I saw, they reminded me of the statue near city hall."

"Do you mean the soldiers' monument?"

"You know about it?" Now that was a bit of a surprise. It didn't seem like the type of thing that would interest her or be anywhere near where she spent most of her time.

"Yes. My parents told me about it when they first unveiled it three years ago. Generals Sheridan, Custer, and Burnside were present for the ceremony, they said. And I've seen a drawing of it as well."

"It's definitely something worth seeing. The octagonal shapes, the eagles on pedestals, the four men standing in place of the Navy, Infantry, Cavalry, and Artillery branches of the U.S. Army. Even the plaques dedicated to the four Union leaders are impressive."

"Don't forget the Indian warrior, Michigan, standing at the top," Felicity pointed out.

"With a sword in her right hand and a shield in her left. How could I miss her?"

"All constructed in bas-relief style, I believe," she added, casting a surreptitious glance to her left.

"That's right." How had she known something like that? That wouldn't be a fact she'd be able to infer from a drawing. He shrugged it off. "And it couldn't be in a better place. Right at the center of five principal streets and at the tip of Campus Martius Park."

"And how do you know so much about it?"

He wondered how long it would take her to ask him that. "I get around," Brandt replied, attempting to keep his tone nonchalant. He contemplated not sharing so much, but he didn't know what else to say. Besides, architecture in the city was a fairly safe topic. "Perhaps I can show it to you sometime."

She hesitated, her eyes flashing with a mixture of sadness and delight. What an odd combination.

"That would be nice," she finally said, her voice lacking the enthusiasm of just a moment ago. Her eyes again looked to the left and right.

Was it something he'd said? Did she want to be with someone else or make sure no one saw them together? No. That didn't seem like her at all. Sometimes having conversations with her had him feeling like he was on the losing end of a guessing game. At any given moment, she could act like two different people instead of the same young woman. Confusion like this could drive a guy crazy.

The song floating from the stage reached their ears, and Felicity tilted her head. Her face didn't register recognition, and a second later, she turned back to him.

"Who is that playing?"

Brandt looked at the two men onstage. "The younger one is Clayton Grinnell. He's attending the university and has a keen interest in pianos. The other older gentleman is Frederick Stearns."

She gasped. "The pharmacist?"

"You recognize his name?"

"Father was sent to his offices once for some special medicine to help his brother with a heart condition. He's on East Jefferson near the MacArthur Bridge, right?"

"Right."

There was no end to the surprises Felicity had hiding up her sleeve. She should pursue a career as a magician with the way she succeeded at throwing him off track. Just when he thought he had her figured out, she threw another twist into his obvious misconceptions.

"Mr. Stearns is a savvy businessman, and I've heard he loves collecting instruments. I'm not surprised to see him here with some of the men and their pieces that have probably been in their families for years."

A well-dressed couple strolled nearby, and Felicity stiffened with a soft gasp. She turned her head in the opposite direction and found the grass next to the cloth on which they sat to be quite fascinating. The pair hesitated a moment and looked at her but continued on their way.

"Is something wrong, Fe...Miss Chambers?" In his mind, he called her by her given name, but it wasn't right to do so out loud.

She peered from the corner of her eye at the path where the couple had been, then slowly resumed her previous position. Her behavior today seemed a bit odder than usual.

"I wanted to keep an eye out for Laura and Brianna. They are likely to return at any moment." She stopped then brightened as if she'd found the perfect explanation. "If they see you here with me, they'll pester you with a never-ending stream of questions."

"Are you saying you'd like me to leave?"

"No!" she answered a little too quickly. "That is...I...uh...I don't want you to be forced to endure their interrogation."

A tinge of pink stained her cheeks, and she ducked her head. Despite her erratic and somewhat befuddling behavior, Brandt couldn't be upset. She was right, though. She'd come with her friends today, and he didn't have the right to command much more of her time.

"Actually, my friends are no doubt wondering where I am, too." He placed his fists on the ground and shoved upward as he stood. "I hope you'll get over and see the mimes. And make sure you sample some of the popcorn from the vendor cart."

Her head bobbed, and she again shielded her eyes as she gazed up at him. He wanted nothing more than to stay by her side, but this was not the time or the place. Extending his hand down toward her, he waited until she placed her delicate fingers against his. He bent at the waist and raised her fingers to his lips, placing a brief kiss on her knuckles.

"Until next time."

The smile she bestowed upon him made all the questions about her behavior today inconsequential. He snatched his cap from the checkered cloth, slapped it on his head, and waved a farewell to Felicity. Seeing her away from the factory again had been quite a treat. Other than her frequent glances around the park, she seemed genuinely intrigued by the facts he shared and the points of interests he described. If he had any say at all, there would definitely be a next time.

Chapter 10

B randt stepped back as Bartholomew Sanderson stepped into the hallway from his office and pulled the door shut behind him.

"Where are we headed today?" Brandt asked as he walked beside the manager down the hall and toward the stairs. It wasn't easy continuing this back-and-forth work between management and the main refinery. Some of his friends had begun questioning his sporadic absences. He'd be glad when he could finally make the switch and put all of this behind him. Just one more week.

Sanderson tugged on the sleeves of his chambray shirt and adjusted the string tie at his neck. It must be an important meeting for him to take such care with his appearance.

"The owner of a new bell-casting shop recently moved to Detroit and is interested in the copper we produce." He walked with a purpose, his carriage tall and erect. "Your father tells me it could mean a great deal of money invested in our refinery and his company should this gentleman like what we have to say."

"I recall Father mentioning a man who had been hired to cast some new bells for some of the churches here in the city as well as near city hall." He preceded Sanderson down the stairs and cocked his head over his left shoulder. "Is this the same man?"

"One and the same. That is, the caster isn't the same man as the one we're going to meet," he corrected, his words beating a staccato rhythm matching his descent on the steps. "This man is the owner of the casting facility."

Brandt pressed down the latch and pushed open the heavy door, holding it for Sanderson, who exited a moment later. "And he makes all the decisions about where to get his supplies."

Sanderson nodded. "Exactly."

"Well, there aren't exactly too many options here in Detroit. If he doesn't agree to partner with us for his needs, he'll have to import them from Canada or even as far away as the Locks up north."

Somehow Brandt had a hard time believing this owner would even consider the expense such a decision would incur. They produced the purest copper and copper elements within a one-hundred-mile radius. The man would be a fool not to invest with them.

"From what I've heard, he's been quite diligent in his research and investigation of the available refineries in the area. This meeting is likely nothing more than a formality, and your father asked me to bring you along for the experience."

Ah, now the truth came out. This might be a bona fide business appointment, but he was only included to learn more about this end of his father's dealings. Brandt didn't mind, though. Felicity had told him earlier in the week that the factory had hired some new workers and the shifts had changed. So she was working fewer hours as the supervisors planned out a new schedule. He would have much preferred sharing lunch with her again, but since she wasn't working today, gaining more understanding of the job he'd soon assume suited him just fine.

"I should have known Father would have arranged something like this."

Sanderson paused at the edge of the refinery gate. "Are you saying you'd rather be back in front of those intolerably hot furnaces and getting covered in soot or burned by the sparks and liquid ore?"

"When you put it that way, I suppose this is the better of the two options." He chuckled and stepped into the street on their way to the nearest trolley line. "But I wish Father would include me in these decisions rather than assuming I'll take part and leaving you to issue the orders."

A rueful expression crossed Sanderson's face. "You do have a point. I'll be sure to bring that up the next time your father comes to meet with me."

"No, no." Brandt brushed off that idea. The last thing he needed was Father thinking he couldn't stand up for himself. "It's only for one more week. I'll speak with him about it tonight. He's always been open to my suggestions in the past. I don't see why this should be any different."

"Yes," Sanderson replied, drawing out the word. "As I recall, you spoke with him not too long ago regarding my overbearing presence in the main areas of the refinery."

Brandt cringed and offered Sanderson an apologetic grin. He probably should have spoken directly to Sanderson, but either way, he knew he was right.

"I did, but only because the other men down there mentioned it more than once. We need to maximize our productivity. Those men felt like they had to keep looking over their shoulders. And when they do that, they're not working."

Sanderson leaned against the lamppost near the corner and crossed his arms. "I didn't say I had a problem with the assessment. I only said that to show you that your father does value your input."

The tinny chime of the trolley's bells sounded, and the horse-drawn cart appeared around the corner. Sanderson shoved off the post and stepped to the curb. Brandt stood beside him.

"All the more reason why I should be the one to speak to him about further instruction where my apprenticeship is concerned."

"Very well." Sanderson shrugged. "If that's the way you wish it to be, I won't stand in the way."

"Thanks. I appreciate that."

The trolley stopped in front of them. The manager climbed aboard, and Brandt grabbed hold of the pole to swing onto the platform. Sanderson shook his head at Brandt's antics. At least he hadn't run behind the cart and hopped onto the rear perch, one hand on the side and the other waving in the wind. He'd been known to do that on more than one occasion.

They rode in silence, and Brandt shifted his thoughts to the conversation he'd have that evening. Father said he was progressing quite well. It wouldn't be long before he could move from apprentice to supervisor. But that meant no more working on the refinery floor. He would soon be overseeing a part of the refinery. The workers under him might not take kindly to the fact that he had worked among them all these months, so perhaps he'd be placed in charge of the initial refining process as the copper was delivered to the plant from the mines.

Once that happened, Felicity was bound to find out. He couldn't exactly avoid the factory. His father had established a solid rapport with the other factory managers along the river. Eventually Brandt would end up meeting with the manager at the factory where Felicity worked. And then how would she react?

Of course, by then Mrs. Gibson could have her baby, and Felicity might surrender her work to leave a possible spot open for Mrs. Gibson. That thought didn't exactly bring a smile to his face. But what if she *was* still there? It could ruin their entire relationship. And he didn't want that to happen. He'd better rethink all this. Maybe he should try to delay his switch to management for just a little longer. At least until he could come up with a viable plan of action.

&

"That went remarkably well, I must say."

Sanderson almost hopped down the marble stairs in front of Mr. Willoughby's home, his steps light and confident. The bell-casting owner had been quite accommodating. In fact, he'd almost been ready to sign at the X the moment his butler had ushered Brandt and Sanderson into the library.

Brandt dashed down the steps behind Sanderson and grabbed hold of the large knob on top of the rail, swinging himself around to step in line with his manager.

"I agree."

Sanderson cast a glance in Brandt's direction and raised his eyebrows. All right, so he still had a bit of boyishness in him. What difference did that make? He'd rather have a little fun in life than restrict himself to being ostentatious and pompous all the time, like some of the men among Father's acquaintances.

"So where to now?" Brandt asked.

Sanderson tucked one hand in the pocket of his pants and pointed at Brandt with his index finger. "You are free to do as you please. I'm returning to the refinery to finish some ledger work, but your father told me to dismiss you as soon as this errand was complete."

"Really?"

If only Felicity were at the factory this afternoon. He could drop by and catch her as she left. Wouldn't she be surprised by that! That wouldn't happen today, though. And since he didn't even know where she lived, he'd have to wait until next week to see her again.

He glanced ahead of them across the street and almost stopped dead in his tracks.

Felicity?

Brandt blinked several times, shaking his head at what he saw. He had been thinking about her, and now his mind had conjured her where she wasn't. Three young women walked side by side in front of the town houses over there. The one in the middle could be Felicity's twin. His eyes must be playing tricks on him. Those three came from the direction of the elite shops nearby. Felicity would never be keeping company with prim and proper ladies like the two on each side of her. And she'd never be in this part of the city.

But it wasn't her. He had to get that clear in his mind. The resemblance was uncanny. He definitely had to do something about this. He couldn't keep going day in and day out wanting to see her so badly that he saw her when she wasn't there. That could lead to all sorts of problems, none of which he wanted to even acknowledge, let alone claim.

One of the other girls said something, and the young woman in the middle looked over at him. He could have sworn a flash of panic appeared on her face. But from this distance, he couldn't know for sure. Besides, why would she react that way? He didn't know any of those girls. They'd have no reason to give him anything other than a passing glance before continuing on their way.

"Mr. Lawson?"

The deep voice shook him out of his contemplative state. He turned his attention back to the sidewalk in front of him. Bart Sanderson. The refinery. A meeting with Father tonight. That was where his head should be. Not on some apparition his mind had conjured.

"You haven't heard a word I've said, have you?"

"What?" He shook his head and turned toward Sanderson. "I'm sorry, Bart. Guess I got lost in thought."

"That's putting it mildly," Sanderson said with a derisive snort. "Your mind drifted the moment those three ladies came into view." He smirked. "You know them?"

"No." Brandt sighed. "One of them reminded me of another young lady I know, but it couldn't be her."

"By the way your entire focus shifted, I'd say this young lady's someone special?"

"I guess you could say that."

Sanderson stopped walking. Brandt took a few steps past him before he realized it, so he turned around.

"Look, son, either she is or she isn't. You have to make up your mind. My Marabelle wouldn't have given me a second thought had I not been determined to win her affections." The manager shoved a finger into Brandt's chest. "You don't trifle with women's feelings, my boy. That'll just get you into a load of trouble."

Brandt pushed Sanderson's hand back to the man's side. "Duly noted, sir."

Seemingly satisfied with Brandt's response, Sanderson continued walking. Brandt might as well accompany him until the time came for them to part ways. No sense taking a different route when the direct way was the most efficient.

If only Sanderson's advice concerning Felicity could be followed that easily.

&

"I do believe I succumbed to the pressure of the clerk and purchased far too many foibles for even *my* tastes." Angela held up the satchels for Felicity and Rachel to see. "How will I ever explain this to Mother?"

"You can't say that we didn't warn you," Rachel pointed out. "Felicity and I both advised you to consider your purchases carefully. I'd say you got what you deserve, spending so recklessly."

"You're just saying that because you weren't able to purchase the items you truly wanted."

"No," Rachel countered, "I'm saying that because I *refrained* from purchasing what I wanted. I intend to return again at a later date to peruse the selections more carefully."

"Sometimes you must simply throw caution to the wind and splurge."

"And sometimes ostentatious expenditures are nothing more than frivolous displays of your wealth."

Felicity glanced over her shoulder again. Her two friends could bicker back and forth the entire length of Beaumont. She had a more pressing matter at hand.

The young man she'd spotted now walked away from her in the opposite direction. He had looked so much like Brandt that she'd stopped to take a second look and almost got tangled in her petticoats. From the way he'd stared for that brief moment, she thought she'd seen recognition in his eyes. But how could that be possible? Brandt wouldn't be walking with Mr. Sanderson. Especially not during the middle of the afternoon. And definitely not in the Pointe district. At least, that's who she thought the man was. No, if he had to meet with Mr. Sanderson, it would be back at the refinery. Even then, the meeting likely wouldn't be a favorable one.

She'd encountered the refinery manager her first day on the job. After signing the work agreement, she'd left Mr. Marshall's office and was almost run over by the man she now knew as Mr. Sanderson. Mr. Marshall greeted him, and even from down below, she had known their conversation was not a pleasant one. The two men exchanged a few heated words, with Mr. Marshall waving his fists in the air. She respected Mr. Marshall a great deal. So the problem must have been with Mr. Sanderson.

"Felicity? Are you all right?"

A hand on her arm made her stop walking. "What?" She turned to see Rachel looking at her with concern reflected in her eyes.

"I asked if you were all right. Angela and I have been telling you about the cotillion you missed last weekend. But you looked like you were miles away."

Just look at what daydreaming of Brandt did. Conjuring him into existence in place of another young man didn't make him appear for real. She had to stop this.

"I'm sorry, Rachel. Angela." She dropped her shoulders and sighed. "I thought I recognized someone I knew, but he turned out not to be the man I believed him to be."

Angela placed her hands on her hips. "Are you speaking metaphorically or in actuality?"

Felicity giggled. She truly needed this. Straightforward, no-nonsense talk to help her clear her head.

"In actuality."

Rachel maneuvered partway in front of her and Angela, giving Felicity a suspicious look. "Is this the same man you mentioned just before summer? The one who has turned your head in his favor?"

"Yes," she admitted in a whisper. What else could she say? Rachel would see through any lie she told, and Angela would devise a plan to get the information out of her one way or another. She might as well be honest. Well, as honest as possible, anyway.

"Ooh!" Angela clapped her hands and bounced up and down as much as her kid boots would allow. "I knew it. Our dear Felicity has a beau, and she's been holding out on us all this time."

"I never said he was a beau, Angela."

Brandt might be the closest thing she had to a beau, but as of right now their relationship was nothing more than friendship.

"No, you didn't." Angela nodded. "But you didn't say he wasn't, either," she added with a smirk. "And that grants us the freedom to pursue this line of questioning much further."

Felicity leveled a glare at Angela, but the girl wouldn't be dissuaded.

"Come now, Angela." Rachel placed herself between Felicity and Angela. "Let's not take things too far."

Ah, good. A voice of reason. At least she had Rachel on her side.

"After all," Rachel continued, turning back toward Felicity with a gleam in her eyes. Angela seemed to pick up on it, too, as her entire demeanor changed from a busybody seeking a little gossip to a sleuth on a mission.

Felicity eyed them both. This couldn't be good.

"If we're not careful, we might cause our dear Felicity to become exasperated and despondent. And then we'd never find out the secret to this mysterious gentleman for whom she's been pining away while our backs have been turned."

All right. Enough of this dancing around. Felicity stamped first her right foot then her left, clenching her fists at her sides.

"Now that is not the way it is at all, you two. You're turning this minor little incident into something of extraordinary proportions."

"But of course!" Angela spread her arms wide. "It's what we do best! How else would we successfully manage to extract the necessary information from you if not by extreme measures?"

Felicity looked back and forth at the faces of her two friends. They couldn't be serious. But their faces seemed to indicate their genuine earnestness. Then the corner of Angela's mouth twitched, and she had them.

"Aha!" She wiggled a hand in both of their faces, mirth bubbling up from inside. "I knew it. You two couldn't fool anyone with that ruse."

Rachel placed one hand on her chest and faked an innocent expression. "Why, whatever do you mean?" The batting of her eyelashes only made it worse.

Felicity pressed her lips tight to hold back the laughter, and it came out more like a loud snort before bursting forth from her mouth. That was all it took.

The three of them bent over at the waist, leaning toward one another as giggles and merriment overtook them. A handful of passersby made their way to the other side of the street, their upturned noses and expressions only making the girls laugh that much harder.

Rachel recovered first, straightening and taking several deep breaths to regain her composure. Angela stood as well, her arms holding her middle as she gasped for air. Felicity struggled to catch her own breath. Her sides hadn't hurt that much in months.

"All right. All right." Rachel splayed her hands, palms down, as if attempting to quiet a rowdy group of children. "Let's take our little party to a less conspicuous location, shall we?"

Leave it to Rachel to get everything back under control. Always the voice of reason. She led the three of them to the nearest bench in front of one of the town houses that lined Beaumont. When they all settled in place—Angela with her packages and purchases in her lap and at her feet—Rachel inhaled then released a single breath.

"Now, Felicity. . .dear," she stated, placing emphasis on the last word as she folded her hands in her lap. "Why don't you finish telling us about this gentleman before our efforts to find out more are waylaid yet again."

No way could Felicity escape this one. She just had to make sure not to give away too much in her response. She tucked her legs beneath the bench and adjusted her skirts around her ankles. Looking straight ahead, she delivered the answer she hoped they wanted to hear.

"It's really not as significant as the two of you make it sound." At Angela's expulsion of breath, Felicity rushed to continue. "Yes, there is a gentleman with whom I've been keeping company of late. He is not my beau," she said with a brief pointed look at Angela, who ducked her head. "But he is a good friend."

"And does he have a name?" Rachel asked. "Or shall we create one from our imaginations?"

"He has a name." Felicity placed her palms on her thighs and slid them toward her knees. "But I don't wish to reveal it to you, lest it provide you with enough information to seek him out on your own."

Rachel gasped. "We would never do that!"

"Oh, I would!" Angela piped up. "Anything to get to the bottom of this intriguing mystery."

Felicity raised then lowered her shoulders. "Well, I do so hate to disappoint you both, but there truly isn't much more to say." Actually, there was, but she didn't intend to tell them now. That time would come. Just not today.

"When are you going to see him again?"

"One day next week, I believe." At least she hoped she'd see him. She was going to notify Mr. Marshall on Monday that this would be her final week. Her family had their annual visit to Mackinac Island to attend, and her factory work interfered with that. Her parents would not allow her to stay behind. "I don't know for certain."

And she didn't. There had been days when he didn't meet her at the corner. It didn't happen often, and he tried to let her know ahead of time. But each day didn't guarantee she'd see him. She'd still make sure Mrs. Gibson had enough to provide for her family until the baby was born and Lucy could return to work. Felicity just hoped she'd have a chance to see Brandt before her final day at the factory.

"Very well." Rachel rose and dusted off her skirts. "Since it appears that you don't wish to share the intimate details of your personal affairs, there's nothing left for us to do but return home."

Angela made her way to the sidewalk to stand beside Rachel. "Yes." She jutted her chin into the air an inch or two. "I'm sure we'll find out eventually. And when we do. . ." A devilish gleam entered her eyes, and she rubbed her hands together like the mischievous soul Felicity knew her to be.

Felicity grabbed hold of the railing and pulled herself up to join her friends. They didn't seem hurt or offended, but she had to be sure. Draping her arms around both of their waists, she turned them toward home.

"When that time comes, ladies, I promise you'll be the first to know."

In the meantime, Felicity had some thinking to do.

Chapter 11

"Must you dawdle so, Felicity?" Mother entered Felicity's dressing room, tugging on a pair of white traveling gloves. "The train for Cheboygan departs in less than an hour." She picked up Felicity's valise and placed it on the padded stool. "Your father will not be pleased if we're tardy."

"Yes, Mother. I know." Felicity forced the impatience out of her voice. How many times would Mother remind her of the ticking seconds? She picked up the powder puff from her dressing table and stared at it. As hard as she tried, she couldn't muster up the excitement she once had for this forthcoming journey.

"Felicity." Mother's voice held that tone. The one that meant the next course of action would be calling upon Father to motivate Felicity into action.

"Mother, I know we go to Mackinac Island every summer. But must I go this year?" She'd better have a plausible alternative if she wanted to persuade Mother to agree. "I could stay behind and work with Rebecca on my cooking and general household mistress duties."

"No." Mother pushed the fabric of her gloves into place between her fingers. "You have been rather distracted lately. I do not attempt to know the cause of this despondency, but your father and I have made special plans and we've worked too hard for it all to be spoiled now."

"Plans? What plans?" What did Mother and Father have up their sleeves now?

Mother paid special attention to the wide array of gowns and outfits that hung in front of the opposite wall. "Oh, nothing too important. We merely contacted a few friends of ours who will also be joining us on the island."

Felicity knew that maneuver all too well. Mother was being evasive. And that could only mean trouble.

"Friends? Why can we not have this little reunion here in Detroit? Why must it be on Mackinac?"

Spurts of air passed between Mother's lips before she gritted her teeth and sucked in a quick breath. "There is no need to mind the reasons. They're of no concern to you. Just know that you *will* accompany your father, your brother and his fiancée, your sister, and me to the island as always. And you will do so with the proper attitude."

Felicity opened her mouth to protest, but Mother waved her off.

"Not another word, Felicity. This discussion is concluded." She brushed past the curtain and stepped into the adjoining bedroom before turning around again. "Finish powdering your face and dressing for travel. I expect to see you downstairs in ten minutes. No more. Is that clear?"

"Yes, Mother," Felicity mumbled.

"What did you say? I'm not sure I heard you correctly."

"Yes, Mother," Felicity repeated, accentuating the two words in crisp tones.

"Very well." Mother disappeared beyond view, but her voice carried through the room. "I shall have Martin fetch your valises. Make certain you have them ready when he arrives."

And with that Mother departed. Felicity slumped against the golden brass bars on the back of her padded chair. She propped her elbow on the dressing table and looked at her reflection. Just once she'd like to feel as if she had complete control over her own life. And she did when she had worked at the factory or devoted herself to her charity work. If only she could spend all her time on charitable services and not on fulfilling the expectations of her mother and every other societal edict that had been placed on her head.

Wait a minute. What was she saying? As much as her charity work fulfilled her, the comforts of the lifestyle afforded her through her parents would not be easy to toss aside. She'd seen the way some of the others without fortune lived. It felt good to be able to select the material she wanted most for a new gown or walk into a shop and purchase what she'd like because she could afford it.

On the other hand, every time she visited Mrs. Gibson or shared meals and conversations with Brianna and Laura, a pang of guilt struck deep inside. And Brandt. He seemed so carefree, despite his existence in a lower class.

Felicity straightened, her arm resting on the edge of the table. If she didn't have her status, though, she wouldn't be able to help people like Mrs. Gibson. So where did she strike the balance?

She sighed. There didn't seem to be an easy answer. And right now she didn't have the time to figure it out. Martin would be here any moment. Mother expected her downstairs in three minutes. And she'd be there. She grabbed her powder puff again and closed her eyes as she blotted it all over her face. Waving the cloud away from her face, she dropped the puff container into her personal valise and stood. With one last glance in the looking glass, she gathered the rope handles of the bag and stepped into her bedroom.

A knock came a moment later. Felicity looked up to see the door push open and Martin peer around the edge.

"Come in, Martin." Felicity pointed to the collection of luggage. "The items are all stacked there against the wall."

"Very good, Miss Felicity." The butler gathered the four pieces under his arms and moved toward the door. "Your sister is already waiting by the front door, and your brother is outside by the carriage. Your mother will likely be in the entryway momentarily."

"As will I, Martin. Thank you."

Felicity snatched her gloves from the small table by the door and slipped them on her hands. At least she had some time of refreshment in the cooler climates of northern Lake Huron. Maybe the fresh air would clear her mind. Getting away for two weeks and a change of scenery just might be the perfect solution to her dilemma.

ஊ

The steam-powered large lake excursion boat bounced through the choppy water. Felicity grabbed tight to the handrail at the bow as she made her way around to the port side. The train ride on the Michigan Central had lasted overnight as they traveled north, and the summer temperatures had dropped considerably. Out on the lake with the wind blowing in her face, it felt like spring again. They could have taken the train farther north to Mackinaw City, but Father had persuaded the engineer to let them off before that stop to catch a private carriage he'd hired to take them east. This leisurely scenic route suited her just fine. It might take longer than the direct route to the island, but Mother and Father took their family this way every summer, and she wouldn't change a thing.

Setting out from Cheboygan, they traveled by boat across the lake to the east past Pointe Aux Pins and around the southeast side of Bois Blanc Island. Once past the confines of land on the left and right, the lake opened up wide, water in every direction. Other excursion vessels and smaller boats sailed with the heavy winds or fought against them on their way back to shore.

"Oh, Felicity, isn't it just beautiful?" Her younger sister shoved against her then lost her footing as the boat pitched. She stretched both arms out in front of her and gripped the handrail to right herself again.

Felicity looked out over the expanse of blue water. She inhaled a deep breath of fresh lake air. The stress and strain of the past few weeks ebbed away, leaving nothing but peace in its place. Yes, this time away would be perfect.

"Yes, Cecily, it's breathtaking!"

If only Brandt could see it all. He'd no doubt thrill at the chance to come to a place like this. He seemed to enjoy God's wondrous nature, and this little piece of heaven would enchant anyone. Oh, how she wished she could bring him here.

"I simply cannot wait until we get to Mackinac. We'll get to dance, play, run, and have a grand time."

"Honestly, Cecily, sometimes you can act like such a child." This came from their older brother, Zach, who sidled up on the other side of Felicity, propping his forearms on the port bow.

Cecily scrunched up her nose and made a face at their brother. "That's because

I *am* a child, silly."

It looked like thoughts of Brandt would have to wait.

"That's enough, you two." Felicity held up her hands between them. Sometimes she felt more like a mediator than a sister. Being in the middle could be quite a challenge. "And, Cecily," she said with a pointed glance, "you're *not* a child. You're almost fifteen. That's a young woman where you're concerned."

"That's right," Zach chimed in. "Which means you should start acting your age."

Felicity whipped her head in the other direction. "And what about you, Zach? You're older than both of us. Shouldn't *you* be ceasing with this childish behavior as well?"

An unladylike snort came from Cecily, and Felicity's mouth twitched. Zach gave them both a sideways glare then turned his attention back to the lake. At his silence, Felicity gave her sister a triumphant grin. Cecily's sharp single nod accentuated their victory. That would teach Zach to mind his own business.

She wished it meant he would think twice before interjecting his opinions in the future. But it'd be a miracle if that happened. He'd been teasing them as far back as she could remember. He claimed it as his older-brother right. But he did it out of love for them. Despite the eight-year span separating the three of them, they were quite close. Felicity hoped that would never change.

"I wonder what type of souvenirs the Chippewa will have for us this year."

"I don't know, Cecily. It will be nice to stroll through the marketplace and browse through their wares."

"I still have that corn-husk doll Father purchased for me seven years ago." Cecily released a melancholic sigh. "It's getting rather worn, though. Perhaps I should see if I can find another to replace it."

The doll sat in a place of honor on top of the cedar chest at the foot of Cecily's bed. A hand-crocheted doily in a circular pattern of thick green and white yarn rested underneath. Although she no longer played with it, it wouldn't be easy for Cecily to part with that doll. Perhaps Mother could find a place to preserve it a little longer.

"I'm certain the dolls will be there, Cecily. They have them every year. I'd like to purchase another reed basket myself. They're woven tighter than the wicker baskets we have back home."

"I'm just hoping they have some big jars of maple sugar," Zach piped in. "Mmm, I can almost taste it."

Felicity laughed. "You'd better have a big jar for your teeth, too, when they rot out of your mouth. You just might single-handedly keep Dr. Wadsworth in business."

"Ha-ha. Very funny." Zach didn't seem too impressed, but he grinned anyway.

"I just wish the local fishermen hadn't run John Jacob Astor and his American Fur Company off the island. Although I can't complain about the quality of whitefish and trout they have here. Still, Astor's beaver hats and pelts are some of the finest I've ever owned."

"I agree." Felicity nodded. "Young men look positively dashing in them." She nudged her brother. "Especially you, Zach."

He nudged her in return. "Aw, shucks, sis. You're making me blush."

"There's the docks!" Cecily's voice interrupted their playful banter. Their sister hopped on both feet, leaning over the bow as she pointed into the distance where the hazy outline of the ferry docks came into view.

Mackinac Island. Or Mishla-mackinaw to the local tribes. Even after all these years, the limestone bluffs and high cliffs still amazed her. Excitement surged from within and made Felicity's stomach quiver. She might have protested about coming, but thank goodness Mother didn't concede. Regret surely would have filled her by summer's end.

No sooner had they docked than Cecily grabbed hold of Felicity's arm and almost dragged her off the boat. The crew had just secured the gangplank, and Cecily led the way for all the passengers onto the island. Felicity had no choice. She ran behind her sister, wincing at the amused glances of both their fellow travelers and those who had come to the docks to greet their boat.

"Cecily, slow down!" Felicity tripped on a dip in the dirt path leading up from the docks, then bit her lip when her ankle twisted the wrong way. When she regained her footing, she planted both feet on the ground and yanked Cecily to a stop. Her sister jerked backward and almost ended up on her rear.

"Why did you do a thing like that?" She pulled her hand free from Felicity's and clamped her hands on her tiny waist. "We were almost there."

Felicity lifted her foot an inch or two off the ground and wiggled her ankle back and forth. It seemed all right. No sprain and no evident injury. Raising her gaze to her sister, who stood about a foot above her on the path, she did her best to imitate one of Mother's reproving glares. "Because you were dragging me behind you like we were running from a blazing fire or something equally life-threatening."

Cecily extended her arms out from her sides in a helpless gesture. "I wanted to be the first one to the top." She turned and rushed up the hill, then stood with a triumphant smile stretching from ear to ear.

Felicity climbed the remaining few steps to join her sister and smiled. "And now what are you going to do?"

Her sister looked past Felicity to where Mother and Father and Zach lumbered toward them at a leisurely pace. She shifted her eyes back to Felicity and offered a sheepish grin. "Stand here and wait for the slowpokes?"

COPPER AND CANDLES

With a shake of her head, Felicity turned around to face the rest of their family and snaked her arm around Cecily's waist. A smile she felt clear from her heart found its way to her lips. They were going to have a grand time.

❧

Strains of a stirring Strauss waltz floated down on the breeze that danced over the outdoor raised platform that had been built two years before.

"Are you ready to enjoy an evening of dancing and gaiety and absolutely delicious cuisine?" Zach stood beside her and extended his elbow.

Felicity smiled up at him then lifted her petticoats to prevent any grass stains around the hem. Her brother looked quite dapper in his top hat and tailored suit. Zach's fiancée would no doubt be quite impressed once he joined her family later. For now, Felicity was honored to be escorted by him. She placed her hand in the crook of his arm as they ascended the hill to join the cavorting hotel guests. The elegant men and women dressed in all their finery sat around small white wrought-iron tables surrounding the floor. Larger tables were positioned on the outskirts of the arrangement.

"Mother and Father said they would have a table for us."

Zach nodded. "Yes. They arrived earlier to meet with some friends from previous years."

Perhaps those were the same ones Mother had mentioned yesterday before they left for the train. She was up to something. Felicity just knew it. She and Father both. But what?

"I see them. Over on the far end."

Zach pointed with his right hand to where their parents stood in a circle with a group of people she didn't recognize. At least not from this distance.

"But they're not standing near a table. Which one is ours?"

Zach looked at each empty table between them and their parents. "Aha. That one." He indicated one of the larger ones where Cecily sat, her blond locks curled and styled to perfection. Despite being the only person sitting at the table, she didn't seem the least bit bored. Instead, her attention seemed to be fixated on the energetic couples twirling around the dance floor.

"Let's make our way there, then. Shall we?"

Zach made a grand, sweeping gesture out from his chest. "After you, my lady."

Felicity curtsied. "Why, thank you, my good sir."

She led the way with Zach placing a protective hand at the small of her back. He had become such a fine gentleman in recent years. Mother and Father had raised him well. They'd raised all three of them well. When her brother married and moved into his own home, she'd miss him terribly.

"It's about time you two decided to grace us with your presence."

Zach stepped behind Cecily's chair and reached out to pinch her cheek. She swatted him away and stuck out her tongue. Felicity just rolled her eyes. Some battles simply should not be fought.

"So what types of songs have they played?" Felicity asked, stepping past Cecily.

Zach held Felicity's chair for her and handed his top hat to a waiter before taking a seat opposite, affording all three of them a clear view of the band and the stage.

"Oh, the usual." Cecily ticked off a list on her fingers. "A few waltzes, a new march by Sousa, and a piece from Rossini."

"There will no doubt be some pieces from Mozart, Beethoven, Verdi, and Wagner throughout the evening as well."

Zach winked at both Cecily and Felicity. "I see the tutelage Mother insisted you two undergo has proven itself rather useful."

"Culture and a solid grasp of the musical greats are essential to any young woman's successful upbringing." Felicity gave her brother a pointed look. "It would do you good to familiarize yourself with these masters of music as well." She grinned. "Especially if you are ever going to impress your fiancée. How you managed to convince her to marry you, I'll never know."

Cecily giggled and covered her mouth with her gloved hand. Felicity held Zach's gaze and engaged him in a visual duel. He held his own and leaned forward, his forearm resting on the edge of the table.

"If you are so concerned about suitable marriage liaisons, then you should be worrying about your own." He leaned back in his chair and interlaced his fingers behind his head. "You'll soon be twenty. I daresay Mother and Father have already taken the necessary steps toward finding you a suitable husband."

"Be that as it may," Felicity retorted, "Father has assured me that he will not enter into any official agreement without my advance knowledge of the young gentleman's identity or my agreement to the union."

"I eagerly anticipate the day I have the good fortune to meet the young man who is worthy of your affections. With your standards set so high, it's going to have to be a man worth his salt to meet them."

Brandt could do it. The thought came unbidden, and Felicity shook it from her head. Mackinac Island society and this entire experience were as far away as she could get from Brandt and the temporary world in which she lived. She had to put him out of her mind.

Felicity changed her position and modified her posture, turning away from Zach and tilting her chin in the air. "There is absolutely nothing wrong with having high standards. It will guarantee me the perfect match. If a young man is unwilling to meet those standards or I find him lacking in certain areas,

I shall know he isn't the right man for me."

"At least you're old enough to be giving marriage a serious thought," Cecily mumbled. "Father said I still have three more years." She stuck out her lower lip.

Felicity glanced at Zach, his eyes full of mirth and his lips turning white from holding back his laughter. She almost laughed as well, but it wouldn't help her sister any.

"Don't be in such a rush, Cecily." Felicity reached over and placed her hand on her sister's arm. "Your time will come. Choosing the one who will share the rest of your life is no decision to take lightly. Besides," she said as she leaned away again and grinned, "whoever this man is, he'll not only have to pass Mother and Father's approval, but Zach's and mine as well."

"That's right," Zach chimed in. "And I don't know how keen I am about some young lad stealing away my baby sister."

That did it—they'd been successful at getting their sister's mind off the grumbling. Cecily placed both hands flat on the table and hopped her gaze between the two of them.

"By the time I'm ready to consider marriage, the two of you will likely have married and settled with a spouse of your own. So I will have nothing to worry about."

"Excuse me, Miss Chambers, but would you honor me with a dance?"

All three of them stopped and stared at a well-dressed young man who stood next to Cecily with one gloved hand extended palm up in her direction.

Cecily didn't waste a second. She placed her hand in his and allowed him to help her to her feet. A moment later the young man led Cecily onto the floor and into a smooth waltz.

"Wasn't that—?"

Felicity nodded. "Yes. I do believe that was Matthew Lodge." She stared at Matthew and Cecily as they glided across the floor. "My, but he's become quite a handsome young man since last we saw him."

"I wonder if Mother and Father are aware of this development."

Zach looked across the table at Felicity, and she looked back at him.

She smiled. "Are you thinking what I'm thinking?"

Her brother stood in haste and came around the table, then bowed. "Would you do me the honor, Miss Chambers, of joining me in this waltz?"

Felicity accepted his invitation and hurried alongside him as they waited for the right moment to merge with the other couples. They might not be able to speak to Matthew Lodge, but at least they could keep an eye on him and their sister.

After two complete sets, Matthew escorted Cecily back to their family's table and bowed over her hand. Cecily nodded with a smile. Zach led Felicity toward them, but she couldn't make out their words. Before they reached their seats, Matthew left.

Felicity placed her hands on the back of her chair. "Did you two have a nice time?"

The smile hadn't left Cecily's lips. "A wonderful one."

Zach took on the older brother role and leveled a warning glance at Cecily. "Well, he'd better be sure to treat you with the utmost respect, or I might have a few words with him."

"Don't be silly, Zach. Matthew did nothing improper. In fact, he—"

"Felicity," Mother's voice interrupted. "I'm so glad to see you've returned from dancing. Your father and I would like to introduce you to someone."

Felicity looked across the table at Zach, who only raised his eyebrows as if to say, "I told you so."

"He comes from a fine, upstanding family," Mother continued, completely oblivious. "And his father has several long-standing investments in the mining and refinery businesses."

So this is what Mother had meant when she said she and Father had been working hard on something. Why did they feel the need to be so secretive? Why not come right out and tell her what they were planning? Felicity wanted nothing to do with Mother and Father's matchmaking schemes. But she owed it to them to at least pretend to go along.

She took a deep breath and turned to face the unknown man.

"Felicity Chambers, I'd like to introduce you to—"

"Brandt!"

Chapter 12

The single word had escaped Felicity's mouth before she could stop it. What was Brandt doing here? And dressed in those clothes? She had managed to see him briefly before her last day at the factory. He'd said he had to go out of town for a few days but would see her upon his return. She didn't have time to tell him she'd be gone as well. Despite the timing being rather vague and parallel to her own itinerary, she hadn't given it much thought. She never would have guessed that journey would bring him here to Mackinac Island!

Mother's gasp sounded distant to Felicity's ears. She'd thought of Brandt several times that day, wishing he could be there with her and see the island. Now here he stood, dressed in a fine, tailored suit with tails on his outer jacket. He looked every bit as out of place as if Timothy, Mrs. Gibson's oldest son, had appeared before her eyes dressed in similar fashion.

"Have you two already been introduced?"

"In a manner of speaking, yes," Brandt said.

She saw his lips move, but she still couldn't seem to make sense of it all. Considering the circumstances, Felicity expected shock from Brandt. Instead, his eyes held a diverse blend of curiosity, anger, hurt, and impatience. Felicity knew the feelings well. Each one of them churned inside her, too. He no doubt had put two and two together when he'd been introduced to her parents. But still, he accompanied them here to meet her and maintain the ruse. Why? So many questions begged to be answered. So many thoughts fought for dominance.

But worst of all, Brandt now knew her secret.

"Felicity, dear, are you all right? Your skin is so pale. Harold, come take a look. I don't believe our daughter is feeling well."

"Davinia, what is it?"

Brandt didn't move. He didn't flinch. His eyes held hers, and she couldn't break the powerful hold. Activity and movement occurred around her, but she didn't hear what they were saying. Then her father's deep voice penetrated through her consciousness.

"If we had known you two were already acquainted, the Lawsons and your mother and I could've saved a lot of time."

Father's words snapped the invisible rope tying Felicity's gaze to Brandt's. A spark flashed in Brandt's eyes, and Felicity shook her head. Her muscles moved like molasses as she turned to face her parents. She did her best to maintain control. "Do you mean to say that you have been planning this meeting for some time now?"

"And that you made all the arrangements behind our backs, without bothering to consult either one of us?" Brandt directed his question at his own parents.

"It seemed like the perfect opportunity, Felicity," Mother offered. "Mr. Lawson came to call one afternoon, and we invited him to share tea with us. Having heard of his tremendous success in the mining industry, your father and I were intrigued about the purpose of his visit."

Father placed his arm around his wife and nodded. "What he had to say surprised us both."

Mr. Lawson—not Dalton as she'd assumed from Brandt's story—looked back and forth between his son and Felicity before settling his attention on his son. "When we spoke a few weeks ago about your progress at the refinery, Brandt, you mentioned Miss Chambers and provided her full name to me."

"If I had known what you would do with that information, I never would have said a word."

Fury seemed to seethe from between his words. Felicity couldn't see his eyes, but as the sound of his voice indicated, the storm brewing inside wouldn't remain contained much longer. Thankfully the band music and clamor of conversations among the other guests drowned out the argument between the two families. For the moment, Brandt at least appeared to have pushed his reaction to her ruse to the side. But the time for that confrontation would come all too soon.

"Now, Brandt," Mr. Lawson continued, his voice calm. He raised one hand, no doubt in an attempt to stay his son's anger. "If you focused more on the practical aspect of these proceedings instead of your irritation, you'll come to see just how providential all this is."

"I'm listening." Brandt said the words, but his tone indicated otherwise.

Felicity didn't know whether to get involved or remain a bystander. She should be planning what she'd say to Brandt when the revelation of their respective subterfuges came to a head. They both had their own reasons for doing what they did, but the fact that their parents had gotten involved in this as well made Felicity want to run away from it all.

Morbid curiosity made her stay.

Mr. Lawson relaxed, the harsh lines in his forehead fading and his shoulders dropping an inch or two. "Very good." He took a deep breath and glanced around the small area where they stood before seeking out Felicity's parents. "Would we not be more comfortable sitting down for this? I daresay the other guests here would find the details of our conversation a bit less interesting if we weren't providing such a public demonstration for them."

"That's a splendid idea," Father agreed.

Oh yes. Have everyone sit down. That way the situation wouldn't seem as serious. But it *was* serious. If only Brandt would look at her. Offer some sort of sign that they were in this together against their parents. She might not be so confused.

Felicity's heart pounded and blood rushed to her head, the steady beat against her temples making it difficult to concentrate. She closed her eyes for a moment, and when she opened them again, Mother's arm came around her shoulders and compelled her to follow Father, who guided the little entourage to a less conspicuous location.

As Felicity walked by her brother and sister still sitting at the family table, they offered sympathetic expressions. But even their support did little to diminish the frustration of being a pawn in her parents' plans.

Once everyone was seated, Felicity attempted to get Brandt's attention, but he refused to look at her. She sat in the middle of her parents, with Brandt on the other side of Father and the Lawsons on the other side of Mother. Mrs. Lawson hadn't said a single word since all this had started. But Brandt hadn't mentioned her much, either. If she was like most society women Felicity knew, she stayed out of conflicts like these. Felicity wished she could do the same.

Mr. Lawson continued, his attention again focused on Brandt.

"Now as I said, you gave me Miss Chambers's name that day. From the way you spoke of her, I could see there were feelings you refused to admit to me. Because of the nature of the position you held, being on the cusp of assuming such integral responsibilities at my factories, I knew something had to be done."

"And so you took it upon yourself to solve the world's problems as you saw fit." Derision laced each word Brandt spoke.

"You left me with little choice in the matter."

"Whatever happened to trusting me to make the right choice and giving me the benefit of the doubt?"

Now that exchange sounded familiar. Felicity had an almost identical one with her parents the first time she had mentioned Brandt's name. Only that time the results had been much more favorable.

"As I watched you each day for almost three weeks, I noticed a change. I believed your emotions were too deeply intertwined for rational decisions to be made." His gaze shifted to encompass both Mother and Father, and he offered a slight smile. "Besides, when I learned the true identity of Miss Chambers and her lineage, I couldn't have been more pleased."

Mother beamed and Father nodded his appreciation of the compliment. But they remained silent. Perhaps they had all four agreed beforehand who would carry the conversation when their plan was revealed. Still, Felicity wished her parents would say something or that Brandt would stop acting like she wasn't even there.

Mr. Lawson continued. "I withheld the fact that you were already acquainted with Felicity and instead sought out a plan for an introduction in your more familiar settings. After further discussion, we all learned we'd be here on the island simultaneously, and it seemed like the perfect opportunity."

Brandt waved his arm out over the table in the direction of his father. "And rather than coming to me to discuss it further, you made my decisions for me."

"Let's not become irrational about this." Father spoke up for the first time since all of them sat down. "We can discuss this in a calm manner."

Mother started to speak, but Father placed his hand over hers, and she closed her mouth, clasping her hands in her lap.

Brandt turned his attention to Father and took a deep breath. "I don't mean any disrespect, Mr. Chambers, but this situation is beyond calm and rational. I don't exactly like the idea of being someone's puppet," he said, swerving his gaze back to his father, "to be controlled at will."

Mr. Lawson acted rather satisfied with what he'd done. No evidence of any regret or remorse could be found in his expression. "You seemed to indicate that Miss Chambers was nothing more than a friend. A passing acquaintance. I didn't see any harm in orchestrating circumstances which might produce more desirable results."

Brandt jumped to his feet, overturning his chair and sending it skidding back a few feet behind him. Fire flashed in his eyes. Mother and Mrs. Lawson gasped. Father started to retrieve the chair only to be intercepted by a watchful waiter standing nearby.

"My relationship with Miss Chambers, whatever it may be," Brandt fumed, "is between Miss Chambers and myself. No one else." He extended his hand, palm up. "What you've done"—his arm moved to encompass both sets of parents—"what you've *all* done is beyond excusable. You should never have interfered."

Felicity had never seen Brandt so angry. If he was this upset about their parents' covert schemes, how much more so would he be with her for her deception? She didn't want to wait to find out.

"I'm sorry," she spoke up, her voice coming out more like a squeak. Hot liquid gathered in her eyes, blurring the faces before her. "I can't bear to listen to any more of this. I. . .I must go."

Before anyone could object, she pushed back her chair, gathered her skirts, and fled the scene. Cries from those gathered at the table reached her ears, but she paid them no mind. The only voice she waited for was Brandt's. Despite the fear of what would happen when the parts they played in this manipulative maneuvering were brought to light, his voice was the only one she wanted to hear.

"Felicity, wait!"

And there it was. But she was too far gone to stop now. Blinded by the rivulets streaming down her face, she half ran, half stumbled down the hill toward the water. She vaguely recalled a gazebo set back a little from the lakeshore. Glancing up at the crescent-shaped moon, she prayed she headed in the right direction. Clomping footsteps sounded behind her, but she didn't stop. Brushing her hand across her eyes to clear some of the tears, Felicity trudged onward. The ethereal glow of the gazebo drew her, its outline illuminated by the waning quarter moon above.

Just as she reached the entrance, a hand grabbed her arm.

"Felicity, please," Brandt huffed, his breathing labored and uneven.

"No, Brandt." She shook off his hand and reached for the railing. "Please. Leave me alone." Tripping up the stairs and giving no thought to soiling her gown, she crumpled in a heap in front of the nearest bench, burying her head in the circle of her arms on the bench's surface. Sporadic sobs escaped her lips as more tears fell from her eyes.

The bottom of Brandt's shoes clacked on the pine steps, and the silky fabric of his tailored suit rustled as he joined her inside. His leg brushed against her arm as he took a seat on the bench. A warm hand touched her shoulder. She wanted to welcome his comfort, allow him to console her. But she couldn't.

For all of his words defending their actions to their parents, she had still deceived him. He had withheld the truth, too, and the acknowledgment of that had to come out.

৯

Brandt didn't know whether to shake her or put his arms around her and pull her close. He'd never really learned to handle a woman's tears. Coming from Felicity, though, it showed at least a hint of remorse and brokenness over the whole crazy situation.

She'd also never looked so beautiful, with her hair piled on top of her head and the elegant gown hugging her slender frame. The dresses she wore to work didn't do her justice. She looked born to wear gowns like this.

He raked his fingers through his hair, feeling the well-groomed strands stand on end. How had things gotten so out of hand?

One minute he was laughing and spending time with friends, and the next he was squaring off against his parents, facing the consequences of his actions.

"Felicity, will you at least look at me?"

"No," came the muffled sob.

"Fine." He slapped his hands on his thighs and stood. "Then I guess there's no reason for me to stay." He took two steps and stopped when he heard her voice.

"Wait."

He turned to face her.

Felicity raised her head and used her fingers to wipe her eyes. For several moments she sat there, not moving or saying anything. Then she placed her palms on the bench and rose from the floor of the gazebo to sit on the bench in the spot he'd just vacated.

Her head remained downcast. She worried the folds of her gown as she mustered up what he guessed were the words she wanted to say. He waited as she lifted her chin and presented tear-soaked eyes to him.

"Why did you not tell me the truth?" she pleaded in a soft voice.

Brandt slapped his hand against his chest, where a shot of indignation burned. "Why didn't *I* tell the truth? What about you?" He made a sweeping gesture of his hand toward her. "The facade *you* presented, working for Mrs. Gibson in the factory and withholding the part about your social status, wasn't exactly honest, either."

Felicity's fingers curled around the edge of the bench where she sat. "I was doing charity work for Lucy. And I didn't see the need to reveal that much information."

He leaned against the post at the entrance and folded his arms. "Charity work that would add another notch to your good-service belt, no doubt."

The second he cast the words out on the wind, Brandt wanted to reel them back. But it was too late.

She gasped and recoiled against one of the whitewashed pine support beams. Her lower lip trembled before she got it under control. "At least what I did and do is out of goodness for those in need. You were misrepresenting yourself to the other men at the refinery. I assume your father owns the refinery, and the only goal you had in mind was the lofty ambition of one day taking over control of the operation."

"Yes, Father does own the refinery. I was learning the way that operation works so I could better understand all aspects before I was put in charge. And I wasn't allowed to reveal who I was. That," he said, leveling a pointed look at her, "was my father's mandate. I merely obeyed and adapted as needed."

"Creatively disguising your true identity so the men working side by side with you wouldn't know they were working with their soon-to-be boss." Her lips trembled, as if she were trying to conceal her hurt, and her words came out choked. "How thoughtful of you."

"Look." He planted both feet on the pine planks beneath him and lowered his arms. "I had no control over what my father required me to do."

"But you *did* have control regarding what you said and to whom," she pointed out.

"Yes, but I couldn't come right out and tell everyone who I was. Father would have found out, and I could have risked my entire future."

"You could have been honest with some."

"And risk those choice people telling someone else? That would've been taking too big a chance. There were consequences either way." He shifted his weight. "Take you, for example. Had I told you who I was from the start, you likely would have never believed me."

This time it was her turn to cross her arms in a defensive manner. "And what makes you come to that conclusion?"

"Think about how I was dressed. There wasn't time to explain the whole situation since I was already late for my first day on the job. And the next day? Anything I said would have sounded false."

"So instead of being honest, you chose what you felt was the easier path and led me to believe you were something you're not."

Brandt nodded. "Exactly the same thing you did to me."

"I—" She opened her mouth then clamped it shut as she stared at him.

He inwardly gloated that she didn't have an immediate retort. He grew tired of this seemingly endless verbal battle anyway. He'd just told her his reasoning. She should do the same.

"Why did *you* feign the truth to the girls in the factory and act like someone *you* weren't?"

She stiffened as her chin jutted upward an inch. Great. So now he'd wounded her pride in addition to angering her. At least they were on even ground.

"Because I didn't want any of them to feel awkward around me or treat me any differently simply because my family had wealth. Working there afforded me a sense of independence. For once I didn't have to concern myself with someone else controlling every aspect of my life. I and I alone decided."

"Did you also decide what you would do when someone discovered your ruse?"

"No. It wasn't going to last long. By the time it became an issue, I would have moved on to other work. But that's neither here nor there. My work at the factory is done."

Brandt pushed off from the post and started to pace. Done? Just like that? She made it sound so trivial. He had become the alter ego because Father demanded it. He had lied, but out of necessity. Now he had to pay the piper for his actions. She had lied as well, but she didn't seem to think it meant a great deal.

"Had you ever planned to confess to anyone?"

"I hadn't thought that far ahead."

He snorted. "That's obvious."

"Why are you so angry at me? It's not like I'm the only one in the wrong here."

She had a lot of nerve asking him that. He stopped in the center of the gazebo. "Why am I angry?"

"Yes."

"Because you didn't trust me, that's why."

Felicity uncrossed her arms and instead planted them on her hips. "Trust you with what?"

"The fact that you came from money." He resumed pacing. "Did you think I'd treat you differently if I knew? That I'd suddenly want to be a friend and get to know you only for your wealth?"

"How should I know?"

"Well, I was nothing more than a refinery worker," he said, flailing one arm wildly in the air. "And the working class doesn't socialize with the upper classes."

She dropped her hands to rest on each side of her legs. "That was exactly the reason I *did* agree to our friendship. You were a refreshing change from the boorish men I knew."

He paused again. That was a switch Brandt didn't see coming. Why couldn't she stick to the topic at hand without changing it again? He had a hard enough time keeping up with the direction of the conversation without her added course alterations.

She continued. "And of course, Mother and Father warned me against it."

"Well, they didn't see what you saw. They only knew I wasn't good enough for you."

She shrugged. "Not as Brandt Dalton, no. But you were as Brandt Lawson."

Brandt paused a moment. Could she be softening a bit, or could his imagination be playing tricks on him?

"The same goes for my father. That is, until he found out who *you* really were."

"And if you hadn't given him my full name, he never would have known, and we wouldn't be in this mess right now."

Great. There went another twist. How did she manage to know just the right words to cut straight to the heart? He crossed his arms again, lest she shoot another piercing remark his way.

"So now this is *my* fault? How did we get back to blaming me again?"

"Not you so much as your father." Felicity's eyes narrowed. "But now that you mention it, you did go along with him. No questions asked."

"He's my father. And I respect him. What else did you expect me to do?"

"You could have found an alternate path to take that wouldn't have been so deceptive or come with so much potential hurt for others."

"And the same goes for you."

She sighed. Her eyelids slowly closed then opened again. "So where does this leave us now?"

A guttural groan rumbled inside him and found its way to his mouth. "I don't know."

"We can't undo what we've done, nor can we go back to the way we were, now that we know the truth."

Did she have to put it in such plain language and state it in such a matter-of-fact manner? As if he didn't already know.

"I think we both just need to go away for a while." Wait a minute. He couldn't presume to speak for her. "No, *I* need to go away. To sort a few things out."

Had he really just said that?

"That sounds like an. . .excellent idea."

The catch in her voice drew his attention to her face. Stone-hardened indifference. That was all he saw. No, wait. A trace of hopelessness and regret also lingered. Could she actually be wishing for a different outcome? One that didn't require them to go their separate ways?

"I think we could both benefit from the time alone," she said.

There went that idea. Obviously she wasn't as broken up over his leaving as he thought. It wasn't as though he wanted it to be this way. So how did she make him feel like it was all his decision? He really did need to put some distance between them. Because if he didn't throttle her, he'd crush her against his chest and never let her go.

Dropping an invisible shield between them, Brandt took three steps and stood in the doorway of the gazebo. For a brief second that regret returned again, and he almost reconsidered. He had to leave now. For both their sakes.

"Very well, Miss Chambers." He bowed and bid her farewell. "I hope you enjoy the remainder of your time here on the island. Good night."

With that he did an about-face and fled, taking long strides and getting away from her as fast as his slippery shoes would take him. There would be time for regret later.

Chapter 13

I can't believe you never told me about him."

Cecily picked up a corn-husk doll and examined it before setting it back in place. Felicity walked beside her sister as they browsed the souvenirs in the open-air marketplace. Local Cherokee were there along with various vendors from Mackinaw City. It was their last day on the island, and Felicity wanted nothing more than to get on the train and return to her normal life back in Detroit. Only it wouldn't be normal. Everything would be different now that her ruse had come to light. She no longer had her work at the factory where she could escape.

"I never saw the need to mention him." And Felicity regretted that decision. Perhaps if she had been honest with her sister, some of this hurt could have been avoided. She ran her fingers over several meticulously crafted quill boxes. She had her reed basket. Now she wanted something more special.

"Ooh! This one is perfect!" Cecily almost draped herself across the table reaching for what seemed like the hundredth doll that morning. "It's almost a perfect replica of the one Father purchased all those years ago."

She bartered a moment or two with the woman at the table, then retrieved some coins and paid for her doll. Cecily held her shoulders a bit higher after making that purchase, yet continued to browse the tables. Felicity followed behind.

"So you meet a handsome young man and spend time with him. And you don't see the need to speak about him to your only sister?" Cecily stopped and turned. "You might think I'm too young to understand all this. But I'd say you either wanted to keep him to yourself or you were afraid of what Mother or Father might say when they found out." She poked Felicity in the shoulder. "Now you know."

Felicity took a step forward and the two started walking again. "But that's just it, Cecily. I *don't* know."

"What do you mean?"

"All I know from Mother and Father is they approve of Brandt Lawson, and they were planning behind my back to arrange an introduction in the hopes that we might form a union together." And if she had met Brandt for the first time under those circumstances, that might have been a possibility. But now? "When Mother and Father learned about Brandt Dalton, they warned me against any liaisons with him."

Cecily shrugged. "That's because they only knew him as a refinery worker. And that would never do. Now, though, he's the heir to his father's holdings. I don't see the problem. You obviously have their blessing."

"He lied to me, Cecily." Felicity adjusted the handles of the reed basket on her arm. "How will I ever know I can trust him again?"

Casting a look over her shoulder, Cecily's lips formed a rueful line. "Don't forget you lied to him, too. He's probably wondering if he can trust you as well."

"Yes, you're right." What a mess she'd made of things. She hadn't intended for anyone to get hurt. But it was too late for that. She and Brandt both had been wrong. Felicity sighed. "I don't know if we can move past this."

"Have you thought of prayer? You used to tell me all the time it was the answer to all my problems. When I didn't know what to do, I should talk to God. Aside from that, the lies are something the two of you are going to have to work out yourselves."

It sounded so simple yet so complex. Amazing how the perspective of someone younger could actually shed light on her quandary. Felicity draped her arm around her sister's shoulders.

"You know, for a child you're rather intelligent."

Cecily gave her a smug grin. "I know. I had an excellent teacher."

Felicity shook her head and chuckled. Despite her mistakes and errors in judgment, her sister still admired her. That proved God hadn't left her alone to fix this dilemma. Sunlight glinted off something shiny just ahead, and she picked up her pace, almost dragging her sister with her. At the sight of the beautiful handcrafted items on the small stand, Felicity froze.

The seller stood next to the display in a tailored suit, his hands clasping the lapels of his coat as he rocked back and forth on his heels. He raised one hand to smooth the thin lines of his short mustache with his thumb and forefinger.

"These pieces are exquisitely crafted jeweled eggs. Each one is unique. No two are alike." He selected one and held it out. "Please. Take a look for yourself."

Cecily pressed against her side. "Oh, Felicity, it's stunning."

Felicity took the item in her hands and observed it from all angles. She ran her fingers across the etchings on the outside and marveled at the intricate detail of the artwork. An entire piece made of gold and clear crystal gem pieces.

The top held a single gemstone surrounded by what appeared to be the roof of a rotunda. Below, a pattern of gold draping tied with bows at the pinnacle left openings in the egg to reveal a small gift box tucked inside. Underneath the bows two sections of scrollwork fashioned after flowers with flowing stems and vines circled the perimeter against a background of pearl-like marble. A hinge connected the two parts. Directly opposite the hinge sat a clasp with a gemstone that duplicated the one on top. The egg sat on a stem that had been welded together and had four oval pearls, one on each side, which gave way to the fanned-out base.

"Do forgive me for interrupting your admiration of the piece, miss, but may I?"

Felicity tore her attention away from the decorative item to look at the seller. "Pardon me?"

"If you will permit me to show you this one thing." He reached for the clasp and opened it. "As an added bonus, there is also a musical melody that plays."

"Ooh!" Cecily clapped her hands. "It's just like a music box."

Felicity stared at the little box as it slowly spun while the tune played.

"Oh, Felicity, you simply must get this one. It will look wonderful next to the handcrafted items in your curio cabinet."

This item had to be costly. The etchings alone must have taken hours. And the intricacies of the designs as well as the music box feature had to raise the price even more.

"How much are you selling these for?"

"Seven dollars and two bits."

Felicity's throat tightened. That amount was more than she had with her. But the piece was so beautiful. She had only to find Father, and it would be hers.

"To own one of these will make you the envy of all your friends. And the value of them will only continue to increase as time passes."

He made it sound so appealing. Could she justify such an extravagant purchase, though? Especially when she knew people like Mrs. Gibson or even Laura and Brianna were unable to afford the basics of life, much less luxuries like this? No. There were far better uses of her abundance than to spend it on another frivolity to add to her collection.

She handed the egg back to the seller, and her shoulders slumped. "Thank you, sir, but I do believe I must decline. Perhaps another time."

The seller bowed. "I shall be here for the remainder of the summer and will likely return again next season." Reaching into an inner pocket of his suit, the man withdrew a small white card. "Should you desire to contact me at any other time, this is my calling card."

Felicity took it from him and tucked it into her handbag. "Thank you very much for allowing me the time to admire your fine collection. We wish you much success."

He nodded. "Good day, ladies."

Cecily remained silent until they had walked about fifteen feet from the stand; then she wrapped her hand around Felicity's upper arm and leaned close. "I can't believe you didn't buy it. What's the matter with you?"

"Life isn't just about buying the things you want, Cecily. Sometimes there are more important matters."

"And I think all that charity work and your time spent at the factory have warped your sensibilities."

"Perhaps."

"No wonder the young men who live in Grosse Pointe never caught your attention and you fell for Brandt as a refinery worker."

Her sister's remark made her pause. Is that why she had found Brandt so appealing? Because as Brandt Dalton he was different from any other man she'd met? She brushed aside those thoughts for another time when she could analyze them at greater length.

"Shall we make our way back to the beginning? I believe I saw some lovely porcupine quill boxes, and I believe I'll purchase one of them to go with this reed basket."

"Very well."

Cecily's enthusiasm seemed diminished, but Felicity refused to take the blame. If her sister had loved the piece so much, she should have bought it. For now it would remain a nice memory of her visit here this summer.

As they passed the display again, Felicity dipped her head in response to the seller's nod. Movement behind the man drew her gaze just up the hill.

Brandt!

Her disloyal heart leapt at the sight of him. Her head told her to keep walking. How long had he been standing there? Was he following her? He was the one who had first said he needed some time away. Surely he could find somewhere else on the island to be. She tried to ignore his presence, but her mind refused to cooperate.

The sooner they returned home, the better.

ஐ

Pain-filled screams reached Felicity's ears the minute she turned the corner on her way to Mrs. Gibson's.

The baby!

She ran past the first two homes and burst through the front door of the Gibson home. Her eyes searched the room. Marianne knelt beside Lucy, a wet cloth pressed to the woman's forehead.

"The pains just started," the younger girl said. "I was about to fetch the doctor."

Lucy had a death grip on the back and bottom front of the couch where she lay. Her five children were all absent. They'd likely gone to a neighbor's or friend's house.

Felicity had to do something. She'd never seen a baby being born. She'd heard the midwife took care of that. If they were back at her home, she'd send a servant for the doctor or call for a buggy to take Mrs. Gibson to the hospital. But here? She didn't know the first thing to do.

Movement around the corner caught her eye, and she looked toward the other room.

"Timothy!"

The lad jumped back, losing his balance and landing on his backside. After he scrambled to his feet, he brushed oily hair in need of a wash and a trim out of his eyes and assumed an uneven stance. "You need something, Miss Felicity?"

God bless the helpful boy.

"Yes, Timothy. I need you to fetch the doctor. You know your mother's going to have her baby, and I'm worried there might be trouble. We're going to need the doctor's help."

Timothy squared his shoulders and slapped his right hand over his heart. "You can count on me, Miss Felicity."

"Go as fast as you can, Timothy. Run!"

The boy stumbled a bit getting started, but as soon as he reached the street, he took off. Felicity smiled. That boy was going to make a fine man when he grew up. She went back inside and immediately to Mrs. Gibson.

"Marianne, why don't you prepare some nourishment for Mrs. Gibson? As soon as Timothy returns with the doctor, Mrs. Gibson might need something to give her strength."

Marianne nodded and stood. "I'll set some broth to heat and fetch some cold water." She stood and backed away, wringing her hands on her apron. "I'm real sorry I didn't send Timothy sooner, Miss Felicity. But someone had to be here with the missus."

Felicity offered a reassuring smile. "You did everything just fine, Marianne. Now pray the doctor arrives soon and tend to the tasks you mentioned."

Just twenty minutes later, the door swung open and Timothy ran inside, a stern-looking man with a medical bag following close on his heels. He quickly assessed the situation, dropped his cap on the chair in the corner, and went to kneel at Lucy's side.

"Has she been screaming long? Have you been keeping her cooled down? Do you have extra blankets and boiling water ready? How far apart are the contractions?"

Contractions? Water? Blankets? Felicity sat back on her haunches, dumbfounded.

The doctor's stern expression softened some as he glanced at her. "How often does she feel the intense pain?"

"Oh!" Contractions. Yes, she understood those. "Every four or five minutes, I believe."

He rolled up his sleeves and dug into his medical bag for a few instruments. Most she didn't recognize, but the stethoscope she knew. He set the two ends in his ears then placed the round piece over Lucy's abdomen and listened.

"Everything sounds just fine, Mrs. Gibson." He placed a hand on her forehead and smiled. Lucy returned a weak smile, her eyes half closed and perspiration dotting her upper lip.

Felicity closed her eyes and prayed everything would go smoothly. *God, we really do need Your divine assistance this day.* Lucy had been through so much this past year. Losing a husband in a boating accident was enough for any woman. She shouldn't have to lose this baby, too.

"Miss Chambers, I'm going to need you to assist me. Are you feeling up to it?"

She almost said she wasn't, but Lucy needed her. "Yes, Doctor. I'll do whatever you need."

"All right. Go into the kitchen and boil a pot of water. Then gather as many blankets as you can from around the house." He lifted the dented metal bowl from the floor. "Dump this out and fill it with fresh cold water. Then bring some extra cloths for keeping her cool."

"Right away, Doctor."

In no time at all, the squalling baby entered the world, and as far as Felicity could tell, without complications. She raised her eyes to the ceiling and smiled.

"Heavenly Father, thank You."

"Amen to that!" came the doctor's hearty reply. He held the baby over a makeshift table by the wall, using the now hot water to wash the newborn. A minute later, he swaddled the child and made his way back to Lucy. "I could never do what I do without His help," he said, kneeling beside the couch.

Felicity peered over the doctor's shoulder. The infant squirmed and fidgeted within its confines. Only whimpers escaped the tiny lips as the doctor settled the baby into Lucy's waiting arms with a smile.

"Mrs. Gibson, you have yourself another healthy baby girl."

The wonder and the joy of life. A miracle in and of itself. Lucy seemed so peaceful now, and the little girl seemed to know her mother now held her. What had begun as heartache and loss for Lucy now ended in wonder and delight. The circle was now complete.

Before long Lucy would be back on her feet and able to work again at the factory. She'd be well on her way toward providing for her family again. That realization brought sudden sadness. Where did that leave Felicity? These past few months had been the longest of any charity service she'd performed. It already felt odd knowing everything was about to change. What would happen when that day actually arrived?

Felicity needed to start thinking more about that. She didn't want to find herself at the end of this current phase without a plan for the next. Today marked the beginning of the end. She truly would miss all of this.

&

Brandt stared at the figures in the three columns for the eighth time. They refused to add up. He must be missing something. He'd been overseeing the work at the refinery for almost a month, and this was the first time he'd had a problem focusing. He didn't want to admit that it might have something to do with catching a glimpse of Felicity earlier when he was outside on his lunch break.

He'd made some well-placed inquiries and learned that Mrs. Gibson had delivered a healthy baby girl the day after he'd returned from Mackinac. She'd been deemed fit to return to work this week. He was glad Mrs. Gibson had recovered, but her return only solidified Felicity's absence. He'd been to the candle factory to discuss business with the manager there at least once a week during the past month, and he'd never seen Felicity. She told him she had quit before the visit to the island. But then why had she returned today?

They hadn't spoken since that fateful day in August. And as he'd figured, the time away from her had helped clear his head.

Today, though, no manner of figures or mindless tasks could take his thoughts away from Felicity. He tried going for a walk, but he only saw the places where they'd talked and shared a picnic. Back in the office, the four walls seemed to close in around him.

Brandt grabbed his coat off the back of the chair. "I need to go home."

After stomping down the back stairs, he shoved the door open with a bang and thudded into the street. All the way home he brooded. How had she managed to bewitch him? Why couldn't he get her out of his mind? He should be worrying about facts and figures and new equipment. Not getting stuck on the image of one girl.

"Master Lawson, sir." Jeffrey opened the front door just as Brandt reached the landing out front. "It's a surprise to see you home so early, sir. Is everything all right at work?"

Brandt shed his coat and dumped it into his butler's arms. "Everything at work is fine, Jeffrey." He jabbed his index finger against the side of his head. "It's up here that there's a problem."

Jeffrey gave him a puzzled look. "Your head, sir? Are you ill? Do you need me to fetch the doctor, sir?"

If Brandt hadn't been so frustrated, he might have chuckled at Jeffrey's concern. If only a doctor could fix this.

"No, Jeffrey. I'm not ill. And no, I don't need the doctor. What I *do* need is a tall glass of lemonade and—"

"And your rather worn copy of *Journey to the Center of the Earth*, perhaps?"

He smiled. How well Jeffrey knew him. If he couldn't be somewhere listening to a band play some of his favorite music, he'd rather be inside with a book by Jules Verne—no matter how many times he'd read it.

"That would be perfect, Jeffrey. Thank you."

"As you wish, sir."

"And Jeffrey?"

"Yes, sir?"

"What did I tell you about the 'sir' business?"

Jeffrey bowed with a half smirk on his lips. "As you wish." He hung up Brandt's coat and disappeared down the hall toward the kitchen.

Brandt made his way to the library. The dark interior welcomed him with the familiar smells of leather, paper, and the ever-present pipe tobacco. He sank into the plush leather seat and propped his feet on the footstool in front of him.

His butler reappeared a moment later with the requested items and placed the glass on the table next to the chair.

"Will there be anything else?"

"No, Jeffrey. That's all for now. Thank you."

"Very well. I shall inform your mother that you're home. I believe she wishes to speak with you."

Brandt nodded as Jeffrey exited into the hallway, leaving the door open to let some light in. What did Mother want to discuss with him? Usually Father had an agenda in mind. But if his mother had something to say, now would be the perfect time. Father wouldn't be there to interrupt.

He waited for ten minutes, but she didn't come. Perhaps he should get some reading done in the interim. He lit a lamp on the small table beside him. As tradition had it, once he settled in for a good read, Mother would interrupt.

Flipping open the well-worn cover, Brandt slid his fingers on the edges of the pages as he turned them. He reached the first page and refreshed his memory about the professor and his family.

Sure enough, as he reached page five Mother's silhouette appeared outlined by the light from the hall. Brandt slapped the book closed and tucked it against his thigh. This likely wouldn't last long. Mother wasn't one to beat around the bush.

"Brandt," she began as she came farther into the study, "I have been meaning to speak with you before now. But the opportunity hadn't presented itself."

He smirked to himself. Exactly as he predicted. She didn't bother with any formalities.

"By all means, Mother." He rested his hands on his thighs. "I'm listening."

Mother approached until she stood directly in front of him. She opened her mouth to speak, then paused. A moment later, she tried again. "Why are you home so early?"

Brandt dismissed the fact with a random wave. "I couldn't seem to stay focused on the tasks at hand. So I came home. Don't worry. I left the refinery in good hands."

The faint glow from the lamp on the other side of him illuminated the look of reprimand on Mother's face. She slid her hands up to rest at her waist. "This wouldn't by any chance have anything to do with Miss Chambers, would it?"

He didn't have to answer that. And he wouldn't. Brandt clamped his lips tight and avoided her eyes.

"Brandt."

He squirmed. Women must receive some form of training or attend a special school to learn how to perfect that tone of voice. The one that made their sons and daughters feel like little children, no matter how old they were.

"All right." He forced out a sigh. "I admit it. I miss her. There. Are you happy?"

She gave him a soft smile. "Only because you've finally confessed your feelings. Now what are you going to do about them?"

Leaning forward in the chair and plopping his feet on the floor, he rested his elbows on his knees. Then he raked his right hand through his hair. "That's just it. I don't know."

Mother pulled the footstool a little ways away from him and sat on the edge, maintaining her proper posture. With her hands folded primly in her lap, her delicate appearance captivated him. "May I make a suggestion?"

"At this point, I'd welcome anything."

"Go to her. Talk to her. Apologize. Work it out."

Brandt gave her a half grin. "That's four suggestions."

She smiled. "You have been brooding around this house for weeks now. Ever since we returned from the island and you assumed responsibility for the refinery. This isn't good for you."

"But, Mother, we both said some rather hurtful things. And we lied to each other."

"Yes, but you both have also admitted those mistakes." She reached out and placed a hand over his. "Don't you believe it's time you laid aside your pride and sought out a way to make amends? To set things right again?"

"I don't know that I can."

"Well, son, I'm afraid that's not something I can help you do. But God can. Have you tried praying and asking for His help?"

Brandt emitted a quiet groan. That was one thing he hadn't done. No wonder his life was such a wreck.

"One thing I will say, though," Mother continued, "is you don't want to let someone like Miss Chambers get away. I almost made a mistake like that once. I don't wish you to do the same."

He snapped up his head, his eyes widening. "You, Mother? But how?"

She took a deep breath and again folded her hands in her lap. "When I first met your father, I wasn't exactly equivalent with him in social standing. It was about ten years before the War Between the States, and some of our family were involved in the local opposition against the cruel acts of the Michigan Central railroad owners." Her tongue snuck out to lick her lips before she continued. "In April of that year, the depot here in Detroit was burned to the ground. I lost an uncle almost immediately. And the way I found out was through a letter informing me that a trust fund had been established for him through my grandfather. As the oldest child of my parents—your grandparents—I was the one named to receive that inheritance."

"But how could you not know about the inheritance? He would've been the brother of one of your parents."

"The opposition to the railroad divided a lot of families, and mine was no exception. This uncle had turned his back on his family because of a disagreement over how to deal with the situation. But that didn't mean the rift couldn't be repaired. So since there were no children to inherit the fund, it went to me instead. The sudden increase in wealth now made me a viable candidate for marriage to your father. Up until that point, however, our relationship had caused a lot of problems. We almost walked away from it all."

Brandt sat back in the chair. "Wow. I had no idea."

"No, and if it weren't for this situation with Miss Chambers, you might never have been told. Your father warned you against a relationship with her because he remembered the struggle he and I faced not long ago. Just like the situation with your brother two years ago. We didn't wish for either of you to endure the same hurt. Now, though, there is no reason for not making amends. I hope this story helps you in making up your mind." With one final pat of his hand, she stood. "Don't allow the mistakes I almost made to be repeated with you. I'll be praying you make the right decision."

The door closed behind her, and Brandt sat alone. He couldn't believe what he'd just learned. His parents had almost lost their chance for the happiness they now knew. And for what? A measly measure of pride? He wouldn't let that happen to him. No matter the outcome, he was going to tell Felicity how he felt.

He only prayed she'd be receptive.

Chapter 14

Brandt dumped the latest refinery file from his father's accountant onto his desk. More figures and columns. Just what he didn't want at the moment. He pressed his fingers to his eyes to rid them of sleep, then slid his hands down his stubbly cheeks and chin. He'd forgotten to shave! How could he have missed that this morning?

With the few winks he'd managed to grab last night, it didn't come as too much of a surprise. During each waking period, Brandt had run several scenarios through his mind about how he'd approach Felicity. None of them sounded plausible.

There had to be an answer.

But he'd have to figure that out later. Right now he had to get over to the candle factory. His weekly meeting with Mr. Marshall was today. Maybe he could take the figures with him and have Marshall look them over. No, the man would likely peer over the rim of his glasses if Brandt made a suggestion like that. He'd get the work done. Later.

In no time at all, he reached the factory and made his way to the upper level. Marshall greeted him at the door.

"Lawson. Good to see you again. Come on in."

They made quick order of pleasantries and exchanged a brief recap of figures from the past week. It was good to hear about the success or failure of another factory. If production was low all around, he'd know it wasn't just his men.

The wooden chair protested Brandt's weight and creaked. He'd just settled back when what sounded like a small explosion and a shout came from the lower level.

"Fire!"

Brandt jumped to his feet and rushed from the office just ahead of Marshall. Rising flames drew his eyes to the far corner of the factory floor. He raced down the stairs, pausing at the bottom to follow Marshall's lead in grabbing a few coarse burlap blankets from one of the supply rooms. As he weaved through the various stations, only one thought crossed his mind.

Please, God, don't let it spread too far.

Most of the young women scattered in all directions, seeing to their own safety. A handful had already begun focusing their efforts on the fire itself by the time Brandt reached the site. Two of the supervisors cleared the area of flammable materials, and another manager attempted to keep the few remaining women at bay. Brandt tossed two blankets to the other men.

"Use them to blot out any new burning from the sparks."

Searing heat rushed in his direction, and flames licked at his clothing as he aimed straight for the center of the blaze.

"Someone get some water over here!"

An immediate flurry of activity followed his command. He prayed they'd have the intuitiveness to organize a line of volunteers, passing buckets of water from the source to the fire. In the meantime, he attacked the flames with a ferocious intensity equal to that of the small inferno.

What felt like hours likely only took about thirty minutes. They'd extinguished the last spark, and everyone breathed a sigh of relief. Black soot and scorch marks now covered everything in the immediate area. The sudden halt to the frantic pace seemed almost eerie.

Then the gradual introduction of the whirring from the machines and lye mixers penetrated Brandt's ears. One by one, the women dispersed as they realized the immediate danger no longer existed. Two or three workers remained, their heads downcast as the other three men gathered close.

Marshall regarded each one in turn. "What happened here?"

A man named Anderson stepped forward. "It appears Miss Morrow spilled a pot of boiling oils and sloshed some lye on it as well."

"But that wouldn't result in something like this." Brandt looked to Marshall for permission to get involved. The man nodded. Brandt waved his hand toward the charred remains. "Who caused the fire to start?"

A young woman spoke up next. "That would probably be my fault. I wanted to neutralize the lye spill, so I grabbed a bottle of vinegar and threw some on it."

"What's your name?"

"Brianna Fleming, sir."

"And Miss Fleming, what happened after you dispensed with the vinegar?"

She cast an eye toward one of the other girls then looked back at Brandt. "I'm afraid some of it splashed into the furnace and caused the sparks that led to the fire." She wrung her hands in front of her and shifted her weight from one foot to the other. "I truly am sorry, sir. I didn't think this would happen from such a small spill."

Brandt took a deep breath and tempered his anger. This wasn't his factory or his place to issue any reprimands. The sincerity in Miss Fleming's eyes proved her remorse. He hoped Marshall wouldn't make it worse for her. A moment later, the manager stepped forward with a reassuring smile and placed one hand on her shoulder.

"Miss Fleming, I appreciate you coming forward with your confession. I don't intend to deduct anything from your pay or Miss Morrow's." He glanced to the other girl involved then addressed everyone present. "But this only proves the necessity of adhering to the highest level of safety when attending to your workstations. We avoided a potentially more serious situation today. There is no guarantee we will be this fortunate in the future. Am I understood?"

All the workers nodded, their faces solemn.

"Now since it appears that no one was harmed, I suggest we—"

"Mr. Marshall, come quick!"

Brandt jerked his head toward the voice as Marshall asked, "Who said that?"

"Laura Price, sir. I'm down here."

Laura? And Brianna? These must be the two girls Felicity had mentioned to him.

Brandt looked at the floor where a young woman knelt beside another figure, partially concealed from his sight by the girth of the midsized furnace. Several gasps came from the young women who craned their necks over the station as he scrambled around the equipment.

He froze as the familiar chestnut hair above a smudged face came into view. "Felicity!"

Miss Price looked up at him, her eyes wide. "You know her, too?"

He fell to his knees and quickly assessed her visible injuries. She wore a plain walking dress, but it was still of finer material than the clothes she'd worn for most of the time he'd known her. Did the girls here know who she really was? It would be best not to reveal anything about her true identity to them.

"Yes, Miss Chambers and I are"—he tried to speak past the lump in his throat—"acquainted."

Pieces of her skirt had been scorched. Soot and ash covered her one arm. Her sleeve had been torn, and reddened skin blistered from what looked like some serious burns.

"How did she come to be here? I don't believe she's worked here for weeks."

"She stopped by to visit Brianna and me, sir. We had just returned from our midmorning break when the accident happened, and she rushed to help."

Always the giver. Whether it was performing charity or lending a hand to a friend, Felicity possessed a heart of gold. How could he have been so blind? He tried to piece together a few frayed ends of her sleeve, then turned his attention to her face.

She didn't move. Didn't moan. Not a sign of life other than the slow and steady rise and fall of her chest. Tenderly he brushed back some hair from her face. A nasty bruise and small cut trickled a little blood near her ear. He withdrew his handkerchief and wiped some of the black marks from her cheeks, careful to avoid the pink areas there as well.

A gasp drew his gaze back to Miss Price. Her face registered recognition, but he didn't see how she could possibly know him. He'd only made brief visits here once a week.

"You're him! You're the refinery worker."

Her voice came out not much above a whisper. This was definitely the Laura whom Felicity had mentioned. Brandt silently pleaded with his eyes for her to remain quiet about that. She seemed to understand and nodded, but a slight grin appeared on her lips.

"I have to get Miss Chambers to the hospital."

Brandt moved into action. Placing his arms beneath Felicity's neck and legs, he scooped her into his arms and stood, shuffling for a moment or two to get his footing.

"Thanks, Lawson, for seeing to the young lady."

"My pleasure, Marshall." If only the man knew the truth. Brandt peered over the machinery. "Could you send a messenger to my father about the incident to tell him what's happened and where he can find me? I'll return if necessary to add my remarks to the incident report."

"That likely won't be necessary, but I'll get in touch with you if it is. You just take care of Miss Chambers."

The young women gaped in awe as Brandt held Felicity in his arms, searching for the quickest exit from the building. As he stepped past Laura, she gave him a quick wink.

He didn't know what Felicity had said about him, but apparently it had met with approval from this young woman.

"All right, ladies. Back to work!" Marshall's voice boomed. The rustling of clothes and the scuffling of feet answered his command.

At least the factory was once again safe and restored to order. Brandt glanced down into Felicity's pale face. If only he was as certain about Felicity.

"God, please. Let her be all right."

⁂

Brandt paced back and forth in front of the private room where the nurse had taken Felicity. The doctor went into the room and came back out again three times. Not once did he provide any information or details to Brandt. When was someone going to give him another update? He just wanted to know Felicity would be all right.

"Mr. Lawson! How is she? Have you heard?"

He turned at the somewhat familiar voice of Mrs. Chambers. Mr. Chambers guided her with his arm around her waist. Worry lines furrowed her brow, and she pinned him with an earnest gaze. His own parents followed directly behind, with his brother and Felicity's sister next. Felicity's brother and another young woman brought up the rear.

The small entourage gathered around him. It pained him to tell them the truth. Perhaps with them here they could get some answers.

"I haven't heard much. It's aggravating having to stand here and watch them walk back and forth as if I'm invisible." He raked his fingers through his hair and groaned. "I haven't pressed the issue, though, as I wanted to allow the doctor as much freedom to work as possible."

"Oh, Harold. Our little girl." Mrs. Chambers buried her face against her husband's chest. He patted her back and whispered a few words to her.

"How was she when you brought her here?"

Brandt met Mr. Chambers's gaze head-on. "I have to admit, sir, she had some bad burns on her arm and a cut near her ear. Her clothes had been scorched in places." With each word he spoke, Mrs. Chambers flinched. Reporting the facts might be difficult, but it had to be done. "Other than that, she didn't seem too seriously injured. She was unconscious, though, so I couldn't tell for certain."

Mr. Chambers looked around their surroundings, appearing to take stock of the people, the hospital workers, and the possible protocol. They hadn't given Brandt a designated place to wait, so he had claimed a bench in the hall near Felicity's room as his perch. Her father turned back to him.

"And how long have you been here?"

"About an hour, sir."

Felicity's father pivoted and deposited his wife on the bench with a few quiet words to her. She nodded and took the handkerchief he offered to dab at her eyes. Mr. Chambers then stepped toward the desk where Brandt had originally spoken to a nurse about admitting Felicity.

"Let me see what I can find out," Mr. Chambers said.

His commanding presence would be enough to get anyone's attention. But the diplomatic manner in which he handled the situation struck a good balance. He reminded Brandt a lot of his own father. When these two men spoke, people listened. Brandt prayed they'd listen enough to give them another update on Felicity.

"She's going to be all right, son." Father came to stand beside him, one hand on Brandt's shoulder. "You did the right thing, bringing her here as fast as you could. Trust the doctor to do his job."

"If only I could've done more."

Father moved to stand in front of him. "You can't live your life wondering about 'if onlys,' son. That will do nothing but pile the guilt so deep you won't be able to accomplish the tasks ahead." Father placed both hands on Brandt's shoulders. "Your mother told me about the conversation you two had yesterday."

"Yes. It helped me make up my mind about Miss Chambers."

"Son, we know you love her. It's in your eyes. Now you just have to make things right again."

Brandt *wanted* to get everything back to where they started before the visit to Mackinac Island occurred. He just didn't know if he could.

"But what if she won't see me?"

Father gave him a half smile. "I have a feeling the young lady in question will be quite amenable once she learns you rescued her."

Brandt looked across the hall at the closed door to Felicity's room. He prayed his father was right.

"All right. I was able to find out a little more about Felicity's condition," Mr. Chambers announced.

Condition? She had a condition? It must be worse than Brandt thought. She hadn't looked too bad when he brought her here. There must have been something else.

Mr. Chambers addressed everyone present, his gaze resting on each one in turn as he spoke. "They have treated her burns and the cut on her face. She was awake briefly, just long enough for them to examine her for further injuries. She had none."

A blended sigh of relief escaped from the members of both families.

Mr. Chambers continued. "A doctor should be here shortly to escort us in to see her. The nurse told me she was given a sedative to ease her pain, so she might be somewhat dazed and might not make sense."

"Since when is that such a change for Felicity?" Zach, Felicity's brother, spoke out.

A rumble of soft chuckles passed throughout the group.

"Zachary." The warning tone that accompanied his name made him flex the muscles in his neck.

Zach gave his father a sheepish grin. "Sorry."

Mr. Chambers just shook his head.

"Mr. Chambers? Mrs. Chambers?" A nurse dressed all in white, complete with a starched white head covering that reminded him of a nun's habit, addressed Felicity's parents. "My name is Nurse Kendall. If you'll come with me, I'll take you to see your daughter."

"Can we come, too?" Cecily stepped forward from the back of the group, pulling on Zach's arm and dragging him to the front as well. "She's *our* sister."

Mr. Chambers looked to the nurse, who smiled. "Of course. Please follow me."

Brandt tracked their progress down the hall and into Felicity's room. The door closed behind her family, and he once again felt like he didn't belong. Who was he to intrude on a moment that should be reserved for family alone? Her parents and brother and sister were here. They no longer needed him. Why didn't he just leave and go home?

He sank onto the bench again, dropping his head into his hands with a sigh. He ruminated on all the reasons why he should go. And he found only one reason why he should stay.

"Mr. Lawson?"

"Yes?" Brandt and his father said together.

The nurse stood before them, looking from father to son. "Oh, I'm sorry. I meant the younger Mr. Lawson."

"Yes?" Brandt repeated.

"Miss Chambers is asking for you, sir."

Felicity? Asking for him? But why?

"If you'll come with me, I'll take you to her."

Brandt cast a glance over his shoulder at his parents. Father gave him an encouraging nod, and Mother smiled softly. He turned back to where Nurse Kendall stood waiting. There didn't seem to be any other option. He had no choice. Isn't this what he'd wanted? Isn't this why he'd stayed and waited? So then why did his feet all of a sudden feel like two large bricks?

"Mr. Lawson? If you please."

Nurse Kendall extended her hand, palm up, toward Brandt. Through no will of his own, he followed. As they reached the door, it opened and out came Felicity's family. Brandt licked his lips several times and swallowed. They all gave him a look he couldn't decipher before moving past him and continuing down the hall.

Brandt took a step forward and stopped when Mr. Chambers placed a hand on his shoulder. The man didn't say a word. He only spread his lips into a slight grin then went to join his family.

The time had come. The moment of reckoning hovered over his head like a cloud.

God, please give me strength and the right words to say.

Nurse Kendall pushed the door open a crack and stepped back to allow him entrance. Brandt placed one foot in front of the other and jumped when the door clicked closed behind him. Rays of light filtered through the sheer curtains at the windows. His eyes immediately sought the single bed and the young woman lying in it.

Her eyes were closed, and she didn't open them at his entrance. Even though she had bandages on her arms and face, he had never seen Felicity look so beautiful. With caution, Brandt approached the bedside where she lay. She mumbled and smacked her lips together. Her left hand raised and settled across her abdomen. A wince accompanied the movement.

Brandt rushed to her side and reached for the pitcher of water on the table. He poured a glass and held it to her lips, slipping his free arm behind her head and lifting her to drink. Any moment now, she would see him there. What would he do then? Her eyelids fluttered as she took a few sips then relaxed against his arm. He laid her back against the pillows and returned the glass to the table.

"Mmm." She smacked her lips again. "Thank you."

"You're welcome." His voice cracked, and the two words came out in a combination cough and squeak. Brandt took a seat in the empty chair next to him, cleared his throat, and tried again. "You're welcome."

Felicity opened her eyes and turned her head to look at him. A soft smile formed on her lips. "Brandt." She slid her hand off her stomach and to the bedside. The muscles in her neck strained as she tried to move her arm more.

Brandt covered her hand with his and placed his other on her forearm, just below the bandages. "No, no. Don't try to move. Just rest."

"I'm so glad you came." Her voice was so soft he had to lean closer to hear her. "Thank you." She swallowed. "Thank you for rescuing me."

"I'm just glad I was there at all." Despite what his father said, Brandt couldn't keep the self-condemnation from his voice.

Felicity closed her eyes for a moment. The soft sounds of her breathing accompanied the faint noises from the hallway. When her eyelids opened again, the same doubt, uncertainty, and fear he felt reflected back at him from her deep pools.

"Brandt, I have something—"

"Shh." He cut her off and touched two fingers to her lips, then removed his hand. She stared at him with doelike innocence. "Let me go first."

An almost imperceptible nod followed his entreaty. All right. He had her undivided attention. Now what should he say?

"Felicity, I have been repeating in my mind the last conversation we had. And I owe you an apology." There, that wasn't such a bad start. "We both made it clear that night that we had our reasons for doing what we did. I am just as guilty as I accused you of being. I was wrong for lying and wrong for getting so angry with you. You deserve more than that." He implored her with his gaze and gave her hand a tender squeeze. "Can you ever forgive me?"

It hadn't come out the way he'd rehearsed it in his head, but it could still work. At least he hoped it would.

Felicity's hand moved beneath his, and she turned her wrist to interlace their fingers. He glanced down at their joined hands then back at her face. Tenderness replaced the uncertainty of a moment before.

"Yes," she whispered. "I forgive you." A small fit of coughs started in her chest, and her body shook.

Brandt poured another glass of water for her. When she finished, she again settled back against the pillows, reaching for his hand once more.

"I was also wrong for being dishonest and in blaming you. Can *you* forgive *me*?"

He didn't hesitate. "Yes. Of course I will." How could he deny her what she'd just given him?

She visibly relaxed. Her entire body sank farther into the mattress, and her expression seemed much more at peace. As she started to close her eyes, Brandt tightened his hold on her wrist. He had to get this out now, or he might lose his nerve. Felicity rolled her head to the left and looked at him.

"There. . .there's one more thing."

Her eyes seemed to tell him to go on, but the words died in his throat. Maybe making her smile would lighten the mood a bit and help him say what he'd come to tell her.

"At least I know I have a captive audience this time."

That worked. Her slow grin turned into a full smile that reached all the way to her eyes. Yes. That's just what he needed to help him get through the next part of his confession. After unlacing their fingers, Brandt clasped her hand between both of his.

"Felicity, it took our parents' schemes to make me realize just how special you are to me. I'm a fool for not seeing it sooner." He sought her gaze and held it. "Maybe I didn't want to believe it. Maybe I wasn't ready. I don't know. What I do know is I don't want to lose you."

A sharp gasp followed his declaration. This was it. He had to say it now.

"Felicity, I love you. I've probably loved you for a while now. I was just too blind to see it."

Her lips moved, but no sound came out. Then she seemed to find her voice.

"Brandt. I love you, too."

This was going better than he thought. He grinned and slid to one knee on the floor. "Then will you marry me?"

"Yes!"

Brandt rose and leaned over her to give her a quick peck on the mouth. He pulled back to look down into her face, seeing the same longing he felt inside. Lowering his lips again, he positioned himself for a better kiss this time.

"Splendid!"

"Excellent!"

"It's about time!"

Exclamations of delight and enthusiasm accompanied the clapping of hands. Brandt whipped around, almost losing his balance. There, crowding the doorway, stood both his and Felicity's families. With wide grins and beaming smiles and the small applause, they gave their obvious approval of this new relationship. Far more than the friends they were, Brandt and Felicity now moved on to a newfound love.

He chuckled and turned his chair parallel to the bed before sitting down. Grabbing her hand once more, he shared a special look with her, emboldened by her nod and the look of love in her eyes.

"You all obviously heard. And we know what you think. Now will you perhaps leave us alone to discuss a few more things?"

Cecily pushed everyone else aside and strode into the room. "There will be time enough for that later. Right now we want to celebrate with you both."

The two families voiced their agreement, and all followed Cecily's lead. Oh well. At least they had their privacy for a few moments.

Brandt pivoted to face Felicity. Amusement danced in her eyes. He shrugged. They could discuss the details of the wedding and their engagement another time. Right now they had their families together, and their relationship had been restored. God had smiled down upon them, despite their bumbled attempts to handle things themselves. Anything else would just have to wait.

Epilogue

Felicity leaned back against Brandt, his arms enfolding her against his chest. "Mmm, I can't believe it's been almost a year already." Normally Molly would accompany her as a chaperone, but Mother had granted permission for them to have this evening to themselves. The rare moment of freedom after a year of being watched was a welcome pleasure.

"A year since what?" Brandt's warm breath fanned across her hair and stirred a few loose strands.

She giggled. "Since you asked me to become your wife, silly."

She felt his smile against her head. "Oh, that."

"Oh, that?" Felicity sat up and pivoted to stare at him. "You make it sound like it's nothing of consequence. Like it's a normal, everyday occurrence." She placed her hands on her hips. "Tell me, Mr. Lawson, just how many women have you proposed to in your life?"

The rumbling chuckle started in his chest and burst forth as a full-fledged laugh by the time it reached his mouth. Amusement danced in his eyes as he reached for her hands, raising first one then the other to his lips. The intensity in his eyes made her quiver inside.

"Only one, my dear. And that's the only one I intend to ask." The corner of his mouth turned up as he smirked. "Besides, with your tendency to masquerade as someone other than your true self, you are more than enough for me to handle."

She grinned. "I haven't engaged in any behavior such as that since last summer. And you know it."

Brandt drew lazy circles on the backs of her hands with his thumbs. They'd come to the lakeshore and chosen this spot by the tree to ensure some final moments of privacy before the wedding tomorrow. At times the year had seemed to drag, but with all the details to plan for the elaborate affair Mother had insisted on having, the time passed more quickly than Felicity had expected. She and Brandt both had suggested something smaller, but Mother would have none of that. Even now a few final details flitted through Felicity's mind, but Brandt didn't seem interested in talking about them. If he intended to distract her, he was doing an excellent job.

All of a sudden he dropped her hands and sat up straight, twisting to reach for the satchel he'd brought with them.

"I was wondering when we'd get around to finding out what you have in there."

Felicity raised her chin and leaned toward him, attempting to see inside.

Brandt held up one finger. "Nuh-uh. No peeking. It's a surprise."

Returning to her previous position, she tucked her legs close to her side. Felicity clasped her hands together and forced them into her lap. Anticipation made her want to squeal for Brandt to hurry, but she managed a docile tone instead.

"I do so love surprises."

Brandt reached into the satchel and withdrew a thin cardboard box. "And this is one I know you're going to treasure." He handed it to her.

Felicity almost dropped it. "Goodness, it's heavy!" She hadn't expected such weight from something that appeared so simple.

"I assure you it will be worth its weight in gold."

She tipped her head and regarded him for a moment. He seemed so sure of himself, so confident she would love this. What had he gone and done now?

"Well, are you going to open it or not?"

He sounded as eager as she felt. "All right." She smiled, allowing her excitement to once again bubble within. "I'll open it now."

Taking great care, she slid her thumb along the edge of the lid and underneath the flap. With that flipped up, Felicity then reached inside to pull out the object, wrapped in white tissue paper and nestled amid a bit of straw. Another quick glance at Brandt showed a light in his eyes as he watched her unveil his gift.

She pulled back the top part of the tissue paper and gasped.

"Brandt! How did you know?"

The jeweled egg! Rushing to pull away the remainder of the tissue, Felicity bit her lip and bounced in place. Moisture gathered at the corners of her eyes, and she raised her blurry gaze to his.

He reached out and caressed her cheek. "A little birdie told me you might want to add this piece to your collection."

"Cecily."

Brandt nodded. "One and the same." He implored her with an earnest gaze. "So do you like it?"

Felicity leaned forward and threw her arms around him. "Oh, Brandt, I absolutely love it!"

He unwound her arms from his neck and settled her back in place. "Well then, there's one more thing I must show you."

"There's more?"

Brandt placed both hands on the egg and opened the clasp. Soft music started to play as the little box turned. He put his thumb on the golden bow at the front and pulled back, revealing another little compartment tucked away within the box. Feeling like a little girl, Felicity tilted the egg toward her. A cry accompanied her sharp intake of breath.

There, set in a tiny piece of velvet, sat a lone golden band. Felicity had no words to say. Emotion choked them off.

"I was going to present this gift earlier, but considering where you first saw this and where we're to be married tomorrow, I altered my plans. I hope you don't mind."

Felicity picked up the ring and held it in her hand for further inspection. The polished gold gleamed in the sunlight. Tears again gathered in her eyes, and one or two spilled down her cheeks. She sniffed and slid her gaze from the ring to Brandt's face.

"Oh, Brandt." She pushed up on her knees and hugged him, whispering against his ear, "You've made me so happy!"

Brandt pulled her close in a tight embrace. They sat there for several moments, Felicity basking in his warmth and the security and comfort of his love.

He cleared his throat. "All right. I think we'd better go for a walk along the lakeshore. Otherwise I might forget that we marry *tomorrow* and do something improper."

Felicity giggled and pulled away. After allowing him to help her stand, she tucked her right hand into the crook of his elbow. He gathered the egg and box and led them out of the gazebo. She held her left hand out in front of her, admiring the beauty and simplicity of her engagement ring again. The gold band would only add to the symbol of Brandt's love. Tomorrow they would speak their vows and become husband and wife. But for now and today, she couldn't be happier.

❧

"As copper must endure a refining process to bring out its luster, as a candle must be shaped and molded before its true beauty shines forth, so your two lives will undergo the same transformation as you grow in love and understanding of each other."

The preacher stood in front of Brandt and Felicity, admonishing them to love, honor, and cherish each other and to place their union second only to their service and devotion to God. They could have been married by the parson on the island, but Brandt wanted Felicity's pastor to do the honors. He'd been attending her church since he proposed. Preacher Westcott had offered some sound spiritual wisdom once or twice, and Brandt could think of no one better.

Felicity's hands fit snugly into his as he faced the woman who would soon become his wife. He couldn't take his eyes off her. Through her veil, he could see a clouded image of her face. Her hair had been styled and gathered on top of her head, with a single wide curl resting over her left shoulder. The sparkle in her eyes no doubt mirrored the light in his.

They'd finally made it.

After they had repeated their vows to each other, the preacher looked at them both and said, "You may now add your personal promises."

At Westcott's invitation, Brandt raised Felicity's hands a few inches and took a step forward.

"We began our journey together as friends, and although we had some rocky roads in the middle, our love saw us through. I chose this spot for us since it's the place where our lives unraveled and everything fell apart." He swallowed past the tightness in his throat and forced his voice to remain strong. "Today we stand here before God, family, and friends to put it all back together. I pledge my undying love to you and will give my life to see you happy."

Felicity inhaled a shuddering breath to speak her answering vows. "From the start, you became a friend, a confidant, and a person in whom I could see true integrity. We survived the fire of our mistakes and arose from the ashes stronger for the experience." She sniffed. "This day I pledge my lifelong love and devotion, promising to honor and respect you above all others, and believing in God to guide us from here forward."

They exchanged rings after the preacher blessed them, and Brandt covered Felicity's hands with his own.

"Having pledged themselves to each other through their individual vows and through the giving and receiving of their rings, Mr. Brandt Lawson and Miss Felicity Chambers are now joined. By the powers vested in me by the State of Michigan and bestowed by our almighty Father, I now pronounce you husband and wife. What therefore God hath joined together, let not man put asunder." Preacher Westcott beamed a wide grin. "You may now kiss your bride."

Those were the best six words he'd heard all day. Brandt fingered the fine lace of Felicity's veil and raised it to reveal her beautiful face. Unabashed tears filled her eyes, but a smile from ear to ear showed her joy. Framing her face with both of his hands, he leaned forward and touched his lips to hers once, then twice, then a final time that sealed the promise of the vows they'd spoken.

Cheers and applause rose from the expansive crowd of family and friends gathered to witness the ceremony. Brandt pulled back—albeit with reluctance—and turned them both to gaze out at the sea of faces. Felicity slipped her hand into his, and he gave it a squeeze. The day couldn't be more perfect. They had God's favor once again and their families' continued support.

From this day forward, they'd weather any storm—together.

HEARTS
AND HARVEST

Dedication

My heartfelt thanks go first to my husband for not letting me get away with any excuses. Thanks also to my family on both sides, my editors (JoAnne, April, and Rachel), and to my local crit group for their honest critiques. I couldn't write my books without all of you!

Chapter 1

Detroit, Michigan
Spring 1894

A nd remember," Pastor Owens said loudly and clearly as he concluded his sermon, "we have placed boxes at the back by the doors for any donations you wish to make on behalf of those who are now farming the public lands in order to provide for their families."

Annabelle Lawson fixed her eyes on the pastor. His crisp, pressed purple robe with gold accents flowed in tandem with his motions as he made a sweeping gesture out over those gathered. The compassion in his light brown eyes only added to his youthful appearance, despite the traces of gray she caught at his temples.

He always looked out for those less fortunate, but never before had his plea compelled her to contribute like it had today.

"Some of you have donated pieces of your land for farming, and I know these families appreciate your generosity. But for those who are unable to do that, you can contribute through the donation boxes. Every bit you give will go toward purchasing farming tools and equipment for these families."

Had Father been one of those the pastor mentioned as having donated land? They certainly had enough to spare. She'd ask him after the service ended.

"And now go in peace and in the knowledge of our heavenly Father's love."

With that the assemblage stood almost in unison, and Annabelle paused as individuals made their way en masse toward the back.

She clutched her handbag in one hand and held her Bible to her chest as she slipped from her family's pew after her parents and entered the center aisle. Her younger brother and sister followed. She stepped aside to let them pass then glanced toward the front of the church at the elaborate furnishings and ornate fixtures, from the hanging chandeliers to the brass candelabras. Marble tabletops sat on hand-carved wooden stands, and rich burgundy carpet adorned the steps as well as the floor of the elevated dais from which the pastor gave his sermon.

That was where the evidence of affluence ended. Annabelle observed the worn pews in great need of whitewashing or a new coat of paint. It almost felt as if a line divided the church from where the congregation sat and where the pastor stood. The people around her wore clothing in a wide variety of quality and style. Here status didn't matter. Even the pastor, in all of his finery, possessed a welcoming personality that embraced everyone equally.

Annabelle again looked at the wide array of appearances in the attendees. How could her family and many who attended this church have so much when others who joined them had so little?

The financial crisis last year had struck in a random pattern. Thanks to the poor investment choices and risky building decisions by the railroad companies, financing had been lost and banks had run out of money. Both the rich and the poor had been affected. Young and old. Businessman and tradesman alike. Annabelle volunteered for one of Detroit's charity services, and her supervisor had recently confided to her that their stores and funds were either depleted or quite low. They had little to give to those in need.

This idea from Pastor Owens could help all the city's charities. And in turn the families could maintain their pride or self-respect as they farmed on their own without accepting handouts. Donations alone wouldn't help. Paving the way for those who had lost much to be able to work would bring fortune to all.

"Annabelle, dear. Don't dawdle." Her mother's voice called to her from a few pews away. "Katie will have Sunday dinner ready by the time we get home. We haven't a moment to spare."

"Yes, Mother."

After a final glance around the haven the church provided, Annabelle made her way to the back. As she passed the boxes, her conscience pricked her rather soundly. Seeing the departing backs of her family, she knew she must hurry. Service had run later than normal. A full half hour, in fact. Without further thought, she reached into her handbag and withdrew all the coins she had. She dropped the money in the slotted box and smiled at the sound of it joining the other money already donated. It wasn't much, but it felt good to help.

"Annabelle!"

The sharp yet soft reprimand made Annabelle start. She looked up to see her mother peering around the doorframe, an impatient expression on her face. If Mother had been standing inside, her foot no doubt would have been tapping against the stone floor. Felicity Lawson normally maintained a cool demeanor. But everyone had his or her limits. No sense making Mother any more upset.

"Coming, Mother."

❧

An hour later the Lawson family gathered around the table. Annabelle picked at her plate while the rest of her family devoured the delicious fried chicken, potatoes and gravy, and canned vegetables from their garden. She didn't want to insult Katie, but she couldn't find much of an appetite.

She stared at how much food they had. Her thoughts wandered to those families going without today. Somehow even Katie's best recipe failed to tempt her taste buds.

"What's the matter, Annabelle?" Her younger brother, Matthew, gave her a poke in the ribs, his voice taking on a taunting tone. "Trying to maintain your graceful figure so some poor, unsuspecting bloke will fall prey to your charms?"

"Matthew! That's enough."

Father's reprimand made her brother straighten in his chair and dip his chin. Brandt Lawson had mediated their little squabbles more times than Annabelle could count. Yet Matthew persisted. The rather tall rascal might be nearing eighteen, but at times he acted like a ten-year-old.

"Sorry, Father."

"It's not me to whom you owe an apology."

"Sorry, Annabelle," he mumbled, not even bothering to look her way.

Annabelle pressed her lips together to hold back a grin, but Father caught her eye and winked. That made her struggle even harder. Father knew what it was like to have a younger brother. Uncle Charles always seemed to be looking for his next victim, and Father had told her he hadn't changed a bit since they were boys. It looked as if Matthew had inherited that streak of mischief from their uncle.

"Now, Annabelle," Father continued in a more congenial tone. "Is there something wrong with the food? Or do you have something else on your mind that's keeping you from eating?"

She set down her fork and reached for her water glass. After taking a drink, she lowered the glass and looked to her left where Father sat waiting for an answer.

"It's not the food, Father. Katie should again be praised for her efforts."

"Then what is it, dear?"

Annabelle glanced at Mother from the corner of her eye. Matthew and their younger sister, Victoria, also waited expectantly. She hadn't meant to interrupt their meal. But now that she had their attention, she'd better take full advantage. Returning her gaze to Father, she attempted to formulate her conflicting thoughts into words.

"This morning. At church. Pastor Owens spoke of the families in need of assistance and mentioned the vacant plots of land being donated for farming use."

"Yes." Mother sighed. "It is difficult to see so many in such dire need. We ourselves aren't without feeling the effects of the crisis, but we fared much better than most, thanks to your father's well-spread investments." Mother looked down the table at Father, and the two shared a silent bond.

"Exactly," Annabelle continued. "And don't misunderstand me. I'm grateful that we were spared for the most part, but somehow thanking God for our abundance feels wrong in light of those we know who have nothing."

"What do you propose we do about that, Annabelle?" Father steepled his fingers and rested his forearms on the edge of the table. "We can't exactly give everything we have in surplus and place ourselves on equal footing with them."

"Nor do I expect us to, Father. I merely wanted to say how inspired I was by Pastor Owens's sermon. The Bible commands us to help our neighbors, and what we do unto the least of them, we do as unto Christ."

Victoria leaned forward. "I put my coins in the box today, Annabelle. Did you?"

Annabelle looked across the table at her sister. Even at twelve she possessed a heart of gold.

"Yes, I did. Everything I had with me."

At times Annabelle felt as if she came in second place to her sister where charity was concerned. Whatever her family did, Victoria was certain to be as involved as possible.

"But I feel we can do more. I just don't know what."

Silence fell upon the table, and her family all wore introspective expressions. Several moments passed. Finally, Father cleared his throat, and all eyes turned toward him.

"Well, I was going to wait until later to announce this, but I suppose now is as good a time as any."

He paused, and Annabelle turned her head to look at Mother, who nodded with a smile. They had done something. Now she was anxious to find out what.

"Following our good mayor's lead of sacrifice, I've put up that vacant plot we own on Marshall to be used for farming. It neighbors several other vacant plots that have also been donated. I gather it will bring about a sizable profit for our city and those in need."

Annabelle clapped her hands and beamed a smile at him. "Oh, Father! That's wonderful. When I heard Pastor Owens this morning mention the need for land, I wanted to ask if we had any to give. When did you donate it? How much land is it? When will the workers arrive to start working? I want to be there to help in any way I can."

The deep sound of Father's chuckle rumbled from his end of the table. "Slow down, Annabelle. I only just spoke with the mayor last week. I daresay it will be another week or more before any families are assigned to our particular plot." He raised a hand, palm out, in her direction. "But I promise to notify you the moment I hear anything further."

"I want to help as well, Father."

"You will, Victoria. You will."

"Father," Matthew inserted, "didn't Mayor Pingree sell his Thoroughbred horse and give the proceeds to the farming fund?"

Father nodded. "Yes, he did. Where did you hear about that?"

Matthew shrugged. "Oh, some of the young men at the copper refinery were talking about it the other day at work. I overheard one of them say it and wondered if they were exaggerating or not."

"It is true. And his act of goodwill encouraged many others to follow suit. Now we have a substantial fund for farming equipment, and we should be able to provide these families with everything they need to get started."

Annabelle listened as Father continued to lay out what he knew would be the plan once the farming commenced. Just this morning she had wanted to get involved and help. Little did she know how close the opportunity would come to her own home. Now she could fulfill God's commandment and at the same time feel satisfied in what she had to offer. Excitement built inside her.

She could hardly wait to get started.

&

William Berringer trudged behind his father as they approached the barren plot of land that would become their place of work for several months, possibly even years. The abandoned factory building at the far edge of the land would house several families working this plot. He sighed. How in the world had something like this happened to them?

One day they were living a comfortable life with plenty to eat and had more than enough money to afford the finer things if they wanted them. The next, their stronghold had crumbled, they had lost their home, and the jobs he and his father held had been stripped away. All because of railroad overbuilding and shaky railroad financing that set off a series of bank failures.

If it hadn't been for the bankruptcy of Philadelphia and Reading Railroad last year, concern over the economy might not have worsened. But it did, and people rushed to withdraw their money from banks. In no time at all, gold and silver reserves were depleted and the value of the dollar had decreased. Their life savings disappeared, and they couldn't meet their mortgage obligations. Everything they had invested was gone. William almost didn't want to blink for fear that something even more disastrous would occur.

"Well, here we are." His father gestured with a wide sweep of his arm. "Our source of income for as long as it takes until we can rebuild what we've lost."

And that could take years if they only had farming as an option. William sneered at the weed-covered ground. Gusts of wind stirred the loose dirt from a bare patch nearby and created a tiny swirl around them. Maybe he could get caught up in one and be taken far away from here. Far away from the gloomy prospect of what the financial crisis had done to him and his family.

"At least we know we aren't alone," his mother chimed in. Her forced cheerfulness was almost too much. "Many others—friends and neighbors—are suffering the same fate. If they can do this, so can we."

Father stepped close and wrapped his arm around his wife. "You are absolutely right, my dear. It might not be much, but our God has provided."

"God?" William couldn't help the derision that filled his voice. "You talk of

God?" He swung out his arm in a sweeping gesture over the land in front of them. "Where was God when the crisis occurred? Where was He when we were forced from our home? Where was He when we lost everything?"

Jacob, his little brother, looked up at all three of them in silence. He moved his gaze from one to another, curiosity and uncertainty reflected in his eyes.

"God is right where He's always been, my boy," Father replied. "With us." Daniel Berringer was nothing if not forthright and stalwart. He led their family with a strength and determination William admired and hoped to have himself one day.

But that strength wasn't what he wanted right now. He wanted answers. He wanted solutions. He wanted a guarantee that this new lot in life would turn out to be a prosperous venture and that they could return to the life they once knew before too long. From what he could see, the likelihood of that seemed as distant as the grouping of various land plots that stretched out to the north and west of the city.

"Well, if God's been right here all along, then He wanted this to happen to us. And if that's the case, I want to know why."

Lucille Berringer came and placed a gentle hand on William's shoulder. "Sometimes, William, we aren't able to ask why. We simply must obey and do the best with what we've been given."

William fought hard not to shrug off his mother's touch. She meant well, but he wasn't in the mood for comfort. "I thought we *had* done the best we could. *Before* all this happened. Father and I had good jobs in finance and industry and had established what we thought was a rather solid family business. I was also looking to expand into manufacturing with some of Thomas Edison's ventures. We worked hard and remained faithful with the fruits of our labors. Was it not good enough to suit God?"

"That's enough, William!" Father's voice took on a hard edge—one William knew brooked no argument.

Jacob's eyes widened, and William regretted his previous words. The last thing he wanted to do was cause Jacob to become bitter. His brother didn't deserve this, either. At least he was young, though. He had his whole life ahead of him. William, on the other hand, had been making plans to move from apprenticeship to management when the crisis struck. He should be furthering his own career right now. He should be courting young ladies and thinking about starting his own family.

Father clenched his fists at his side, then relaxed them. "I realize how difficult this is for you. It's difficult for all of us. We have all lost a great deal. But I will not have you allowing your anger at the situation to poison the hope we have, thanks to a generous donor who has given us this land. There are many others who have not been as fortunate, some who even now are headed west with nothing left here in the city." A sigh, full of acceptance, blew forth from his lips. "You would do well to remember that."

William lowered his head. Father was right. His best friend growing up had done just that. Unable to see any hope in Detroit or any of the areas nearby, Ben's family had packed up and headed west toward Seattle or Portland. Others went to Denver or Salt Lake City or even San Francisco. Anywhere but here. For a moment William wished his family had followed. But no guarantees existed there, either. So for now at least they had a roof over their heads—drafty and run-down though it was—and the opportunity to grow food. He might as well make the best of it.

"I'm sorry, Father. I know we're not the only ones who are suffering. I'll try not to be so negative."

Father's expression softened and relief spread across his face. "Thank you."

Mother gave his shoulder a squeeze before once again stepping to her husband's side. William looked down at Jacob and smiled. The lad put his hand in William's and grinned. William reached out and tousled his brother's hair. At least they hadn't lost each other. Other families he knew hadn't been as fortunate.

❧

William had been working in this field for more than six hours. The overhead sun beat down upon his back, and sweat made his shirt stick to his skin.

He lowered his hoe to the ground and leaned his full weight on the farm tool. Reaching into his back pocket, he grabbed his handkerchief and swiped it across his brow then down his face. Without the benefit of a looking glass, he had no idea if he managed to rid himself of the dirt and grime. But it had to be far better than he looked a moment before.

Then he saw her. A brown-haired young woman moving from worker to worker, carrying a pail of water with a dipper. Perfect. The last thing he wanted was another benevolent society member reminding him of where he'd been before the panic and all that he'd lost. Fresh water sounded good. He just didn't want it to come from someone like her. Yet here she was, headed in their direction.

William glanced down at Jacob, who worked alongside him. At least for his brother's sake, he'd remain cordial. But he didn't have to like it.

Chapter 2

Thank you." William accepted the dipper and took a long drink. The liquid quenched his thirst and cooled his overheated body. Immediate relief filled his limbs and made him feel as if he could work another ten hours. "You are quite welcome," she replied. "I can imagine how difficult it is to spend so many hours in the sun. Would that I could offer more than just water."

What about some financial assistance or a job other than farming? William asked the question in his mind, but he didn't speak it aloud. "The water is enough. Thank you."

The young woman dipped her chin in acknowledgment and bent to offer the pail to his younger brother. Jacob hesitated and looked at William, as if seeking permission or asking if it was all right. Before William could respond, the woman set down the water and knelt in a dry patch of dirt, puffs exploding around her. She didn't seem too concerned that her well-pressed skirts were getting soiled or that her styled hair had fallen into slight disarray, though. Instead, she focused her entire attention on Jacob as she reached out to touch his shoulder. Jacob startled, but his attention went straight to the young woman. She smiled and held out the dipper again.

"Don't worry. You can have as much as you like. There is plenty here for everyone."

William watched the transformation on his brother's face. The lad went from uncertain to eager in a matter of seconds. He reached out a grubby hand and took the dipper, guzzling its contents in one gulp. Melodious laughter bubbled from the young woman's lips as she filled the dipper again and held it out to Jacob, who accepted more without hesitation.

For weeks Jacob had worked hard and done his part. He had dug in with gusto, never once complaining and always right there by William's side. The only concern William and his parents had was Jacob's lack of interest in people. He no longer sought out other lads his age, and when anyone approached, he held back and attempted to disappear. He didn't speak to anyone but his family.

Today, however, was different. This young woman managed to coax a reaction from Jacob—quite a feat in and of itself. Her attentiveness and soft-spoken words must have gotten through to Jacob. Perhaps William had been wrong to make such a hasty judgment of her. And those beguiling blue eyes paired with the kind smile made him want to get to know her better.

She had already served his parents. Jacob was the last of his family. If William didn't do or say something, she would leave them and move to the next family. He had to keep her here, even for just a few extra moments.

"His name's Jacob."

The woman rocked back on her heels, then stood in one slow, fluid motion, coming about seven inches below his six-foot height. Not a drop of water sloshed from the pail. Hooking the dipper on the edge, she extended her free hand toward Jacob. William widened his eyes and raised his eyebrows. Jacob showed his surprise as well, his expression no doubt mirroring William's. A rather bold move on her part. Young women never offered a hand to anyone they met. Maybe she was making an exception for Jacob.

"My name is Annabelle Lawson. Pleased to meet you, Jacob. You may call me Miss Annabelle."

Again his brother glanced up at him. He gave a sharp nod. Jacob reached out and struck hands with the young woman.

"Nice to meet you, too, Miss Annabelle."

Annabelle. The name suited her. William searched his memory and years of study for the Latin origin. *Graceful.* Yes, she had been named well. In fact, William felt rather awkward in her presence. He'd never had a problem speaking with the fairer gender before. But standing in his oversized breeches that felt like coarse burlap, the loose-fitting shirt in need of washing, worn and dirty shoes, and a ragged cap, he lacked the confidence he normally possessed. His previous wardrobe contained nothing appropriate for working the fields, so he'd been forced to resort to handouts from some of the charitable donations. Good thing his brother seemed to hold her interest for now. He certainly didn't feel ready to venture into conversation at the moment.

"And how old are you, young Jacob?" Annabelle released Jacob's hand only to tap the edge of the boy's cap.

Jacob warmed to her immediately. Puffing out his chest and snapping his suspenders, he rocked back and forth on his heels and beamed a wide smile. "I'm eight."

"Well, now, you're quite a grown-up young man already. Your parents are no doubt proud to have you working alongside them. I would surmise that you probably do the work of two young lads your age."

William chuckled at the image his brother presented. If Jacob's chest got any bigger, he'd explode with all the proud air he'd inhaled. But William was impressed with how quickly Annabelle had set his brother at ease. Jacob could be the inquisitive sort, but since they'd lost everything, his demeanor had dampened in a substantial way. William gave his brother a pat on the back, which caused Jacob to relax and release the breath he'd been holding.

"And how about you?" Annabelle switched her attention from Jacob to him. "Do you have a name as well?"

William opened his mouth to speak, but no sound came out. Despite the water he'd drunk a few moments ago, his mouth felt as dry as the ground he now dug would be in summer. He swallowed several times and attempted to bring moisture back to his tongue. Before he could speak, though, Jacob chimed in.

"His name's William. William Berringer. And he's my brother."

Amusement danced across Annabelle's face. She no doubt thought him quite the fool for not being able to answer for himself. "William and Jacob Berringer. Such fine, strong names. Your father and mother chose well."

William cleared his throat and managed to croak, "Thank you."

Great. Was that all he could say to this young woman? It was the third time he'd uttered those words in almost as many minutes. She might believe him a half-wit with a limited vocabulary if he didn't figure out how to get his tongue and head to work in tandem instead of fighting with each other.

He tried again. "How did you come to be distributing water at this farm plot? You're the first nonworker I've seen around here in days."

Annabelle looked away. William thought he saw a hint of pink steal into her cheeks. But she composed herself and returned his gaze. "This land belongs to my father. He donated it to help with this crisis. I learned of it two weeks ago and was eager to help in any way that I could. But Father forbade me to come unaccompanied, so I had to wait until he made his weekly visit before I could venture over this way."

"You mean you own all this land?" Jacob swung his arms wide and spun in a circle as he gestured toward the expansive plot where at least six families farmed. "You must be rich!"

"Jacob!" William scolded.

His brother ducked his head and scuffed the worn toe of his shoe in the dirt. "Sorry," he mumbled.

It was bad enough their family had been reduced to this type of work. They didn't need to act like the migrant workers they were and present the appearance of discourteous behavior as well.

Annabelle didn't seem to mind, though. The soft smile on her lips and twinkle in her eyes proved that. "Your apology is accepted, Jacob, but I would still like to answer your question, if I may."

She looked to William to obtain silent permission. Amazed at her forthrightness and the fact that she had no qualms about speaking with them, he could only nod.

"My father has made some very wise decisions over the years. But that doesn't mean our family is better than anyone else. We might be rich compared to some, but that could all change. In fact, that's why I've come to help. It could be me and my family here instead of yours."

"We used to be rich, too. But now we're not."

"Jacob," William warned, keeping his voice low.

Annabelle stayed his protest with her hand. "It's quite all right, Mr. Berringer. As my mother has quoted many times, 'Out of the mouths of babes.' A lot has happened in recent months. This past year has been rather difficult for everyone. Your brother is merely saying what so many are feeling."

"Well, I appreciate your understanding, Miss Lawson. And you can call me William. We might as well dispense with the formalities around here. We aren't exactly being presented at court."

The young woman tilted her head and regarded him with a curious expression. She pressed her lips in a line for a moment then smiled. He thought she might agree. "No, I don't believe we are. . .Mr. Berringer. However, we have only just met, and it wouldn't be proper." Obviously not.

William nodded. "Miss Lawson it is, then."

"Why do I have to call you Miss Annabelle?" His brother crossed his arms over his chest.

William gave Jacob a playful punch. "Calling her Miss Annabelle is a sign of respect."

"But don't you respect her?"

Heat rushed to William's face, and for once he was grateful for the hot sun that had already made his face a bit red. It seemed his brother had found his precociousness again.

Annabelle's laughter set William's mind at ease. She leaned down so she was almost at eye level with Jacob and smiled. "I'll make you a deal. When you are old enough to own your own piece of land, you may drop the 'Miss' and just call me Annabelle. All right?"

So she was giving Jacob permission to be informal yet insisted William abide by society's dictates? William recalled some from his younger days who had allowed him to address them in a similar fashion, but this was different. Why did William feel as if he'd picked the shorter straw?

Jacob scrunched his face and was silent for several moments as he pondered her offer. Then a grin split his lips, and he stuck out his hand. "Deal."

Annabelle struck hands with him again. "Deal," she repeated.

William thought about how long it would be before that time came to his little brother's life. He hoped by then they would have figured out how to regain their standing in society once again. Right now that possibility seemed too far away to even fathom.

And what about Annabelle? Jacob was sure to remember and hold her to her promise. Would she even be around? Would she even care?

Wait a minute. What was he thinking? He had no business contemplating his future and wondering if she would be in it. He shouldn't even be taking up so much of her time right now. She was here to bring water to everyone, not just him and Jacob. He should step aside and allow her to continue on her way.

"So do you have any other brothers or a sister perhaps?" Annabelle again faced him. "Or is it just the two of you?"

She didn't seem in any hurry to leave, but more families needed water. Who was he to monopolize so much of her time when he was nothing more than a dirt farmer with no land or possessions to call his own?

"Don't you think you should see who else might need some of the water you're offering?" William cringed at how abrupt that sounded. He tried to soften it somehow. "I'm sure there are others who would appreciate it as much as we."

Annabelle hesitated, a mixture of hurt and uncertainty crossing her features. She looked between Jacob and him and back again. Finally, she nodded. Schooling her expression into one of nonchalance, she grasped hold of the bucket and dipper and took one step away.

"Very well. I shall see to the other families. Thank you for taking the time to introduce yourself and speak with me for a few moments. I am certain our paths will cross again."

"Good-bye, Miss Annabelle!" Jacob called to her retreating back.

She pivoted and gave him a soft smile. "Good-bye, Jacob. You behave yourself." With a final glance at William, she was gone.

William closed his eyes and clenched his teeth. What a fool he'd been. She was only attempting to bestow some kindness on him and his family, and he'd run her off. If what she'd said were true, it would be another week before he'd see her again. That gave her plenty of time to devise a reason to avoid this area of her father's land. She might even decide to send someone else in her place.

At least Jacob had made a good impression. Maybe that was enough to bring her back. William hoped so. Otherwise he'd blown his only opportunity.

❧

Annabelle resisted the urge to turn around again and watch the two brothers. The abrupt change in William's demeanor couldn't have shocked her more had she been splashed in the face with the very water she carried. She could see the tumult of emotions warring within the young man the moment she approached. At first he looked like he would dismiss her and tell her to go back to where she came from.

His desire for the water she brought superseded whatever thoughts he might have had to turn his back on her, though. And despite obvious reservations, he remained cordial. It wasn't until she spoke to his brother that William warmed a little.

She understood his protectiveness. She'd do the same for Victoria in an instant. It was his mannerisms and choice of words that replayed in her mind.

"...*dispense with the formalities...presented at court...*"

He spoke as one whose normal life involved expectations and activities such as those. Considering how widespread the effects of the panic were, the Berringer family could have once been equal or greater in station than she. William might not wear the clothes of other gentleman she knew and his face might be smudged with the evidence of his hard labor, but she knew a true gentleman when she saw one.

And William was it.

In fact, his mannerisms fell second only to the appeal of his nervous behavior and rather boyish charm. It seemed almost comical on a man who stood nearly six feet tall and possessed a build familiar with some form of hard work. With his sandy-colored hair that blew in the breeze and fell in stubborn locks across his forehead, the slight tilt of his mouth when he grinned, and the deep chocolate eyes, he possessed a number of charming qualities. The dimple in his cheek only heightened the attraction. He and his brother had been the first to engage her in any way. The rest of the workers gave her nothing more than a cursory nod as they accepted the water. Some averted their eyes, while others appeared to sneer as if she chose to be here in order to flaunt her superiority or make a mockery of them. That couldn't be further from the truth. Yet knowing that and living with the reality were two entirely different things.

As she finished making her rounds, Annabelle felt compelled to return and continue their conversation. What good would that do? He'd made it clear he didn't want to spend any more time with her. And he did have work to do. If she interfered, it would only make matters worse. No, she'd have to wait until next week. Perhaps by then William would be in a better mood.

"Annabelle!" Father called from one of the supply stations nearby.

"Yes, Father?"

"Are you about finished? We should be heading home soon."

Yes, she was done. She'd had more than enough for one day. If it hadn't been for William and his brother, she might have decided not to return. At least they appeared genuine. And that made her service more than worthwhile.

If only she didn't have to wait a full week before seeing them again.

"Coming, Father!"

Chapter 3

"All right." Mrs. Jennings clapped her hands to get everyone's attention. "Let's bring this meeting to order, shall we?"

Annabelle looked around the courtyard. A large number of maple, oak, and elm trees with sparse branches and new buds offered little shade or privacy. Sunlight filtered through the trees and shone bright at the very middle, providing warmth to the otherwise chilly day. She recognized most of the women gathered. Some chose to sit on the whitewashed iron benches at the edges of the cobblestone pathways, while others surrounded the center where Mrs. Jennings stood. Mother and Victoria flanked Annabelle's sides.

"The reason we're gathered here today," Mrs. Jennings continued, "as you all likely know, is to discuss possible ways we can bring additional assistance to those working the potato patches throughout the city."

The self-proclaimed leader of this meeting had been an active member of the nation's first Ladies Aid Society since its inception more than thirty years ago. At that time, she was no older than Annabelle. With her ingenuity and self-sacrificing endeavors, many women looked up to her for leadership and inspiration. She had earned the right to be deemed the honorary matriarch. Annabelle admired her a great deal and was excited to participate today as an active member.

"What about organizing a rotating group of volunteers to make sure the workers receive food at mealtimes?"

This came from Mrs. Olson. Annabelle didn't know her all that well, but her husband was an influential business owner like Father.

Mrs. Jennings gave Mrs. Olson her undivided attention, nodding and showing approval of the suggestion. "Are you speaking of arranging the preparation and distribution of the meals at each of the lots throughout the city?"

"Yes."

"I believe that sounds like a splendid idea." Mrs. Jennings gazed out over all the women gathered. "Do we have a volunteer or two who might be willing to supervise the others involved? You would need to develop a schedule and arrange for the collection of foods prepared as well as oversee the various teams of ladies at each plot."

Mother stepped forward. "I would be both pleased and honored to accept that position."

Annabelle's eyes widened at her mother's offer. It wasn't that she didn't feel

Mother could handle the responsibility. On the contrary, she'd never seen another woman so willing to get down in the dirt to help or so able to balance multiple tasks at once with apparent ease. No, she simply thought Mother had more than enough other commitments without adding one more. But perhaps some of that work had diminished in light of the current economic state.

"My daughters, Annabelle and Victoria, will assist me." Mother moved to place a hand on both Annabelle's and Victoria's shoulders.

What? Not only had Mother volunteered to oversee this new idea, but now she was offering Annabelle's services as well? What about the charity work she already performed or the water she had already committed to deliver? She glanced first at Victoria, who merely shrugged with an amused grin, then up at Mother, who glanced down with a soft smile. It was difficult to deny the unspoken request. They would be working together as a family, after all. She only wished Mother had sought her input first. Well, perhaps she could figure out how to deliver the water and distribute the food at the same time.

"Excellent." Mrs. Jennings nodded once to confirm the arrangement and looked directly at Mother. "I trust you will have no trouble securing more than enough ladies to help. But I'll leave you to that."

All right, so that was done. No backing out now. Annabelle simply had to share her concerns about the water delivery with Mother and work that into this new responsibility. Mother had always been supportive of charitable endeavors, no matter how small. They could come up with a compromise here, too.

"Very well," Mrs. Jennings continued. "With the food distribution arranged, does anyone have other ideas for how we can assist those in need?"

"We could go around again collecting old or extra pieces of clothing."

"What about making sure the seed sacks and potato sprouts for planting are available to the workers?"

"With school coming to a close soon, there is a need for care for the younger children who are unable to work."

The suggestions flew among the group like bubbles rising from a boiling pot of water. Annabelle had a difficult time keeping up with everything. Mrs. Jennings seemed to have no trouble, though. In no time at all, at least one woman had been assigned as the head of each project, with promises from others to assist in the area they took the most interest in.

It felt good to know they would be helping in every way possible. Annabelle knew the Ladies Aid could accomplish quite a lot when they put their minds to it, but she'd never seen the progress in action on such a grand scale before today. It was exhilarating. And she could hardly wait to get started.

Mother placed pressure on Annabelle's shoulder, including both of her daughters in her gaze. "So do you have any ideas for how we can organize such a substantial amount of food in a short time?"

"We'll cook it," Victoria offered in her simplistic viewpoint.

Mother's tinkling laugh resembled the chimes they had hanging from the trellis in their backyard. "We will be doing some of the cooking, Victoria, but not all of it."

Annabelle tilted her head to the left and tapped her finger against her lips. "Well, for starters we could determine how many plots there are and which ones will be the center for meal distribution."

"That's putting your mind to work." Mother pressed her lips together and raised her eyebrows in apparent pleasure. "I had a feeling securing your assistance would be a wise decision on my part." A twinkle entered Mother's eyes, and Annabelle returned the smile.

"At first I was surprised you volunteered so quickly. I will help, but I wish we could have talked about it all first."

Mother drew her eyebrows together. "You aren't regretting our involvement, are you? Since you jumped at the opportunity a few weeks ago to get involved, I figured this would be the perfect way for you to accomplish that."

"Oh no." Annabelle rushed to assure Mother. "I don't mind at all. In fact, I am happy to be able to be there among the workers, helping them get the nourishment they need. They work so hard and have so little."

Actually, if she used her previous experience of delivering water as an example, distributing food might not be any easier or produce any better results. But it would mean she'd have yet another excuse to see William and Jacob again. And they were sure to show their appreciation, even if no one else did.

"What is troubling you?" Mother touched her cheek. "I can see something is. You have that crease in your brow above your right eye, and that only appears when you're worried."

"Well. . ." Annabelle paused and looked down at her feet. "You know I've already agreed to deliver water when Father makes his weekly visits to the land he donated."

Mother nodded. "Yes."

"If we get involved with food distribution, will that mean I have to give up that task?"

"I don't see why." Mother shrugged. "We'll likely make the land your father owns our primary station and put other ladies in charge of the other plots of land. That will mean you'll be there quite often at mealtime. You can arrive early or stay later to see to the water dispensing as well."

"I can help deliver water, too." Victoria planted both fists on her hips, her duplicated creased brow evidence of her displeasure with being ignored.

Annabelle flicked one of her sister's curls. "Yes, Victoria, you can help as well.

But only on the days when we are all there together."

What Mother detailed would work perfectly. Not only could she visit the plot more often, but she could be there for longer periods of time. Father's trip there didn't last long on her first round. Working with Mother sounded better and better with each passing moment.

Annabelle threw her arms around Mother in a quick hug and stepped back. "Thank you."

"For what, dear?" she asked with a smile.

"I admit, I wasn't too sure about this new venture with the food."

"And now?"

"Now I look forward to it. With so many in need these days and without a lot of activity in the city due to the lack of funds available, we need something to keep us busy."

Mother chucked Annabelle's chin with a forefinger. "Somehow I have a feeling you will not suffer from lack of things to do, my dear." She turned away and looked over her shoulder. "Now I must see to the other ladies who will be working with us. Do feel free to mingle if you wish. Or you can join me over there." She gestured toward a small gathering of women awaiting her instruction.

"I believe I will make my way to the other side of the courtyard. Victoria can come with me. Caroline and Rebecca are there with their mother. I'm sure we can find something to talk about."

"Of that I have no doubt." Mother waved them on their way. "Off with you now. We'll meet back together again in about half an hour over by the south entrance."

"All right."

"Bye, Mother," Victoria called.

Annabelle led her sister around the path and raised a hand to signal their friends. About halfway there, she overheard some murmurs coming from a group of three women standing off to the side. From their pinched faces and curled upper lips, it didn't appear they wanted to be there. They took no notice of Annabelle and Victoria.

"I don't see why so many are eager to get involved helping these families," one woman sneered. "If they lost their investments, they probably weren't wise when making them in the first place."

"Exactly," another agreed. "If you ask me, I think they got what they deserved. They no doubt squandered what they had, and now they're paying the price for their actions."

"How can you say that?" The words were out of Annabelle's mouth before she could stop them.

All three women snapped their heads in her direction. Victoria gasped but otherwise remained silent.

"Excuse me?"

Annabelle stepped closer to the trio. "I asked how you could say such a thing about these families in need. Not all of them come from undesirable backgrounds." She thought of the Berringer family. "Some truly are suffering from uncontrollable circumstances."

The first woman looked Annabelle up and down and raised one eyebrow. "Aren't you Felicity Lawson's daughter?"

"Yes." Annabelle stood tall, proud to be associated with her mother.

"That explains the outburst then," the second woman said.

"I beg your pardon?" What did Mother have to do with her behavior?

"Well, it's no secret, my dear," the first woman began with disdain in her voice, "that your mother has been rather heavily involved in charitable causes for many years now. And that work has taken her into some rather questionable areas of the city. It's no surprise that some of the manners of the people she encounters would rub off on you as well."

The woman's words raised Annabelle's hackles. How dare she insult Mother that way? If she weren't concerned about the repercussions, she might give these ladies a piece of her mind. But that would only give credence to their already misguided allegations. So, instead, she took a calming breath and squared off against the women.

"I don't believe you know my mother well if you feel her manners are anything but impeccable. And I honestly can't understand why you would come to today's meeting if you didn't agree with the purpose. You obviously have no intentions of getting involved." She took a moment to look each woman in the eyes. "However, be that as it may, I'm sorry you feel the need to insult others in order to make your lack of participation justified. As for my sister and me, we will continue on our way and do our best to forget this little altercation even occurred." Annabelle offered the most congenial smile she could muster. "Good day, ladies."

With one hand lifting her skirts and her other at Victoria's back, Annabelle encouraged her sister to again head in the direction where they had started in the first place. They were almost out of earshot—but not quite—when one of the women muttered loud enough for Annabelle to hear, "As I said. Poor manners and an obvious show of disrespect for her elders. That young woman is on her way to following the same footsteps as her mother."

Annabelle smiled. The final remark couldn't have been more accurate, nor provided her with more pleasure. If she became even half the woman her mother was, she'd be pleased. What a shame those women didn't understand the blessings that could come from giving.

❧

"Come on, Berringer. Admit it. You or your little brother here threw dirt at us, and now you're lying about it."

William stood not three feet away from the two men about his age making false accusations against him and Jacob. Their greased-back hair and clothing with holes in it made them look the part of the ruffians they attempted to be. They'd been inventing stories and causing problems for several days now. And William was nearing his tolerance point.

"Yes," the second hoodlum echoed. "We saw you do it."

With a sigh, William glanced down at Jacob to be sure his little brother stood behind him. Then he looked between the two accusers. "That is a bald-faced lie, Charlie, and you know it. Neither Jacob nor I did anything of the sort."

The first man snorted in derision. "Are you saying we made it up?"

"That's exactly what I'm saying, Johnny."

"Then how come the dirt was flung from this direction? There ain't no one around who could've done it except you two."

William clenched his fists and ground his teeth. These two weren't going to go away, but he refused to give in to their taunts. "If dirt truly did fly in your direction, perhaps it was blown by the wind as a result of your digging in it."

"Or you digging and making certain it landed at our feet," Charlie piped in, "instead of keeping it on your own bit of land."

Johnny took a step closer. "You've been swaggering around here for weeks now, acting superior with your fancy talk and making the rest of us feel like scum under your shoes. But you're no better than us, and we're gonna prove it."

Charlie thumped his right fist into his palm. "Right here, right now. Let's see how much of a man you really are."

William fought hard not to roll his eyes at their attempts to intimidate him. Two against one should have made him a little wary, but these two were more filled with hot air than true mettle.

"Come on, Willie," Jacob said from behind. "Show them what you got."

The other two chuckled. "You even got yourself a cheering section."

"Jacob, you stay out of this," William growled. "Father will have both our heads if we get into a fight."

"Oh, so you're still answering to Daddy now, are you?" Johnny taunted. "Why don't you send little Jacob here running on home to tattle on us? Then maybe you won't have to hide behind your kid brother instead of facing us like a man."

The tic in William's jaw started pounding like crazy. His lungs expanded and contracted at a faster pace, despite everything he did to calm himself. These two were asking for trouble, and he'd give it to them if they didn't stop. Then he remembered that Jacob stood right there behind him. If he did send his brother scurrying to Father, he'd never hear the end of it. But if he lowered himself to fight Johnny and Charlie, Jacob might learn the wrong way to deal with men like these two bullies. No, he had to stay in control—for both their sakes.

"So what's it gonna be, Berringer?" Johnny narrowed his eyes then kicked dirt at William. "The way I see it, you got two choices."

"You're right, Johnny, I do." William swallowed, fighting hard to keep back the growl in the back of his throat. "You can say whatever you wish about me. You can even make up lies about things that never happened." He took a step forward and stared directly into Johnny's face, clenching his fists again until he could almost feel his nails puncturing the skin. "But I will not engage in any form of a fight with you. Not now or ever."

A flash of hesitation appeared in Johnny's eyes then disappeared. The man swallowed, not once but twice, before taking an almost imperceptible step back. William tried not to grin at the obvious show of anxiety. He might not agree to fight Johnny, but at least he could leave the man with his dignity still intact—what little there was, anyway.

Several moments of silence passed. Johnny didn't break his gaze, and Charlie stood there waiting to see what would happen. The leader of the two was clear.

Finally, Johnny released a slow breath. "Come on, Charlie. These two just ain't worth our time."

Charlie took a moment for the words to sink in. "You mean we aren't gonna fight today?"

"Not today, no." Johnny leveled a menacing glare at William. "Maybe another time when little boys aren't around to get in the way."

As if Jacob could stop William if things got too out of hand. Sure, he'd do what he could to spare his brother from such violence, but he had his limits, too.

Johnny turned to leave, and Charlie followed, but not before delivering one final parting remark.

"You just watch your back, Berringer. Because when you least expect it, we'll be there."

William had no doubt Charlie spoke the truth. And if that time came, he might not have much of a choice. For now, though, he had managed to avoid the immediate problem. Oh, how he wished he could've taught those two a lesson.

Chapter 4

"Look at all this food, Annabelle!" Victoria walked up and down the length of the table, eyes wide. If she weren't attempting to maintain her ladylike appearance, she'd likely be licking her lips as well.

"Yes, I only wish it hadn't rained so hard last night." Annabelle lifted her boot again and grimaced at the mud caked on the bottom. The hem of her skirts had become soiled the moment she set foot on the land from the stone-paved sidewalks.

The fare being set out on the solid tables tantalized her taste buds. From bean soup, braised beef, and boiled asparagus, to great mounds of mashed potatoes and cherry pie for dessert, the ladies had worked hard to create a delicious meal sure to have the workers coming in droves.

"So when will we begin serving?" Victoria nearly bounced in excitement. "I love the idea of being a food angel."

Annabelle smiled, her heart warming at her sister's tenderness. It helped having someone else eager to serve working alongside her. Most of the women had willingly prepared the foods and even helped transport them. All but a few of them ceased their efforts or were unwilling to engage when it actually came to interacting with the workers. But that's where Annabelle knew the true joy came. To see the gratitude on their faces and know they were getting a warm meal meant a lot to her.

At least she hoped she'd see their thankfulness. A part of her wondered if the reception would be as cold as last week with the water. No sense fretting about that now, though. She had work to do.

"Annabelle," Mother called from a few feet away, "make sure you tie an apron over your clothes. I know we aren't wearing anything that can't get soiled, but we should still do our best to remain as clean as possible."

"I will."

Annabelle stepped away to reach for her apron and tied it around her waist. Then she made a final perusal of the tables to make sure everything was in order. With only ten minutes until the noon break, her hands started twitching. She wanted the workers to come in droves for a hot meal, and she wanted to be busy doing something. But there didn't seem to be anything to do.

"Take this, Annabelle," Mother said from behind her as she carried a pot of braised beef.

Annabelle had been so lost in her own anxiousness that she hadn't heard Mother approach.

"Stir the gravy and make sure to spoon it across all the meat."

Finally! Something to do. She glanced over her shoulder to see her mother smiling.

"The time will pass much faster with a task to complete."

She left before Annabelle could reply. How well Mother knew her. No wonder they worked so well together.

"Can I help with something, too?" Victoria wrapped a hand around Mother's arm and followed along beside her.

"Yes, dear." Mother wrapped an arm around Victoria's waist. "You can help me stir the potatoes and set out the tin plates for serving."

Their words faded as they moved farther away. With spoon and serving fork in hand, Annabelle soaked the pieces of beef farther into the gravy. At least the chill of the morning had turned into another warm day. Otherwise they might not have been able to promise a hot meal to the workers. They'd been spreading the word for several days to make sure everyone knew.

A bell rang and sounded to everyone that the meal was ready. Annabelle shifted from one foot to the other and drummed her fingers on the table in front of her. No one came toward them, although many did stop their work to take a break. She glanced around at those she could see. They were definitely curious, but they didn't make an attempt to investigate. If they waited too long, the food would be cold, and all their hard work would have been for naught.

So Annabelle got an idea. She left her station and headed for the end of the table. Grabbing a tin plate, she put a small portion of each item on it and moved her way toward the end, where she grabbed a fork and knife. The other women watched, and one nodded when she realized Annabelle's plan.

With a deep breath, she stepped away from the table and headed toward the nearest worker. It happened to be a young father with his wife and two sons, who clung to their mother's skirts and hid partially behind her.

"The hot meal is for everyone," Annabelle began. "Please. Take this and bring your family to get plates of their own." She extended the plate toward him, praying he wouldn't allow his pride to turn down the offering.

The man swallowed several times and looked from the plate to Annabelle and down at his wife. Almost a minute passed before the man slowly raised a hand and took the plate from Annabelle.

"Thank you," he choked out.

She released her breath in a soft sigh and gave the family an encouraging smile, winking at the two boys who seemed to be in awe of her. One of them curled his fingers and gave a little wave then ducked behind his mother again.

"Make sure you get your fill, now. There is more than enough food for everyone. We don't want anyone to leave hungry."

The family followed her to the table and continued on to the far end. That seemed to be the trigger for the other workers. Before long, a line stretching back at least sixty feet had formed. Parents and children all gathered for the midday meal and a break from their work.

For the next forty minutes, the women filled the plates presented by each worker. With each passing person, Annabelle became more and more delighted to be there. Far better than last week, this endeavor seemed to be paying off in a great way.

In the frantic pace to see everyone fed, Annabelle didn't recall William or Jacob coming to get any food. When the line dissipated, she took a moment to brush her hair back from her face and wipe her hands on her apron, now smeared and in dire need of a good scrubbing. Susannah was going to love doing the wash this week.

Annabelle stepped back and surveyed the small groups of families eating together. Some had already finished and were back at work. Others, no doubt, enjoyed their respite from the backbreaking labor. Her gaze took in each and every cluster of people until she finally located the person she sought.

William crossed a particularly muddy piece of land, with Jacob trailing behind him. Both held a plate, but William walked with purpose in his step. Annabelle followed their progress until they stopped in front of a young lad who couldn't be much more than seven or eight. She couldn't hear the verbal exchange, but the boy dipped his chin toward his chest and shook his head at whatever William said to him. A moment later, William handed the boy his plate. The boy hesitated then took the food and nearly inhaled it.

Why hadn't the boy come through the line like everyone else? Surely he had family somewhere who could have brought him. And why had William not filled up two plates if he intended to give one to the boy?

"What are you looking at, Annabelle?" Victoria appeared at her side and stared across the land in an attempt to identify the source of her sister's attention.

"Nothing, really." Annabelle checked the line and saw that only a handful of workers remained. Some latecomer volunteers had just arrived to help with the cleanup afterward. "Victoria, would you mind taking over my station here and serving anyone who's left?"

"I can do that. Where are you going?"

"To help a friend," was all she said to her sister. Victoria didn't need to know any more. It would only start a slew of questions Annabelle wasn't ready to answer just yet.

After filling another plate, she made her way to where William and Jacob had settled, sharing one tin plate between them. They'd located some higher ground and were able to sit on a clear patch of dirt. William looked up and stood when she approached, but he didn't offer a greeting of any kind.

Jacob turned his head when his brother moved and beamed a wide grin at her. "Good afternoon, Miss Annabelle." His face was smeared with gravy, and his fingers bore evidence of the rather large piece of cherry pie he'd sampled.

Annabelle giggled at the adorable sight, retrieving a clean napkin from her skirt pocket for him. "Good afternoon, Jacob. I see you're enjoying your lunch."

"It's the best meal we've had in weeks." He tilted his head and regarded her with a curious stare as he eyed the plate of food she held. "Did you come to eat with us, too?"

William narrowed his eyes. That wasn't exactly a welcome invitation if she *had* intended to join them. Did he just not want her around, or was there some other reason for his seeming distrust?

"No, Jacob. I actually brought your brother an extra plate since he gave his away."

At this William averted his gaze and looked down at the ground.

"He saw this little boy who didn't have anything to eat, so he took his plate to make sure the boy wouldn't go hungry. His papa didn't want to come and take the free food, and we felt bad. So we gave him some of ours."

"Well, that was very kind and generous of you, Jacob." She raised her eyes toward William, who had returned his gaze to her. "Of both of you." Focusing again on the plate she held, she continued. "Will you accept this plate from me, then?"

He took the plate and split portions of it with Jacob before partaking on his own.

"Why did you go to all the trouble to bring this to me?"

So he was still sore about something. And he couldn't accept a gift for what it was. He had to question it. Annabelle had no idea why, but she figured the honest answer would be the best way to go.

"Because the Lord commands us to help those in need and watch out for the ones among us who have fallen on bad times."

"That's what the Bible says," Jacob announced, pride evident in his voice.

"You're exactly right, Jacob. The Bible does teach us that." So they had some exposure to the teachings in the scriptures. That was a start. "It also commands us to love our neighbors and even do good to those who hurt us."

"Mama used to read to us all the time before we had to come here to work. Now we don't get to hear the stories as often because she's so tired at night that she falls asleep right away."

"Well, she works hard, Jacob," William interjected. "You can't expect her to do

all the things she used to do when we had our house and lived a different life."
He grunted. "Besides, a lot of what she read was just stories of people who lived
a long time ago. We've got more important things to do these days."

More important things than reading the Bible and learning from what God
has to say? Annabelle couldn't imagine anything that could take the place of God
in her life.

"Do you mind if I join you? I've been standing for quite some time and would
love to take a rest."

"Sure!" Jacob scooted over and made a grand show of brushing a clear spot in
the dirt beside him.

Annabelle hesitated and looked to William before making a move. He didn't
say a word, only nodded. She gathered her skirts in her hands and settled next to
Jacob. William took a seat as well and continued eating.

"Jacob, you say that your mother used to read a lot to you. What was your
favorite story?"

"Umm. . ." He scrunched up his face and pressed his lips together, thinking
hard. "Well, I like the story of Jacob, but that's only because we have the same
name." He grinned. "The other one I like is the one about the boy who only had
two fish and five loaves of bread, but the men who followed Jesus fed thousands
of men with it."

"Yes, that's an amazing story, isn't it?"

"You fed a lot of people today with the food you brought, and it was much
better than fish and bread."

"They fed a lot of people," William interjected, "because they all made a lot of
food and brought it. God had nothing to do with it."

"Actually, William, God has everything to do with it."

William waved her off and remained intent on the food still left on his plate.

"We wouldn't be here if God didn't command us to be. And we wouldn't spend
any time at all with those in need if we weren't following His commandments."

"So you're saying you don't really want to be here. That you're only doing it
because you feel you have to or because of some obligation?"

All right, so that didn't go exactly as she'd planned. She wanted him to see that
she cared, as did all the other women, and that's why they came. But he was being rather hardheaded about it.

"No," she corrected. "We *do* want to be here. At least I do. My mother and
sister do as well. The three of us are organizing the food distribution. We enjoy
helping those who are working hard here at the potato patches and farm plots.
It's an added bonus when we can get involved in others' lives instead of just sitting at home and collecting items for people we'll never see."

"Well, don't feel you need to spend any more time than necessary with us.

We're doing just fine on our own and don't need your charity."

Annabelle almost recoiled from the bitter tone in his voice. His words stung. On the one hand, he appeared to appreciate her efforts. On the other, his words and attitude said something entirely different.

"I don't consider it charity at all, Mr. Berringer. In fact, I see it as a partnership in many ways."

William wrinkled his brow. "How so?"

"Well, you and many other families are spending your days working this land and cultivating it for fresh food that will be harvested and used to feed those in the city who need it. Some of what you harvest will replenish the depleted stores that are in desperate need of restocking." She gestured back over her shoulder toward where the women were cleaning up the food. "It's our pleasure to provide a hot meal for you as our way of saying thank you." Annabelle shrugged. "A partnership."

He regarded her for several moments, as if he couldn't believe someone like her would bother to spend time with someone like him. But she'd seen passion in him that obviously ran quite deep. And despite the heartaches of recent months, she knew that spark still existed. She also longed to know more about his life before they lost everything. And she'd only find that out if she spent time with him. If he didn't welcome her presence, she could always come to visit Jacob instead. Jacob watched his brother with interest but remained silent. She prayed William's sour attitude didn't rub off on Jacob. That innocence suited the boy well and didn't deserve to be tainted.

"You make some valid points, but I still don't agree that God is involved in any way."

"What makes you say that?"

"If He were making it possible for you to be here, then why didn't He make it possible for the banks to survive the crisis or the railroads not to lose their investments? Why did He cause so many families to lose their homes and their entire livelihoods?" William balanced the plate on his legs and flailed both arms out away from his body. "God caused the selective ruin of many families who didn't deserve to suffer the way they have. He picked and chose at will, while others came out of this just fine. If He is so intent on helping, why didn't He help then?"

Annabelle remained silent for several moments. He asked a lot of good questions. Questions she didn't know if she could answer. After all, she was among the families who fared far better than his had. What could she say to him that would ease the obvious anger and resentment he felt?

"You make some valid arguments, and I know I don't have all the answers—"

"Look," he cut her off. "I appreciate all that you're trying to do. The food was delicious, and you managed to feed a lot of people. But no matter what you do, you can't cure everything. And regardless of what you might find to say, it's not going to change our circumstances any." He gathered Jacob's plate and stacked it on top of his own then handed them to her.

She took them and stood there, waiting for what he might say next. The pain he felt was evident, yet she could see he kept his emotions somewhat in check and made certain to deliver a respectful response to her. No retort came to mind to what he'd said already, yet he seemed to need to get a few things off his chest. So she lingered.

"The truth is, God decided we must have needed some sort of reprimand or punishment. Maybe we weren't doing good enough to please Him. Whatever the reason, we lost what we had, and your family didn't." He schooled his expression and reached out to take Jacob's arm. "So thank you for coming and bringing the extra plate. But we can't stand around and talk all day. There is work that needs to be done." Bending to retrieve his cap, he straightened and slapped it on his head. "Good day, Miss Lawson."

Chapter 5

N ow wait just a moment."

William didn't pause at Annabelle's retort, but he grimaced at the predictable response. He knew she wouldn't just leave his good-bye at that. She didn't seem the type. He fought against a grin that threatened to pull at his lips at the appealing prospect of continuing conversation with her. Despite her pleasing appearance, he didn't look forward to more talk of God.

"William," Jacob said in a loud whisper. "Aren't we going to wait for Miss Annabelle?"

"She'll be able to keep pace with us, Jacob. We're not walking all that fast."

"But why did we walk away? I don't think she was done talking."

"Mr. Berringer, I don't believe we were finished with our conversation." She spoke as if she'd heard Jacob.

William wanted to say that a woman like Annabelle could probably find any number of reasons to talk, but that wouldn't be fair to her. He'd only had two encounters with her, after all. Too soon to be making assumptions like that.

"We left because our break is over, and we have to get back to work. I know you might want to stay and talk with Miss Annabelle, but our ground isn't going to till itself. And if we want to make sure we have something to show for the first harvest, we have to put our backs into it."

He turned his head to look down at Jacob, but in his peripheral vision, he caught sight of Annabelle still trailing behind them, stepping gingerly through the mud patches. She'd somehow dispensed with the tin plates he'd handed her, so perhaps another volunteer came to take them. He and Jacob just tromped along, mud and all. If his mother saw him right now, she'd box his ears for leaving a young woman the way he had.

A groan rumbled in his throat.

"What's the matter, Willie?"

"Nothing. We should stop, though, and wait for Miss Annabelle. It's not nice to leave her trudging through the mud on her own."

Jacob immediately halted in his tracks and turned, beaming a wide smile in Annabelle's direction. "We'll wait for you, Miss Annabelle. Come on. The mud isn't that bad."

William grinned. Leave it to Jacob to make an unpleasant experience sound like fun. He paused as well but didn't turn around as he allowed his brother to draw Annabelle into their circle. His brother even reached out a hand to help her attain the last step that brought her to their sides. How could an eight-year-old boy make him feel like such a lout?

"Thank you very much, Jacob."

She raised the hem of her skirts just enough to view her boots, stamped each one of them twice to shake off the caked mud, and then lowered her skirts again. Giving her blouse a somewhat discreet tug, she appeared to have herself back in order. At least they were on dry ground now for the remainder of their trek.

"Shall we continue?" William extended his left arm out, palm up in front of them.

It was more of an instruction than a question, and he resumed walking without waiting for a response.

"I would like to pick up our conversation where we left off, Mr. Berringer." Annabelle sounded a little winded, but she kept up with them.

"And I would like to get back to work, Miss Lawson." He almost cringed at the harsh tone to his voice. It was true, though. "Fields don't plant themselves, you know," he added, repeating what he'd said to Jacob only moments before.

"I realize that, Mr. Berringer. And be that as it may, there still remains the issue of your beliefs regarding the role God played in the ruination of your family and so many others."

She didn't give up easily, did she? He'd have to add persistence to the list of qualities he'd begun making in his mind. Only he didn't know if that one went under positive or negative attributes.

"Willie, do you really think God caused us to lose our money?"

Jacob spoke with such curiosity, yet a tinge of worry accompanied his question as well. William scolded himself for allowing his younger brother to overhear the exchange. It was bad enough he struggled with understanding the situation. Jacob didn't need to be dragged into the quandary as well.

William paused and crouched next to his brother, placing a hand on his shoulder and looking up slightly to meet his brother's eyes. "Hey, Jacob, why don't you run on over and see if Father has a new job for you to do? I bet you're tired of digging holes in the ground. Maybe they have the extra seeds for the parts we've already dug."

"Really?" Jacob's eyes brightened, and he seemed to forget the question he'd just asked. "Do you think he'll let me plant instead of dig?"

"Won't know unless you go ask and find out, now will you?" William grinned in hopes of enticing his brother even more.

"Yes!" Jacob threw his arms around William's neck. "Thanks, Willie."

And off he went, racing across the expanse of land and carefully avoiding the rows that were already done.

Annabelle watched alongside him. A moment later she spoke. "That was sweet of you to do that for Jacob."

William shrugged. "He's been clamoring to switch up his tasks for several days now."

She kept her gaze on Jacob and tilted her head to the right, pressing her lips into a thin line. "There is such a difference in your ages, yet you treat him like any older brother would."

He closed his eyes and sighed. "Mother and Father actually lost two others between Jacob and me." Yet another reason to be angry at God.

Annabelle released a soft gasp. "Oh, Mr. Berringer, I'm so sorry."

William opened his eyes to see the stricken look on her face. A part of him wanted to respond to her compassion, but the other part didn't want to get into anything else. The latter won.

"It was a long time ago," he said with a shrug. "But we are a bit protective of him." Then there was the obvious reason. "And he didn't need to be here listening to this conversation."

"Does that mean you're willing to continue our discussion?"

He paused and looked at the sky. The sun blazed overhead, unimpeded by clouds or shade of any kind. After the recent rains and chill in the air, the warmth brought a welcome change. He then turned his attention to the seemingly endless stretch of land they had been given to farm. Finally, he shifted his attention to Annabelle.

"Miss Lawson, I will be honest with you. This topic of God's involvement is one I'm sure you would love to discuss at great lengths. But as I told Jacob and as I mentioned a moment ago, there is a lot of work to be done. I just can't stand around all day talking."

"Then show me what needs to be done, and I'll help."

William started to open his mouth then snapped it shut. Had she really just offered to work alongside him? And if so, why? It couldn't only be so she could share her point of view and hope to change his mind. Because if that was the case, she was wasting her time. And what about her mother and father? Surely they wouldn't approve of her working alone with him out here without supervision.

"I, uh. . .I don't know that there's anything you can do." Her simplistic solution to the closed door he'd attempted to present on the discussion unsettled him. And he didn't want to invite unnecessary trouble from her parents should they learn of her whereabouts.

Annabelle looked around. "There are a lot of women working in these fields. I'm not exactly as delicate as I might appear. Besides, with me working as well, you will have no excuse left to avoid conversation."

Or so she thought. He could remain silent and refuse to answer her questions if he so chose. Something told him, though, that she wouldn't be deterred so easily. It seemed he had no choice but to go along with her.

"All right." He pointed to an untilled section of land to their left. "I began working there this morning. Let me fetch some additional tools and seed, and we can work those rows."

"Very well." She didn't waste a moment before heading in that direction where he'd pointed.

William marched off to do as he said. If she was that determined to work alongside him, so be it. Perhaps he could get so involved in the tilling that he wouldn't be required to say much in response to what he was sure would only amount to preaching.

Five minutes later, he met her at their work plot and dumped a heavy bag of seed at her feet. After that came a bucket of water. The liquid sloshed over the sides when he dropped it on the ground. His hoe and digging stick remained nestled in the hollow of his shoulder.

"You'll be using the seeds to fill the holes I dig. Then you'll need to pour a good measure of water over them to moisten the soil."

"I believe I can handle that."

William thought he detected a hint of sarcasm in her voice, but he didn't bother to look at her to find out if his suspicions were correct.

"All right, then. Let's get started."

He dug the hoe into the earth and broke apart the clumps of dirt. With the digging stick, he pressed down the dirt and made a suitable hole, then stood back and waited for Annabelle to fill it. She did as he'd instructed, refilling the hole and pouring water over it.

"Good. Let's continue."

It was the closest he could come to a compliment. Best not to encourage her too much. She learned fast, though—with just the right number of seeds and an appropriate amount of water. She worked as if she had done this before. But that was ridiculous. From what he could tell, they'd both grown up in similar households. She was a lady. Servants most likely performed the menial tasks of planting and gardening. Still, she didn't seem to mind the labor.

He moved on to the next hole and then the next. After digging and filling at least a dozen, he tilted his head and regarded her from the corner of his eye. She reached into the seed sack and withdrew two handfuls. Curious, he paused as she deposited the seeds into a front pocket of her apron, which still bore evidence of the meal she'd helped serve for lunch.

William cleared his throat. "Impressive," was all he could manage. He still hadn't come to terms with her offer to help. And now she seemed to be making the best of things.

"If we are to be as productive as possible, this will help our pace. The sack can be left at the end of each row, and I can replenish as needed." She smiled, obviously pleased with her ingenious solution.

"Good thinking," he said cautiously, determined not to tip the tone of this forced situation one way or the other. He moved ahead to dig the next hole. "The work is not done with digging and planting, though. The seeds must be tended and nurtured each day. Then the weeds will need to be cleared away to allow room for the seeds to take root and sprout. After that, there's the elimination of any pests that might take up residence on the leaves or the plants." He looked down at the ground and spoke low. "There will be much to do long after you're gone."

Annabelle dug into her pocket for more seeds, but not before William caught the flash of disappointment in her eyes at his intentional barb. She waited in pronounced silence until he had the next hole ready, then dumped in the seeds, filled the hole, and poured the water.

It was just as well. The less communication they had, the easier it would be to get lost in his work. But the longer the silence lasted, the more his conscience was pricked by guilt. If she said something, he might be tempted to deliver an insult in order to protect himself. That went against his grain. He might not be sure where he stood as far as God was concerned, but he was still a gentleman. And as such, he had a duty to be courteous and respectful.

If only she didn't make it so difficult.

As she filled the most recent hole, she paused and stared at the wet area left behind by the water. "These seeds are a lot like us," she muttered almost to herself.

He drew his eyebrows together as she turned her head to look up at him.

"These seeds. They are a lot like people." She reached into her apron and pulled out a few, holding them in her palm. "In their present state, they are like a newborn baby. After we are born, we need a great deal of care and attention in order to grow in the best environment possible. Our roots are formed from the instruction of our mother and father and other people in our lives."

He moved down the row, working as she spoke. A stolen glance at his companion's face revealed bright eyes and an eagerness in her expression. She obviously assumed that he was interested in what she had to say. He may be, but he didn't intend to tell her that.

"When we are ready," she continued, "we break free from our family—like what you will do when the vegetables are ready for picking—and we become mature plants. We are independent, but we came from the same roots. If conditions are right, the seeds at the core of the vegetable are strong enough to be replanted in the ground in the hopes that they will grow to produce healthy plants. Just like their sources before them. And so the cycle continues, does it not?"

William rammed the hoe into the ground and separated the dirt. "I never thought of farming and family in that way."

"Our faith in God is almost the same."

He gripped the long end of the hoe, making a fist around the rough wood. *God again*, he groaned inwardly. Why did she insist upon making such an analogy to his faith? It would have been fine to leave it as a parallel to their physical growth. He didn't want to hear anything about God or how the roots his parents had instilled in him still ran deep.

Besides, his life couldn't possibly be compared to these seeds or the way they would be tended as they grew. God had uprooted him and his family from the comfort of their home and left them to wither and die without sustenance. It was by pure chance they had happened upon this opportunity to farm in order to have a way of life again.

"We begin as little seeds when we first believe. By reading the Bible and going to church with others who believe, we receive the nourishment and the care to grow healthy and strong."

William tried to ignore Annabelle's words, but no other noise existed to drown them out. It was impossible not to hear them.

"We live each day to the fullest and plant seeds in others to help them grow as we grow. If our faith is strong, when the rain and winds and storms come, we will survive."

The winds and storms hadn't stopped since the runs on the banks had ripped the rug out from under his family and forced them to lose their home. Sure, they were surviving, but not by God's help. He'd had to compromise his own goals, dreams, and desires. He'd been forced to use his own innovation to make the best of the situation. He was working hard, just as his parents and his brother were, all so they could start rebuilding what they had lost. No matter what Annabelle said or how much time she took to extend her charity to others, she wouldn't change the facts.

Although, if he had to admit it, he was enjoying her company far more than he thought he would—more than he should, all things considered. As they moved up and down the rows, his mind focused on Annabelle. She didn't have to be here working with him. And she didn't have to get mud and sweat and dirt all over her pretty clothes. Yet she was here doing exactly that. And for what? For him? That possibility seemed too far-fetched to even consider. What if it was true, though? He couldn't do anything about it. He had nothing to offer a fine lady like her. Not now, anyway.

"Is everything all right, Mr. Berringer?"

Her voice interrupted his musings.

"Your face is rather flushed. I do hope you aren't suffering from heatstroke or even from the food we prepared for your lunch."

William shook himself free from his trailing thoughts. He risked a look in her direction. Loose tendrils of her chestnut hair framed her face, and the slightest bit of perspiration formed on her brow. Despite the soiled state of her clothing, she presented a rather appealing picture. For a fleeting moment, he entertained thoughts of the many possibilities. But the worried expression gracing her delicate features reminded him of the folly of those thoughts and brought him back to the present.

"No, no," he rushed to assure her. "There was nothing wrong with the food, and I am feeling just fine. I promise."

William took note of the progress they'd made. If they continued at this pace, they'd complete at least five rows before the hour was done. Had it not been for her creative use of the pocket in her apron, they no doubt would have been slowed considerably. If only she didn't feel the need to ramble on and on about faith and God and strong roots.

"In that case," she replied, "I had another thought regarding your comments earlier."

And there she was, back on the religious talk again. Rather than respond, he remained quiet and focused on the planting. *Let her continue to talk to herself. Perhaps that audience will be preferable to my participation in the conversation.*

She continued as if she didn't even notice his silence. "You seem to believe that God has forgotten all about you. Or that He's too busy to notice that your family is in need and suffering like so many others."

Annabelle followed behind him, focused on her part of the work and what she felt the need to say to him.

"But God doesn't forget the tiniest sparrow, and He hasn't forgotten you or your family, Mr. Berringer. Why else would you have this land to farm and the help of others in this city to assist you in rebuilding? Why else would your entire family have been left healthy and able to work to recover from the loss?"

His mind drifted back nearly twenty years to his childhood and a time when he sat on his mother's lap listening to her read from the Bible. He remembered the story of the sparrow, as well as the lilies in the field. His mother had told him that God valued him far above those items and that he should never worry about tomorrow. God had it all under control.

"You realize, Mr. Berringer, that you could have been more than crippled in your finances. Illness, injury, or any number of other setbacks could have incapacitated you or one of your family members. And then where would you be?"

William wanted so desperately to say something to her. But words failed him.

What would he say, though? He couldn't exactly throw off everything when deep down in his heart he knew she spoke the truth. Still, there was a rather large gap between what he'd learned as a child and what he lived today as an adult.

Annabelle didn't press him in any way. And soon, assuming either his disinterest or his inner struggle, she lapsed into silence as well. The silence chilled him like the cold April rains that had recently fallen. At least they agreed on something. Not talking would prevent any disagreements or arguments. And since their conversations to this point seemed to end in some form of conflict, maybe silence was the answer.

"Annabelle!"

They both looked up at the calling of her name. It took William a moment to locate the source. A young girl, who looked to be four or five years older than his brother, stood about seventy-five feet away, shielding her eyes from the overhead sun and looking in their direction.

"That's my younger sister, Victoria," Annabelle explained. "She's no doubt coming to say it's time to go home."

William looked back over their progress. They had reached the end of the sixth row. More than he had expected they'd do in the time they'd been working.

Annabelle made a point to carry the nearly empty water pail to the start of the next row. William followed her as she walked toward where they'd left the seeds. She reached into her apron and emptied the seeds back into the sack. Then she dusted off her hands and stood staring at the ground.

He couldn't tell if she was trying to think of something to say or waiting for him to say something. Again, his conscience pricked. He couldn't let her leave without at least thanking her for her help.

"Uh, Miss Lawson? I, uh. . ." Why wouldn't his brain work? This should be a simple task. He cleared his throat and waited for her to look at him. "Thank you. For your help and for what you shared today about faith and God."

Oh no. Where had that come from? He had only intended to mention the work. Yet for all he tried, he couldn't stop the tumbling words from his mouth. "I know I didn't say much, but I did hear every word you said. You've given me a lot to think about."

Hope filled her eyes, making the dark blue hue lighten a few shades. "Mr. Berringer, if I only succeeded in making you rethink where you stand with God, then that's enough for me. I don't wish to preach, but I believe in my heart that God will never leave or forsake us. I would love for you to see that, too."

Her innocence struck a chord with him, and her open expression compelled him in ways he didn't understand.

"I can't promise anything except that I will continue to think on it."

She nodded. "And that's more than enough." With a glance over her shoulder and a raised arm, she signaled her sister then returned her gaze to him. "Thank you for allowing me to work beside you today, Mr. Berringer. And I hope we see each other again." She grasped her skirt in her hand and smiled. "Good day."

"Good day, Miss Lawson," he said as she walked away toward her sister.

At least that parting hadn't been as cruel as the one he'd delivered right after lunch. This one left them with a chance to at least remain cordial. Although, after all that she'd said to him and the time she'd spent working at his side, they were now beyond mere polite exteriors. Where they stood, he couldn't say. But he admired her tenacity and hoped their paths would cross again soon.

Chapter 6

Annabelle accepted the assistance of the footman as she descended from the carriage onto the sidewalk. Victoria, Matthew, and her parents followed. The five of them approached the impressive home of Mayor Pingree on Woodward. It was quite a few blocks from their home on Marietta, but the ride had passed quickly.

Now, standing in front of the house for the first time, Annabelle studied the Italianate-style architecture with French influence. She'd heard about the mayor's taste for things French and read a great deal about the French influence in some of the major cities throughout America. However, she had no idea he'd go to lengths such as this to bring a taste of France to Detroit. Even the mansard roof seemed out of place among the other structures.

"Isn't it beautiful, Annabelle?" Victoria came to stand next to her sister, transfixed and staring at the home in front of them.

"Yes, Victoria. It's stunning."

A handful of elm trees grew tall and protected the home, set back about forty feet from the street. Two brick walks wound away from Woodward, one to the mayor's home and the other to the carriage house that sat farther back. It was the middle of May, and the wide variety of flowers planted at the front of the home blossomed in an array of colors, shapes, and sizes.

"Come now, girls," Mother reprimanded softly. "Let's not dawdle and appear impolite. I am certain many of the guests have already arrived, and we don't wish to be tardy."

The five of them walked up the five stone steps to the front porch where a butler swung wide the door and ushered them inside. After taking their wraps, he directed them into the parlor to the right. A maid weaved her way through the other guests and held a tray of glasses filled with punch, wine, and champagne.

Annabelle took a glass of punch and sipped it as she stepped away from her parents to observe the furnishings of the room. The deeply tufted sofas and chairs were covered in crimson and black satin damask. The rosewood frames, delicately carved, had recently been polished until the wood gleamed. A grand piano sat in the corner, where a young gentleman tinkled out soft strains of a pleasing melody. Even the satin drapes that hung from the doorway at the far end matched the crimson of the carpet under her feet. And the oval end tables were graced with sienna marble instead of the white slab marble they had at home.

The various items placed here resembled their parlor, but the quality far outshone anything they had. Annabelle could only imagine the expense involved if the entire home had been decorated in the same manner. The quality alone likely cost the mayor twice as much as what her parents had paid to decorate their home. The only aspects that seemed to parallel her home were the wallpaper patterns and the chandelier that hung from the ceiling in the center of the room.

Annabelle felt almost like an imposter. It seemed wrong somehow to be standing in a room this ornate when families such as William's shared the open space of an abandoned warehouse near their farm plot with at least four or five other families. She'd been serving the families on the land her father had donated for more than a month now, and she'd even begun to view her own home in a different light.

Victoria sidled up to her. "Feels strange, doesn't it? Seeing all the expensive things here," her sister said as if she'd read Annabelle's thoughts.

"Yes, it does. The mayor must have spent a small fortune to decorate his home. I don't suppose we can fault him much, though. This house was built twenty years ago and paid for with money he'd accumulated through his business ventures prior to becoming a mayor. He's done a lot of good for the city and those in need since the financial panic last year."

"He has, I agree." Victoria nodded. "And a man as important as Mayor Pingree shouldn't have to live in anything less simply because others are struggling."

"Still, I can't help but think of the people who are working on Father's land."

"You mean families like the Berringers?"

Annabelle looked down at her sister to see a gleam in the young girl's eyes and a grin on her lips. "Why do you mention them?"

"Father has a list of all the families who are working on that acreage. When I came to find you a couple weeks ago, I asked a few questions and found my answers."

Quite the little detective. Annabelle was impressed. "Well, yes. That family is one in particular. But there are many others working there as well."

"What's so special about the Berringer family, then? You seem to spend a lot of time with them each week or mention them more often than others."

Annabelle shrugged. "I met the two sons the first day I delivered water to the workers, and they were among the only ones to show any true form of gratitude. I guess they stick out in my mind." No reason to make any more of William than necessary. Otherwise her sister would never let it rest.

"Oh. Okay."

She looked about to say something else, but they were interrupted by the arrival of the butler.

"Dinner is served, ladies and gentlemen. Please make your way to the dining room."

Annabelle and Victoria joined the flow of guests as they moved from the parlor and headed toward the dining room. If the first room had been impressive, this one was extraordinary. Several large mirrors with gilded frames flanked two of the three walls. A large portrait of Mayor Pingree adorned the wall behind the head of the table, and three stately windows with brocade curtains were spaced a few feet apart on the fourth wall.

The polished mahogany table in the center of the room gleamed, and when Annabelle found her seat, she could see her reflection in the surface. She smiled at seeing she had been seated next to Mrs. Jennings with Mother on her right. Across the table, Matthew faced her with Victoria and Father flanking his sides. Oh, if only William could be here. Then again, how would that be possible? She knew his family had lost a great deal, but she didn't know for sure just where they stood financially before the crisis. He might not have been included in the guest list for this evening. And being here, or even hearing about it, would only increase his bitterness about his present circumstances.

Her thoughts were once again interrupted by the arrival of their host. Mayor Pingree stood behind his seat at the head of the table and rested his hands on the high back.

"I'd like to thank everyone for coming this evening. From all reports, many of you have been involved in helping launch the efforts to establish the potato patches throughout the city. Others have provided additional clothing, food, and funds, which have gone far toward replenishing our depleted stores." He looked down the table, his gaze resting on each guest on both sides of the table. "I couldn't think of a better way to thank you than to invite you and your families here to enjoy a delicious meal."

After pulling out his chair and taking a seat, he extended his arms out toward his guests.

"Please. Sit. Let's get this dinner under way."

Several servants assisted the ladies present then reached for the napkins on the table, fanning them out before placing them in the ladies' laps.

In a matter of moments, the soft din of voices rose from the table. Mrs. Jennings leaned close.

"My dear, I am quite pleased at the company in which I find myself. I cannot imagine a more giving or industrious family than your own." The woman smiled past her at Annabelle's mother. "Felicity, you have set a fine example for both of your daughters, and it's wonderful to see them following in your footsteps."

Father winked across the table, while Mother nodded at Mrs. Jennings. "Thank you, Olivia," Mother said, pride reflected on her face. "I am quite honored to have two such dutiful daughters and ones so willing to help wherever there is a need."

Salads were placed in front of them, and they halted their conversation for a few moments. After waiting for everyone to be served, they looked to Mayor Pingree to take his first bite. He did and waved his fork in the air to encourage everyone else to do the same.

After eating her first forkful, Mrs. Jennings picked up where they'd left off. "I do know for a fact that the food schedule you have set up, Felicity, is a big success. I haven't seen a more organized distribution since I began working with the Ladies Aid."

"Well, I can't take all the credit," Mother said. "I have a reliable group of ladies who bear the brunt of the work. My daughters and I only work the one plot owned by Brandt. The other areas are under the supervision of many more volunteers."

"Regardless, your work is greatly appreciated."

Father took that moment to speak up as well. "I have heard various positive discussions from the workers who remained at the factories that were able to stay open regarding the charitable contributions of those who managed to avoid serious declines in their holdings."

"Yes," Mr. Jennings said from Victoria's right. "I'm fortunate the railroad car shop where I serve as supervising manager is still managing to function. After most of the other railroad shops closed along with the stove factories, fear raced through the remaining shops until workers speculated whether or not their job would be next."

"Yet through it all," Mrs. Jennings began, "we as a whole have managed to survive. And I believe a great deal of thanks is owed to our mayor for his innovative ideas."

"I agree," Father echoed. "When the hoped-for revival of business failed to come earlier this spring and the city's poor funds were exhausted, he knew something different was needed."

Matthew leaned forward, his face reflecting interest. "I heard the mayor had analyzed the real estate market from the previous boom in our economy. When he saw all those plots of land being held for a rise in value standing idle all over the city, he made a public appeal to the owners."

Mr. Jennings nodded. "Yes. The mayor asked for permission to use their properties for vegetable gardens, both big and small."

Annabelle had been following the entire story in the newspapers each week ever since the day at church when the pastor had put out a call for donations. Although she didn't often engage in the detailed discussions surrounding the idea, she had found the affectionate name given to the plots rather humorous.

"Pingree's potato patches is what they're being called," she said with a smile.

"It does have a nice ring to it, doesn't it?"

Mrs. Jennings chuckled. "It does at that, Annabelle dear. Several other cities have even taken the model and created similar farming or gardening systems to help their own residents. But it's our very own mayor who is now known as a champion for the needy. It makes me quite proud to be living here in Detroit."

Their salads were removed and replaced by steaming bowls of french onion soup. Considering the home where they were eating, the choice of flavor came as no surprise to Annabelle. She eagerly dug into the delicious broth.

Silence fell upon the table as many took their initial spoonfuls of the second course. A few minutes later, Father resumed the conversation.

"And let's not forget the mayor's fight for municipal ownership of our city's street transportation system."

Mr. Jennings had made quick order of his soup and laid his spoon in the empty bowl, then rested his forearms on the edge of the table. "Yes, he's built more than fifty miles of new track to help our streetcar system."

Victoria sat up straighter in her chair and grinned. "I like that I can ride one for three cents now instead of five like it used to be."

Her childlike fascination with the modernized method of transportation was infectious. Annabelle had ridden on the conveyances on more than one occasion, but Victoria took every opportunity. And since the electric cars had recently replaced the previous horse-drawn ones, Annabelle had to admit enjoying the ride even more.

"Well, if things don't improve with the American Railway Union," Mr. Jennings announced, his face pinched and full of concern, "we might be back to horse-drawn transportation when departing from the confines of a city."

"What do you mean?" Mother asked.

Mr. Jennings's eyes widened. "Have you not heard of the Pullman strike taking place right now? It just started a week ago, so news is only just starting to reach everyone."

"Ah yes." Father nodded. "I read an article about that just this morning in the *Detroit News*."

The next part of their dinner was a refreshing serving of lime sorbet to cleanse their palates in preparation for the main course. Conversation stalled for just a moment as each of them took a small spoonful of the sweet treat.

"Pray tell; do not keep us waiting in suspense much longer, dear," Mother pleaded as soon as her mouth was clear.

"Well, it seems the lack of demand for train cars and the drop in their revenue caused the Pullman Palace Car Company to cut wages by 25 percent recently."

"Cut wages?" Matthew's face reflected the horror his voice conveyed. "That's not going to help anyone!"

"I agree," Mr. Jennings stated. "And it seems the workers do as well. Because of their rebellion, this recent strike has brought all transportation west of Chicago to a screeching halt."

Chicago. Annabelle recalled something she'd read a while back regarding the railway car company. Ah yes, it was the small town that was built. "Isn't Mr. Pullman the man who built a company town near Chicago and paid high wages to the workers who agreed to live there?"

Father looked across the table at her with surprise and pride in his eyes. "I'm impressed, Annabelle, that you're aware of that. And yes, Mr. Pullman is that very same man. The town features attractive houses, complete with indoor plumbing, gas, and sewer systems, plus free education through the eighth grade and a public library."

"Yes," Mother interjected, "but with all that is the reality that Mr. Pullman is controlling everything in that town. He prohibits such things as independent newspapers, public speeches, town meetings, or any speeches that haven't been preapproved by him or his inspectors first."

"Doesn't sound like a desirable place to live," Mrs. Jennings remarked.

Annabelle could think of at least a dozen places that would be more appealing. "It's no wonder the workers have chosen to strike."

"And the strike is gaining popularity rather rapidly." Father sighed. "If something isn't done, it could spread all across the nation. With refusal to load Pullman cars or run trains containing those cars, we could see far-reaching effects even here in Detroit. I pray that doesn't happen."

Silence again fell upon their little group. Annabelle contemplated what some of those effects might be, as if the economic state wasn't enough. It seemed some of the larger companies were bent on making things worse for those already suffering. Didn't they realize the workers were the reason their companies even existed in the first place?

Without workers, they'd have to close their doors permanently. If the owners had been wiser about their investments, they might not have to resort to cutting wages. No guarantees of that existed, but if even a few jobs could be saved, it would be worth it.

From that point forward, talk continued to focus on the improvements being made right there in Detroit and the efforts of so many to rebound from everything. Before Annabelle knew it, the evening had come to a close and they were again in a carriage taking them home.

Father rested his head against the back wall of the carriage and rested his hands over his abdomen. "Well, I must say I enjoyed the evening immensely."

"I never knew Mr. and Mrs. Jennings were so well informed about current events."

"They'd have to be, Annabelle," Mother answered, "if Mrs. Jennings wants to stay abreast of the current needs in the city to inform the Ladies Aid, and Mr. Jennings wants to make certain his factory remains in operation."

"True." Annabelle could understand that reasoning. And it made for entertaining discussion, even if some moments didn't pique her interest as much as others. It was during those times that her mind drifted to William.

"Father, do you know how many affluent families were affected by the financial crisis?"

He took a deep breath and looked up toward the roof of the carriage. "Well, let's see. Some I know had all their investments tied up in one area. Take the railroad, for instance. When that failed, they lost everything. Others had their money invested in more than one company. But if the majority of those closed due to the railroad failures or the bank runs, they also would have lost a substantial amount."

Annabelle nodded. "And then there is us. We suffered, but not as heavily as some, right?"

"Exactly. Thanks to the investments made by my father and Grandfather Chambers, our surplus was spread out in a diverse number of companies. Some of them fared rather well when the panic struck. Others didn't. But because we had spread out our investments, we weren't hit as hard."

She wondered if William's family had been one of the ones to have everything tied up in one company or in several that came to ruin. Either way, he and his family were forced to work the land her father had donated while she and her family remained in their comfortable home. They had seen the need to cut back on certain frivolous spending, but they were in no danger of losing anything that might cause a drastic change in their lifestyle.

For once she wondered how much truth there was to William's feelings on the matter. Just how had God decided which families would suffer and which wouldn't? The misfortune did seem to strike at random. What made their family worthy of being spared?

Of course, that started another line of thought—the purpose in everything. She firmly believed everything happened for a reason. While she might not be able to figure out the reason, she still had a duty to take what had happened and make the best of things. If that meant serving out of her own abundance or blessing others in need when she had something to give, she would do it. God's Word said if she served even the least of those she encountered, she served as if unto Him. Meeting folks like Jacob and William was just a bonus.

Chapter 7

"Watch the ball, Jacob," William instructed his brother. "I might switch my pitch or drive it straight down the middle at you. But if you keep your eye on it, you'll be able to catch it no matter what."

"All right, Willie. I'm ready."

Jacob thumped his fist into his palm several times and assumed a rigid stance, poised on the balls of his feet. William smiled. He was ready. No doubt about it.

"Here it comes."

He wasn't sure why he gave his brother the warning. Jacob had already proven himself on more than one occasion to be an excellent catcher. His throws were getting stronger with each practice session they had together. It wouldn't be long before Jacob's skill with both bat and ball would exceed his own. Father joined them from time to time but admitted he didn't possess as great a skill at the game as his sons. So he stuck to instruction rather than actual play.

William could still remember the times he and his father had spent hours at the park near their old house throwing the ball back and forth to each other. Father had taught him and Jacob both how to hit. Not a bad legacy to pass down the line, even if Father spent more time correcting them than participating. William loved the chance today to work with his brother. They didn't often get the opportunity to make it to the old park and see Jacob's friends. Maybe once they rebuilt their holdings, they and Father could bat the ball to each other—for old time's sake.

"Are you going to throw it or not, Willie? My legs are getting tired from standing like this."

William shook his head. It looked as if he had let his thoughts wander. He gripped the ball in his hand and placed two fingers over the top, just like Father had once shown him. He cocked his arm back behind his head and prepared to release. Jacob would never know what hit him.

"Is this a boy's-only game, or can I watch as well?"

William let go of the ball just as Annabelle's voice reached his ears. He didn't have time to maintain a hold before it left his hand. His breath caught in his throat as the baseball zipped through the air toward Jacob.

God! Please let Jacob catch it.

Wait a minute. Had he just prayed? Yes, he had. And right now he needed the extra help.

A few seconds later, though, he realized he had no reason to worry. Jacob shifted his stance and caught the ball with ease, his grin beaming from ear to ear.

"I got it. I got it." The boy puffed out his chest. "See, Willie? I told you I could catch anything you threw!"

"Yes, I see that." William breathed a huge sigh of relief.

"Hi, Miss Annabelle." Jacob tossed the ball back and forth between his hands and approached. "When did you get here?"

Annabelle's soft laughter added a nice layer to the tense moment her sudden appearance caused. "I only just arrived." She reached out and ruffled the boy's fine blond hair. "In time to see you make that amazing catch."

Jacob puffed out his chest again. "That catch *was* amazing, wasn't it?"

"You did a fine job, Jacob." William turned to face Annabelle. "What brings you out to visit us today? You don't have a water bucket with you."

He held back the grimace at how callous his words sounded. Thankfully, Annabelle didn't seem to notice. Or if she did, she didn't show it.

"No, I took a quick break from meal preparations to come extend an invitation to you both."

"An invitation?" That sounded intriguing.

"You mean you want us to come somewhere with you?"

"Yes, Jacob." She looked back and forth between them. "And I am quite confident it's a place you both will love very much."

"Tell us! Tell us!" Jacob barely managed to contain his excitement. And he didn't even know where they might be going yet.

"Yes," William added. "By all means. Don't make us stand here and guess."

Instead of answering them, Annabelle reached into the pocket of her skirt and pulled out several identical items that looked like tickets of some sort.

"What are those?" He nodded at the items.

She extended her hand toward William. "Why don't you take a look and see for yourself?"

William held them in front of him to read what was printed. He gasped. How had she gotten ahold of these? Better yet, how had she known it would be like a dream come true to go?

"What are they, Willie?" Jacob took a step closer and craned his neck, trying to get a glimpse beyond William's hands. "Can I see? Can I? Please?"

William's voice caught in his throat. He opened his mouth several times and tried to speak. Nothing but air came out. Clearing his throat, he tried again.

"They're—" His voice cracked. He had to get it together. "They're tickets, Jacob," he managed, feeling like someone had landed a blow to his head.

"Tickets to what?"

"To a baseball game at Boulevard Park."

"A game?" Jacob sounded amazed. "A real, honest-to-goodness baseball game? With players and gloves and uniforms and everything?"

Annabelle laughed. "And everything, Jacob."

The sound of her voice broke through the cloud of disbelief surrounding William. "How did you manage this?"

"My father has a few connections with some rather influential people."

She spoke as if it wasn't a big deal. Then again, she likely had no idea just how important something like this was.

"I heard that the Western League had reorganized this year and that there was a club in the city that has established themselves as a charter member. Never in my wildest dreams did I think I'd actually be able to see the team play."

Annabelle shrugged. "Well, I remember another visit where you, Jacob, and your father were tossing and hitting the ball back and forth. I could see how much fun you were having and how much you seemed to love it. So I asked my father to make some inquiries. When he came back with the tickets, I could hardly wait to come here and give them to you."

"And your father didn't ask you why you had this sudden interest in baseball or why you needed three tickets?"

"Five, actually," she corrected.

"Five?" Who else was coming?

"Yes. In order to get these tickets I've given you, I also had to agree to bring my brother and sister as well."

"Oh." That didn't sound so bad. William figured it was more so she would have a chaperone. After all, he had yet to officially meet her parents, even if he was certain they knew about him. And that brought back the question about her father and the number of tickets. "You didn't say whether your father asked about the number of tickets."

"Yes, about that." She ducked her head, and a becoming blush spread across her cheeks. "He and my mother were rather curious when I gave your names, but I assured them the tickets were for two friends." She looked up at him, a pleading expression in her eyes. "I hope that was all right."

"We're your friends, Miss Annabelle," Jacob piped in before William could reply. "Of course it's all right."

William grinned and jerked a thumb toward his brother. "What he said."

"So you'll go then?"

As if he'd turn down an opportunity like this. He'd be daft to refuse. "Of course."

"Excellent." She took two steps backward. "Very well. I can't tarry much longer. I only came to make sure you wanted to come and to give you the tickets." Annabelle pointed toward the tent and tables off yonder. "Lunch will be served soon." She stepped away and turned.

"Will we meet you there?" The park was quite a ways from where they worked, but if they left early enough, they could make it in time.

"Oh, I hadn't thought about that." She glanced over her shoulder, pressed her lips into a thin line, and tilted her head. The way one corner of her mouth quirked, it made a dimple appear in her left cheek, giving her a pixieish quality. "Since we have to pass by here on our way, we'll take you in our carriage. Otherwise you'll have to walk quite a distance. And you might not make it in time."

A carriage. He hoped it wouldn't be enclosed. An open one suited them just fine. Dressed the way they'd be, the plainer the transportation the better. He didn't need to tell her that, though. Whatever carriage she sent would be fine with him.

"That sounds good."

"Very well." She nodded. "It appears to be all settled, then."

"Are we really going to a baseball game, Willie?"

"Yes, Jacob. And we have Miss Annabelle to thank."

"Thank you, lots and lots, Miss Annabelle. Willie talks about games all the time. We're going to have a great time. I just know it."

Annabelle ruffled the boy's hair again. "I certainly hope you do, Jacob. I hope you do."

Just before she turned to leave, William caught her eye and held her gaze. "Thank you," he said with all the sincerity he could muster. "You have no idea how much this means. . .to both of us."

A soft smile formed on her lips. "I believe I have some idea."

And with that, she left.

Four days. How in the world would he manage to wait that long?

❧

The park at the corner of East Lafayette and Helen was even larger than he imagined it would be for a team just getting on their feet again. Nothing like when the team in the city was the Wolverines, but every charter had to start somewhere. From what he'd heard, the owner was determined to make this team stick. They'd been without a professional team for almost six years. It was high time another one came back.

"Would you look at all the people, Willie!" Jacob ran ahead of them but not too far. "And the field. It's so big."

Annabelle walked right next to him. Matthew and Victoria ambled alongside her on her left. The carriage had arrived right after lunch. And just as he'd hoped, it wasn't enclosed. But another surprise came when the carriage deposited them at the nearest trolley stop and Matthew paid for their fares. He could accept that better than if Annabelle had covered them. From there they followed Jefferson to Helen and Helen to Lafayette.

"Annabelle tells me you and your brother really love the game of baseball." Matthew craned his neck forward to speak to him as they made their way to their seats. "Same here."

"Yes. A few years back, I followed everything I could read about the Wolverines, including the National League pennant and the exhibition championship they won seven years ago. Then the team disbanded, and Detroit has been minor league ever since. Until this year, that is."

"No kidding?" Matthew paused and moved to William's other side, no doubt to avoid talking around Annabelle and her sister. "Does this mean they're back at major league status again?"

"Not yet. They're only a charter member this year. But I have no doubt they'll be major league before too long. From what I've heard of their owner, George Vanderbeck, it's only a matter of time."

"Here we are," Annabelle announced as they reached the wooden benches where they'd sit.

William looked out at the playing field where the two teams were practicing and warming up for the game. It wasn't the best vantage point, but he couldn't complain. Just being here was the best gift he'd received in a long time. He ushered Jacob in first and made sure he got the seat closest to his brother. Matthew followed with Victoria and Annabelle bringing up the rear. The two girls immediately lapsed into a conversation all their own.

"So," Matthew continued once they were seated, "it appears you know far more than I about this game. What else do you know about this particular team?"

William almost laughed. He knew just about everything there was to know, short of being an actual member of the team. "What do you want to know?"

"Well, how about the players? Are any of them the same as when the Wolverines played in the city?"

"Not as far as I know. But then again, this is the first game I've attended, and this club is just getting started. I haven't heard much about who is playing on the team." He thought back to when the major league was there. "I do know that there was a high percentage of turnover during the eight years they played as the Wolverines. Only one member made it through all eight seasons, and that was Ned Hanlon."

"Hmm, I believe I heard his name once or twice."

"Well, you might not have heard much about baseball when it was here last. At least when it was worthy of front-page news."

Matthew nodded. "You've got a point there." He paused and looked out at the field. "What made them disband?"

"They didn't have enough fans to remain a major league team."

"Yes, I remember reading that Detroit was actually one of the smallest cities in the National League to have a baseball team."

"Right." William ticked off other cities on his fingers. "Boston, Chicago, Cleveland, and St. Louis all had thousands more fans than Detroit did. And since they couldn't keep up, they had to quit." He searched his memory for some other tidbits. "There were two attempts a few years ago to revive the team through the International League and the old Northwestern League."

Matthew chimed in. "But both ended after one season."

Annabelle's brother obviously had more than a rudimentary knowledge of the game. Perhaps they could have a rousing discussion today.

"Willie, look." Jacob tugged on his arm and pointed out at the field. "They're about to start. Come on. Let's watch."

William chuckled. "That's why we're here, Jacob. To watch. It would be hard not to."

His brother was so fixated on the field, he hadn't picked up on William's teasing. And that was just as well. The more enamored the lad was in the game, the less he'd have to be concerned with keeping an eye on him. He wouldn't likely get into too much trouble if he didn't take his eyes off the players.

Once the game began, the five of them watched everything with unabashed interest. William managed to glance out the corner of his eye to find Annabelle appearing to enjoy herself as well. At least the tickets proved worthwhile. He'd hate it if she went to all the trouble to get them and then didn't have a good time.

At several points in the game, Matthew demonstrated a true interest in baseball that almost mirrored William's. But he also had a lot of questions. William answered them all amid their banter on what they each knew. If he didn't miss his mark, he figured Matthew would become even more of a fan by the end of the day.

"You weren't kidding when you said you knew a lot about this game." Matthew shook his head. "I don't think it's possible to stump you."

William grinned. "Well, can I help it if I used to come to every game they played in town?"

"Wow! Every game? I only managed to make it to one or two."

"Well, you see, my father knew the owner, and our family had a standing invitation to the games. Since I loved it so much, we came."

He shifted his gaze to find Annabelle staring at him, her mouth parted slightly and her eyes registering surprise. Had he said something wrong? He tried to retrace his words. She spoke before he could put his finger on what caused her shock.

"Your father used to know the owner of the Wolverines?"

Ah, so that was what caught her attention. And she'd paid attention earlier when he had stated the old name of the team when they played at the major league level. Yes, he could see why such an admission would garner that type of reaction.

"Yes. They were good friends, in fact." No sense lying about it. She might as well know a bit more about his family's past. "Baseball has always been a favorite pastime of mine. When my father saw this, he managed to persuade the owner of the old team to allow us access to every game. We came every chance we could get."

"So what happened?" Annabelle leaned forward, her attention focused intently on him.

William shifted on the hard bench. A moment ago he thought it might be wise to share some details about his past. Now he wasn't so sure. It only brought back memories he'd much rather see remain buried. He'd been the one to open Pandora's box, though. Talking more about what his family once had wouldn't exactly unleash a swarm of evils upon them, but it would make him dwell on all they had lost.

"I'm not really sure," he finally managed. "Once the Wolverines disbanded, the owner seemed to disappear with them. A few others came and went with the attempts to start a team again during the years when we only had minor league status. But I never saw Mr. Stearns again."

"Do you think he might have left and moved to another city?" Matthew asked. "Maybe he switched to another team somewhere."

William hadn't thought of that, as it didn't happen too often with owners. "I suppose that's possible. All I know is my father never spoke of it, and I soon came to realize it was a mystery that wouldn't likely be solved anytime soon."

"That's so sad." Victoria sighed. "To think that a friendship like that could just fall apart. I mean, it sounds like he was an important person in your life when you were younger."

"Yes, he was." William had almost come to see him as part of the family. And then he was gone.

"It makes you wonder if there had been a disagreement of some sort." Annabelle tapped a finger to her lips as she often did when she became contemplative. "Or it's possible the disbanding of the team hit the owner really hard, and he wasn't able to handle it all."

"Well, whatever the reason, I only know I spent a lot of years wondering and waiting, hoping one day to see the return of a major league team." William extended his right arm toward the field. "Now it looks like I'll finally get that chance again."

Annabelle paused and licked her lips. She opened her mouth to speak then closed it, sitting back on the bench. "It does seem like that's a strong possibility."

Had she been about to say something else? William wasn't sure. But her remark seemed to put a period on that topic of conversation. No one else offered anything more, and their attention focused again on the game.

It was just as well. Talking about the past had made William a bit melancholy. Remembering what once was only made him question the reasons why again. They'd had everything.

Oh well. He didn't want to spoil a good thing by dwelling on the negatives today. Being at this game was a dream come true. And he intended to enjoy it.

Chapter 8

For several weeks following the baseball game, Annabelle devoted all of her spare time to assisting the farming families. So many of them had endeared themselves to her and found a special place in her heart. Most of all, she'd come to love the time she spent with the children.

The Cooper family had a little girl with a soft voice and a favorite doll that she took everywhere with her. When Annabelle had first brought water to them, Emily had tugged on her skirt to get her attention. Annabelle looked down to find a blond-haired girl of about three or four standing at her feet.

"Are you an angel?" Emily asked.

"No, I'm not. But I am doing what I feel God would like me to do." She set down the pail and squatted in front of the child. "My name is Annabelle Lawson. What's yours?"

"Emily Cooper." The girl stuck her thumb in her mouth and clutched her doll to her chest.

Her hair had been fashioned in two braids that draped across her shoulders, with flyaway strands framing her face and wispy bangs nearly hiding her dark blue eyes. Annabelle couldn't remember a more adorable child.

"And does your dolly have a name?"

Emily pulled her thumb from her mouth, glanced down at the doll, and offered a tentative smile. "Her name is Lizzie. And she's my best friend."

"It's important to have a best friend." Annabelle nodded. "You know she'll always be there with you. Make sure you're extra special nice to her, and if things get scary or hard, you can talk to Lizzie."

"Mama says that, too." She peered up at Annabelle with a curious expression. "Are you a mama?"

Such innocence. It tugged at Annabelle's heart. "No, Emily. Not yet. But I will be someday, I hope. And when I am, I pray I have a little girl just like you." She flipped one of Emily's braids and touched her cheek.

"You'll be a good mama. I know. 'Cause bad mamas don't talk to girls like me. They're mean."

Unbidden tears formed in Annabelle's eyes. "Why, thank you for that, Emily. It was very sweet of you to say. And it means a lot to me."

"You're welcome." Emily reached out one arm and gave Annabelle a quick hug, crushing her doll between them. Then she pulled back. "I have to go now. Thank you for the water."

The little girl scampered off to play with some other children. Many more encounters had been similar to that one. Each one imprinted itself on Annabelle's memory and brought a smile each time she recalled it. From the rambunctious and mischievous Pennington boys who had unruly hair and a smattering of freckles across their faces, to the shy or hesitant kids who took a little bit to warm up to strangers—each one made her work that much more enjoyable.

She'd even started volunteering to watch the children under eight years old two days each week while their families and older siblings worked the fields. Thanks to the other women and some of the older children who came to visit, they had plenty of games for the children to play and books to read. Plus, one day a crate arrived full of slates, paper, chalk, and pencils.

They spent their days playing hopscotch, quoits, marbles, bilboquette, and pick-up sticks, or having fun with wooden building blocks. Some days they had races with rolling hoops and sticks to see who could get to the finish line first. When they weren't playing or reading, they sang songs and Annabelle kept watch while some of the children napped. It was such a rewarding time. Anything Annabelle could do to help keep their minds off the bleakness of their day-to-day lives, she'd do.

One afternoon Annabelle arrived and started to head for the main warehouse where the children stayed. But she heard her name being called and turned toward the voice.

"Miss Annabelle, come quick!" It was Mrs. Cooper, Emily's mother. The woman had worry written across her entire face, and she had obviously run all the way there.

"What's wrong, Mrs. Cooper?"

"It's Jacob Berringer," she said, trying to catch her breath. "He's been missing for over an hour. We can't find him anywhere."

Oh no! Not Jacob. William and his parents would be beside themselves. They no doubt already were.

"Well, what are we waiting for?" Annabelle hiked up her skirts, ready to run. "Let's go find him."

In no time at all, they gathered with the spontaneous search party that had been formed. Annabelle did a quick search of the faces, some familiar to her and some not. She caught sight of William and offered a smile with as much encouragement as she could. The elder Mr. Berringer stood next to him with his arm around his wife, who wrung her hands on the apron covering her simple working dress.

Annabelle hadn't officially met them, but there was no denying their identity.

"All right. Now that we've all gathered, let's split up to cover more ground."

Mr. Pennington eyed the assemblage. "I suggest at least pairs, if not three or four to a group. But spread out and fan out from your assigned areas. We don't want to miss anything."

Mr. Pennington began making assignments. Annabelle waited to hear who would become her partner. Then all of a sudden William was standing next to her. She almost jumped when he touched her arm and spoke.

"Would you like to join my parents and me?" He made a loose gesture toward the others gathered. "I'm not sure how well you know the other workers, but we could use a fourth in our group."

Annabelle almost said she knew most of the ones who had come to help by name. If he wanted her to accompany them, though, she wouldn't turn him down. She didn't want to do or say anything that might make him change his mind. Perhaps it would give her a chance to get to know his parents better.

She smiled. "I'd like that very much."

He paused, and his expression took on a soft yet odd appearance. "Good. Follow me."

With a hand at her back—a gesture she'd never have imagined might come from him at a time like this—William led her around behind the others and brought her to stand in front of his parents.

"Father, Mother, I'd like to introduce you to Miss Annabelle Lawson. As you know, she dispenses water to the workers or stands at the food line on the days the hot meals are provided." He looked at Annabelle again with that softness in his eyes. "Miss Lawson, these are my parents, Daniel and Lucille Berringer."

Not a hint of superficial propriety existed in his tone. In fact, he seemed almost proud to introduce her. She wasn't sure if she should curtsy or simply incline her head. Mr. Berringer saved her the trouble though by extending his hand toward her.

"It's a pleasure to meet you, Miss Lawson. Jacob's spoken highly of you."

"Yes," added Mrs. Berringer. "Thank you so much for coming and offering your assistance to help find him."

"It's my pleasure, I assure you. Your son has become quite special to me. I'll do whatever I can to help."

Mr. Berringer flashed a quick glance and grin at William, who in turn looked at her then immediately back at his father with wide eyes and an almost imperceptible shake of his head. It took a moment for the silent communication to make sense. When realization dawned, heat rushed to her cheeks. She *had* meant the younger son, right?

"Very good," Mr. Berringer continued as if nothing was amiss. He looked over his shoulder to an area behind him. "We've already covered our plot, so we've been assigned the one adjoining ours. It starts here and goes to the northern edge of the property. Then it covers about seventy yards each to the east and the west."

"If each one of us takes a quadrant," William suggested, "we'll cover more area simultaneously."

"Yes, you're right, son. Let's do that." Mr. Berringer turned to his wife. "Lucille, why don't you take the east, and Miss Lawson, you can take the west. I'll cover the quadrant here to the south, and William, you take the part to the edge of our plot."

With their assignments made, each of them split in the four cardinal directions. Annabelle took each step carefully and looked up and down the many rows of vegetables. The others in the search party fanned out all around her. Some called Jacob's name, while others simply made their way through the various plots.

What had once been nothing more than an extensive, bare piece of land now thrived with rows and rows of fresh, green plants as far as the eye could see. From green beans and tomatoes to squash and the prime crop of potatoes, the workers had done a fine job of turning this property into a productive part of Mayor Pingree's potato patches.

It had been nearly three months since the first seeds were planted. Already the vines and roots showed signs of a substantial crop once everything could be harvested. If this land resembled the other plots throughout the city, it looked like the mayor's idea would be a grand success.

Annabelle stepped with caution across one row after another. She tried to stay within the cleared area surrounding the plants as much as possible. Could Jacob really be out here in the middle of the fields somewhere? If so, where would he be? She sent a silent prayer heavenward for God's angels to protect the young lad, wherever he was.

More than that, she prayed he hadn't been harmed in any way or somehow gotten lost. Detroit was a rather large city. Folks with less than honorable intentions existed everywhere. Oh, how she prayed something like that hadn't happened.

"Father," she said aloud. "Please guide our steps as we search for Jacob. You know where he is, Lord. I'm sure You have him under Your watchful eye. A lot of people here care about him and want to see him safe again with his family. I ask that You show us the way to find him so his parents can once again have their little boy safe and sound. In Your name, amen."

As soon as she finished, she crossed into yet another row of vegetables. This time staked tomato plants came up almost to her waist. Small green balls had formed on some of the vines. She was amazed to see the growth in such substantial amounts.

About halfway down the row, something caught her eye. From where she stood, it looked like an empty seed sack, but she couldn't tell. Pivoting on her heel, she almost lost her balance and tumbled onto a few plants. After she righted herself, Annabelle took careful steps toward the object in question.

"Oh my!"

She covered her mouth with her hand. Then she giggled as she looked down upon the angelic sleeping form of Jacob Berringer. Curled up near one of the tomato plants and using a seed sack for a pillow, he rested his head on his arm and appeared to be lost in dreamland. He looked so peaceful that she didn't want to disturb him. But his parents and brother were worried. She had no choice.

Annabelle knelt beside the boy and placed a hand on his shoulder.

"Jacob," she called in a soft voice. "Jacob. Wake up."

He mumbled and curled his legs tighter against his body, bunching up the seed sack under his head.

"Jacob," she said again, only louder.

This time he smacked his lips together as his eyelids fluttered several times. Annabelle put pressure on his shoulder again. After a few seconds, his eyes opened, and he squinted under the bright sun. She shifted so her shadow would cover him. When he was able to focus, he gave her a sleepy grin.

"Hi, Miss Annabelle. Where did you come from?"

Poor thing. He didn't even seem to be aware he'd fallen asleep in the middle of the field.

"Hello there, Jacob. I was walking up and down these rows of vegetables, and I found you asleep in the middle of them."

Jacob sat up with a start and looked around. He reached up and ran a hand through his hair, making the sleep-rumpled locks even more of a mess.

"You mean I've been sleeping here?"

The incredulous look he gave her elicited another giggle. "Yes, and you've caused a lot of people to be out looking for you. Come on." She reached out her hands and took hold of his as she stood, pulling him up with her. "Let's get you back to your parents so they can call off the search. They'll be happy to know you're all right."

He dragged his feet a bit as he followed, and his head remained downcast. "I'm sorry, Miss Annabelle," he mumbled. "I didn't mean to scare anyone."

Annabelle tousled his hair and draped an arm around his shoulders. "It's all right, Jacob. Everything will be fine when they see you're safe and sound again. You'll see."

Everything *was* all right. Just as Annabelle had predicted. Mr. and Mrs. Berringer threw their arms around their youngest son, showering him with affection and words of reassurance. William also showed his happiness to see his brother back with a mock punch to his cheek. Several of the volunteers from the search party heard the commotion and came to investigate.

"It's all right. We've found him," Mr. Berringer announced. "Spread the word. And thank you so much for your help."

In no time at all, everyone dispersed and went back to their duties. Annabelle watched the tender family reunion and felt like an outsider. She slowly took a few steps backward. It would be best if she just slipped away unnoticed and returned to the other children.

Mrs. Berringer looked up before she could escape.

"Oh, Miss Lawson. We were just about to partake of our noonday meal when we noticed Jacob was missing. We'd like to invite you to join us." She paused and looked to her husband, who nodded. "That is, if you don't have somewhere else you need to be."

"We also want to thank you for taking time to find our boy," Mr. Berringer added.

Annabelle looked at Jacob's parents; then she glanced at William. His face showed a spark of interest and perhaps even eagerness, but he didn't say anything. Well, she couldn't count on him for help in deciding. So she shifted her focus to Jacob. His wide smile and the way he nodded his head up and down in rapid succession gave her more than enough reason to stay. Now why couldn't William be that transparent?

"Very well," she finally said. "I accept your generous offer."

"Splendid." Mr. Berringer roped Jacob with his arm and pulled his son close as he wrapped his other arm around his wife and led the way toward a makeshift encampment. It was simple yet functional.

William hung back and allowed her to precede him as they followed his family, his hand again barely touching the small of her back. She couldn't tell if he was just being a gentleman or if it meant something more. Mrs. Berringer immediately set about stirring the stew that had been set back away from the fire. It smelled delicious, and Annabelle's stomach rumbled in response.

Jacob laughed. "I guess you're hungry, too, huh, Miss Annabelle?"

She placed her hand over her abdomen as her cheeks warmed. "Yes, Jacob. It appears I am."

"Well, don't worry," Mrs. Berringer said without looking up. "We will have hot stew in a matter of moments. It's not as nice as the meals you and the other ladies provide, but—"

"I'm sure it will be delicious," Annabelle rushed to assure her.

A few horse blankets had been spread out on the ground to cover the dirt. Jacob tugged on her sleeve for her to sit next to him, so she obliged. William lowered himself on her other side, taking pains to maintain a respectful distance. His actions seemed so contradictory, and his silence didn't help, either.

Once the bowls were filled and passed around, Mr. Berringer bowed his head, and his family followed suit. Just before she closed her eyes, she glanced at William, whose eyes remained open.

He was in so much pain and so confused. She wished she could come up with the answers that would ease his troubled mind and set him back on the course toward faith once more. It wasn't up to her, though. She could only be a friend and continue to share God's love any way she knew how.

Once the simple prayer ended, the family all dug into their late lunch. Annabelle raised her spoon to her lips for her first taste. Amazed to find chunks of meat mixed with vegetables amid a seasoned, thick, gravylike base, she swallowed it all and eagerly dipped her spoon for another bite.

"We are so blessed to have such generous families working alongside us each day," Mrs. Berringer said between bites.

Mr. Berringer set his spoon in his bowl and looked up. "Whenever extras of anything are discovered, most of the families share from their abundance. One of the older sons works for a meat shop in the city and managed to secure a donation from the shop owner," he went on to explain. "Thanks to that, we've been able to make a meal from the portion given to us on more than one occasion."

"It's not much," Mrs. Berringer continued, "but it fills our stomachs and gives us strength to keep working."

"Stew is my favorite." Jacob spoke with his mouth full and received a silent reprimand from his mother. He swallowed and gave everyone a sheepish grin. "Sorry."

"It's delicious," Annabelle said, taking another generous bite to prove her declaration. "I haven't tasted stew this good since I don't remember when."

The compliment made William's mother brighten and sit up straighter. "If nothing else, being without has caused us to rethink our priorities and determine what is truly important in life." She sighed. "I'm afraid we once placed money and prestige above the blessings our heavenly Father had provided. But now. . ." She let her voice trail off as she ate another spoonful of stew.

"We're not saying we didn't appreciate what God had given us," Mr. Berringer rushed to add. "We're just saying our current situation has given us a fresh outlook on life. I'm confident we'll again establish ourselves, but for now I'm thankful we have work to do and a place to live." A frown formed on his lips, and his eyes filled with sorrow. "I'm afraid others didn't fare as well."

Annabelle was impressed with their positive attitudes, despite all they'd lost. For the first time, she had a glimpse of what life had been like for William prior to the panic last year. Although he seemed to have turned his back right now on the faith that he'd been taught or even believed, at least he still had his family to support him.

"I know exactly what you mean," she said. "Seeing so many in need has given me new insight into how I can follow the commandment to love my neighbors as myself." She wiped her mouth. "I dearly love what I'm able to do and the wonderful people I've met as a result."

Mrs. Berringer's eyes sparkled with a sheen of moisture. "It's thanks to your willing service that we have the strength to push through the tough times no matter what."

Annabelle didn't know how to respond, so she smiled softly and nodded. The Berringers had quite a legacy built around them. Despite their recent loss, they maintained their faith and continued to be a light amid the dark circumstances surrounding the city. They had many reasons to be proud of the paths they now chose. If only William could see the benefit in continuing to trust God, even through the storms.

She looked at him for a moment only to see he kept his head down and focused on his bowl. He hadn't participated at all, but at least he hadn't gotten up or walked away. Annabelle prayed he listened to what his parents had said. Perhaps their words could serve as water to the seeds she'd planted a few weeks ago. The foundation was there in his life. She could see that. He just needed time.

God had brought them into her life and her into theirs. Nothing happened without a purpose. Annabelle looked forward to seeing how it all played out.

Chapter 9

"Where are we headed first?"

William walked alongside his father on a Sunday afternoon a week later as they ventured into some of the more affluent areas of the city. Even though they both had taken great care with their grooming that morning and wore some of their better Sunday clothing, he still felt shabby and insignificant. It didn't matter that they might look the part. Inside he didn't feel it.

His father looked down at a piece of paper where he'd scribbled some names and addresses. "We'll pay a visit to Amos Shepherd."

"Are you sure these men won't mind us barging in like this? I mean, we didn't exactly notify them in advance that we'd be coming. There was a time when we'd leave a calling card first."

Father sighed. "Yes, I know. However, we don't have the luxury of planning ahead like we once did. We have no other choice but to seize the opportunities as they arise. And that means today."

William wasn't quite sure he could grab hold of the same determination or zeal his father had managed to find, but he'd do his best. It couldn't be easy for a man like Father to resort to this. They were asking for special favors, plain and simple. A dozen scenarios played out in his head about how they'd be received by those who had once openly welcomed them into their homes. He only hoped the worst of them wouldn't come true today.

Walking up the six steps to the front door of the Shepherd home, William noted that the windowpanes lacked their former decor. It appeared as if Amos and his family might have been affected as well.

A moment or two after Father knocked, the latch clicked and the door swung open.

"Good afternoon," the butler said in a formal tone, eyeing them both from head to toe with disdain in his eyes. "How may I help you?"

They still were able to afford their butler? Perhaps they weren't as affected as William had thought.

"We are here to see Mr. Shepherd," Father replied. "You may tell him that Daniel and William Berringer have come to call."

A barely perceptible nod on an almost emotionless face was the only sign that the man had even heard them. He stepped back to allow them entrance.

"You may wait in the sitting room," the man instructed as he closed the door behind them. "I shall inform Mr. Shepherd immediately."

William and his father made their way into the front room and took a seat in opposite chairs facing the windows. They had a clear view of the doorway so they'd know when Amos appeared. Two minutes later, the sound of shoes clicking on the hardwood floor in the entry preceded Mr. Shepherd's arrival.

"Daniel!" Amos stepped into the room, aided by a polished beech wood cane with a brass handle. His slicked back, silver-lined hair and tailored suit made him appear every bit the dapper gentleman. "I must admit, your presence this afternoon is quite a surprise."

William didn't like the forced jovial sound to the man's voice, nor the reserved smile that didn't quite reach his eyes. Nevertheless, he and his father stood to shake hands with Shepherd as etiquette demanded.

"Yes, my friend. And I apologize for arriving unannounced."

Shepherd dismissed Father's comment with a wave of his hand. "Nonsense. You are always welcome in my home." He hooked his thumbs on the pockets of his vest and rocked back on his heels. "So tell me. What brings you here today?"

William took a tiny step back to allow his father to control the conversation. He was only there for moral support and to plead his own case if it became necessary.

"Well," his father began, "this isn't the easiest thing for me to do."

Shepherd moved toward a wingback chair. "Please," he invited, "sit down, and start from the beginning."

After they sat, Amos perched on the edge of his chair, one leg extended out in front of him while the other remained bent at a perpendicular angle.

Father cleared his throat. "I'm sure you're well aware of the effect the crisis had on my family."

"Yes, and I'm sorry I haven't been in touch lately to extend my condolences. So many of our previous acquaintances have lost so much."

"We've made out better than some. That much is certain." Father took a deep breath. "We're here today to ask if there is anything at all with which you're aware for either myself or William to do in order to get back on our feet. You're well acquainted with our work habits and our ingenuity. We're not afraid of starting small to begin, either."

Shepherd started to respond, but Father continued.

"I know you might not have anything yourself. But if you know of someone who does, we'd be appreciative of your direction or even a good word on our behalf."

William watched Shepherd with a wary eye. Something about the man's demeanor didn't sit right. He went through all the motions of appearing to consider

Father's request, but his actions and his facial expression didn't seem to line up.

"Daniel, you know me as well as anyone. If I had any resources at all at my disposal, I'd be the first in line to open any doors I could for those who needed it."

Here it comes. William tried not to roll his eyes at the predictable response from someone who didn't want to exert any effort toward helping someone who had fallen on hard times as his father had.

"However, although we fared measurably better than others, the current economic situation has not looked favorably upon us, either. We are barely managing to make ends meet. Two of my associates and I are working long hours at the bank in an attempt to find anything extra from which we can pull to help ease the city's burden." He sighed. "Most simply aren't able to afford additional help at this point."

The words were delivered with just the right measure of regret and sympathy, but William still wasn't convinced of the man's sincerity. Call it a hunch. He just didn't believe him.

"I understand," Father said with a note of obvious resignation. "We weren't certain what the result would be of our efforts today. If there is anything out there, we're going to find it, though."

Shepherd leaned on his cane and rose. Father and William did the same.

"I do appreciate you taking time out of your day off to see us." Father extended his hand, which Shepherd took.

"Of course. It was my pleasure."

"And if you do hear of anything, or if circumstances change in any way, be sure to come find us at the Lawson plot to the north."

The man rested both hands on the handle of his cane and nodded. "Of course. Of course. You know I will."

Father took a step toward the front door. "We'll see ourselves out."

"It was good seeing you again, Daniel. Give my best to your wife and young son."

William followed behind his father and gave Shepherd a polite dip of his head in farewell. "Thank you, sir."

"William," he returned.

Once they closed the door behind them and descended the steps, William had to bite his tongue to keep from speaking aloud his thoughts regarding Shepherd. From the moment the man had entered the room, William knew what the end result would be. He and his father were begging. There was no other way to put it. Accepting assistance freely offered was one thing. Seeking it out in this manner was quite another. It went against everything inside him. Still, his father needed his support. He'd give it no matter what.

"All right," his father said with a bravado William was sure he didn't feel, "that didn't turn up any possibilities. Let's move to the next one on our list."

It pained him to see his father reduced to this. What else could they do, though? Fighting back was the only solution. If they accepted their fate and did nothing about it, they'd be right where they were for years to come.

"Whom do you have written down for our second visit?" William nodded his head toward the paper his father held.

Father consulted the list of names. "Samuel Jacobson." He looked down the street from where they stood. "That's only two blocks away."

"Let's get moving, then. We don't have all afternoon." William gave his father a grin he hoped would be an encouragement. "The sooner we make it through that list of names, the sooner we can return to Mother and Jacob, perhaps even with some good news."

"You're absolutely right, my boy." Father clapped him on his back with a solid thump. "Time's a wasting."

Fifteen minutes later, they were back on the sidewalk again. That visit hadn't gone much better than the first. Jacobson didn't even invite them past the foyer. He at least waited to hear what they had come to ask before hastily interrupting to tell them he had no answers for them. Based on how eager he seemed to see them leave, William could tell those doors wouldn't be open for them anytime soon.

So they crossed off that name and moved to the one in the third spot. That meeting lasted less than three minutes, and this time they weren't even invited into the house.

After three hours and eleven different stops, they still had no offers extended and no opportunities available. With each door that closed behind them or in their faces, William watched the position of his father's shoulders fall lower and lower. A man who had started out the day with a spring in his step and expectation in his eyes now stood next to him with the light dimmed and his feet dragging. Hopelessness had definitely begun to seep into his demeanor.

Placing a comforting arm around the man who had been a rock for as long as he could remember, William forced as much encouragement into his voice as he could muster.

"Well, we seem to be striking out today, that's for sure." He chuckled, but it sounded hollow. "We're not giving up, though, right? I mean, since when have the Berringer men taken defeat lightly?"

His father offered a grin that came out looking more like a grimace. "Never," he said without conviction or emotion.

"Right." William thumped his fist into his palm. "So we won't start now." He searched his memory for some of the inspiring advice his father had given him growing up. "You've always said that God is watching out for us. That He has our best interests at heart."

Father nodded. "I have at that."

"So that means there's still a chance out there somewhere that something will break in our favor. Just because we didn't have success from one afternoon, that doesn't mean we're down for the count. We'll just reorganize, rethink our plan, and start again next weekend."

It broke William's heart to see his father in such a state. What had he honestly expected from today, though? Surely he didn't think they'd solve their entire financial future with just a few visits to the homes of previous business associates. It couldn't be easy, though, calling on the men once considered trusted confidants, only to have them turn their backs on sincere pleas for help. He just hoped his words didn't sound as false to his father as they did to his own ears.

A long sigh escaped from Father's lips before he looked at William. "Thank you, son. It means a lot to me to have your support. I might not be the best company right now, but having you here beside me makes all the difference. If you hadn't come along, I might have given up after the first few stops."

William wished he deserved the praise his father bestowed upon him. He felt like such a hypocrite, spouting off words he himself was only recently coming to believe so that he could offer what reassurance he could to a man who needed to hear them. Perhaps William needed to hear them, too.

"Why don't we call it a day and head back to the farm plot?"

"I think that's an excellent idea," William agreed. "Maybe tomorrow we'll have another idea." At least he hoped so.

&

"Am I doing it right, Willie?"

Jacob stood at the edge of the pond at the far end of the farming land, holding a fishing pole so tightly that his knuckles had turned white.

William had to laugh. "Yes, you are, Jacob, but remember to loosen your grip on the pole. If a fish bites, you'll be too tense to reel it in properly."

"Oh," was all his brother said. He did adjust his stance and his clasp, though.

About twenty feet away, William had his own line cast into the murky waters. If they had any luck today, maybe they could cook up some fresh fish for dinner.

"Have you caught anything yet?"

William started at the sound of Annabelle's voice and jerked his head to see her approach from behind him. With her hair pinned atop her head and her clothes pressed free of wrinkles, she looked the very picture of elegance. Still, he couldn't deny the breath of fresh air she brought to an otherwise wearisome day.

"Not yet, no," he answered her. "Between the two of us, though, we're hoping for something."

"I hope you don't mind my coming. Your mother told me I could find you here."

He shrugged. "Not at all. Did you have something on your mind?"

"Not particularly, but after speaking with your mother for a few minutes, I learned about the visits you and your father paid to some old friends yesterday."

Friends? If you could call them that. From the way they treated his father, he'd be more likely to call them enemies or adversaries. "Yes, we were looking to see if things had improved yet in the various financial markets. I thought it might be too soon, but Father wanted to try anyway."

"You never know with things like money. From all appearances, the situation might appear bleak, but there could be a tiny crack that leads to something more." She stepped into the peripheral line of his vision. "You just have to find the crack."

"We didn't have much luck at that yesterday. And I have a feeling it took quite a toll on my father."

The words were out of his mouth before he realized it. Why was he admitting something like that to Annabelle? She didn't need to hear about their failures. It wasn't as if she could do anything anyway.

"How so?"

Now he'd done it. He'd opened the door, and she'd stepped right in. In truth, what could it hurt?

"When you try again and again for something only to have the door slammed in your face, it gets to you after a while."

She nodded. "I can understand that. He isn't giving up, though, is he?"

William cast a quick glance at her to see concern etched across her delicate features. He warmed at the thought that she cared enough to ask.

"No, but I've never seen him so dejected. He's always been the strength of our family, and yesterday I watched each refusal weaken his resolve."

"Still, the fact that he even took the chance of doing what he did speaks of great inner strength. If the results were as bad as they seem from what you've said, it's bound to take its toll on anyone. I admire you both for even trying."

He reeled in his line, adjusted the lure, and recast. "I told my father that the Berringer men don't give up easily. He agreed that we just have to try again."

"And you're absolutely right. One day doesn't represent the full extent of opportunities. You'll find the right door soon enough. I'm sure of it."

"Yes, but how soon?" A tinge of anger found its way into his voice. "We paid a visit to almost a dozen different people who were supposed to be friends of my father. Not a single one offered any hope whatsoever." He'd been a comfort to his father yesterday. Today, though, he wasn't in the mood to pretend. "What makes you think any future attempts will yield different results?"

"Because I know God rewards the diligent," she said simply.

"Then why are we stuck here working as farmers when we spent years being industrious and conscientious enough for three families? Why are we being forced to pay the price for others' mistakes and lapses in judgment? How did we get selected to be among those who have to bear the brunt of the financial depression instead of the ones who are responsible for the economic downfall?"

Shock appeared on Annabelle's face at his rant, and her mouth fell open slightly. He almost rushed to apologize, to erase that hint of hurt on her face and bring back a smile, but he didn't have it in him.

"I—" She swallowed twice as she seemed to struggle finding the words to say.

"Look, Miss Lawson," he began, softening his words. "I appreciate your attempts to infuse a measure of hope into an otherwise hopeless situation. The fact of the matter is that you truly don't have any answers. So let's forget about trying to paint a rosy picture, all right?" He groaned and looked away from her.

That hadn't come out as he'd wanted it to. Discouraging her completely was not what he had in mind. He enjoyed her company too much to dismiss her or risk losing her interest. She'd managed to temper his anger more than once and helped him see he wasn't alone in this. He tried again.

"I do appreciate your concern, but if you don't mind, I think I just need some time alone."

William still didn't like how selfish he sounded. Maybe Annabelle wouldn't take any of this personally.

"Very well, Mr. Berringer." She interlocked her fingers in front of her for a moment. "I'll leave you to your solitude. . .for now."

He looked at her.

"Don't expect it to last forever, though. In the meantime, I'll be praying you either find a solution or a way to make peace with the way things are." She turned on her heel and called over her shoulder. "I hope you catch something. You or Jacob."

William watched her leave. Good thing Jacob seemed to be preoccupied with his own pole and fishing, or he might have gotten upset that William had sent Annabelle away like that. He silently rebuked himself for not asking her to stay and for his attitude. Something about her caused him to act far from his norm. He could generally keep his emotions under control. With Annabelle, though, and the more time they spent together, staying in control became harder and harder. Had she stayed any longer, he might have said something he'd regret or even done something impulsive like asked her to take a walk with him.

Now where had that come from? One moment he was upset about the results of yesterday's visits, and the next he was thinking about taking afternoon strolls with her. Annabelle affected him like no other young woman had. She was gone, though, and he could again get back to the matter at hand—catching something for dinner. There was time later to dwell on his feelings for Miss Lawson, whatever they were.

Chapter 10

Come in, Annabelle. Come in," her father beckoned when she knocked on the open door to his study.

She stepped inside the dark interior and wrung her hands together. "I'm sorry to disturb you, Father, but there is a matter of great importance I wish to discuss with you."

He looked up from the ledger he was reading and quirked an eyebrow. "It sounds serious." Leaning back in his chair, an amused expression crossed his face. "I don't wish to cause my daughter distress, so why don't you take a seat and we'll have ourselves a little chat?"

Good. She had hoped Father would be willing to see her now instead of putting it off to a later date. From what she'd gleaned after talking with William yesterday, he and his father could use a little spark of hope in their plight.

"Now tell me what this is all about. I'll see if I can't help erase that look of concern from that beautiful face."

Perched on the edge of the padded leather chair opposite her father's mahogany desk, the two options for presenting her request came to mind. Licking her lips, she chose straightforward and direct.

"Father, you know I've been volunteering a good portion of my time at the land you donated for the workers to farm."

He nodded. "Yes. Go on."

"I love everything I do there. The families I've met, the children I've supervised. It's been an incredible blessing to have the chance to get involved in their lives in such an intimate manner."

Her father pressed his lips together for a second or two and regarded her. "Something tells me there is an exception coming. Perhaps involving one particular family or something else for the children, such as more slates?"

She should have known he would ascertain her reason for coming before she got around to saying it. He didn't hold commanding positions in several operations by being oblivious to the needs or opportunities around him.

"Yes, there is one family I have gotten to know quite well—the Berringers. A father, mother, and two sons," she explained. "Their dedication and hard work ethic have impressed me a great deal, not to mention the sustaining faith of Mr. and Mrs. Berringer, despite all that's happened in their lives recently."

Father leaned forward and propped his elbows on the edge of his desk. "So where do I come in? How might I be of assistance?"

"Yesterday I paid them a visit and learned that the oldest son, William, and his father had spent a substantial amount of time Sunday afternoon visiting old associates and friends from before the financial devastation."

"Hmm. I would hazard a guess that they didn't exactly get the reception they'd hoped for."

She sighed. That was putting it mildly. She wasn't there, but she could tell from William's face and tone that it hadn't gone well at all. "No. In fact, they had no success whatsoever. They were only making inquiries to see if any opportunities existed anywhere for them to get their feet back in the door. Only they returned empty-handed."

"Times are tough for everyone, Annabelle. I know you're aware of this." He steepled his fingers. "Still, that's no reason for previous friends to turn their backs on someone simply because a family has fallen on hard times."

"That's exactly what I thought." Annabelle was grateful her father seemed to be seeing things the same way. "That's also why I've come. To see if you might be able to help in some way." Before he could respond, she rushed on. "I know you can't guarantee anything, but if you could just make a few inquiries of your own and test the waters, it could be a start."

"Do you know anything specific about this family? Perhaps what the father or son were doing before last year?"

Thinking back to the conversations she'd had with William, she tried to recall if he'd mentioned any specifics.

"I believe they were connected to the railroads at the investment level and in manufacturing, but I'm not sure."

"And you say their last name is Berringer?"

"Yes. Daniel Berringer is the father."

Father nodded. "That will help a great deal. I'm sure I can find out exactly what he did and where he was working before."

Her breath caught, and she inhaled a sharp breath. "Does that mean you'd be willing to assist them?"

Removing his elbows from the edge, he folded his arms on the desk and splayed out his hands. "I can't make any promises, but I will promise to do my best to exhaust my contacts and uncover the potential opportunities beneath every rock I find. . .no matter how small," he added with a grin and a wink.

She grinned as well and stood. When he rose from his chair, she came around the desk and threw her arms around his neck, burying her head against his chest and inhaling the blended scents of peppermint and tobacco.

"Thank you so much, Father."

He wrapped his arms around her and returned the hug. "You're more than welcome, little one. Anything I can do for my favorite daughter."

Annabelle pulled back and looked up into his teasing eyes. She lowered her arms and planted her fists on her hips. "Well, I *am* your first. I *should* be your favorite." Lowering her voice, she added, "Let's not tell Victoria, though."

He chuckled. "I agree. That would be quite unwise."

"I'm not so little anymore, either."

A melancholic expression crossed his face. "No, you're not." He reached out and touched her cheek. "My little girl is all grown up, right before my eyes." His eyes narrowed as he looked down at her. "So how old is this oldest son in the Berringer family?"

Annabelle looked off to the left. "Umm, I believe he's twenty-three. Why?"

Father stepped away and back behind his desk, where he reached for the ledger he'd been reviewing when she'd arrived. "Mere curiosity is all."

Something about his mannerisms told Annabelle there was more to it than that. He and Mother had no doubt talked about William, but they had yet to say anything to her. Maybe they didn't mind her spending so much time with him.

"All right." She finally shrugged. "Is there any other information you need from me?"

"Not at the moment, no." He glanced down at the book in his hands. "But could you go find your mother and tell her I'd like to speak with her, please?"

She was going to ask if she could tell Mother the reason for the request, but that was none of her business. She'd simply do as Father asked.

"I'll tell her straightaway," she said as she moved toward the hallway.

"Thank you," he said without looking up.

❧

"Afternoon, Miss Annabelle." Jacob greeted her as soon as she approached the section of rows he and William were tending.

"Good afternoon. Are your parents nearby?"

William turned his head and looked up from his kneeling position beside a tomato plant. He plucked off a few tomatoes with black rotting on the bottom and removed what appeared to be wormlike creatures from the stems.

"They're about ten rows over."

Annabelle stepped closer and peered into the pail where he tossed the worms. Their green bodies blended so well with the plants, she was amazed he could even spot them.

"What are those?"

"Hornworms," William answered. "They feed on the leaves and tomatoes during the day, and they are so well camouflaged, it is hard to see them. We've also found them on some of the potatoes, peppers, and eggplant."

She wrinkled her nose and stepped back. "Do they cause a big problem?"

"They can. There usually aren't too many hanging around. If we don't catch them now, when they become adults, they turn into moths and eat the leaves."

"Here, I've got one, Miss Annabelle. Wanna see?"

She turned and came face-to-face with a fat, four-inch caterpillar that Jacob held up to her. Concealing a shriek as she stumbled backward, Annabelle slapped her hand over her heart. "Gracious, no!"

William laughed out loud and returned his attention to his task. "They're actually quite harmless to us."

"Be that as it may," she began, "I still have no desire to have any further surprise meetings with them."

"What is it you've come to speak to my parents about?"

She kept a wary eye on Jacob and cautiously approached the two of them again. There was no telling what other surprises he might have hiding nearby. She determined to keep the boy within her sight. Glancing out the corner of her eye, she turned again toward William.

"My family is going to be spending Sunday afternoon on Belle Isle. I came to ask if your family would like to join us. You'll be invited to Sunday services as well."

"Oh." He didn't make eye contact with her in any way, instead remaining focused on his task. "Yes, that's something you'll need to ask them. I'm not sure what they might have planned for that day—if anything."

She had a feeling his lackluster response had to do with the mention of church more than the idea of spending a day relaxing with a lot of other families. That was fine. He didn't have to show great enthusiasm about her invitation. But she did hope he would come.

"You said they're working ten rows away?"

"Yes. To the north." William pointed in front of him.

Annabelle rose up on the balls of her feet and peered through the plants. Mr. and Mrs. Berringer were crouched low, like William and Jacob.

"Thank you. I'll leave you two to your work and go speak with them." Gathering her skirt in her hands, she stepped sideways through the first row of plants. "Have fun."

Neither one of them responded. She didn't expect them to, either. As she headed toward Mr. and Mrs. Berringer, she couldn't resist a peek at the plants to see if she could spot any of those worms herself. It took her searching four different plants before she finally found one. William was right. Those critters were quite adept at disguising themselves. Thankfully, her volunteer work didn't involve that task. She'd never be able to handle it.

After making her way through several more rows, she came upon Mr. and Mrs. Berringer kneeling in front of the stalks and leaves much like William had been.

Mrs. Berringer looked up when Annabelle kicked a dislodged rock in her path.

"Miss Lawson, how good it is to see you today."

"Good afternoon, Mrs. Berringer. Mr. Berringer," she added with a nod at the man only a few feet farther down the row. "I just spoke with your sons, and they told me where I might find you."

Lucille shielded her eyes and peered up at her. "Was there something in particular you needed? Forgive me for not greeting you properly, but I'm afraid my hands are rather soiled," she said as she gave her hands a self-conscious swipe through her apron. "As are my clothes. I don't wish for any of that to get on you."

Annabelle waved off the excuse. "No, no. It's fine, I assure you. Don't feel the need to rise on my account. I only came to extend an invitation to you and your family for this coming Sunday."

"An invitation?" Her expression changed to one of piqued interest. "To where, might I ask?"

"My mother came to me yesterday and mentioned there would be several families gathering on Belle Isle to enjoy our day of rest. She suggested that it might be a refreshing change of pace for all of you, and I offered to come personally to tell you about it."

"Belle Isle?" Mr. Berringer spoke from beyond his wife's shoulder. "That's a popular place for many affluent families here in the city."

"The very same." Annabelle nodded. "There is a host of activities for everyone to enjoy. I know William and Jacob like to go fishing, so they could bring their poles. And there are the paths for taking leisurely strolls or areas where we'll be setting up a picnic. We're praying the weather cooperates and remains as nice as it's been lately."

Mrs. Berringer hadn't protested or refused yet, so Annabelle continued.

"We usually attend services in the morning at Memorial Chapel near Jefferson. We'd be especially honored if you would join us there first. Then we can all venture together to Belle Isle."

Mrs. Berringer looked down at her clothing with a grimace. "We still have our Sunday outfits, but we are sure to attract far more attention than I would be comfortable with, especially among those who knew us before. . ." She trailed off.

Annabelle silently scolded herself for not thinking of that. She should have known appearance would be of prime concern when mingling with others at a social event, whether it be church or a picnic.

"Nonsense," she rushed to reassure the woman. "There are many families who attend each week who are dressed exactly as you are now. Some own only two outfits. Others come dressed in finer clothing, but I can state with absolute certainty that you will not stand out in any way nor draw any unnecessary attention by your presence."

Mrs. Berringer shifted and looked over her shoulder at her husband. Annabelle couldn't see the woman's face, but by the shrug Mr. Berringer gave her, she assumed the silent conversation the two shared meant an acceptance would be forthcoming.

Lucille turned again to face Annabelle. "Miss Lawson, thank you so much for taking the time to come and invite us. We would be both pleased and honored to join you and your family this coming Sunday." A soft smile formed on her lips, and the sheen of tears appeared in her eyes. "Is there anything I might bring?"

Annabelle made a mental note to thank her mother for the foresight regarding the picnic items they'd be providing. "No, nothing. Our cook, Katie, is going to be preparing a feast that is sure to delight, so you needn't worry about the food. And there is sure to be a variety of games being played throughout the afternoon. I'm certain the other families will provide the essentials there." She smiled. "You just come with your family, and everything else will be taken care of."

"Thank you," the woman managed beyond a catch in her throat.

The look of appreciation Mrs. Berringer bestowed upon her meant more than any words could say. And the soft thanks she spoke said everything necessary.

"You are more than welcome. Mother will be pleased to hear of your acceptance. I'll hurry home to tell her the good news." Annabelle started to leave then turned and stepped forward, placing a hand on Mrs. Berringer's shoulder. "You won't regret it. I promise."

"I'm sure we won't. And thank you again. The good Lord surely has sent many angels to us this season."

Annabelle only responded with a smile before taking her leave. Funny that Mrs. Berringer should mention angels. She didn't feel like one, even if others saw her in that manner. One thing she did know, though. God truly was at work here.

Chapter 11

*R*egardless of where you are now or what has happened, God has not forgotten you."

William repeated that line from the pastor in his head over and over again on the ferry ride over to Belle Isle. When the invitation to join Annabelle's family also included a visit to church, he wanted to make his excuses not to attend. However, they were being gracious by even associating with his family. At the very least, he could be cordial.

The rhythmic dips and plunges of the ferry on the water sent his mind back to the sermon from that morning. The pastor had a way of taking his listeners to a low and contemplative state by reminding them they were but specks compared to the mighty and powerful God. Then he'd raise their hopes and faith by promising God knew each and every one of them by name.

"Are not five sparrows sold for two farthings, and not one of them is forgotten before God? But even the very hairs of your head are all numbered. Fear not therefore: ye are of more value than many sparrows."

He'd heard scripture verses such as that one for years growing up. Even Annabelle had used a similar comparison as a way to remind him that the struggles he and his family now faced were not missed by God. Yet for all the promises he'd been told and all the reassurances he'd been given, he still had trouble determining the hidden purpose underneath it all.

"Oh, Mother, Father, look!" Victoria's elated voice drew his attention to the railing where the young lady pointed. "You can see the lighthouse from here."

"Lighthouse? Where?" Jacob strained his neck to see over the rail.

Matthew came alongside and gave him a boost with his knee. "Right over there. See where Victoria is pointing?"

As if Matthew had asked the question of him and not Jacob, William's eyes followed the invisible line that extended from Victoria's finger and stopped at the impressive structure standing tall and high above the ground. He'd only been nine when the lighthouse had been built, and he'd begged Father to take him to the unveiling. Recently he'd learned there were plans for the building of a newer lighthouse made out of marble, but it seemed the actual construction was still a few years away.

A few minutes later, the ferry docked and the passengers disembarked. William waited for Annabelle's family and then his to step off before him. For some reason, he felt like remaining at the back of the assemblage. It often ended up being his position anyway. Why change things?

They all walked along the main paved road that looped around the park, opposite the typical flow of carriages. About one hundred feet into their stroll, Annabelle glanced over her shoulder and gave him a questioning look. He mustered a smile for her. It must have worked. She returned the smile and a moment later resumed her original position.

When she wasn't preaching at him, Annabelle actually had many appealing qualities. He'd never forget the squeal when Jacob held that hornworm up to her face. The interest she had shown in baseball at the game and her thoughtful gesture in getting those tickets still impressed him. Her infectious enthusiasm was contagious. Just a few minutes in her presence and William found himself relaxing or even once in a while forgetting about his problems.

That spelled danger. Her sparkling blue eyes, beautiful smile, melodic laughter, and unassuming behavior made him want to do nothing more than remain in her presence as long as possible. Every time she appeared, though, it became harder and harder to maintain his seeming disinterest.

"Mother, do you think we might picnic near Muskoday Lake today?" Annabelle tucked her hand around her mother's arm and leaned close. "We always go to Tacoma Lake, but Muskoday was just formed last year. I'd love to enjoy the island from a different perspective."

"I don't mind if your father doesn't," Mrs. Lawson replied. "Brandt, dear? Shall we alter our standing plans and try something new this afternoon?"

Mr. Lawson shrugged. "As long as the Berringers are all right with that, I have no objections."

"We are fine with wherever you would like to settle," William's father answered on behalf of his family.

With their new destination decided, they stopped and changed direction toward the east instead of the west. They'd be farther away from the lone wooden bridge and casino, but they'd have a much closer view of the lighthouse.

Annabelle fairly bounced at her request being accepted. The ruffles of her skirt swayed to the left and right as she walked and drew William's attention. She seemed so carefree and full of life. And why not? She didn't have to work a farm plot or share living space with eight other families. That brought him back to the folly of thinking about her as anything but a friend.

After all, what did he have to offer her?

William scuffed his shoe on the gravel beneath his feet and kicked a few tiny rocks out in front of him. He couldn't take her on carriage rides or invite her for an afternoon stroll through the park. Today was the closest he and Annabelle would come to what life might have been like had his family not lost everything—and they were surrounded by both of their families.

He knew she was interested, but his present station made him hesitate. It wasn't that he didn't want to pursue something with her. On the contrary, he didn't feel comfortable just yet. Being a lady, she'd never initiate anything with him. So he was right back where he'd started—wondering and chastising himself for even thinking of her in that way.

"Well, here we are!" Mrs. Lawson announced.

William had been so lost in thought that he hadn't even noticed they were close to the new lake. Three large blankets were unfolded and spread out on the ground. A minute or two later, the two large picnic baskets Mr. Lawson and William's father had been carrying were set down and opened.

Jacob stood at the edge of one of the blankets. "I want to go see the horses and the stables and take a pony ride."

How had his brother heard about the riding stables? They'd only been constructed earlier that year.

"Victoria told me about them when we were on the ferry," Jacob added as if he'd heard William's unspoken question.

"After you eat some lunch, dear," his mother stated.

"But I'm not hungry."

"Jacob." His father's tone brooked no argument, and Jacob knew it. The frown he made and the way he crossed his arms said he didn't like it, but he'd obey.

William almost laughed. There were times he forgot just how much of a boy his brother was. He worked hard on their piece of farmland and seemed so grown-up at times. Today, though, he was all boy.

As the two families shared the delicious meal of roasted chicken, coleslaw, potato salad, and almond-glazed sponge cake the Lawsons' cook had prepared, conversation flowed on a number of different topics. William knew he should try to keep up with them and offer some input, but between the sermon that morning and being here with Annabelle and her family, he couldn't. There was so much circling in his head—he needed to make sense of it all. The sooner he finished, the sooner he could excuse himself and take a walk. Maybe that would help clear his thoughts.

After tossing the final bone on his plate, he wiped his mouth and hands and stood. Everyone looked up at him, and his parents shared a joint curious expression. He'd better make this quick so they could all return to their socializing.

"Mr. and Mrs. Lawson, you must extend my compliments to your cook. The meal was quite tasty. But if you'll excuse me"—he allowed his gaze to roam over each person in turn—"I believe I'll take a walk and enjoy this fresh air."

Jacob immediately jumped up, almost upsetting his plate, and looked at his parents. "Does that mean we can go see the horses now?"

"And maybe the verandas on the outside of the casino, too?" Victoria looked to her own parents, a hopeful yet pleading look on her face.

Great. If the other adults agreed, he'd likely end up being asked to escort them. So much for his solitary walk. He really needed some time alone to sort out a few things.

"I'd be happy to go with them," Matthew offered. "That is, if Mr. and Mrs. Berringer approve."

That was something William didn't expect. He might be free of the others after all. And that meant he could still take his walk.

Both sets of parents did agree. In what seemed like seconds, plates were abandoned and the threesome headed toward the road. Maybe he should ask Annabelle if she'd like to join him. Then again, that would defeat the intention of being alone.

"I believe I'll join them all as well."

So much for that idea.

Annabelle wiped her mouth and gracefully stood. After stepping around behind her parents, she caught his eye.

He tried to read her expression, but he could only decipher a confusing mixture of disappointment and acceptance. As she walked by him to join Jacob and her brother and sister, William had second thoughts. Should he have invited her anyway? What about their parents all watching and listening? That would have started them talking for sure.

Avoiding the temptation to see if anyone still paid him any mind, he took off toward the outer loop. The rest of them had chosen Central Avenue as a more direct path to where they were headed, but he preferred to circle Lake Okonoka and walk by the pier on the south side of the island.

William had no idea how much time had passed when all of a sudden he found himself at the eastern edge of Tacoma Lake. The casino Victoria had mentioned earlier wasn't too much farther. If William kept walking, he might run into the four of them.

Instead, he found a shady spot under a big oak and settled on the grass, staring through the trees to where he could just make out the roof of the casino. Even though he hadn't been there in two years, he could still see it in his mind's eye.

The two-story Queen Anne-style building with its corner towers and covered exterior walkways was a popular meeting place for many on the island. Its gabled wood structure had even been where William's cousin had gotten married two years ago. The residents of Detroit had begged the city to turn Belle Isle into a public park emulating the tree-lined boulevards of Paris. Following in the pattern established by Frederick Olmsted, this meetinghouse for social events added just the right touch.

"Would you mind some company?"

William startled at Annabelle's hesitant voice behind his left shoulder. She sounded and appeared rather nervous. He hastened to his feet and faced her.

She held her hands clasped together with fingers hooked. "Forgive me if I interrupted your solitude. I was just walking around the perimeter of Tacoma Lake when I saw you. But I can continue on my way if you'd rather be alone."

"No, please." He almost spoke without thinking and said that was exactly what he wanted—for her to leave him in peace. One look at her face, though, and all thoughts of dismissing her flew from his mind. He extended his arm toward the space he'd unofficially claimed. "Sit."

After gathering her skirts in her hand, she settled on the ground and assumed a most ladylike perch, legs tucked underneath and to the left. He wished he had a jacket he could have laid down for her so she wouldn't have to soil her pretty blue dress. It set off her eyes perfectly. He joined her on the ground and couldn't take his eyes off her. If anyone happened by, they'd just assume the two of them were courting. For the first time since they met, William wished they were.

Silence fell between them. He wanted to say something, but his tongue was tied in knots and his brain refused to register any coherent thought beyond how pretty she looked.

"Amazing to think that a man who also designed Central Park in New York came up with the plans for Belle Isle as well. Don't you agree? Did you know this island actually belonged to Chippewa and Ottawa tribes and they named it Wahnabezee, or Swan Island, to start?"

William released a sigh. At least she managed to come up with something to start the conversation again.

"It was owned by the French and then British before American settlers finally claimed it. Then the city of Detroit bought it just fifteen years ago and named it Belle Isle."

Her voice trembled a bit. Could she be as nervous as he was right now? If so, maybe things weren't as hopeless as he'd thought. There was only one way to find out.

He cleared his throat. "Yes, and I much prefer Belle Isle to Hog Island, like the French had named it."

Annabelle covered her mouth and giggled. Turning her head to look at him, she lowered her hand and smiled, a twinkle making her blue eyes shine. "I would have to agree with you there. Naming a beautiful island such as this after a pig doesn't exactly seem like the proper choice."

The tension seemed to be broken. Laughter almost always had a way of helping.

Extending his long legs out in front of him, William leaned on his hands.

"You mentioned the designer when you first approached. Frederick Olmsted. Did you also know he resigned before any of his designs for this island were actually begun?"

Her eyes widened. "No, I didn't. What happened?"

"The city had already approved everything, so they went ahead with his plans anyway."

Annabelle looked out over the lake. He followed her gaze as she shifted it to the north where the tree-lined path offered shelter to numerous couples out enjoying the day.

"I'm glad they did," she said a moment later. "I can't imagine this island as anything other than what it is. My family has been coming here for years."

"It reminds me a lot of Mackinac Island," he said without thinking.

Her head swung toward him once more, and surprise spread across her face. "You've been to Mackinac?"

Oh no. He hadn't intended to let something like that slip. Then again, why not? She knew his family hadn't always been living the way they were now. What harm could come of sharing a little from life prior to the current state of affairs?

Shifting to lean back on his elbows, William crossed his legs at his ankles and stared straight ahead. "Yes. In fact, we used to go at least once every year near the end of the summer. Just two years ago, we were at the hotel to witness a demonstration by an agent of Edison Phonograph of their new invention."

"On the front porch? I've been there to see that, too!"

He glanced over to see her close her eyes and draw her hands up to her chin.

A sigh slipped from her lips. "It's the most beautiful hotel I've ever seen. The tulips, daffodils, and geraniums all create such vivid color."

For a fleeting moment, William wondered if they might have been on the island at the same time. Perhaps they even stayed at the hotel during the same week. No, that wasn't possible. He would have remembered someone like Annabelle.

"My parents were actually married in a gazebo on the island before the hotel was built." She opened her eyes and tilted her head toward him with a soft grin on her lips. "And it was on that island where they both realized neither of them had been honest about who they really were."

William drew his eyebrows together. "What do you mean?"

She placed her hands in her lap. The grin turned into a full-fledged smile. "Oh, it's one of my favorite stories to tell." Shifting so she faced him, she continued. "When they met, they both were pretending to be someone they weren't. Mother took a job at a candle factory to achieve some independence and assist a woman who was part of her charity work. Father assumed the position of a simple refinery worker to appease his own father before achieving a management position there."

That seemed logical enough. "So how does Mackinac Island factor into everything?"

"Well," she began, flattening her hands on her lap, "at the end of the summer the year they met, their families both traveled to the island. And unbeknownst to them, their parents had already met behind their backs to plan their meeting. Their entire pretense came to a halt the first night they were both there."

William could imagine what type of meeting it must have been. If they had been lying to each other all that time only to learn they both belonged to elite families, it must have been a miracle they ended up together. Something didn't quite make sense, though.

"If they found out they were both from upstanding families, then wouldn't they be happy?"

"Well, that's just it," Annabelle replied. "Mother thought Father was nothing more than a refinery worker, and her parents had already cautioned her against pursuing a relationship with him. And Father had a similar edict issued from his father regarding Mother. My uncle Charles had already caused a bit of a scandal with a young woman not of his class. Grandfather Lawson didn't want to see a repeat of that."

William nodded, starting to understand. "Ah, so despite their attraction, neither one of them thought they could do anything about it."

"Exactly. And when they came face-to-face on the island, dressed in formal attire, well, you can probably imagine the result."

He could imagine it, all right. Only he wasn't thinking about her parents' meeting. All he heard was the clash that resulted between two families when they believed their status in society didn't match. If even a hint of that remained with Annabelle's parents, he didn't stand a chance.

"I never have agreed with all the conflict, though," she said, interrupting the negative turn his thoughts had started to take. "I mean, if two people care about each other, where they live or who their families are shouldn't matter." She pinned him with a direct gaze. "What do you think?"

Her question caught him off guard. "I. . .uh. . .uh. . ."

For the life of him, he couldn't come up with a logical response. What *could* he say to that? Trying to break the hold her gaze had on him so he could compose himself, he found it impossible. Her eyes seemed to be saying something he didn't dare hope to assume. Could this be her way of saying she considered him more than a friend? Or was he simply imagining it?

William didn't want to read more into the situation than actually existed, yet he had to fight not to reach across and take one of her hands in his. He could throw caution to the wind and tell her he agreed. Or he could take the safer route.

"I think it should be up to the two people involved." Yes, the safe path was best. . .for now. "They should be honest with each other first and take it from there."

"Oh," she replied, her voice containing a hint of disappointment.

Had she wanted him to say more? To get more personal, perhaps? He wanted to, but would she accept what he had to say? William opened his mouth to test the waters, but another familiar voice interrupted before he could begin.

"There they are! Come on, Jacob. Hurry, Matthew."

Victoria. William sighed. He looked toward the northern side of the lake to see his brother running behind Annabelle's sister with Matthew bringing up the rear. Annabelle also shifted her attention to the trio approaching.

No sense trying to continue their conversation now. Hopping to his feet, he stood and turned to extend a hand down to Annabelle. She looked up at him and hesitated. A second later, she placed her soft hand in his and allowed him to help her to her feet. The change in position brought her just inches away from him.

As she lifted her chin, her mouth parted, drawing his eyes to the charming pink of her lips. Shoving that idea to the back of his mind, William again found her eyes and searched them for a sign—any sign at all. She didn't waver in her gaze, and that was when he saw the spark.

"Oh, Annabelle," Victoria called, interrupting the moment. "You missed seeing the geese and the swans. They were so beautiful."

The spell was broken, and Annabelle turned to face her sister, pulling her hand free from him. William took a step back and tried to get involved in the ensuing conversation. His mind refused to cooperate, though. Annabelle felt something for him. That much he knew. He just didn't know what or how much.

Still, even a little made a difference. And that helped him sort out his feelings somewhat. Maybe God had a greater plan in all this after all. Maybe his circumstances weren't as bleak as he thought. Only time would tell.

Chapter 12

Annabelle couldn't help the smile that formed on her lips. "Have you heard the news?"

William stood in front of her and held out his plate at the last station in the food line. She normally worked closer to the center. Today she hoped it would work to her advantage.

"What news?" William asked, his eyes appearing to pick up on her enthusiasm.

"About the Pullman strike."

It had been two weeks since their afternoon on Belle Isle, but her work had kept her too busy to follow up on their conversation since that day. Perhaps today would be better.

She placed a rather large slice of berry pie on his plate. It was hard to believe he wasn't aware of the outcome of the strike. Even with his limited exposure out here in the fields, he always seemed to have extensive knowledge about current events.

Two lines formed on his brow as he drew his eyebrows closer together. "No, I haven't. Has there been another development?"

Annabelle looked at the next person in line. She'd love more than anything to stand and talk with him, but other workers needed to be served. With a quick glance behind her then back at William, she made an attempt at nonverbal communication.

It took a second or two, but understanding dawned on his face, and he nodded. "Pardon me," he said to the worker waiting next to him. "I'll be out of your way in just a moment."

William stepped to the end of the table and selected a patch of dirt about five feet away. Annabelle served pie to the worker in front of her.

"Enjoy," she said with a smile as he took his plate and left.

William crossed his legs like an Indian and settled his plate on his knees. It hadn't been all that difficult to persuade him to stay and talk. He could have just taken his meal and left. Obviously she hadn't imagined his interest that afternoon on the island. As he took his first bite, she continued to serve.

"So tell me," he said after swallowing a bite of beef. "What is this splendid news you have to share about the strike?"

She glanced from the corner of her eye but maintained her focus on the workers. "Well, you know the results of the strike during this recession and how it affected transportation west of Chicago."

"Mmm-hmm," he replied as he took another bite.

"Mr. Debs and the American Railway Union have tried hard to sustain their momentum."

"Yes, and they even resorted to violence in order to achieve their goal. At least supporters did," he added.

She'd read the horrific reports of some of the tactics used. The obstruction of tracks and walking off the job was one thing, but attacking those who broke the strike and setting fire to buildings was quite another. Those who continued to work were only looking out for their own interests. They didn't deserve to be treated cruelly for that.

"I don't understand how the loss of life would help aid their cause. If anything, I'd think it would cause more complications."

"Well, sometimes people don't always think before they act." He took a long gulp of water. "Sometimes their ultimate goal makes them blind to the pain they might cause by acting on their passions."

"I wish they could somehow achieve their goals without all the violence."

"That's how we eventually end up with wars."

"This is true." Annabelle sighed. Only in a perfect world would violence cease to exist. As long as men were left to their own devices, hostility and bloodshed were sure to be the end result.

"You were going to tell me about the recent news."

"Oh my! You're absolutely right." How could she have gotten so off track?

William chuckled and speared a forkful of vegetables. "It's all right. But if you don't share this exciting report, I might be forced to seek my information elsewhere."

Annabelle turned her head to catch sight of the grin William tossed her way and the teasing gleam in his brown eyes.

"Very well." She pursed her lips. "Now, where did I leave off?" She honestly couldn't recall.

"I believe you had mentioned something about the strike workers doing what they could to maintain their momentum."

"Ah yes. Two days ago, I overheard Father and Mother talking. It seems the strike has now collapsed, and the plant has reopened."

"What about the workers who went on strike?"

"I believe Father said they're now in jail. Something about ignoring an injunction that forced them to cease their activities or risk being fired."

His eyebrows rose. "Injunction? That means the company must have managed to secure counsel on their behalf."

Leave it to William to understand the procedures and have a better grasp on the details than she. Annabelle tried hard to remember what Father had said. Perhaps she could impress him with that.

"Yes, and President Cleveland actually stepped in to send in the army and a U.S. marshal, saying something about the strike interfering with the delivery of the United States mail."

"Oh, you know, I hadn't thought about that." William rubbed his fingers over his chin. "But I can see how that would be the case." He grinned. "I mean, you can't stop the mail service. That alone should be a federal offense," he said with a wink over the rim of his cup as he took a drink.

Annabelle planted one fist on her hip. "You're teasing again, aren't you?"

He laughed. "Yes, Miss Lawson, I am. But that doesn't take anything away from the fact that you have paid excellent attention to the developments of late and provided sound information." Then he sobered and nodded toward the other side of the table.

She turned back around, pleased. Her memory hadn't failed her, and William was indeed impressed.

"Can I have two pieces?" asked the young lad in front of her. He couldn't be more than twelve or thirteen, and that meant he had a healthy appetite, too.

"Of course." Annabelle served the boy and glanced down at the thinning line. Only a few more minutes and they'd start the cleanup process. There was more than enough pie left. Maybe she'd even save a second piece for William as well.

"You know, you have just the right disposition for something like this."

His remark took her by surprise. Was that a compliment?

"What do you mean?"

"The way you respond to the workers and those who make special requests," he explained. "You return the right amount of kindness and generosity that keeps folks coming back for more."

She fought hard not to look at him or react in any significant manner. He certainly had made a sudden about-face regarding his treatment of her. If she had to pinpoint the moment it happened, she'd never succeed.

"And you're persistent, too," he added. "Especially with folks who can be a bit stubborn."

Annabelle had to strain to hear that last part. He spoke it under his breath, and from the way he ducked his chin to look at the ground, she had no doubt he was referring to himself.

"Mother would say I come by it honestly," she replied in an attempt to put him at ease. "Father would say it's all part of my charm."

"I might be inclined to agree."

She started to respond, but he didn't give her a chance.

"This pie is delicious." He held up his fork with a rather large piece of pie sitting atop it, but he didn't quite meet her eyes.

Annabelle couldn't tell if he was attempting to cover up the remark he made about her charm or if he didn't consider the remark anything out of the ordinary. She didn't have much experience with men. Today she wished she did. Being able to interpret hidden meanings might make this conversation easier.

She heard the scrape of fork on plate and looked down to see that he'd just finished the pie.

"Would you like another piece?" She pointed at the table then reached for one of the two pies remaining, holding it up for him to see. "There is plenty here. And I certainly don't intend to consume the leftovers."

William paused as his gaze traveled from her face to her feet and up again. Her cheeks warmed at his open admiration and perusal. In fact, if she didn't miss her guess, he actually approved.

"Mr. Berringer?"

Her father's voice startled her. How long had he been standing there? Not long enough to have witnessed William's bold and obvious assessment of her appearance, she prayed.

William presented the picture of calm control as he stood and set his empty plate on the table next to Annabelle then shifted his attention to Mr. Lawson.

"Yes, sir?"

"Could you tell me where your father is? I'd like to speak with him for a few moments."

"Um, I believe he and my mother are eating with Jacob over at our plot."

"Excellent. Thank you." Father nodded then turned toward her.

She held her breath, wondering what he might say and praying it wouldn't be asking her to leave her place to help Mother.

"Annabelle, you did a fine job today. I know the workers," he said with a quick glance at William, "appreciate your dedication."

Exhaling, she relaxed a little. He could have said a lot more, especially where William was concerned. Annabelle said a silent prayer of thanks that he hadn't.

As Father stepped away toward the main fields, he again gave her a pointed look. "Will you be ready to accompany me home when I return?"

Only clearing and wiping down the tables remained. "Yes, I should be."

"Very good. Then I shall make a point to stop here before leaving."

She and William both watched her father head away from them. No doubt about it. Father had observed the exchange between William and her prior to announcing his presence. He didn't have to come out and say it. She could tell. And if she didn't miss her guess, there would be a conversation about it later.

"Well, I didn't expect to see your father here. Do you know the topic of that conversation?"

Annabelle hoped it wasn't a direct result of what Father might have witnessed between William and her. On the contrary, she prayed it was because Father had found a lead or two in the business world for Mr. Berringer.

"I'm not certain," she said truthfully. "He did seem rather intent on finding your father, though."

"Miss Lawson," William began, pivoting to face her. "Do allow me to apologize for anything I might have said or done that could be improper."

He obviously had seen the same thing she had from her father. Why else would he be asking for her forgiveness? *Had* he done anything wrong? She didn't think so.

"There is no need for a confession or defense of your actions, Mr. Berringer," she said softly. "But if it helps ease your mind, your apology is accepted."

"Thank you." He visibly relaxed.

Annabelle understood his trepidation. Her father could be a rather intimidating man when he wanted to be. It only endeared William to her more to see how much he respected her father and how eager he was to clear his conscience or make certain he was held in high esteem in her eyes.

"Now," he said, smacking his hands together. "How can I help?"

ها

The soft murmur of voices traveled into the front hallway as Annabelle made her way toward the sitting room. Just as she'd predicted, Father wanted to speak with her. During the carriage ride home from the potato patches, he'd asked her to join him for a meeting before dinner. He made it clear Mother would be present as well.

Whatever they had to say, she prayed it wouldn't be something she didn't want to hear. But first she had to face her parents. There were a lot of possibilities, and only one way to find out.

Before she stepped into view, she took a deep breath and willed her heart to settle down to a more even pace.

"Ah good," Mother announced as soon as Annabelle walked into the room. "Please, dear, come take a seat and join us."

Well, she didn't sound upset. That had to be a good sign. In fact, she actually sounded quite pleased.

Annabelle's feet sunk into the woven carpet as she headed straight for her favorite settee. By all appearances, her parents were giving her no reason to be concerned. Each of them sat in wingback chairs opposite her and presented the image of relaxation. Father leaned back in the chair and rested his hands on the arms. Mother tucked her legs underneath her with her hands folded in her lap. When neither of them said anything, Annabelle swallowed and wet her lips.

Finally, Father spoke.

"Before we get to the primary reason for asking to speak with you, your mother and I want to make it clear that we are more than pleased with the work you've done at the fields."

"Yes," Mother added. "In fact, your selfless acts of service have gone far to ensure the continual high spirits of the workers."

"Compared to reports from other plots, the productivity levels from that area of the city have even caught the attention of the mayor."

Annabelle didn't know how to respond. They made it clear that complimenting her wasn't the purpose of this conversation. She appreciated the fact that they made it a point to begin with that, though. Still, anticipating what might come next made her heart race again. If that didn't give away her nervousness, her erratic breathing would.

Father again resumed control. "Now, for the matter at hand."

A matter? Annabelle shifted her legs to cross her left ankle over her right. She slowly smoothed her hands on the folds of her skirt. It helped absorb the dampness of her palms as she awaited Father's next words.

"Annabelle, you know your mother and I only want the best for you. But before we present several opportunities to you, there is something we must know."

First there was a matter. Now they had a question about that matter. Then they had an opportunity for her? Just where were her parents heading with all this?

Father leaned forward and clasped his hands together, resting his forearms on his knees. "You came to me a few weeks ago asking that I make a few inquiries on behalf of the Berringer family. As a result, we suggested you invite them to join us for a picnic on Belle Isle."

Ah, so that invitation had been extended for more than mere socializing. They were looking to learn more about the Berringer family. Well, at least the day had been a good one—even if her parents had ulterior motives.

"But it has come to our attention that a good portion of your time is spent in the company of the eldest Berringer son."

Annabelle shouldn't be too surprised to see the focus on William. The thought *had* crossed her mind earlier near the end of lunch. She just didn't think it would be treated in such a serious manner. They hadn't done anything untoward.

"With that in mind," Father continued, "we'd appreciate your honesty in answering the following question."

She knew what was coming, but she wasn't sure she could provide an answer that would satisfy her parents.

"What are your feelings regarding William Berringer?"

Annabelle opened her mouth to speak, but no words came out. She swallowed twice and tried to gather her thoughts. Considering William more than a friend had only been a viable option as of their visit to Belle Isle. Now her parents expected her to make sense of her feelings and put them into words?

"Annabelle, dear," Mother interjected, breaking the silence. She narrowed her eyes and peered into her daughter's face. "Do you simply not know how you feel?"

Clearing her throat, Annabelle tried again. "Father, Mother, I must confess. Up until today, Mr. Berringer and I had been nothing more than friends. Other than attending the baseball game, nearly every one of our conversations has centered around his anger for what had happened to his family or where he stood in his faith."

"And now?" Father pressed.

"Now?" She wet her lips again. "Now I don't know. I admit that I'm attracted. Any more than that, I don't believe I can say for certain."

There. She might not have given them the response they sought, but she had been honest.

Several moments passed as Father and Mother exchanged silent communication with each other. Father angled his body toward Mother and raised his eyebrows. Mother nodded in response. Annabelle sat in silence, awaiting what felt like a sentencing, even if she knew that was a rather substantial exaggeration.

Finally, Father returned to his original position. "It's clear to us that you have been nothing less than honest, and for that we are grateful." His expression brightened then, and he again sat back in his seat. "Now that we have that settled, we're faced with the issue of your social activities with eligible men."

Her heart fell, and her shoulders dropped. She should have known this conversation would present itself again. And on the heels of asking her about William, it made perfect sense. Her parents wanted her to pursue other relationships.

Mother sat up straighter, eagerness replacing the previous concern. "We have been speaking with several of our friends and believe we've found several young men we'd like you to meet. Each one of them is quite poised to assume solid positions either in their father's footsteps or in a venture they've begun on their own."

She wished she could muster up a bit more excitement in response to this announcement. Although she couldn't say for certain where she and William stood, she wasn't eager to pursue a relationship or possible romantic entanglement with someone new. Nevertheless, her parents had gone to all the trouble on her behalf. As their daughter, she owed them her respect and cooperation. And that's exactly what she'd give.

"Is there anything you'd like to say in response?"

Annabelle took a deep breath. "Well, I must confess that this comes as a surprise today. I have no doubt that you do have my best interests at heart," she added with a soft smile. Best to do what she could to set them at ease. "I am, after all, eighteen."

"A fact that hasn't been lost on us, I assure you," Father said, his voice a mixture of remorse and pride.

"Be that as it may, I'm well aware that my friends are all married or engaged or headed in that direction. I'm just grateful you were more patient than other parents regarding any arrangements."

"We're well aware of what can come of wanting to force certain outcomes," Mother replied. "As you know, your father and I endured that very thing not long ago. We agreed that we didn't want to do the same to you."

"I appreciate that, Mother. But I suppose it's time for me to take the matter of my relationships a bit more seriously." She looked at them both before continuing. "You've both given me so much. How could I not honor your wishes?"

Maybe with this shift in her priorities, she could continue to explore possibilities with William as well.

"However," Father stated, "where Mr. Berringer is concerned, we must caution you."

What? Just when she thought her parents were providing the perfect opportunity for her to answer all the questions floating in her mind regarding William, Father throws this into the mix?

"But, Father, it isn't like that at all." She unclasped her hands and extended them in a placating gesture. "I already said he is only a friend." At the moment that much was true in reality. Her thoughts, however, were another matter. "Are you saying that I can no longer spend any time with him or his family?"

Father pressed his lips into a thin line. "What I'm saying is that prolonged interactions with him on a social level might prevent you from seeing certain possibilities with the other gentlemen you meet. I've done what I can in regard to possible job opportunities for both him and his father. Anything further is up to them."

He hadn't set William apart from the class of a gentleman. That had to be something.

"But how will I avoid spending time with him when his family works at the very area where I volunteer all my time?"

Annabelle knew very well what the answer might be. She prayed the actual one would be different.

Father hesitated, and she could tell what he was about to say wasn't easy for him. "Then I suppose we have no choice but to limit the time you spend volunteering." Father inhaled and released his breath in a loud sigh. "For the time being, let's say only once a week."

Mother nodded and pursed her lips. "I do not see any cause to end your charity work completely, Annabelle, dear. But I agree with your father. William might be respectful and possess exceptional manners, and we know he's simply fallen on difficult times, but until he can reestablish himself, anything beyond friendship is not wise. At least not at the moment. There are more than enough young men right here who I'm sure will provide a suitable distraction."

She didn't come right out and say it, but Annabelle could read between the lines. It wasn't that William might distract her from the other men. It was his current status as a farm worker, not a member of their elite society. After what her parents endured in their own lives, she'd have thought they'd be more lenient. At least they didn't forbid any association at all with him. They were only limiting her. That left her with no choice but to abide by their wishes—no matter how much it pained her.

"Thank you, Mother. Father." She regarded them each in turn and dipped her head in acknowledgment, maintaining a polite exterior. "I admit I will miss the time I am giving up, but I promise to devote appropriate attention to the potential suitors I might meet as well."

Her parents both stood, seeming pleased with the outcome and Annabelle's promise.

"That is all we ask, dear," Mother said.

"Now let's adjourn to the dining room where I'm sure Katie has an appetizing meal ready."

Annabelle allowed her parents to precede her from the sitting room. That conversation hadn't gone as she'd have liked. It could have been much worse, though. At least she was still permitted to continue her volunteer work. Of course, once a week didn't leave opportunity for much. If anything more was to happen with William, God would have to work a miracle. She had to trust Him and leave it at that.

Chapter 13

William brushed his hands over the tops of the tomato plants as he moved from those rows into the potatoes. He might not be the best farmer, but any man would be proud to walk among the results of their months of hard work.

Movement to his right caught his attention, and he looked up to see Annabelle crossing the field toward him. He started to smile and call out to her. Then he noticed her demeanor. She didn't look anything like the same vibrant young woman he'd seen only a week ago. With slumped shoulders and head down, this Annabelle was like a completely different person.

"Good afternoon, Miss Lawson," he greeted in an attempt to ease whatever might be bothering her.

The way she dragged her feet and the fact that she had yet to make eye contact with him said a lot. What could have possibly happened to cause such a drastic change? She hadn't responded, so he tried again.

"Is something the matter?"

This got her attention. Slowly she raised her eyes to look at him. A frown marred her pretty face, and her eyes had lost all their shine.

"Mr. Berringer," she began in a hesitant voice, "I've come today to let you know that you'll only be seeing me once a week from now on."

"Once a week? Is everything all right?" He'd gotten rather used to seeing her several times a week. Knowing that would no longer be the case interrupted the sense of calm he'd begun to have where she was concerned.

"Well, to be honest, no. At least not to me."

"What happened?"

The sigh she released was full of regret. "Remember when Father came last week?"

"Yes."

How could he forget? When his own father had told him about the meeting and shared they might have found an open door or two, he'd been thrilled. That Mr. Lawson would go to all that trouble on their behalf meant a lot to him. His father had seemed impressed as well. How could anything following that meeting cause Annabelle to be so unhappy?

"Later that afternoon, just before dinner, my parents invited me into our sitting room to speak with me. And the result of that conversation was to tell me two things."

She lowered her eyes again. He had a hard time believing the ground held much fascination, so he waited and gave her time to say what she'd come to say.

"The first was to inform me they had several young men they'd like me to meet."

Oh no. Parents arranging meetings for their daughters with eligible men usually meant one thing. They were intent on finding a good match and would likely encourage a short engagement period once one was found.

"The second was to say that my volunteer time here would be limited to once a week."

At least they hadn't forbidden her entirely. They would just have to make the most of the time they did have. It didn't seem as hopeless as she made it seem. He opened his mouth to respond, but she held up a hand and raised her gaze to his. The sheen of tears took him by surprise.

She sniffed. "That means the time we spend together will likely be during the noon meal I'll be serving and nothing more."

By her reaction, he could tell she didn't like what her parents had to say. Yet, as a dutiful daughter, she could do nothing less than obey. A sense of honor like that wasn't easy to find these days.

"Did they give a reason for this abrupt change?" William had his own ideas, but he wanted to hear Annabelle say it.

"Only that spending more time with you might hinder me from seeing the merits in the other gentlemen they wish me to meet."

Well, those weren't exactly the words he assumed Mr. Lawson had used, but the meaning was the same. He might have gone the extra mile to speak with his associates and done so out of the goodness of his heart, but that didn't change how the man obviously viewed him and his father.

"I tried to reassure them they had no reason to worry about our friendship. But they were convinced that restricting my time here would benefit everyone involved."

Sure it would. William stared beyond her to the expansive fields. If they prevented her from spending time with him and limited even the time they *were* together to supervised areas, it would be quite difficult for them to share any private moments. By enforcing this edict, everything would go according to her parents' well-thought-out plan. Eliminate the possible competition—him. He had to admit, they seemed to have thought of everything. And they appeared to have noticed the attraction even before he had a chance to speak of it with Annabelle or hear her respond in kind.

"Do you not have anything to say, William?"

The sound of his first name coming from her lips shook him from his thoughts. Had she even realized what she'd said? He returned his gaze to her face, only to find a silent pleading in her eyes combined with a lone tear that slipped down her cheek. If he had any doubts about her feelings before, he didn't have any now.

"I'm afraid I don't know what to say, Miss Lawson."

He almost used her first name as well. Only if he did that, he might forget himself. Or worse, he might fool his mind into believing that something more between them already existed. He wished it did, but neither of them had spoken of it yet. No, maintaining his distance was the best option at this point.

"It's clear how your father feels about me." He sighed. If only things were different. "And to prove that I'm unsuitable, he's not only forbidden you from spending unsupervised time with me, but he's also cut back the frequency of your visits."

"He hasn't completely ruled out all my visits, though," she retorted with hope in her voice. "I'm still able to come here once a week."

"Yes." He looked down and kicked at the dirt beneath his feet. "Once a week. That seems more like a charitable allowance on their part so they can say they didn't put an end to your work entirely."

William hadn't intended to take out his frustration on Annabelle. She didn't deserve to be the recipient of the misplaced irritation directed at her father, especially when he was more upset with himself for not doing something sooner. And she didn't deserve to have what little hope she still held dashed by his doomsday frame of mind. He couldn't seem to stop himself, though.

"Miss Lawson, I believe it's best if we see the current turn of events for what it is." He risked a glance at her and forced his expression to remain unaffected—at least where her tears and pleading were concerned. "A sign from God that our friendship will have to remain just that. A friendship. Nothing more. Your parents have made sure of that."

She flinched with his final words. Her lower lip trembled, and it tore at his heart. He refused to put her in a position, though, that might require her to defy her parents. There was only one way to ensure that.

"Miss Lawson, we should both accept things the way they are and make do." Letting her down like this wasn't what he wanted to do, but it was for the best. If he didn't put an end to this now, he might rethink his decision and confess his feelings. "Now, if you'll excuse me, I have work I must do."

"But—"

William didn't give her a chance to respond. Instead, he kicked the dirt again then removed his cap and slapped it against his thigh. A part of him wanted to turn around to see if she would follow him or leave. But if he did that, he'd lose all resolve. He did have things to do, and he couldn't allow her sentiments or emotions to interfere. Otherwise he might not succeed.

One week later, Annabelle made her dutiful appearance at the potato patches to serve the noonday meal. She did her best to offer a smile to each worker. Kind words or conversation of any kind beyond a simple "You're welcome" or "Have a nice day" were out of the question. Her heart simply wasn't in it.

Last week when William had stormed off and left her standing there alone, she thought she'd crumple in a heap right then and there. She had hoped he might protest with more force or, better yet, tell her he wanted more than friendship and ask her how she felt. What he said and did, though, had caught her off guard, leaving her with no response. Instead, she'd returned home dejected and asked her mother to move forward with the introductions to her first gentleman of choice.

She might not be able to be with William, but at least she could conceal her hurt and pain behind the guise of social engagements and the pretense of getting to know the men her parents insisted on parading in front of her. If she played her role well, no one would be the wiser.

Not even the excitement of hearing the state fair would once again take place in Detroit could penetrate her self-inflicted despondency. Whenever anyone spoke of it, she remained silent, nodding where appropriate and displaying a smile she didn't feel.

She hadn't counted on facing Mrs. Berringer or Jacob again, though. It made sense. They did have to eat, after all. She just figured they might skip this week. Well, hoped anyway. It looked as if that wouldn't be the case today. Only this time, Mr. Berringer and William were notably absent. She glanced farther down the line to see if they just might have arrived late. No, they weren't there, either. Was William avoiding her? If so, why was his father gone as well?

"Afternoon, Miss Annabelle." The little boy greeted her with a smile as wide as could be.

One look at his face, complete with the customary dirt marks and unkempt hair falling in his eyes, and she nearly lost all control.

"Hello, Jacob," she managed through the thickness in her throat.

"I'm extra hungry today, so give me lots and lots."

In spite of herself, she smiled. Even so, she didn't feel it. "Very well, Jacob. You'd better eat it all, though. I don't want to see you throwing any of it away."

"Oh, you won't," he said, licking his lips. "I promise."

"I have a feeling he means what he says, Miss Lawson," Mrs. Berringer added. "So you had better take him at his word."

Annabelle did as he asked then turned to his mother. "The normal amount for you, I assume?"

Mrs. Berringer tilted her head and regarded her for a few moments. "Yes," she finally answered, sounding distracted. "Tell me, dear, is everything all right?"

"Everything is fine, Mrs. Berringer," she lied, averting her eyes. Perhaps Jacob and his mother would take their meals and leave her be.

"Somehow I have a feeling that's not entirely true, Miss Lawson." Mrs. Berringer reached across the table and placed a hand on Annabelle's arm. "Come find me when you're through here." She started to usher her son farther down the line then paused and pinned Annabelle with a meaningful look. "Please," she added.

Annabelle wanted to make her excuses and say she had to clean up afterward and might not have the time. However, the words wouldn't come. Instead, she nodded, touched by the tenderness she saw in the woman's eyes. Perhaps Mrs. Berringer would have some answers to her dilemma.

છ

About an hour later, Annabelle swiped her cloth across the table and stacked the last pot in the wagon headed back to the collection center. Her heart pounded as she made her way around the tent where most of the other remaining workers were. If she took care, she could slip away without her mother noticing. She just wasn't ready to answer any questions about her destination.

Besides, her parents hadn't said she couldn't talk to the Berringers at all. They simply cautioned her regarding William. And he wasn't even here today.

Placing two fists at the small of her back to work out a few kinks from all the bending and scrubbing, Annabelle made her way across the field to the Berringers' land. Mrs. Berringer hadn't said she'd be there, but it was the most logical place to look first. As she approached, she caught sight of a lone figure walking slowly up and down the rows and inspecting the various plants. For a moment Annabelle had thoughts of those little worms she'd seen William and Jacob plucking from the leaves. At least Jacob wasn't here to provide a repeat performance.

As she observed Mrs. Berringer further, she noticed the woman appeared to be saying something. Or perhaps she was singing to herself. No—there was no sound coming out of her mouth. Then Annabelle realized what it was. Mrs. Berringer was praying. Annabelle almost didn't want to intrude, so she stopped.

Mrs. Berringer looked up when she was still fifteen feet away. It was almost as if she'd been expecting her right at that moment. A welcoming smile broke out on the woman's lips.

"Miss Lawson, I'm glad you decided to come. I was beginning to wonder if I needed to come find *you*."

Now that certainly would have caused a scene. Mother would have been sure to see Mrs. Berringer and ask a lot of questions. She intended to speak with her mother very soon but not today. All things considered, Annabelle was glad she came here.

"Why don't you join me on the blanket I have set out there, and let's have ourselves a little chat."

Annabelle peered over Mrs. Berringer's shoulder to see the coarse horse blanket laid out on the ground. The woman obviously had this all planned out. A dented and worn teakettle in desperate need of a polish sat on one corner of the blanket with two tin cups next to it. She'd thought of everything it seemed.

Again words failed her, so she nodded and followed Mrs. Berringer's lead. Zipping a quick prayer heavenward, she petitioned God to give her the strength to get through this conversation without completely breaking down.

Lucille dipped her hands in a small bucket of water set off to the side then dried them on her apron. "Feel free to do the same if you wish. Although I'm sure you had ample opportunity to do that back at the food tent."

"Yes," Annabelle replied. "But thank you just the same."

Mrs. Berringer tilted her head to the side and pursed her lips. "You have a lot of weight on your mind. I can tell. Something troubles you, does it not?"

William's mother was nothing if not direct. Now she knew where Jacob got it. For a moment Annabelle thought about making up something different to tell Lucille. But one look at the kindness and wisdom she saw in the woman's eyes disarmed her. Perhaps if she shared her heart with Mrs. Berringer first, she'd be better prepared when she spoke with her own mother. Maybe it would help her sort out a few things in her mind.

"Yes, as a matter of fact, it does. Am I correct in assuming that's tea in there?" She nodded at the kettle.

"Yes," Mrs. Berringer replied, reaching for one of the cups. "Would you like some?"

"If you don't mind, I'd love some."

"But of course, my dear. I prepared it just for you." She poured and handed Annabelle the cup. "So you see, it's a good thing you did come. Otherwise I might have been forced to either drink everything in this kettle or dump it out. And I do so hate to waste anything if I can avoid it."

How long had it been since she'd sat with her mother like this, talking about anything and everything? A few months at least. And that was too long. A pang of guilt struck her that she wasn't confiding in her mother. She'd do that at the earliest opportunity. For now she'd make the most of this situation.

William's mother settled in place and gave Annabelle her undivided attention. Her motherly demeanor reached out and touched Annabelle's desperate longing to share her innermost struggles.

"Drink your tea and tell me what's on your mind. . .or perhaps your heart."

Yes. No doubt about it. Lucille was straight to the point, just like Mother. The build up of concerns that burdened Annabelle's weary soul teetered right on the edge of her lips, wanting to spill forth like water from an upended pail. Her thoughts scattered in every direction at once.

"I. . .I'm not sure. I mean, I don't know," she babbled, trying to gather her thoughts into some semblance of coherency. "I hardly know where to begin."

"Maybe I could help somewhat?" the kindly woman asked.

"Please," Annabelle encouraged.

"I am quite certain a good bit of what is plaguing you is somehow connected to my son. If I'm not correct, stop me now."

Annabelle dipped her chin and whispered. "No, you're correct."

"And if I haven't missed my guess, it's because you have feelings for my son yet are torn because your parents have limited your time here at the fields."

Annabelle could hardly believe it. All those emotions tumbling around inside her wanting release, and William's mother had summed it up in just a few words. Sometimes hearing it spoken from someone not involved in the mess proved beneficial. Meeting Mrs. Berringer's gaze over the rim of her teacup, Annabelle blinked back the tears that had gathered.

"I can see the purpose behind Mother and Father doing what they did. I mean, they are only looking out for me, keeping what they believe are my best interests at heart." She shook her head and wiped away the overspill from her cheek with the back of her hand. "And I truly believe that of them," she declared. "I just don't agree with how they're going about it."

"Have you spoken with them about this and told them how you feel?"

"No. Not yet."

"Then I strongly encourage you to be honest. It's clear your parents love you, but how can they truly know what's best if you don't share the truth in your heart?"

Mrs. Berringer was right. She had told them only what she knew they'd wanted to hear, so her current situation was as much her fault as theirs. "You're right. They had asked for my input, but I didn't refute anything. And William"—Annabelle sighed, remembering their last conversation—"he didn't even allow for a rebuttal of any kind from me. He just reacted and walked away."

Instead of acting surprised, Mrs. Berringer simply nodded. She no doubt knew her son quite well, and this behavior wasn't unexpected.

"Unfortunately, William gets his impatience and impulsiveness from his father. But he means well, even when he doesn't show it."

"Yes, I know that. The last time I saw him, I could tell he was fighting a battle all his own," Annabelle said hesitantly.

"I will confess," Mrs. Berringer began, "William did come to see me after he spoke to you that day. He confessed everything he was feeling and even shared about your sadness, but he knew that moment was not the right time to do anything about it. I could tell that hurt him a great deal." The regret in her tone spoke volumes. "He always wants to fix things, to come up with solutions. Feeling like his hands are tied is not a good place for him to be, nor a comfortable one."

William? Hurt by her sorrow and what she had said that day? She thought back. There had been a definite melancholic quality in his mannerisms. And if she called it what it was, she had seen the hurt his mother now mentioned. He'd covered it so quickly, though, she hadn't been sure at the time. Then he'd stormed off and was now nowhere to be found, leaving her to interpret his true feelings.

"I'm so sorry, Mrs. Berringer. I would never intentionally hurt William. But he deserved to know what my parents had dictated."

"He cares a great deal for you, you know."

Care for her? After the way she'd initially shoved all those Bible verses at him instead of waiting to get to know him better? Then again, there was the afternoon on Belle Isle and the teasing moments they'd shared at various times. Still, hearing it from his mother felt odd. She had wanted to hear it from William first.

"You must be mistaken."

Lucille squared her shoulders. "I know my son, Miss Lawson."

Now she'd done it. Annabelle should know better than to imply to a mother that she was wrong about one of her children. "Please forgive me, Mrs. Berringer. I didn't mean to imply that you don't, but William hasn't exactly given me a lot of substantial evidence to prove that statement. There have been moments when it's seemed clear, but I'm still not sure."

William's mother placed a warm and comforting hand on Annabelle's arm. "He tries to hide it, but a mother knows the heart of her son." She took a final drink of her tea and smiled. "Give it a few days. And trust God. I have a feeling everything isn't quite as hopeless as it might seem right now."

Annabelle continued to ponder those words long after she left and returned home. As she'd confessed to Mrs. Berringer, there had been times when William appeared to feel the same as she, but he'd never spoken the words aloud. Besides, how could he possibly care about her if he was intentionally avoiding her?

What was a girl to think? She sighed. As Mrs. Berringer had said, there was little left to do but wait on the Lord. If no one else knew what was on William's mind, He would. Now she had just one thing to do. Wait. All right—two things. She had to speak with her Mother.

❧

Felicity reached out and wiped a tear from Annabelle's cheek and smiled. They sat facing each other in the two wingback chairs in the study, their knees almost touching.

"Why didn't you speak of this sooner? The conversation your father and I had with you would have been the perfect time."

Annabelle offered a rueful grin. The confession had gone a lot smoother than she thought it might. Thanks to the brief preparation during her earlier chat with Mrs. Berringer, she had been able to share her heart with Mother with more clarity.

"I am sorry I didn't say anything then, Mother. But I thought you and Father had already made up your minds. And I suppose since I myself didn't know where William stood, I didn't feel comfortable at the time." Even now the explanation sounded weak. In truth, she didn't have a good reason for holding back.

"I could tell something wasn't quite right that day," Mother said with her keen understanding. "When you didn't protest at all, though, I assumed you were being forthright as usual. I'm glad you've decided to be honest this evening."

Remorse filled Annabelle. She should have told Mother how she felt from the start. She'd made foolish decisions in the past, and this would be added to that list. "I know. And my reasons don't even make sense now." It felt like a great weight had been lifted from her shoulders. "I'm so relieved I didn't allow this to go on any longer."

Mother clasped one of Annabelle's hands in her own, giving her a loving squeeze. "As am I. We have always been able to talk about anything. I don't like it when I feel there's an unexplainable rift."

"Nor do I." Annabelle sighed. "But where does that leave us now?"

Mother pressed her lips together in what appeared to be an apologetic expression. "Well, I cannot cancel on some of the meetings that have already been put in place, but I promise not to arrange any further ones." Amusement danced across her face. "I only ask that you at least give these young gentlemen a chance."

"I shall remain cordial at all times." Annabelle giggled. "Unless, of course, one of them becomes insufferable."

"Your father and I have chosen these men quite well. I highly doubt you will encounter a circumstance such as that." A twinkle entered Mother's eyes. "But if you do, I give you full permission to put an early end to the outing."

It felt so good to relate like this again. The past few months hadn't been a good measure for the depth or closeness she shared with Mother. Now things had been put right again, and they could move forward from here.

All she needed now was to hear William admit his feelings himself. She prayed it would happen soon.

Chapter 14

Everything seemed to be falling into place. One of the open doors turned into an opportunity beyond his wildest dreams. All because Mr. Lawson had taken the time to make a few inquiries. William could hardly wait to find Annabelle and tell her the good news. He should probably thank Mr. Lawson as well, but he wanted to start with Annabelle.

Of course, she'd have to agree to see him first. With the way he'd left things the last time they spoke, he might have ruined his chance of that.

Only one way to find out.

"Berringer, do you have a moment?"

William paused on his way out the door of the Edison factory and turned to see the man who would soon become his supervisor.

"Sure, Mr. Hudson. Something on your mind?"

Ralph Hudson came to stand before him, a serious look in his eyes and his mouth formed into a thin line. Had William done something wrong already? He hadn't even started working yet. That couldn't be possible. Could it?

Hudson motioned to a bench near the main walk to the building. "Shall we sit?"

This sure felt important. At least half a dozen possible scenarios ran through William's mind.

"Mr. Berringer, first allow me to reassure you this has nothing to do with our interview earlier this morning."

William released a silent sigh. All right, so that answered one question.

"But there was something I gathered from your response when I remarked about the kindness of Mr. Lawson in informing us of your name in the first place." Hudson put up one hand in a staying motion. "I could be way off base, and if I am, I invite you to correct me."

With a shift of his arm from the back of the bench to his lap, William wasn't sure if he should respond or wait for Mr. Hudson to continue. William was thankful the man decided for him.

"I know the Lawson family rather well through our various business dealings. Although this recent financial recession has left us not keeping in touch as much as we once did, I know Mr. Lawson to be a rather devout Christian, putting his love for God above everything else. Your acquaintance with Brandt made me speak with Mr. Edison on your behalf." Hudson kept his gaze direct and steady.

"When I remarked that God had brought you to our company, your disposition changed. Do you perhaps not agree?"

That was the last thing he expected Mr. Hudson to ask. "Pa–pardon me, sir?"

"I assure you that your response to my question bears no weight whatsoever on my decision to hire you as my assistant. This is strictly for my own benefit."

William looked down at his lap then stared out across the street. So it wasn't something he had done; rather, it was his reaction. Returning his gaze to Mr. Hudson, he took his time in formulating a response. After all, God and His plan had been the very thing that had plagued him for weeks—ever since hearing that sermon the Sunday they went to Belle Isle. In fact, a lot had happened that day.

"Sir, I will not disagree with your assessment of Mr. Lawson's character and devotion. In fact, his entire family follows his lead. I have no doubt it's what caused his daughter to speak to her father on my behalf in the first place."

"His daughter?" Hudson quirked an eyebrow. "Annabelle?" A slight grin formed on the man's lips as he nodded. "So that's the real connection, then. I had wondered how Lawson managed to find you."

"Yes, sir. Miss Lawson has spent a great deal of time helping the workers on the land where my family farms." William brought her beautiful face to mind, an easy feat considering how often he'd thought of her lately. "She has given so selflessly, while at the same time making no attempt to hide the fact that her faith in God is what led her to get involved."

"Was that the reason, then, for the change I mentioned?"

"That was part of it."

William wasn't sure how much he should share. He didn't know Hudson at all. Then again, the man had taken the time to seek him out to speak on matters related to God. Perhaps it was God's way of saying He was indeed still looking out for him.

"As you are no doubt aware, Miss Lawson can be rather persuasive when she sets her mind to something."

Hudson chuckled and rested farther against the bench, draping one arm across the back. "Well, I don't know her as well as I know her father, but from what I hear, yes. That is true."

"And I'll confess, sir, that when my family suffered so greatly following the failed banks, I blamed God."

"That's understandable."

"When Miss Lawson arrived and seemed to make me her target for her personal crusading, it only angered me further."

Hudson seemed to follow his thought process. "And now?"

"Now?" William appreciated Hudson's desire to get to the point. "Well, sir, how could I not see God's hand in everything that's happened lately? I never fully turned my back on Him. I was just angry." He thought of how persistent Annabelle had been and how often evidence of God's involvement had almost smacked him in the face. "I highly doubt this all happened by chance."

"You are right about that. And don't misunderstand me. Your qualifications are the reason you were hired. However, hearing what you've confessed, I see it was God at the center of it all."

William offered a slightly nervous chuckle. "Guess I have some thanks to be giving."

"Perhaps to a certain young lady as well?" Hudson suggested with wisdom and an acute perception in his eyes.

A lazy grin formed on William's lips at the idea of resuming his original plan to go find Annabelle. "Yes. I believe that's in the works as well."

Hudson stood, and William did the same. The man extended his hand, which William took. "Mr. Berringer, I look forward to having you join us on our team. This company is poised right on the edge of some amazing developments. I don't know about you, but I'm looking forward to being a part of these exciting times."

"As am I, sir." William dropped his hand. "Now if you'll excuse me, I do believe there is someone I must seek out."

Hudson held up both his arms in surrender. "By all means, my boy. Don't let me delay you any further."

As William walked away, Hudson called to him.

"We'll see you first thing Monday morning."

Monday. After the past year and a half of struggling, it almost seemed impossible that his life was about to change in such a profound way. Yet it would. For that, and so much more, he owed God, Mr. Lawson, and Annabelle his gratitude.

※

William paused just outside the door to Mr. Lawson's study. The butler had directed him down the hall and said Mr. Lawson was expecting him. Of course he was. William had requested this meeting. Now that he was here, though, his stomach clenched and tension rippled across his shoulders.

With a quick prayer for strength, he took a deep breath and raised his hand to deliver two short knocks to the closed door.

"Come in!" came the immediate response.

He turned the knob and pushed the door open, stepping into the darkened interior and immediately removing his hat. His eyes searched the room and found Mr. Lawson standing next to his desk. The man's expression was too difficult to read from this distance, though.

"Mr. Lawson," William plunged forward. "Thank you for seeing me on such short notice."

"It's my pleasure, Mr. Berringer."

Annabelle's father didn't make any attempt to move from where he stood, so William approached him instead.

"I know you probably have a lot of business to attend to, so I won't take up too much of your time. I just wanted to come here today to thank you in person for all you've done on behalf of my father and me. You're no doubt aware that we have both secured positions at Edison Illuminating Company, and for that we owe you a great deal of thanks."

"I'm pleased to hear everything has worked out. And I was happy to do what I could to help."

The man William thought might be intimidating was anything but as his congenial expression became clear. Whatever preconceived notion he'd formed in his mind about Annabelle's father that might paint him in a less than appealing picture vanished. In its place was a man William looked forward to getting to know better. If things went the way he hoped, he'd have ample opportunity in which to do so.

"Father and I both begin work Monday. In fact, I have just come from the meeting where the job was offered to me. I didn't want to wait any longer before letting you know how much I appreciate your interventions."

"I'm glad you did come, son. It says a lot about you and affirms so much of what my daughter has said when she's spoken of you and your family."

William licked his lips and shifted from one foot to the other, turning his hat in his hands. Mr. Lawson's approval meant so much, but standing before the man still put him on edge.

"I won't deny the fact that I've been aware of her feelings for you for quite some time now. And I won't make you any more uncomfortable than you are by asking your intentions toward my daughter. I am certain they are honorable."

"Yes, sir."

Mr. Lawson nodded. "Very well. We'll leave the rest for another time." The hint of a grin tugged at the corners of the man's mouth. "I have a feeling a more personal conversation with my daughter at the center of it will be forthcoming before too long."

Annabelle's father was astute. William had to give him that. He swallowed and nodded, unable to speak beyond the tightness in his throat.

"Now if you'll excuse me, I do have some rather important matters that require my attention before supper." He winked. "And I don't want to upset Mrs. Lawson by being late."

"No, sir!" William grinned, grateful he'd again found his voice.

"I trust you don't mind seeing yourself out?"

"Not at all, sir." William turned toward the door then glanced over his shoulder. "Thank you again, Mr. Lawson."

"You're quite welcome."

❧

All right. That was it. Annabelle had just ended her outing with her most recent suitor—and her last. As Mother had requested, she'd seen these engagements through to fruition. Now she was glad to put an end to them. None of the men she'd met held any appeal, nor did she see them anywhere in her future.

On the contrary, the only man she consistently saw in that future hadn't been around for several weeks. That didn't mean he hadn't been far from her thoughts. In fact, with each new social event, William became more and more a forerunner in her mind. With this last outing, she had even imagined William's face across from her instead of the man who escorted her.

Being patient was getting her nowhere. Annabelle had promised her parents to go to the potato patches only once a week. But she couldn't avoid it any longer. She had to find William.

As Annabelle marched across the adjoining plots, resolute and focused, her tunnel vision prevented her from seeing anyone or anything around her. Before she realized it, her trek had brought her to the Berringer land and straight into the solid form of William Berringer.

"Umph!"

William immediately placed his hands at her waist and saved her from a fall. She looked up into the amused eyes of the very man she'd come to see. After all this time and how easily it seemed he had made himself scarce every time she came to the fields, Annabelle thought she'd have plenty to say. Unfortunately, her tongue refused to cooperate.

"Mr. Berringer!" was all she managed to get out.

"Tell me, Miss Lawson, do you often make it a practice of not looking where you're going?"

His eyes crinkled with laughter, and the brown in them lightened as his lips quirked into a grin. Her heart raced at the appealing image he presented. Then she remembered all the pain of the weeks of separation. He might have been helping her abide by her parents' wishes, but to her, he'd abandoned her. Plain and simple.

She took a step back, forcing him to drop his arms, and planted both fists on her hips and frowned. "Well, under normal circumstances, no. However, you've been absent every other time I've ventured onto your land in the past few weeks." She shrugged, doing her best to remain unaffected by his nearness. "I didn't expect to run into anyone."

William winced as her words hit their intended mark. Annabelle didn't truly desire to hurt, but even she felt the sting delivered by her response. Still, he needed to know.

He sighed, and his shoulders drooped. The mirth in his eyes dimmed as well.

"Miss Lawson, I do apologize for my behavior since we last spoke. Please believe me when I say that you have not been far from my thoughts, despite how we parted."

She almost admitted the same thing. Instead, she held her tongue and waited for him to continue.

"There really is no excuse for my deplorable actions, and I was actually planning to come find you today so I might tell you so." He implored her with true penitence in his eyes. "I also came to ask for your forgiveness in the hopes that we might repair whatever rift I might have caused."

Well, that confession certainly took the wind out of her sails. How could she deny a request like that? In spite of herself, the hurt and pain she'd been feeling at what she'd viewed as his desertion vanished. His sincerity reached deep and touched her heart. Her puffed-up desire for some form of vindication deflated, leaving behind the soft spot she'd reserved only for him.

"Mr. Berringer, I appreciate your honesty. Your apology is accepted." She nearly smiled at how he visibly relaxed. "Might I ask for your forgiveness as well?"

Confusion wrinkled his brow. "My forgiveness? For what?"

"I harbored some resentment after you stormed off that day, and prior to that, I hadn't been the best example of patience regarding your anger at God or your slip in faith."

"About that," he began. William licked his lips and swallowed twice then offered a sheepish grin. "I've finally been able to make peace with everything and realize that God indeed has been looking out for me and my family all along."

Annabelle gasped. That confession seemed to come out of nowhere. It was the last thing she would have expected to hear from him today. Yet she could see in his boyish demeanor and the expression in his eyes that he meant every word.

"But how. . .I don't under—" She paused to gather her thoughts, unable to keep the surprise from her voice. "What happened to bring about this change?"

Almost instantly a wide smile transformed his face. It reached all the way to his eyes. An answering smile started to form on her lips as hope made her catch her breath.

"That's the other reason I wanted to come find you. I've got a job!"

Heedless of propriety, Annabelle jumped forward and threw her arms around William's neck. A second later, his arms came around her waist. He swung her once in a circle as his laughter sounded in her right ear.

"Oh, William, that's wonderful!" she spoke over his shoulder. Then realizing where they stood and what she'd just done, she released her hold and put a little distance between them, tucking her chin against her chest. "I'm sorry."

He chuckled. "Don't be. I didn't mind."

Annabelle looked up to see that his eyes had darkened. He now regarded her with an emotion she didn't dare name. Not when it bordered so close to what she wanted to show as well.

"So tell me," she began, attempting to return her pounding heartbeat to normal. "What is this job, and when do you begin?"

"It's for Edison Illuminating Company, and I started three weeks ago as the assistant to one of the supervisors. You might even know him. Mr. Ralph Hudson."

"Oh my! Yes. At least I know who he is. Father is more familiar with him than I. But I have met him on more than one occasion." She drew her eyebrows together. "He's rather important with the Edison Company, is he not?"

William nodded. "From what I gather. What's even more amazing is the fact that my father has been offered a position as a financial consultant for the company. So not only do I have a job, but he does, too." He reached for her hands, holding them lightly in his own. "So you see? With the abundance of good fortune, God and I had ourselves a little chat." He grinned. "I hadn't exactly been fair in my anger at Him. Tossing aside years of faith because of present circumstances doesn't say much of me. It took the wisdom of another believer, my parents' steadfast faith, and the admittance of my own stupidity to get me back on track. Now God and I are back where we used to be."

Annabelle gave his hands a slight squeeze. "You have no idea how glad I am to hear that, Mr. Berringer."

"What's with the formality? A moment ago you used my first name."

She had? Perhaps the hug they'd shared blotted that out. "Oh," she muttered, lowering her eyes.

William dropped one of her hands to touch her chin and raise her gaze to his once more. "As I said, there is no need for apologies. I liked it. And I'd like it if you did it from now on."

"I don't believe that would be proper," she protested. Then again, this would be a step in the right direction if what she thought might come next truly did.

"On the contrary, I must disagree. After all the time we've shared and the conversations we've had, I would say it's entirely proper." His eyes regarded her, mirth again dancing in his brown depths. "Would it help if I said please?"

A giggle escaped from her lips at how adorable he looked. "Very well."

His voice lowered and became quite gentle. "Very well, what?"

"Very well. . .William," she whispered.

"There, now that wasn't so difficult, was it, Annabelle?"

Hearing her name coming from him sounded so nice. She could see why he preferred it.

"All right, now that we've got that out of the way, there's only one more issue to address."

"What's that?"

"Gathering our families to celebrate the recent good fortune and share in the gratitude my father and I owe your father."

"That sounds like a splendid idea!" Annabelle already knew Mother would agree. With a little persuasion, she was sure Father would, too.

"I've already thanked your father privately, but—"

"You have?" When had he done that? And why hadn't Father told her about it?

"Yes. I believe a dinner would be the best way to commemorate everything."

He made it sound so uncomplicated, speaking of meeting with her father and now moving forward with plans to gather their families together again.

"It sounds as if you've given this a great deal of thought."

"I have. In so many ways." He squeezed her hands. "And before we discuss the details of the dinner, there is another matter I wish to discuss. No—make that confess."

Annabelle's breath hitched. Was he about to say what she'd been hoping he'd say for a while now?

"I haven't been all that great at sharing what I've felt." William grimaced and released a nervous chuckle. "Unless of course it was my anger at God." He held her gaze with his own and licked his lips. "Despite my boorish behavior, you never gave up and in the process became quite important to me."

Annabelle bit her lower lip, trying hard to contain her excitement.

"So before I make a mess of everything, I'm going to come right out and say it." He inhaled once. "I care a great deal for you and need to know if you feel the same."

"Yes!" she immediately replied, fighting the urge to embrace the man in front of her again.

William saved her the effort by pulling her to him instead. "That's the best word I've heard all day," he said, wrapping his arms around her back.

She nestled against him. It would be so easy to stay there forever. But she remembered how she hadn't told anyone she'd even come here today.

"Oh no!"

William stared at her with a quizzical expression in his eyes and eyebrows drawn. "That wasn't exactly what I expected to hear next. Annabelle, what's wrong?"

"I shouldn't be here today. Mother and Father are sure to wonder where I've gone."

"Oh, is that all?" He visibly relaxed and grinned. "Then let's make sure you get home safely, shall we?" He maintained his hold on her left hand and turned. "We don't want to jeopardize anything we've accomplished to this point, do we?"

William winked, and a blush warmed her cheeks. They hadn't yet made any promises, but at least their feelings were out in the open. Beyond that, they'd discover it together. For now Annabelle basked in the joy of Willam's returned affection. Anything else was mere icing on the cake.

Chapter 15

Are you sure everything is in place?"

Annabelle peered at the break in the curtain then glanced back at William, worry etched across her face.

"Relax, Annabelle." William stepped away from the table where he'd been setting up a few items loaned to him courtesy of the Edison Company. "You have worked hard with that handful of women from the Ladies Aid and managed to accomplish quite a lot in a short amount of time."

"I know." She inhaled a deep breath. "But there is so much about this evening that must go right."

He walked up behind Annabelle and turned her gently to face him. Taking her hands in his, he gazed down into her blue eyes. "Everything will go just fine. Do what you told me many times to do not so long ago."

"Trust God," they said in unison.

She smiled. "I do. I'm still nervous, though."

William raised one hand to trail a finger down her soft cheek. "So am I. However, this is all going to work out just fine. It *is* the state fair, after all. We didn't have one last year, and it hasn't been here in Detroit for eleven years. That's bound to make everything better." He implored her with his eyes. "Even if there are any glitches."

"I pray you're right," she replied, the tremble in her voice belying her lingering doubts.

He leaned forward and placed a kiss on her forehead. "I am. Trust me." Tapping her nose with his finger, he grinned. "Why don't you head on over to the stage area so you can be sure your parents make their way here without delay?"

She nodded. "All right. We'll be back shortly."

After she left, he returned to see to the final details.

He and Annabelle had indeed worked hard the past two weeks. They never would have made it happen without the help of his newly formed connections at the Edison Company. Not to mention his own parents. When they learned of his plan and the promise of seeing Annabelle more often, they'd eagerly agreed to help.

With everyone working together as a team, they had secured the private area now cloaked in the thick, tentlike curtain on all four sides. The candelabras on the tables in the center cast a soft glow, and the place settings had been transported from one of the finer restaurants in Detroit. Even now the tantalizing aroma of the dishes prepared for this meal reached his nose and made his stomach rumble in response.

William cast an analytical look around the makeshift room, a sense of pride filling him at all they'd achieved. He sent a silent prayer of thanks to God, along with a request that His hand remain on all that would be taking place in a matter of moments.

All he needed to do now was make sure his special guest was in position.

◆

"Annabelle, where are you taking us?" Mother demanded.

"I must admit, your cryptic invitation on behalf of young Mr. Berringer has piqued my interest," Father added. "But I also hope it involves food. I'm famished."

Annabelle grinned. She did her best to hide it from her parents, though. The more secretive she could be, the better. The less they knew, the better the surprise would be.

"You will both be quite pleased, I assure you," she promised.

The rest of the trek took place in silence. As they reached the entrance to the curtained room, she prayed for peace. If only her heart would return to its normal position instead of lodging in her throat. It made breathing rather difficult.

At that very moment, the curtain parted and a maid dressed in black with a white apron stepped outside.

"Mr. and Mrs. Lawson. Miss Lawson," the young girl greeted. "Please come in."

The gasps from both of her parents as soon as they entered filled Annabelle with pride. She caught sight of William standing at the opposite side. His wink sent her heart racing.

"Oh! It's all so beautiful," Mother gushed.

"I *am* impressed." Father inhaled an appreciative breath through his nose. "And if the meal tastes half as good as it smells, I will say you and Mr. Berringer have outdone yourselves."

"Yes." Mother looked all around the room. "But the question still remains. What is all this about?"

"If you will take your seats, Mother and Father, you will find out in just a few moments."

As soon as they sat, William opened the curtain where he stood and ushered in his parents along with Jacob, followed by Mr. Hudson and his wife. Matthew and Victoria brought up the rear. Annabelle smiled at her brother and sister, who moved with the entourage to gather at the table, each one sitting where his or her name card indicated.

William walked to the head of the table and cleared his throat. All eyes turned toward him, waiting expectantly.

"First, I want to thank all of you for agreeing to come this evening." He caught Annabelle's eyes for a brief second. "Miss Lawson and I appreciate your presence. We both agreed to begin with the purpose of this evening."

Annabelle took her eyes off William long enough to look at Father, who regarded William with obvious pleasure. Mother smiled as well.

"Now," William continued. "If you will indulge me a moment longer, I need to preface our remaining guest by way of an introduction."

He had originally suggested they wait to bring in their guest of honor until after the first or second course, but Annabelle had pleaded with him to start the dinner by introducing him. She would never make it through her first bite otherwise. And it would only add to the enjoyment of the evening.

Everyone looked to the two chairs that still remained empty, one where William stood and the other immediately to the right, next to where Annabelle sat. William pinned his gaze on Father. His throat muscles moved as he swallowed several times, and his hands gripped the back of the chair in front of him hard enough to make his knuckles turn white.

"Mr. Lawson. You and I already spoke about this that day in your study, but I felt a celebratory dinner would better demonstrate the full scale of my appreciation and that of my family for all you've done to help us. And as you surmised that day, the other topic has indeed become an issue."

William relaxed his grip on the chair and inhaled a deep breath. Annabelle did the same, sharing his apprehension. There was no going back now.

"Sir, I am well aware of how much you love your daughter. I also know that considering my former state of affairs, I was not deemed an acceptable suitor."

Father didn't show any surprise at hearing that word, and Mother grimaced. They shared a private look between them that spoke volumes. Chagrin fleeted across both their faces, and Annabelle was glad to see they regretted discounting William simply because of his current status.

William forged ahead. "However, as I said that day, my intentions are completely honorable, and I would not dare to make this request if I didn't feel you would even consider it a possibility." Another deep breath preceded the final rush of words. "You see, I have come to care a great deal for your daughter. Now that I am settled into my new position, I feel the time is right to pursue a further relationship with her. With your permission of course," he hastened to add.

Ripples of delight rumbled through those gathered. Mother and Father remained stoic, but Annabelle caught the sheen of tears beginning in Mother's eyes. Mr. Hudson sat back in his chair, a measure of satisfaction reflected on his face. The others made no attempt to hide their reactions.

"Before you respond, though, and without further ado"—William raised his voice and turned toward the opening where he'd at first been—"I'd like to invite our remaining guest to now join us."

The curtain parted, and in stepped Thomas Edison. As he approached the table, Father, Mr. Berringer, Matthew, and Mr. Hudson all stood.

Annabelle had never met the gentleman, so she took the time to observe his appearance. Dressed in a tailored suit and a bit older than she'd expected, Mr. Edison's receding hairline was parted on the side and brushed over. He carried an air of importance about him and commanded immediate attention.

Mr. Edison immediately approached Father. "Mr. Lawson," he greeted as they shook hands.

"Mr. Edison." Father nodded. "It is good to see you again."

Annabelle couldn't remain silent a moment longer. "Do you mean you know each other?"

"Yes, as a matter of fact, we do." Father acknowledged Annabelle then returned his attention to Mr. Edison. "Although it has been some time."

Mr. Edison agreed. "When Mr. Hudson extended the invitation for me to join you all this evening, care of Mr. Berringer, I was delighted to accept. Am I to understand this charming young woman and one of my newest employees are responsible for this evening?"

Pride reflected in Father's face at Mr. Edison's favorable remark. "Yes, I do believe that is correct."

"Well then, my compliments to you both." Mr. Edison dipped his head with a smile at Annabelle then turned to face William. "Mr. Berringer, allow me to say to you directly that I am happy to have you working at my company and look forward to the benefits you and your father both will bring to the team."

"Thank you, sir."

Father cleared his throat. The attention then shifted to him as he prepared to speak. "And before we are all again seated to begin partaking of a meal that promises to be just as memorable as this evening already is, I would like to say a few things."

He stepped around his chair and moved to stand next to Annabelle. With a slight motion of his hand, he beckoned William to approach.

"Mr. Berringer, I would be remiss if I didn't acknowledge all the hard work you and my daughter have put into making this evening rather special. And I would also be quite the fool if I denied your request from a moment ago." He lightly clasped Annabelle's chin in his hand and bestowed a loving smile upon her before again directing his gaze at William. "You have more than proven yourself as a worthy suitor. I am impressed with your tenacity and unwillingness to give up on something you obviously wanted so much." Extending his hand toward

William, who accepted it, Father continued. "It's clear to me that you two make an excellent team. You may continue with my blessing."

Annabelle's heart soared at the final pronouncement. Joy filled her to the core. "Oh, Father, thank you!" She placed a kiss on his cheek and threw her arms around him in a quick embrace. Relaxing her hold, her eyes drifted to William, whose face reflected the satisfaction she also felt at their attempts resulting in success.

Father again stepped back to allow them to move closer together. Mindful of all the other watchful eyes, Annabelle simply bestowed a kiss on William's cheek before leaning against him as he wrapped one arm around her waist and pulled her to him.

"Mr. Lawson," William began. "I am grateful for the trust you've given me." He glanced down at Annabelle with a smile. "And the treasure. I promise to treat both with the utmost care and attention."

Father wagged a finger in William's direction. "See that you do, my boy. I'll be keeping my eye on you."

William chuckled. "I wouldn't expect anything less, sir."

Mr. Edison moved to his place at the head of the table, again drawing everyone's attention his way. "Now that that's settled, let's eat, shall we?"

Hearty exclamations of agreement sounded. A blur of frenzied activity accompanied the verbal responses. Annabelle stood within the protective and warm circle of William's arm, watching their friends and family.

It all felt surreal. She had fully expected Father to protest a bit more, or for some other hitch to happen in their plans. But nothing did. It flowed so well, there was no doubt God was at the center of everything. All of her worrying and fretting seemed like such a waste of time and energy. As William had said, she should've trusted. Ironic that he would have to remind her when she was the one to help bring him back to his faith.

"Looks like everything has worked itself out. I have your father's blessing, a good job, and a promising future." He tightened his hold. "And best of all, I get to share it with you."

Annabelle turned and looked up into William's eyes. His smile was reserved only for her. "Who would have thought that such a blessing would have come out of such adversity?"

"Yes." William stepped back and drew Annabelle with him until they were a few feet from the table. "I spent so much time being angry, and God still brought you into my life in spite of it. I don't deserve you, but I sure am glad you're here."

She giggled. "Me, too." Annabelle wrapped her arms around his waist and grinned, "I know I chose the best."

He chuckled and drew her closer. "And the best is what you're going to get.

I promise. Just make sure you remind me to trust God when times get tough again."

"I will." She cast a look over her shoulder at the table. Everyone seemed to be oblivious to their absence, but that didn't mean they shouldn't participate.

William nodded toward the others. "Do you think anyone would miss us if we took our plates and ate in private somewhere else?"

Annabelle jerked her attention back to him to see if he was joking or not. The twinkle in his eyes gave her the answer. "I believe they would. But perhaps we can enjoy our dessert alone later."

Casting a quick look to the left and the right, William touched his forehead to hers, a crooked grin appearing on his lips. "That sounds like the perfect end to the evening."

"Now, will you join me, Mr. Berringer?" She held out her hand, palm down, in his direction.

He took it and tucked her arm into the crook of his elbow and bowed. "Yes, Miss Lawson. I do believe I will."

PATTERNS
AND PROGRESS

Dedication

Many thanks go out to my husband for assuming baby duty while I finished this book. To my readers who faithfully ask for the next book. And to JoAnne Simmons, Rachel Overton, and April Frazier, my editors. This book wouldn't be what it is today without your help. Top gratitude goes to my heavenly Father though, for the gift of writing and doing what I love.

Chapter 1

"Are you certain you're up to the responsibility, Mr. Berringer?" Henry Ford's solemn voice commanded attention. "I don't offer this opportunity to you lightly."

Jacob Berringer stood erect, his eyes locked on to those of his boss. He tried hard to calm his trembling legs and shaking hands. He'd only been a supervisor for a few months. Had Mr. Ford really just asked him to take the newest Model T out for a test run?

"Yes, sir," Jacob replied, hoping his voice didn't sound as squeaky to his superior as it did to his own ears.

"You have shown exemplary performance here in the plant. The care you have taken with each automobile and the manner in which you lead your team of workers has not gone unnoticed, I assure you."

"Thank you, sir."

Mr. Ford reached into his vest pocket and withdrew a shiny gold pocket watch on a chain. He snapped open the cover and looked at the face. "I shall be timing you to measure just how long it takes to make the journey from origination to destination."

Jacob gave a sharp nod. "I will provide you with the exact roads I take and any other necessary details for the report."

"Very well." Mr. Ford tipped his head toward the large door where the automobiles normally exited the plant onto the street. "Mother Mitchell is already waiting by the car. See that she reaches her home safely, and return here once the task is complete."

Anticipation raced through Jacob's veins, yet he maintained his calm exterior. No sense tipping his boss to the excitement, although knowing Mr. Ford, the man already knew how Jacob felt.

"You can trust me, sir. I will treat the Model T as if she were my own."

Mr. Ford clapped a firm hand on Jacob's shoulder. "See that you do, my boy. I look forward to hearing from you upon your return."

With a final nod, Jacob almost ran outside toward the waiting automobile and the important passenger he'd be transporting. The dowager woman tapped her shoe on the sidewalk and gave him a disapproving glare.

Great. He wasn't even on the road yet, and he'd already managed to disappoint Mr. Sorenson's mother-in-law. Charles Sorenson was second in command to the production chief, Peter Martin, with the Ford Company. Jacob loved his work and didn't want to do anything that might jeopardize his employment.

After helping Mrs. Mitchell onto the front seat and closing the door, Jacob bounded around the back to the driver's side. He grabbed hold of the body frame and vaulted from the running board to the cushioned seat. For a few moments, he sat and stared at the wheel, running his hands over the patchwork-style seat and marveling at the design. Then he shook his head and jumped down again to the ground.

He'd get nowhere if he didn't shift into action.

But he couldn't resist letting his fingers travel along the body's sleek contours, admiring the shiny, black vanadium steel that made up most of its parts. As he stepped toward the front of the car, he folded back the hood cover with deft precision and familiarity. The four-cylinder solid block engine gleamed in the late-afternoon sunlight. Just seeing how much cleaner this engine looked from the ones with individual cylinder castings made Jacob wonder why the other factories didn't adopt this style. The flywheel magneto connected to the trembler coil, where the current would pass from the timer to the firing cylinder.

Every part on this motorcar was brand new, straight off the assembly line. And Jacob had been selected to test it.

"Would it be possible for us to please move a bit faster, young man?" Mrs. Mitchell's voice shrilled from the front seat. "I *am* on a tight schedule."

Jacob popped his head around so he could make eye contact with her. "Yes, ma'am. We'll be in motion in a jiffy."

He sighed as he once again covered the engine. There would be more time to admire it later. Right now he had a job to do. And he'd best not upset the boss.

Cupping the crank handle in his right palm, Jacob reached for the choke wire on the bottom of the radiator. He'd had a lot of practice on other automobiles inside the Highland Park plant, but he'd never driven one to great lengths on the city streets. With a silent prayer for the car to start on the first try, he rotated the crank.

The engine sputtered a few times then rumbled to life. Jacob patted the side of the car and smiled. Vibrations pulsed beneath his fingertips, charging his own excitement to get behind the wheel and go for a drive. He stood for a brief moment to make sure the car wouldn't stop running before he stepped onto the floorboard and settled again into the seat. This time he wrapped his hands around the wheel and looked down the road ahead. No time like the present to get moving.

Placing his foot on the far left pedal, Jacob reached for the lever mounted next to the seat. He pressed the pedal and held it forward, putting the car in low gear. A jolt immediately followed as it jerked forward. This model had a top speed of an amazing forty-five miles per hour, but Jacob didn't dare risk anything that reckless. He'd start slow and run the car through its paces first. For all he knew, having to transport Mrs. Mitchell might be more than a mere favor. If word got back to Mr. Ford that he was being less than responsible, it might be a long time before he was asked to test a new automobile again.

They maneuvered through the streets in silence. Mrs. Mitchell sat ramrod straight, her hands clutching the purse she held in her lap. Not talking suited Jacob just fine. He could enjoy the rumblings of the car pulsating under his feet and focus on his driving.

After a few minutes, though, Mrs. Mitchell's voice broke the silence.

"As surprising as this may sound, I don't much care for these machines. But Charles has assured me they are perfectly safe, and I have no reason to doubt him."

"Mr. Ford and Mr. Sorenson make sure the cars that come out of their factory are of the highest quality, Mrs. Mitchell."

"Yes." The woman pursed her lips. "They are mighty proud of their work. That much is clear. I admire Henry's ethics and his devotion. He has achieved a great deal and worked hard to get where he is today. I know he will continue to go far." She paused and smiled. "And of course, having my son-in-law serving him in such an esteemed position doesn't hurt, either."

Jacob agreed with everything Mrs. Mitchell said. Mr. Ford set a rather intimidating yet inspiring example. The same for his two top associates. He didn't know what to say in reply, so he remained quiet. It turned out he didn't have to worry about keeping up the conversation, though. Mrs. Mitchell managed quite well on her own. She rambled on about her daughter's marriage to Mr. Sorenson, annual vacations at Niagara Falls and Mackinac Island each August, and even added her thoughts on the merits or disadvantages of progress.

In no time at all, he had reached Mrs. Mitchell's house. After stopping the car, Jacob hopped down and hastened to the other side to offer his assistance as she descended from the car. Tucking her hand into the crook of his elbow, he escorted her up the sidewalk to the front door of her home.

Mrs. Mitchell held out the key to the door. "Thank you very much, young man. The ride was a pleasant one."

Jacob took the key and opened the door, giving it a light shove. He turned back to the woman, tipped his hat, and inclined his head. "My pleasure, ma'am. Have a good day."

"And you as well."

After waiting to see that she had entered her home safely, Jacob returned to the Model T and put it in gear once more. That went quite well, and he prayed it would mean a favorable report back to Mr. Ford.

As Jacob headed back toward the Highland Park plant, another specific destination formed in his mind. It would be the best place to truly test the car and not endanger anyone else. Returning to the busy city streets with its eight-miles-per-hour speed limit wouldn't afford the same guarantee. So when Jacob reached the next intersection, he pointed the car toward the outlying fields to the northwest.

Once free of the confines of the city, he enjoyed the way the land seemed to spread out before him. A flock of birds took to flight ahead of him, and two horses beyond the fence to his left galloped away from the road. He inhaled the fresh scent of farmland and relished the cool breeze of the evening air. Invigorated, Jacob decided to be bold and raise his foot off the left pedal, setting the car into high gear. Another jolt occurred as the car increased speed.

Jacob's knuckles turned white, and his heart pounded as he prayed for safety. The fields on his left and right zipped by in a blur. A little voice in his head told him to depress the pedal once more or put his other foot on the right pedal and bring the car to a stop. He ignored the voice and instead savored the feeling of freedom.

If only he made enough money to afford one of these cars for his very own. His brother William had just purchased one two months ago for his family, and Father owned one as well. Jacob might only be twenty-six, but seeing his older brother and father driving around the city fueled his desire to join the league of motorcar owners. Perhaps in a few more months, his pay as a supervisor would amount to enough. For now at least he could pretend.

The crack of a rifle sounded to his left, and Jacob jerked his head toward the echo. It effectively jarred his thoughts from his little pleasure ride and brought his boss's face to mind.

"Mr. Ford! I have to return the car!"

Jacob had no idea how long it had been since dropping off Mrs. Mitchell, but he had no doubt he was expected back long ago. Frantic, he returned his attention to the road. Good. An intersection. He could turn around there and head back to the city. With his attention on the upcoming maneuver, he didn't see the horses and wagon until too late. The team was on a direct collision course with his car.

Jacob tensed and shifted into survival mode. Visions of a crumbled heap of steel and wheels flashed before his eyes. He immediately rammed his foot down on the right pedal and yanked the steering wheel in the same direction.

The driver of the wagon screamed and pulled back on the reins, causing the horses to rear up and paw at the air. If it didn't get into a wreck, the model might end up with hoofprints on the engine instead.

Skidding only a few feet on the dirt-packed road, Jacob released a whoosh of breath when the car came to a complete stop mere inches from the nearest fence. He jumped down from the running board and raced to the front of the car to check the suspension and wheels as well as the engine. Barely giving the wagon driver a passing glance, he groaned.

"Could you not see that I had the right-of-way?" He folded back the hood. "Why don't you watch where you're guiding that antiquated wagon of yours?"

"I beg your pardon?" came a distinctly incensed feminine voice.

PATTERNS AND PROGRESS

Jacob tilted his head and looked over his shoulder at a woman not too much younger than he standing next to the horses, her fists planted on her hips and reins held loosely in one hand. A bank of gray clouds partially concealed the sun and cast eerie shadows on her face. He couldn't tell if it was the temporary minimal light or his faulty perception that made her look so livid. Then again, considering the circumstances, she might very well be furious.

Before he had a chance to say anything further, she spun away and stepped close to the horses, speaking in low, soothing tones. The horses sidestepped and pranced a bit, snorting and continuing to paw the ground. Under her calming voice, the animals soon ceased their nervous behavior and settled once again.

Jacob observed the young woman in silence. Honeycomb hair fell in a single braid down her back. Her straw hat was tied beneath her chin but now sat askew and partially cupped her right shoulder. A smirk formed on his lips as he allowed his gaze to travel from her head to her feet, taking note of the way the simple material of her dress hugged her trim figure. She certainly didn't appear to be injured in any way. In fact, from her sharp retort and the fire in her eyes, he'd say the exact opposite was the case.

As if divining his thoughts, she whirled to face him again, the fury in her narrowed eyes marring what he considered a rather attractive face.

"Just what do you think you were doing, driving so recklessly? Do you not realize you could have caused any number of accidents or even killed someone with that"—she gestured wildly toward the Model T—"that...contraption? I think *you* should be the one who should have been watching where *you* were going instead of daydreaming or attempting to break some sort of record in speed."

"Me?" Jacob slapped his hand to his chest. "I didn't exactly creep up to the crossroads in silence. In case you haven't noticed, this 'contraption' as you call it makes a rather substantial bit of noise when it's running. If I was the one daydreaming, what exactly were *you* doing that prevented you from hearing the approaching motorcar?"

A flash of guilt appeared on her face before she erased it and tapped into her anger once more. "If you must know, I was minding my own business and making my way toward home when all of a sudden you came out of nowhere and ran me off the road."

Jacob leaned back against the car and folded his arms across his chest, giving her a leisurely perusal as he quirked one eyebrow. "Well, from what I see, you don't appear to be any worse for the wear. Of course, I'm no doctor, so I can't tell if there might be internal injuries. That would require closer inspection."

The young woman dipped her head toward her chest. If more light were available, Jacob was certain there'd be a blush on her cheeks. Maybe she was coming around. A beat later, she raised her head and glared.

Then again, maybe not.

"You, sir, are quite bold in your assumptions and your suggestions. I will thank you not to make such audacious statements. We don't even know each other."

Jacob pushed away from the car and stepped toward her. "That can easily be remedied." He stuck out his hand and inclined his head. "Jacob Berringer, at your service."

Chapter 2

S hannon Delaney stared at the extended hand and then at the man who owned it. She drew her coat tightly around her to ward off the chill of the late March air. He must be completely crazy to think a mere exchange of introductions would cure his reckless driving escapade. Had her reaction been one second slower, the consequences could have been far more serious. But she wasn't the only one at fault. It would take more than a simple apology to make up for this—even if the young man in question possessed a certain charm and boyish appeal.

Well, perhaps it wouldn't hurt to at least pretend to be cordial.

"Shannon Delaney," she replied, reaching her hand toward Jacob's.

Before she could shake with him, he did a quick flip of his hand to grasp just her fingertips. Raising them to his lips, he bowed slightly and brushed an airy kiss across her knuckles with another grin.

"It's a pleasure to meet you." Jacob released her fingers and straightened. "Much better than almost running into you."

Shannon caught herself before she giggled at his quick wit. This Mr. Berringer was far too appealing for his own good. Besides, he drove a motorcar. He was obviously enamored with them as much as her brother. And that placed them on opposite sides.

Schooling her expression into one of displeasure, she gave him the sternest look she could muster. "Yes, about that." She returned her fists to her hips. "I do hope in the future you will be more careful about where you direct that mechanical contraption. You managed to avoid an accident this time, but that won't always be the case. There may very well come a time when you can't steer away quickly enough to avoid it. And what will you do then? Those things are a menace to society and a danger to everyone. Not to mention the smoke they cause—and the noise. I simply can't believe so many people prefer them to the quieter ride in a wagon. Faster isn't always better, and if people would take a moment to realize—"

"If you'll take a moment to *breathe*, I might be able to answer you."

Shannon paused. The way he'd emphasized the word "breathe" made her do a mental review. Had she really just rambled on that much without allowing him a word? She so easily got incensed over issues that mattered to her, and this one mattered a great deal.

Dipping her chin, she mumbled, "I'm sorry."

Jacob waved off her apology. "Think nothing of it." He took a step back and leaned against the car, folding his arms across his chest. "Besides, had I been more careful about my driving, we might have been nothing more than passing modes of transportation on a country road. And I never would have met such a delightful lady as you."

Oh, he was smooth. Shannon had to give him that. She wondered what other sweet talk he might conjure up in an effort to appease her. Then, all of a sudden he shrugged and assumed an air of nonchalance. Quite opposite from what she expected.

"Now, why don't you tell me what you have against such fine automobiles as these?" He reached over to rub the fender and then nodded toward her wagon. "Unless of course you're in a rush to be somewhere? I see your load of supplies there. I don't want to make you any later."

She glanced over her shoulder to where her horses stood. They seemed none the worse from the near accident.

"No," she said and returned her gaze to Jacob's face. "There is nothing in that wagon that can't wait. I was merely returning from my weekly visit to town to replenish our supplies."

"And I'm already behind schedule." He stared off blankly into the distance and mumbled, "At least I was able to deliver Mrs. Mitchell to her home safe and sound."

It sounded like he was talking to himself. He couldn't be speaking to her. She had no idea who that woman was. A second later, he shook his head as if clearing his mind from a haze.

"When I explain the circumstances to Mr. Ford, I'm sure he'll understand."

Shannon narrowed her eyes. "Mr. Ford? Mr. Henry Ford? Owner of the Highland Park plant?"

"Yes. I'm a supervisor there. Why?"

"He's just as responsible for the current circumstances as all the other motorcar owners and manufacturers."

"What do you mean?"

She threw out her arms in a wide arc. "Look around you. Do you see all of this beautiful farmland and wide-open space?"

Jacob did as she asked and gave her a dispassionate nod to continue. She should have figured he'd have no appreciation for the very things she loved and held quite dear.

"Well, thanks to men like Mr. Henry Ford and the other motorcar factories around here, we are losing our farms so the land can be used to build more factories and produce even more of those infernal contraptions people are buying left and right."

"But they aren't putting people out of their homes. They're only buying land where people are willing to sell."

"Not necessarily."

"Do you know of a situation where someone was forced to move?"

"I. . ." Shannon almost told Jacob about the offer her father had received but thought against it. She had no reason to involve this young man in her personal affairs. He was nothing more than a stranger to her. Besides, her family hadn't been forced yet. "I can't say for certain, but those men who own the factories have a lot of money and power. If they want something badly enough, there isn't much that can be done to stop them."

Jacob peered at her with a questioning look in his eyes. One side of his mouth pressed tight, causing a dimple to appear in his right cheek. He looked like he wanted to press further.

"It all depends upon the situation, I'd think," he said.

All right, so he obviously had decided against getting more information out of her.

Jacob continued. "If the circumstances weren't favorable to both sides, I would think the family who owned the land wouldn't be forced to do anything against their will."

Shannon thought about the letter and the wording that was used. It wasn't Mr. Ford who was behind it, but a rival car company. Her family did still have a choice, but there were other farms that weren't doing so well economically. And those prime pieces of farming land weren't valued as much as this so-called progress.

"That may be true, but I can't help being heartbroken knowing that some families who have been farming for generations now face losing everything because they're not turning enough profit. And all to make room for yet another factory."

"The factories and the motorcars aren't the evil you make them out to be," Jacob countered.

"No?" Shannon took a step toward the two horses and smoothed her hands across their jowls, then scratched their forelocks. The horses responded by ducking their heads toward her skirts. "Can motorcars take sugar cubes from your hand or nuzzle your pocket for a carrot?" She reached in and presented the treats to each animal. "Can they show you affection and respond to your voice?"

"Well, no."

His voice held a tinge of regret. Shannon turned to see him watching her with a wistful expression on his face. Perhaps he wasn't all bad.

"But motorcars present a unique opportunity to explore this land around us in greater comfort. In fact, machines in general have increased productivity a great deal."

He quirked a grin. "And you have to admit, they do make a bit less of a mess."

She couldn't help but smile at that remark. "You do have a point. But they are still loud and smelly."

Jacob's eyes twinkled at her return teasing. A second later, he glanced up at the sky as if to ascertain the time. "Miss Delaney, I hate to cut this short, but as I said, I was already running behind schedule when we met. As long as you're certain you're not hurt, I'd like to excuse myself and be on my way."

A part of her was glad to see him in a rush to leave. Another part wanted him to stay so they could continue this conversation.

She didn't know why, but she had a feeling he might actually be slightly sympathetic to her family's plight. As a supervisor, he might have some influence with the Ford Motor Company.

And other than Johnny, he was the first man not related to her who had shown any interest in conversing. Still, she had a few ingredients for supper among the supplies she needed to get back home, and she shouldn't keep him any longer.

"I am fine, Mr. Berringer. And I'm glad your motorcar didn't suffer any harm, either. I would hate to see you get in trouble with Mr. Ford for ruining one of his newest Model Ts."

Jacob jerked his head back and raised his eyebrows at her words. Shannon mentally scolded herself for showing her knowledge of the various models. At least she hadn't let slip its "Tin Lizzie" nickname. She might not like the cars, but she did try to stay informed. How else could she argue against their invention? Thankfully, Jacob remained silent about it.

"And you said you come into the city every Saturday?" he said instead.

"Yes. Some weeks I don't purchase much. Others I have a full load in my wagon."

"Well, maybe we'll bump into one another again sometime."

"Perhaps." She reached for the reins and prepared to climb into the buggy. Jacob was there in an instant to assist her.

"Thank you." She nodded down at him and offered a smile. "Next time I hope our meeting doesn't cause quite so much alarm."

He returned the smile and tipped his cap at her. "Good day, Miss Delaney."

"Good day, Mr. Berringer."

Shannon flicked the reins and clucked her tongue to get the team moving. She almost looked back to see if Jacob was watching her. If he was, then he would see her looking. No, it was best if she acted as if their chance encounter was nothing more. He might possess a great deal of charm, but she should leave it at that.

Jacob stood on the other side of the desk from Mr. Ford, trying hard not to display the nervousness he felt. Mr. Sorenson flanked the desk to the right and maintained an imposing stance, arms folded across his chest as he peered at Jacob with an unreadable expression. Ford pressed his lips in a thin line as he perused the report Jacob had presented not five minutes ago along with his apology for returning late. Finally, the man spoke.

"I'll admit, Mr. Berringer, that I was not pleased to see you take such a long time to perform such a simple task." He glanced up from the report. "It's fortunate that one of the workers in your division was able to step up and see to your duties in your absence. I don't like to see any area of my plant left unsupervised for long."

Certain this wasn't the time to interject anything or respond in any way, Jacob remained silent and simply met Ford's gaze. At least he could show his boss he was willing to accept whatever penalty might be levied against him. He only prayed it wouldn't mean a demotion from his supervisory position.

"However," Ford continued, raising the report and giving it a couple shakes, "you do provide a thorough accounting for your lengthy excursion and the reasoning for it." A congenial smile formed at the corners of his lips. "And I can't help but acknowledge your assertiveness in deciding to test the model free from the city's boundaries."

Perhaps the punishment wouldn't be all that severe after all.

"There's also the matter of Mother Mitchell."

Jacob drew his eyebrows together at this. He couldn't tell if Ford was pleased or upset. But instead of continuing, Sorenson stepped forward.

"Mother Mitchell phoned not long after arriving home and had nothing but praise and adulation for your courteous escort and pleasing company during the drive to her house. For that, I am extremely grateful."

So, Mrs. Mitchell had spoken highly of him. Jacob stood taller at hearing that news, and his confidence began to build again. "It was my pleasure, sir. She provided entertaining conversation during the time we were together." He left off that she had just about been the sole source of dialogue. Neither of the men who stood before him needed to know that.

Sorenson grinned. "I have no doubt that she did." His wink told Jacob he was well aware how talkative his mother-in-law could be.

"But back to the matter at hand," Ford said, effectively focusing attention on him again. "The good you accomplished does outweigh the tardiness, but it doesn't erase the fact you were substantially late."

"Yes, sir." Jacob nodded.

"You did account for everything. However, these models are not toys, and although you managed to avoid an accident or any damage to the car, you diverted from the original instructions. As it stands, I will only dock you a day's wage. Nothing more."

Well, there went one more day he'd have to work in order to save his money for a car. It could have been worse, though.

"Thank you, Mr. Ford," Jacob said, his gaze steady and direct as he silently paid the piper for his somewhat imprudent decision. "I assure you it won't happen again."

Ford leveled an admonishing stare in Jacob's direction. "See that it doesn't, my boy. I'd hate to lose such a valued member of my supervisory staff." He dismissed Jacob with a wave of his hand. "Now, back to work."

"Yes, sir." With that Jacob turned on his heel and left the office. Once outside he breathed a sigh of relief that the consequences hadn't been any worse. At least he still had his job. So, the unfortunate—or rather fortunate—meeting of Miss Delaney might prove beneficial after all. He just had to devise a plan to see her again. With her regular visits to the city, that shouldn't be too hard.

Chapter 3

W hat else can I get for you, Miss Delaney?"

The stout yet congenial owner of the corner store placed the most recent item on Shannon's list into a crate on the counter. She'd had to wait a few moments upon arrival for Mr. Mulligan to finish a phone call, but he'd gathered everything in quick order once he began waiting on her.

Shannon looked in each of the boxes on the floor and consulted her list. "Umm, I need ten pounds of sugar and flour and three boxes of nails. Oh, and of course any of those leftover fabric scraps you usually keep."

"For your quilts?"

"Of course." She smiled. "I couldn't make them without those pieces. And since you also generously agreed to sell some of my quilts here, I'm happy to put those scraps to good use." Shannon checked the final items off her list with a pencil then tucked it behind her ear. "After that, I do believe we have everything."

His receding hairline and slight gray at the temples were the only indication that he'd been working for more than half his life. The ever-present smile and good-natured personality made him seem so much younger than his fifty-three years.

She loved coming to this store each week for supplies. The scent of cinnamon and cloves from the spices in the nearest aisle mixed with the aroma of fresh bread from the bakery next door, providing an invigorating blend. The floors were always swept clean, and the aisles were arranged in neat array. Mr. Mulligan always greeted her with warmth, and she had yet to find any better costs for the items she needed. It gave her a sense of being in a small town rather than an ever-growing and booming city.

"That should do it," Mr. Mulligan stated as he hefted the two sacks in place beside the crates on the floor. "I'll have Johnny come and help you load these crates into your wagon."

"No need for that, Mr. Mulligan. I'll help."

The familiar voice made Shannon turn her head toward the door only to see the young man who'd almost run her off the road last week. What was his name? Jason? James? Jacob? Jacob! That was it. Jacob Berringer.

"Ah, Mr. Berringer," the owner greeted much louder than necessary. "So nice to see you here this fine day."

Something in his voice sounded odd, so Shannon turned around again in time to see what she thought was a wink from Mr. Mulligan to Jacob. Now why would he be winking at Jacob? She glanced back at Jacob and saw nothing unusual in his expression, so she brushed it off as her overactive imagination.

"Yes," Jacob replied. "It seemed like a good day for a walk, so I came over here on my break from work. Mother wanted me to pick up some flour, and I figured now is as good a time as any."

"Well, help yourself to a sack, my boy. I'll finish tallying Miss Delaney's order."

Jacob nodded at her as he headed for the burlaps in the corner. For a fleeting second, she caught a twinkle in his eye; then it was gone. She couldn't help but follow his movements and stare at his broad back. His dark hair curled at the collar of his shirt. Why did he have to be so attractive?

"I have your total, Miss Delaney."

Shannon shook her head and started at the gruff voice of the shopkeeper. It sounded like he'd just cleared his throat to get her attention, only she hadn't heard it.

"I'm sorry, Mr. Mulligan." She returned her attention to settling the bill. After handing the money to the shopkeeper, Shannon lifted the lightest crate in her arms. "Thank you again for gathering my supplies. It saves me a lot of time and helps me get back to the farm faster, which makes my family happy."

Mr. Mulligan waved off her thanks. "Think nothing of it. I could never allow a young lady such as yourself to tote and carry such things while I stood idly by and didn't help. That goes against everything I was ever taught."

An airy giggle escaped from Shannon's lips as she shifted the crate she held. "Well then, be sure and thank your mother for me for raising her son right."

The owner touched two fingers to his brow and gave her a mock salute. "That I will do." He turned toward the corner where Jacob still stood. "Jacob, my boy, I believe Miss Delaney is ready for your help now."

"Yes, sir." Jacob jumped into action, tossing the twenty-pound sack of flour he held on the counter like it weighed nothing more than a feather. He then bent and grabbed the heaviest of Shannon's crates and headed for the door, barely pausing to readjust the added weight. Stopping just as he reached the front of the store, he looked back over his shoulder at Shannon. "Miss Delaney, if you'll point me in the direction of your wagon, I'll get these crates loaded in the back in a jiffy, and you can be on your way."

Shannon stared, still dwelling on the obvious strength this man possessed. Oh, but he was waiting for her response. "Umm, it's the one that's, um, next to the hitching post to the left." She pointed in the general direction and waited for Jacob to disappear outside. Where was her brain? And could she sound any more addlepated? She knew where she'd left her wagon. There was no need to stutter.

A few moments later, Jacob returned for the next crate. Shannon felt useless standing there and watching him tote her supplies from the store, so she pulled the crate she held closer to her chest and headed for the door. No sense letting him do all the work.

"Umm, thank you," she began as she met him at her wagon. "You didn't have to use your valuable break to help me with this menial task." In fact, she had to wonder just why he did. She hadn't exactly been cordial to him when they'd met.

He paused and tipped back the same cap he'd worn the day they met. "It's my pleasure, Miss Delaney." Averting his eyes, he dipped his chin toward his chest. "Besides, it's the least I can do after the unfortunate way we met at those crossroads."

Ah, so that was the reason behind his offer. Was she imagining it, or had his voice just taken on a sheepish quality? He seemed genuinely regretful for the circumstances surrounding their first encounter. The sincerity in his tone made him that much more endearing. As if she needed another reason for him to fill her thoughts.

"I beg your pardon if this is out of place, but why don't you have a farmhand or other hired help come to town for supplies? Or at least come with you so you don't have to tote all this alone?" He made a sweeping gesture over the three crates now in the back of the wagon.

Shannon bristled and squared her shoulders. "My family and I work very hard to keep the farm we own running and producing enough to meet the demands of property taxes, not to mention other everyday costs. We don't have enough left over to pay anyone else or even hire them on a short-term basis. Since my father and brothers all have to work the land, that leaves me to come to town. My mother is busy preparing food for everyone, and my sister is too young to venture into the city on her own."

Jacob held up his hands in mock surrender and took a step back from her. "Hey, I meant no harm in asking and didn't intend to insult you or your family in any way. I just wanted to make sure someone wasn't taking advantage of you by sending you to fetch supplies."

His quick apology took the wind out of the sails of Shannon's staunch defense. She narrowed her eyes. He didn't appear to be making up a story to placate her. Maybe she shouldn't have overreacted so much.

"I'm sorry for that outburst. I never have been good about things people say that I perceive as being a slight against my family."

"Don't worry about it. I'd react the same if I felt someone was insinuating things about my family." He disappeared inside and returned a moment later with another crate. "So, how many brothers and sisters do you have?" The last part of his question came out more in a grunt as he hefted the crate into the wagon and arranged it with the others.

"I have two brothers and one sister. The brothers are older, and the sister is younger."

"Being groomed for taking over the farm one day?"

Shannon tilted her head. "I honestly hadn't thought about it, but I suppose so, yes."

Jacob shrugged. "It's inevitable, isn't it? The natural order of things?"

"Well, yes, but I guess I always imagined my father being around forever."

Shannon didn't want to think about it. If one of her brothers assumed ownership, she might be pressured to marry and leave everything she'd ever known. Of course, if that other car company had their way, the farm wouldn't need any owners. It would be destroyed in the name of progress. All their dreams and hopes and hard work would be for naught. All the years they'd invested would be wasted. If only their farm were farther out from the city, then they might be safe from such concerns. Perhaps if they could maintain a profit or find ways to increase production, the company would look elsewhere for their land and cease their attempts to negotiate.

"Might also be you and your future husband if you marry. Depends on who wants to stay living there."

"What?"

Shannon jerked her head toward the store front door where Jacob exited to join her on the sidewalk. He had the final crate in his arms and a smaller box stacked on top. When he loaded them with the other crates, Shannon tried to recall what he'd just said. Had she misheard, or had he just mentioned marriage and living somewhere?

"I mentioned one or both of your brothers becoming owners of your farm." He took out a rather worn handkerchief from his back pocket and swiped it across his brow then tucked it into his shirt pocket. "Then I said it might be you if you're the one who wants to continue living there."

"Oh, right." She really needed to stop letting her mind wander or get distracted. "I have no doubt it will be one of my brothers, though. They are both rather fond of our land."

Jacob hopped up into the back of the wagon and wedged all the crates close together. "And well they should be. Farms bring us a lot of what we need to survive."

Shannon hadn't expected a philosophy like that to come out of Jacob's mouth. He seemed to be one who would prefer the manufactured goods over the natural and fresh produce that came from the land.

"Do you want this box settled with the crates or up on the seat with you?"

She shielded her eyes from the sun as she looked up to where Jacob held out a small box, awaiting her further instruction.

"What's in it?"

He dunked his hand inside and rummaged a bit, then held up a piece of fabric. "Just some mismatched pieces that look like leftovers from a bunch of shirts or dresses or something."

"Oh! Scraps for my quilts. Yes. Please put them on the bench at the front."

Jacob twisted at the waist and stretched over the crates to do as she asked. With both hands resting on the back of the seat, he peered at her over his shoulder. "Quilts? You mean those patchwork things you sew together?"

Shannon resisted the urge to laugh at his basic and obviously uneducated description. Then again, he worked at a motorcar company. Why would he have any knowledge of such things?

"Yes. It used to be a hobby of mine, but a couple years ago, a friend of my mother's visited and saw one of the quilts I'd made draped across one of our chairs." She moved toward the front of the wagon and reached for a single piece of scrap, already envisioning its place on a new quilt. "She asked about it and ended up taking it home with her after paying me handsomely for it. When a similar thing happened two more times, I realized I could make a profit from doing something I loved."

He nodded toward the quilt draped across the bench. "Is that one you made?"

"It's one of my earlier ones. I've since relegated it to helping make the ride a little more comfortable."

The corners of his mouth turned down as he assessed the sample. "Even with it being an early attempt, it looks good to me."

Shannon beamed under his praise. "I've managed to learn a few things over the years that have made the results of my work a bit more attractive to potential buyers. And now Mr. Mulligan carries a few in his store."

"Sounds like you've merited a good measure of God's favor."

She stared up at him and drew her eyebrows together. "I beg your pardon?"

Bracing himself with one hand, Jacob vaulted over the side of the wagon and down to the sidewalk to stand next to her. "Well, it isn't often that folks can get paid for doing something they love." He shrugged. "I just figured you've been rewarded for your diligence."

Rewarded by being able to do what she loved? She'd never considered that before. "I suppose it can be seen that way. I know I'm grateful. Far too many do work they don't love simply to earn money. I hope I never have to live that way."

He let out a chortle. "You're not kidding. I thank God every day for my work at the Ford plant. In a flash, it could all be gone, so even when I mess up, I'm quick to ask for forgiveness—from both God and my boss."

Shannon didn't have a response, so she remained silent. Jacob didn't say anything either at first. All of a sudden, he smacked her wagon where his hand had rested and looked at the crates in the back. "Looks like we've got everything loaded.

Are you sure you're going to be all right getting it all back to your farm?"

"I should be fine."

"Because if your father and brothers will be in the field, I could come with you and help unload."

Her breath caught in her throat. Ride all the way to the farm alone with him sharing the seat with her? A sudden increase in her heartbeat made it quite clear what her mind thought of that prospect. As much as she would enjoy the company and the opportunity to get to know Jacob better, there would be far too many questions at home if she agreed. Perhaps another time.

"I appreciate the offer, Mr. Berringer, but my family will be there to help move the crates into the house." She put on what she hoped was an encouraging smile. "Thank you for your concern, though. You've provided more than enough assistance today. Besides, I wouldn't want to keep you any longer from your work." Shannon looked down the street to the south in the direction of the Highland Park plant. "Speaking of which, shouldn't you be returning soon? I believe you mentioned you came here to the store on your break. You can't have much time left."

Not that she wanted to see him leave. In fact, it would be nice to continue this conversation. Today just wasn't that day.

"No, you're right. I had another supervisor step in for me during my absence to allow me enough time to get the flour. I don't want to take advantage."

"Then I shall bid you good-bye and let you be on your way." She reached for the reins and raised one booted foot to the board only to find Jacob right there to assist her into the seat. Just as he had done at their first meeting. "Thank you," she replied once she was seated and could turn to look at him.

He nodded, placing his thumb and index finger on the brim of his cap. "Miss Delaney, it was a pleasure. At least this time our meeting wasn't surrounded by misfortune. I hope our future ones will be the same."

"As do I, Mr. Berringer. Thank you again."

With a quick snap of the reins and a cluck of her tongue, she set the horses in motion. Shannon kept her attention in front of her, but her thoughts remained behind and focused on the man she was certain still stood on the sidewalk outside the store watching her depart.

Future meetings? Did that mean he wanted to see her again? She certainly hoped so. They might be at cross paths in regard to how they viewed the world, but that didn't take away from his charm and handsome appearance. At least for now, they could be friends.

Chapter 4

Jacob stood across the street from Mulligan's Grocery and observed the activity inside. Shannon took a slow walk up and down the aisles. The owner had said she came in every Saturday for supplies. Once in a while, she made a midweek visit, but her regular schedule remained. Jacob could probably set his watch by it.

Yesterday he'd managed to get approval to work only a half day today at the plant, but he'd worked thirteen hours the day before to make up for it. And oh, how his friends had teased him when they found out the reason. They'd used one of their break times while Jacob continued overseeing his department. He could still play out the scene in detail in his mind.

Kendall Waverly propped his elbow on the metal conveyor belt where Jacob observed the progress. "A girl, huh?" He smirked. "She must be quite a looker to make you want to miss work and spend time with her. I can't remember you ever doing that. It's about time."

Bryce Gallimore nudged Jacob in the ribs. "You mean the mighty Jacob has finally been bit by the smitten bug?"

"It's not as serious as you two make it sound," Jacob countered. "We met when I took the newest Model T out for a test run and almost had an accident." He shrugged and pushed a crankshaft more to the center as it passed. "I only want to apologize and make amends."

The two guys snorted and exchanged knowing looks.

"Make amends?" Kendall didn't look like he believed it. "You can do that with a quick apology. No need to spend time with her."

"Yeah, so fess up," Bryce added. "This gal has caught your eye. No sense denying it."

Jacob sighed and rolled his eyes. "You two are a real piece of work. The way you gossip, you'd give some girls I know a good bit of competition."

"This isn't gossip," Kendall denied. "You're standing right in front of us. If we were gossiping, you wouldn't be here."

"Besides," Bryce continued, "you're our friend, and we have to look out for you."

"Yeah, yeah." Kendall nodded and jerked his thumb toward Bryce. "What he said."

Jacob signaled one of the workers to flip the lever that would bring the next set of parts their direction. "Call it what you want. But you're making this out to be more than it is. Trust me."

"Any time a man chooses a girl over work, it's something." Kendall pressed a mock punch into Jacob's upper arm. "We'll be waiting for a report first thing Monday morning."

"Don't disappoint us." Bryce mimicked Kendall's action on Jacob's other arm. "We know where to find you."

Jacob lifted his pocket watch from where it was hooked to his suspenders and flipped open the cover. "Speaking of work, don't you think you two should get back to it? Your break is about over."

His friends gave him one parting glance obviously meant to intimidate, but Jacob only laughed as they walked away. They meant well. He had to give them that. And a guy couldn't ask for two better friends. Maybe one day soon they'd also become supervisors of their own areas. With his attention again on this part of production, he began formulating how he'd explain Shannon to them.

Now as he watched the subject of that entertaining conversation, Jacob had no idea what he'd say come Monday morning. What exactly were his feelings where Shannon was concerned? Could it be more than just making amends? Kendall had been right. She was a looker. A moment later, she stepped outside and gave him a better view.

Her hair was again gathered in one long braid down her back, and her straw hat sat a bit crooked on her head. A white apron over a simple brown skirt and light blue top didn't exactly command all eyes to turn her way. But her face— that was the feature to make him stand up and take notice. Smooth and round with wide blue eyes and long eyelashes. Add to that her rosy cheeks and full lips curved into a half smile and it all blended together in a rather appealing package.

No, he couldn't say for sure how he felt, but he would have fun while he figured it out. It wasn't fate that brought them together. God played a part in there somewhere. And Jacob wasn't about to waste the opportunity.

He started to take a step off the sidewalk when another girl joined Shannon by the wagon. Johnny, the grocer's assistant, followed close behind with the first crate of supplies. The younger girl looked to be about sixteen and resembled Shannon in many ways. This had to be her sister. Every bit as pretty and possessing the same smile.

The two appeared to be engaged in an animated discussion of some sort. The younger girl waved her arms several times and pointed off in the distance. Shannon responded in a more reserved manner, but her face reflected her passion as well.

Johnny stepped around them to load another crate then said something to Shannon. She nodded and smiled as Johnny tipped his hat and disappeared back inside. That was likely the last of her supplies. She'd be leaving any minute. After she stepped toward her wagon and grabbed hold of the reins, she paused to glance up and down the sidewalk in both directions. It appeared like she was searching for something. . .or someone.

Maybe she was looking for him.

Jacob grinned at the thought and pushed away from the lamppost where he'd been leaning. Only one way to find out.

Careful to avoid being too obvious, he approached the wagon and almost managed to get right next to her before she turned toward him. Avoiding detection by her younger sister, though, proved much harder. The young lady caught sight of him just as he reached the sidewalk where they stood. She hadn't alerted Shannon, only watched his progress with slightly narrowed eyes and keen interest.

Jacob tapped Shannon on the shoulder then shoved his hands in his pockets and rocked back on his heels. "Looking for someone?"

Shannon gasped and turned toward him, her face immediately flushing. Could he have been right? It wasn't as if he had made it a habit to be there when she came to town. He'd only done it once. Not enough for her to expect a repeat occurrence. The fact that she might, though, made him grin again.

"Mr. Berringer." Shannon quickly hid what he considered guilt at being caught and replaced it with pleasant cordiality. "What a nice surprise. Are you here for more flour?"

She recovered well. "No," he replied. "I was across the street there and thought I'd come over to say hello." Jacob pointed in the general direction of where he'd been standing. No reason to give away that he'd been watching for her. Shifting his attention from Shannon to the younger girl, he tipped his cap. "And who is this pretty little lady with you today?"

Shannon extended her free arm toward the girl who stepped into Shannon's embrace. "This is my younger sister, Maribeth." With a quick glance at her sister before returning her gaze to Jacob's, Shannon continued. "Maribeth, meet Mr. Jacob Berringer."

Maribeth gave him a sly smile then bobbed a short curtsy and nodded. "Pleased to meet you."

Jacob held her gaze a moment or two. She wasn't obvious about it, but Maribeth had a streak of mischief in her. He should know. He'd been the perpetrator of a number of schemes through the years.

"Mr. Berringer and I met two weeks ago at that intersection near Mr. Holstead's farm."

Recognition lit up Maribeth's face. "Oh! So *you're* the one with the motorcar and the careless driving skills."

Shannon hid her giggle behind her hand. The amusement in her eyes belied exactly how the retelling of their encounter had occurred. The two sisters no doubt shared a few laughs over the story. Good thing her brothers weren't with her, or they might've demonstrated their protective nature and put him in his place.

Well, no reason not to go along with how Shannon had relayed the incident. Jacob swooped off his cap and bowed. "Guilty as charged." Straightening, he gave Shannon a wink. "Although your sister might not have told my side of the story the way I would have."

A twinkle in Shannon's eyes told him he'd guessed right. No matter, though. At least it put a positive slant on their meeting. He could work with that. A negative one would be harder to overcome.

"So, are you going to come with us this time to help with these crates?" Maribeth was bold enough to ask. "Shannon's not alone with me here."

"Maribeth!" Shannon spoke low and gave her sister a reprimanding glance.

Maribeth didn't see it, though. Her attention stayed focused on Jacob. The young lady didn't waste any time. And she certainly wasn't the least bit shy. In fact, *precocious* came to mind as Jacob regarded the younger version of Shannon. This girl could be a real handful if he wasn't careful. At the same time, she could also be an asset. Shannon obviously kept nothing from her sister. Or her sister pestered her until she told everything. Either way, Maribeth knew about last week as well.

"I don't know, Maribeth. I suppose that's up to your sister." Jacob slanted his eyes toward Shannon to gauge her reaction. "I offered last week, and that offer still stands. In fact, I have already finished work for the day, so my time is yours if I can be of any help."

Shannon bit down on her lower lip and chewed it for a moment or two. Her inner thoughts reflected on her face and were rather easy to read. A part of her revealed her desire for his company, and another part showed uncertainty.

"As I said last week, Miss Delaney," he jumped in to possibly aid her in making up her mind, "consider me nothing more than an extra pair of hands to help tote the crates wherever you need them delivered." He glanced between the two sisters and smiled. "Besides, with two such charming ladies, the ride is sure to be quite enjoyable."

That last remark sealed the deal for Maribeth. The young lady's eyes brightened, and a wide smile beamed across her face. All of a sudden, she seemed rather eager to get moving and made her way to the back of the wagon where she climbed up and knelt behind the front bench before Jacob could even think to offer his hand to help her up.

"It's all settled, then," Maribeth stated with a tone of finality. "Let's get home, Shannon. Or else Mama and Papa will be wondering what took us so long."

Shannon looked from Maribeth to Jacob and back again twice. The indecision on her face kept her rooted to the sidewalk. Finally, she shrugged and stepped toward the footboard on the side of the wagon.

Jacob rushed forward to offer his assistance, placing one hand at the small of her back to give her a slight push and allowing her to hold his other hand for balance. Once she was settled, he climbed aboard and took his seat beside her. Maribeth rested her forearms on the bench's back and positioned herself between the two of them. Jacob almost chuckled. Shannon had no reason to worry. They had a chaperone. And one he was sure would watch their every move.

"Is everyone ready?" Shannon peered over her shoulder at Maribeth, then glanced at Jacob.

"Almost," Jacob replied.

He reached for the reins at the same time as Shannon. She opened her mouth to protest, but he cut her off before she could.

"I'm no stranger to a horse and buggy, Miss Delaney. I haven't always driven those metal contraptions, as you like to call them. Besides, I couldn't sit here while you drove the team. Goes against everything my mother taught me."

That final remark must have worked because Shannon relaxed and nodded, giving her silent permission for him to take the lead. Good. She needed to know he was a gentleman first and foremost. If she hadn't realized that before today, she knew now.

Jacob snapped the reins and set the wagon moving. Silence settled over them, and conversation ceased. With deft precision and knowledge of the streets leading out of the city, he guided the team past the Grosse Pointe district where his family lived and headed north.

"It's so fascinating, don't you think, to see the blend of so many forms of transportation all vying for their place on the streets?" Maribeth turned her head to the left and right, looking at everything as they clip-clopped past. "I wonder how long it will be before wagons such as ours become extinct."

"It never ceases to amaze me that the horses don't frighten from the roar of the motorcars," Shannon replied. "Or worse, that there aren't more accidents from so many different types of transportation all in a hurry to get somewhere."

"The motorcars have been in the city for a number of years, Miss Delaney. And they aren't any louder than gunshots or any more startling than the bells on the trolleys." Jacob tried hard to settle on something that would help. "In fact, their low rumbles are steady enough that horses wouldn't be distracted by them. Whether you're in a buggy or a motorcar, it's the sudden movements of people or other travelers that cause accidents." He shrugged. "Besides, horses can adapt."

"Mr. Berringer is right, Shannon," Maribeth agreed, coming to his aid. "Our horses hear far worse things out on our farm with things like rifles firing, hammers banging, Papa's table saw, and other tools in the barn, not to mention the clanging of the triangle Mama rings for mealtime."

He'd have to thank Maribeth at some point for her defense. She didn't seem to be one who would be rushing out to buy a motorcar anytime soon, but she did appear to be more willing to consider its benefits. Perhaps he had a solid ally in

Shannon's sister. It certainly couldn't hurt.

"I suppose you're both right." Shannon pursed her lips and regarded the easy way the motorcars paused to allow buggies or wagons to pass and vice versa. "But I prefer the simplicity that a horse and wagon offers. There is no cranking, no monitoring pedals with your feet, and no maintaining control of a wheel or the smoke of the exhaust."

Jacob paused. If she was so opposed to automobiles, how did she seem to know so much about them? Maybe she had ridden in one and the experience turned her against them. He wanted to find out more.

"No, but with a horse and wagon you need to be careful of holes and ruts in the road or the condition of your axles and wheels. You also have to hold tight to the reins and manage the brake as needed." Jacob raised the leather he held in his hands and nodded at the horses as they passed the invisible city line and made their way toward the farmlands. "Which way?"

"Just let the horses lead," Shannon replied. "They can navigate this route blindfolded if necessary."

That suited Jacob just fine. The less he had to think about, the better. He could focus more on the discussion at hand. Loosening his hold, he leaned against the bench.

"Your horses are amazing and obviously of great value. Another thing to consider is that the power behind your buggy or wagon needs hay and a clean stall, plus shoes and a good brushing on a regular basis, among other things, to perform at optimum level."

"Wow. You make it sound like so much work." Maribeth sighed. "We do all that and don't even think about it. And Papa or our brothers make sure the wagons and all the parts are in excellent condition."

"I was only pointing out that maintaining a motorcar isn't too much different than maintaining a pair of horses and a wagon," Jacob added, casting a glance at Shannon to see how she was responding. "It's just different."

"Yes," Shannon agreed, her lips set in a firm line, "but a motorcar can't respond to you or have any sort of personality. It's a cold, unfeeling machine that seems to reflect the insensitive nature of its designers."

Ouch. Jacob knew she didn't like automobiles, but he had no idea she felt this strongly about them. There had to be some other reason for her aversion.

"People who own those contraptions," Shannon continued, "seem to be more interested in the latest model or the state of production and advancement in technology than they do about each other. From what I've seen, these machines cause nothing but trouble and make people more selfish. I'll take the simple farming life any day over being wrapped up in machines. At least we still have neighbors who genuinely care about us instead of worrying about some status symbol."

"Not everyone who owns a motorcar exhibits behavior like that." Jacob transferred the reins to one hand and extended his other toward Shannon. "And not all machines cause problems. Industry and development have brought a great deal of improvement to our lives. We have electricity to light the dark, telephones to call people who live in a completely different state, and phonographs for playing music."

Shannon interrupted before he could continue. "But those are all valid benefits to us. I wasn't talking about inventions. I was referring to noisy machines."

She obviously was going to need more specific and practical examples. And those Jacob had. "All right. Let's talk noisy contraptions," he began, using her negative description to keep her attention. "Take the farms you love so much. It's those machines that make it possible for the expansive irrigation of farmland, saving time for the farmers and enabling them to plant more crops. Those machines also plow the land faster to provide a more substantial harvest in less time."

"You might be right, but they are still intrusive and threaten our livelihood in other ways."

"Aww, Shannon," Maribeth said in a somewhat defensive tone, "they're not that bad."

Jacob almost shied away at how fast Shannon whipped her head around to glare at her sister. Had her arm flailed out, it would have hit him. The restrained anger in her eyes looked about ready to burst.

"Maribeth, you are only saying that because you don't fully understand everything about them."

Maribeth pushed back from the bench and jammed her fists to her waist. "I am not a child, Shannon. I'm sixteen. You are only four years older, and that doesn't make you an expert."

"Maybe not, but there are a few things you're obviously not remembering."

"Such as?"

Shannon paused, as if weighing whether or not to reveal her thoughts and pursue this topic of conversation. Jacob alternated between maintaining control of a team that seemed to know exactly where they were going and watching Shannon. Finally, she licked her lips and opened her mouth.

"Such as the fact that Papa's cousin was killed while driving one of those infernal pieces of metal." She bluntly delivered the statement and avoided all eye contact.

Now that was something Jacob never would have expected. No wonder she felt the way she did.

Maribeth stared, mouth wide open and eyes reflecting a shared hurt. "You're right. I'd forgotten about that."

Shannon closed her eyes for a second and took a deep breath then turned to face her sister. "I'll never forget Mama and Papa talking to us that evening last year. You didn't know him as well as Jeremiah, Matthew, and I did, but that was only because he stopped visiting when you were still quite young."

Maribeth placed a comforting hand on Shannon's shoulder, her expression changing to sympathy. "It's understandable why you always look so upset whenever mention of automobiles is made. With Matthew going on and on about how he wants to save his money to buy one, I'm surprised you don't speak up more often about that."

"Well, it wasn't as if it happened to one of us," Shannon offered without conviction. "Besides, there are far more important matters at hand. Papa received another letter recently from that other car company expressing interest in our farm. They want the land so they can build a second factory in an attempt to increase production." She grunted. "As if we need another factory this far outside of town. It will only make more noise and more smoke and destroy the fresh air we enjoy away from the city."

Jacob refrained from mentioning anything like manure or the normal smells produced by livestock, barns, and farming in general. He needed to tread lightly where these two ladies were concerned. And in light of what he'd just learned about their family, remarks like that would do him no good. No sense putting himself in front of the firing squad on purpose.

"Not to mention the peace and quiet we have out here," Maribeth added. "I had no idea Papa had received such requests."

"That's only because Mama and Papa didn't want to upset anyone."

"So how did you find out?"

Shannon's face softened as she adjusted her position in her seat to face her sister.

"The same way I learned of Papa's cousin. When I asked, they had no choice but to explain everything." Shannon reached out and touched one of Maribeth's hands. "And believe me, whoever it is that is contacting them is not being kind about it. In fact, they could almost be considered threatening in nature."

Maribeth gasped. "You mean if Papa doesn't sell to them, they could force his hand in some way?"

Shannon nodded. "That's one way of putting it."

Threatening letters from another car company in the city? Jacob could hardly believe it. He was relieved to know it wasn't Ford clamoring to buy that land. But how had something like this gone unnoticed or unchecked?

He turned to face Shannon and caught her eye. "Letters like that can be considered harassment. Has your father spoken to anyone else about this?"

"Do you mean a lawyer or perhaps someone in law enforcement?"

"I'd start there, yes." Jacob almost said he'd volunteer to do that for them, but he didn't want to hurt her father's pride—or Shannon's for that matter. "Your father shouldn't allow whoever it is to bully him like this." Shannon stiffened and was about to protest when he held up his hand. "From what you've told me about him, I'm sure he can hold his own." She relaxed again. Good. He'd recovered from his initial blunder. "Your brothers will no doubt stand on their own as well."

Maribeth giggled. "Yes, and even issue their own threats if necessary."

Jacob had almost forgotten she was there. He hadn't noticed a farmhouse had come into view, either, and now it was right in front of them. Considering how the horses had pretty much led the way, this had to be the Delaneys' farm. He made a quick glance around what he could see without making it obvious and was quite impressed. The farmhouse featured a large covered front porch with two swings that sat at each corner, reminding him of some of the more elaborate homes he'd seen in the Grosse Pointe district. Wide enough to have at least four or five bedrooms and well kept, its appearance spoke volumes about the pride this family took in their home.

Of course, seeing the farmhouse meant their ride had come to an end and he might be meeting the rest of Shannon's family—including these brothers Shannon and Maribeth had mentioned.

"I haven't met any of your brothers and don't know much about them, but if they're helping run a farm of this size, I can come to my own conclusions. They will be an asset to your father. There's no doubt."

"Oh, they're all grand." Maribeth gave him a sly glance from the corner of her eye and quirked her lips in a half grin. "And they love Shannon and me a great deal. They'll go to great lengths to protect us."

Jacob couldn't be sure, but it sounded like Maribeth was insinuating he had an interest in Shannon beyond helping her with the supplies. And did he? If so, he'd do well to heed Maribeth's unspoken warning. Maybe he should see them safely home and do what he came to do. Unload the supplies and be on his way.

That brought another dilemma to mind. How was he going to get home? He hadn't thought about that at all. He'd been so caught up in spending time with Shannon that he hadn't made plans for a return to the city once he was done. Oh well. It wasn't that far. He could use a good walk.

"Well, we're here," Shannon announced unnecessarily. "And it's still early. Papa, Jeremiah, and Matthew will still be in the fields. We're on our own to get these crates inside."

Jacob hopped down and immediately turned to offer a hand to both Shannon and Maribeth. As soon as they were on the ground, he headed to the back of the wagon and dropped the gate.

"Just point me in the right direction, and I'll take care of them."

It only took three trips to the porch where Shannon assured him they could take it from there.

"Nonsense." Jacob pressed his palm flat against the beam next to the steps. "When I do a job, I see it through to completion."

"That's an admirable quality to possess," an unfamiliar voice spoke from behind the screen door.

"Hi, Mama," Maribeth greeted.

Jacob licked his lips. This was it. He might not meet Shannon's father or brothers, but he was about to meet her mother. As the matriarch of the family pushed on the door and stepped onto the porch, Jacob withdrew his handkerchief and wiped his hands before offering his right one to Mrs. Delaney. She let the door smack shut behind her and took his hand without hesitation.

"Mr. Berringer, I presume? My name is Rachel Delaney."

Jacob started. Did everyone in Shannon's family know about him? He glanced toward Shannon, who averted her eyes as the slightest pink stained her cheeks. This really was a close family. "Jacob Berringer, ma'am," he said, returning his attention to the woman whose hand he still held. He cleared his throat and ended the handshake.

Standing there surrounded by the three women made him want to say or do something to alleviate the awkwardness. Ah, the crates. Perfect. He could use a task right now to keep him busy. Bending, he hefted the nearest one into his arms and stood. "Where would you like these supplies, ma'am?"

Mrs. Delaney reached for the door, but Maribeth beat her to it. The woman smiled at her daughter then looked at Jacob. "The foodstuffs can be placed on the table in the kitchen. The rest can be set in the front room. My husband and sons will sort through the items when they come in from the fields."

"Very well." Jacob didn't waste any time and got right to work.

The ladies left the path clear for him to get the crates placed where Mrs. Delaney had requested. They didn't attempt to engage him in conversation, just busied themselves with supper preparations and putting things away. For that he was grateful. However, he did notice a silent exchange more than once when he looked up between leaving a crate and heading to the porch for another. Once he was gone, he had no doubt he'd be the immediate subject of conversation. That alone motivated him to get finished.

After stacking the last crate in the front room, he brushed his hands together and again reached for his handkerchief to clean off any dirt. "I believe that's all of them," he announced.

Mrs. Delaney came into the front room, shadowed by her two daughters. She assessed his work and smiled. "This will do quite nicely. Thank you, Mr. Berringer."

Jacob wanted to tell her to call him by his first name, but considering the circumstances, it was best he keep things somewhat formal. . .for now.

"You're more than welcome, ma'am. I'm glad I was able to help." He shifted from one foot to the other. Should he bring up the issue of a way back to the city? He *did* live on the east edge, so it wasn't far. "Guess I'll be going, then." He glanced between Shannon and Maribeth. "Thank you for the entertaining conversation on the ride here." Placing his hand on the wooden edge of the screen door, he pushed it out and stepped onto the porch.

"Wait!" Shannon cried.

Jacob paused and turned to face her. She and her mother exchanged a few quiet words he couldn't hear before she focused her eyes on him.

"I just realized you didn't bring a horse or a motorcar with you. How will you get back home?"

He shrugged. "Figured I'd walk." With a sheepish grin, he added, "I could use the exercise."

Shannon looked aghast at that remark. "Oh my, no! I couldn't allow you to do that." She rushed toward him and peered over his shoulder toward the fields. "Let me send Maribeth to fetch one of our brothers to give you a ride." She paused and shifted her attention to the barn. "Or you could borrow one of our horses."

Her proximity and the sweet scent of her rose water perfume muddled his thoughts. "No, no. I don't want to put you out in any way," he managed around the sudden lump in his throat.

Mrs. Delaney stepped forward. "But you aren't at all, Mr. Berringer. It's the least we can do for your assistance with the crates," she said with a vague wave toward the stack near her feet.

Which would be better, borrowing the horse or riding with one of her brothers back to the city?

"Well, I suppose the horse would get me home faster. I can bed him in our carriage house until someone can come get him. And I don't want to take your brothers away from the fields. Farming is hard enough without interruptions and having to stop to take a stranger back to the city."

Shannon tilted her head at this remark. She no doubt believed him to be ignorant of what it took to run a farm. He hadn't run one this size, but he at least understood the underlying requirements.

"Then it's settled." She pointed toward the barn. "You can take Blue Aster in stall three. He'd probably appreciate a good stretch of the legs. I can always retrieve him next week during my trip to the city."

He paused before agreeing. If he took her horse, they'd have to meet next week to make the transfer back. And that would mean another guaranteed conversation. That option sounded better than him having to come up with another reason to talk to her.

"Sounds good." He nodded. "And I'm sure I can find everything I need in the barn to saddle the horse. You go ahead and tend to your supplies." He stepped fully onto the porch and reached the edge of the steps before stopping and pivoting on his heel. Shannon remained at the door, watching his departure. "It really was a nice ride, Miss Delaney." He tipped his hat toward her then looked past her to Maribeth and their mother. "Mrs. Delaney, Miss Delaney. It was a pleasure to meet you both. I'm sure we'll see each other again."

"I look forward to it, Mr. Berringer," Maribeth replied with a coy smile. "Good day."

"Thank you again, Mr. Berringer," Shannon added.

With that, the three ladies turned away and disappeared from view. Jacob resumed his path toward the barn and headed inside to find Blue Aster. The animal's coat gave him away, and he immediately nuzzled up to Jacob. This horse had a great disposition. As he hauled a saddle from the hook and set about preparing for his ride, he made a mental note to thank Shannon for recommending this mount. She could've given him a more volatile one and tested his riding skills.

Not that he wasn't up to the potential challenge, but he looked forward to a leisurely ride home. This way he could formulate his plan to learn more about the monetary offer from the other car company. Maybe there was some way he could help without appearing to interfere. Working at the Ford factory gave him some connections she and her family might not have. At the very least, he could get things rolling in the right direction. And that might work in his favor in more ways than one.

Chapter 5

Shannon's throat closed, and a heavy weight descended upon her heart. The news had just been announced, but the report couldn't be true. A ship the size of the *Titanic*? Sank in the middle of the ocean on the fifteenth of April, just five days after leaving England? And on its maiden voyage.

Her hands crumpled the edge of the newspaper as she stood outside the grocery while Mr. Mulligan filled her order. She listened to newsies hawk the latest edition, heralding the front-page story. If she hadn't come into the city today, she would have had to wait until Saturday to find out. Without a telephone, they had to rely on someone paying a visit to the farm during the week or the occasional postal mail delivery. She'd be the source for this, though. She only wished she had better news to share.

This ship was supposed to be one of the safest and best engineering creations of its time. Those behind the building of it had touted the ingenuity for months. "Unsinkable" is what they had said. Shannon had read the stories and heard of the boasts. The ship had become a legend even before it sailed. And now this.

More than fifteen hundred passengers and crew had been lost at sea with the ship. For what? Yet another advancement in technology to show off to the world? Despite the pain in her heart at the loss of so many lives, Shannon couldn't help but blame the engineers behind the *Titanic* for deceiving so many people. She was sure they hadn't intended to lie; nevertheless, their promises had led to the deaths of more than a thousand people. How would they ever get this off their consciences?

"I see you've read the news." Johnny nodded at the paper Shannon held as he arranged a few crates of apples outside Mulligan's Grocery.

"Yes." She sighed. "Such a tragedy."

"But did you see the article right below it?"

Shannon drew her eyebrows together and raised the newspaper again, scanning for what Johnny might mean.

"There's a brief story about Harriet Quimby," he went on as she read, "and her flight across the English Channel."

Shannon read the quick blurb. The first woman to accomplish such a feat. But who would read that article when the one about the *Titanic* all but covered the front page?

"I probably wouldn't have seen this until much later if you hadn't pointed it out. Thank you, Johnny." Shannon wasn't much for yet another noisy contraption like an airplane, but she had to admit, the concept of flight seemed thrilling. "It's a shame Harriet Quimby's story had to be relegated to the bottom of the page instead of a headline for such a triumph."

"I know." Johnny reached for the broom leaning against the wall and began sweeping the area around the front door. "Just one day after the *Titanic* sank."

"She loses the notoriety she deserves because some builders wanted to show off their creation and boast about its safety." Shannon tapped the newspaper right at the headline. "Looks like reports of how careless they were will be filling the news now."

"Oh, I don't know that they wanted to show off."

"What else would you call it?"

"Well, they were proud of the ship. It makes sense they would want to celebrate it being ready to sail. They couldn't have known it would strike an iceberg on its way to New York City."

He made a good point. No one could predict the future. She took a moment to observe Johnny as he worked. He'd always been there to help her during the past several months since he took the job of grocer's assistant. And they'd talked about so many things in their brief conversations while he loaded her supplies. She could always count on an intelligent topic with him. A lot like what she'd expect with Jacob, only she and Johnny never argued as much.

"But they could have made sure they took all the precautions, just in case." Shannon held up the paper. "It says they didn't have enough lifeboats to save everyone if an emergency happened. Why would they do that?"

Regret drifted across Johnny's face. "They didn't think it would sink."

"Exactly. For all their hard work in constructing the ship, they didn't plan for the worst."

"The worst of what?"

Shannon and Johnny turned to see Jacob stepping onto the sidewalk. She couldn't stop the smile that appeared on her lips at seeing him. A few seconds later, he stood opposite her. Just like he had four days ago, he appeared at the same time she was in town. How had he known she would be here at this moment? It wasn't her regular day to come for supplies. And why would she be feeling guilty about standing alone with Johnny outside the store? It wasn't as if Jacob had any claim on her.

"Johnny and I were discussing the headline in today's paper."

"You mean about the *Titanic*?"

"Yes." She tilted her head. "You've heard as well?"

He nodded. "I'm sure most of Detroit has heard by now. At least anyone who can read. And even many who can't."

"Word does spread rather quickly in a city this size." The sinking happened in the middle of the Atlantic Ocean early on Monday, and the full details were in their paper today, just two days later.

Jacob chuckled. "It spreads fast no matter where you are. Especially news like this."

"This is true." She laughed. "Some of us on the farms are spread out by miles, yet no one seems uninformed."

"That's because folks out there rely on the gossip of their neighbors."

Shannon opened her mouth to protest, but Jacob held up a hand.

"Now don't take offense. I didn't mean anything by it. I was a farmer at one point, too, so I know how difficult it can be."

Now that was a surprise. Jacob Berringer, a farmer? The mere idea seemed impossible. The image that formed in her mind's eye actually made her giggle.

"What's so funny?"

Shannon covered her mouth with her free hand to gather her composure. "I just have a hard time seeing you behind a plow and horse. You talk of how great motorcars and modern technology are, and your clothing doesn't exactly give any hint that you might know anything other than success."

A melancholic expression crossed his face, and his eyes took on a faraway look as he smoothed his hands down the front of his suit jacket. "Well, don't be fooled by my appearance. You were likely too young to remember the financial crisis about eighteen years ago, but my family suffered a great deal and were forced to farm for a time until my father and brother could rebuild and start fresh."

"Oh. I had no idea." She wanted to feel more compassion for the situation he'd just described, but he also said they'd been forced to farm. As if farming was a burden to bear. Then again, to a young boy it very well might have been. Forcing a brightness to her voice, she decided to give him the benefit of the doubt. "At least you rallied and managed to thrive despite the challenges. That's the most important thing."

"That we did." Jacob slipped his hands into his pockets and rocked back on his heels. "I was only about eight, but I still remember how hard it was for Willie and my father. Even after they found steady jobs again, it took us a while before we could rebuild to our prior standing. Mother enjoyed farming, so we held on to the plot awhile longer." Surprisingly, he grinned. "And Willie still managed to find himself a girl to marry, too."

Mirth filled Shannon again. Thankfully, Jacob didn't seem too upset, and he'd turned the conversation to a more lighthearted topic.

"Sounds like your brother made the best of what happened and prospered in more ways than one."

"That he did." Pride and contentment reflected in every aspect of his face. "And I couldn't ask for a better sister-in-law than Annabelle." He chuckled. "Of course, my niece and nephew round out the blessings rather well, too."

Blessings? People who used that word to describe something good usually had a strong faith that guided their lives. She knew Jacob had some belief in God, but she wondered how those in support of technological advancement could possess a deep faith when they were so seemingly consumed with progress. Then again, Jacob did have a quiet strength about him and a peace that said otherwise.

"Do you have any other brothers or sisters?"

"No. My parents lost three in between my brother and me. Mother took it rather hard for a number of years."

"I can imagine." Shannon had known other women who had lost babies. Two girls who finished school the same time she did had even lost one each. The heartbreak had to be deep.

"That's why William is so much older than I. My oldest nephew is already sixteen." Jacob shook his head. "Hard to imagine."

"Time does pass quickly. I'm amazed your mother recovered well enough after such loss. She must be a very strong woman."

The obvious affection he felt for his mother softened the expression in his eyes. "Yes, she is." His voice also reflected the emotion. "If it hadn't been for her strength during those difficult times all those years ago, I don't know that my father and brother would have had the desire to pursue rebuilding with as much ferocity as they did."

"Tragedy and loss tend to bring families closer together, and the strength of one rubs off on the rest." Shannon should know. Their farm hadn't always been a success, but they worked together and relied on one another to keep it going.

"Brings to mind all the families who have lost someone in this mishap with the *Titanic*," Jacob mused, the corners of his mouth frowning.

Images of those passengers and what they must have been feeling or thinking as they fought for their lives in that frigid water flashed through Shannon's mind. "They don't have the full count yet, but from the way things sound, there will be a lot of families who will need to be contacted."

"And in some cases, next of kin," Jacob added. "My brother said he received a call from an associate in Washington that *The Post* ran a story with the most information available so far. *The Detroit News*," he said as he flicked the edge of the paper she held, "only reported the basics."

Bitterness once again surfaced as bits of the article she'd read came back to her. "So much pain and suffering, and all because some men were both careless and overconfident in their rush to herald their new engineering marvel to the world." Shannon tried, but she couldn't keep the disdain from her voice.

Jacob opened his mouth as if to reply then stopped and closed it a second later. He regarded her with keen interest, removing one of his hands from his pocket to lightly tap his upper lip.

"Well," he began cautiously, "their confidence was merited. A slew of prominent engineers and maintenance personnel thoroughly checked that ship before deeming it sail worthy."

"That's almost what Johnny. . ." Shannon stopped and looked around. "Where did he go?"

Jacob's eyebrows knitted. "Who? Johnny?"

Who else did he think she meant? There was no one else around. "Yes. He was here when you arrived and was still here when we began talking."

He shrugged and waved his hand absentmindedly in the air. "Oh, he disappeared inside a few minutes ago. Somewhere around us discussing farming, I think."

How had she not noticed him slipping away? She didn't recall being that focused on Jacob that she'd miss something as obvious as a person leaving her company. But it was apparent she had, as Johnny no longer stood with them. Shannon hoped she didn't offend him or make him feel less important than Jacob. She really needed to be more careful.

"All right," Shannon began. "You say the *Titanic* had been checked for safety. Then it appears those in charge of performing the inspection didn't do a very good job."

"Why are you always so quick to blame technology as being the problem?"

"Because it seems no matter how great a new invention is, there are always drawbacks and possible dangers with the unveiling of it."

Concern entered his eyes as he held her gaze. "Are you speaking in a general sense, or is the memory of your father's cousin still the primary source for your aversion?"

She wasn't prepared for the softness in his tone or how he genuinely appeared to care about what her answer might be. That alone made her want to come up with some other story to back up her bold statements. But she didn't have one. And she wasn't about to lie merely to elicit continued interest. "I will admit that learning of that cousin lent to my existing hesitancies. But I have also witnessed what so-called progress has done to many people I know. It corrupts them, makes them want more and more. They are never happy with what they have. They are always striving to make things better and faster and bigger."

Jacob ran a hand through his hair and sighed. "I can see your point. . .somewhat. But that's not the real issue here, is it?"

"What do you mean?"

"I mean, the invention and launching of this ship or even the heralding of it being so safe isn't the reason why you're so upset."

Shannon bristled. "I don't—"

Jacob held up a hand to silence her. "You're upset because it appears as if all those people lost their lives for no reason. You blame the engineers and the ones who boasted about the safety of the ship, yet deep down, you wish more people could've been saved." He paused and sighed again. "I do, too. I'd be callous and unfeeling if I didn't."

The way Jacob saw right through her anger and got to the heart of her feelings unnerved her. If she didn't guard herself, he could melt all her defenses and leave her rather exposed. A man like him just didn't seem the type to be so sensitive. The two different sides of him fascinated her. She wanted to know more.

"You're right," she conceded. "I'm only thinking of how much heartache has been caused and how many people have no more tomorrows to await."

"I wouldn't expect anything less of a lady as tenderhearted as you." He reached out and brushed the back of his knuckles across her cheek. "I'm sure those involved are doing everything they can to notify the families, and there is sure to be a long investigation into the accident. So, how about we turn our attention to a more immediate topic?"

Shannon tilted her head, the path on her cheek that he'd traced still tingling. "Such as?"

He grinned. "Such as me returning Blue Aster to you safe and sound."

She drew her eyebrows together. "We agreed last week to meet on Saturday for that." She wondered again how he had known she'd be here today. Could it really have been a chance meeting?

Jacob shrugged. "Yes, but since we're both here, why don't we go ahead and send him back home today?"

All right. She had to know. "Yes, about that." Shannon tilted her head to the left, quirked one corner of her mouth, and narrowed her eyes. "How did you happen to have Blue Aster with you today and be here at the same time as I?"

He gave her a sheepish grin and shoved his hands in the pockets of his pants. "I was actually wondering when you would ask about that."

She'd half expected him to brush off her query or make up some story, but it appeared as if he intended to be direct. Yet another quality to admire in him.

"I hope you don't consider me intrusive in any way, but I've had Mr. Mulligan ring me at the plant when you're here in the city. After his call, I rushed home to retrieve your horse and came straight here."

Shannon raised her eyebrows as her mouth slipped into an amused grin.

"Seems foolish now, standing here and explaining it to you." Jacob glanced down at the sidewalk then raised his eyes to her again. "You had me intrigued, though. You don't mind, do you?"

"Not at all," she answered immediately. Better to reassure him and set him at ease. He might be quite endearing in his chagrin, but she didn't want to cause him any further embarrassment. "In fact," she continued, "I'm flattered. You must be highly favored at Ford, though, if you are able to leave on such short notice."

He winked. "Well, so far your visits have been well timed, close enough to my usual breaks that I've been able to find someone to cover me."

Shannon giggled. "I'll do my best to continue doing so, then."

"So. . ." Jacob nodded at her wagon. "Can I get Blue Aster tied up?"

"That sounds fine to me. I'll be happy to have him back home. I got so caught up in the news and dialogue, I hadn't given it much thought." She looked over his shoulder and all around where they stood. "Where is he?"

Jacob jerked his thumb across the street. "I tied him up over there." He winked. "Figured he might get into trouble if I let him get this close to the apples."

She giggled. "You are absolutely right." Shannon relaxed at the lighthearted turn to their conversation. She was grateful, too. All the talk of lives lost and families mourning those losses made for a rather melancholic aura surrounding them. Jacob seemed to know what they needed to turn things around.

"Well, how about you go ahead and gather whatever items you have waiting for you inside? I'll take care of Blue."

"Yes, that will work nicely. Thank you."

Shannon started to turn toward Mulligan's Grocery as Jacob pivoted on his heel and headed for the street. Then he stopped. She did as well.

"By the way," he called. "I saw some of your quilts for sale in there. They're magnificent. Might make a great gift for my mother or Annabelle."

"Thank you." Pride filled her at his high compliment. Once again, he'd managed to surprise her. "If you decide to purchase one or more, let me know. I'll be sure you receive a discount."

"I'd appreciate it."

Although she hesitated to say good-bye, there was no reason to tarry any longer. Still, she couldn't keep the regret from her voice. "Good day, Mr. Berringer."

"Good day, Miss Delaney." His voice held a similar tone to hers as he performed the customary tipping of his hat and again turned to cross the street.

Shannon allowed her gaze to linger a few moments on his back as he headed toward her horse. When Jacob reached the other side, he paused and turned to look over his shoulder, catching her watching him. She stiffened and rushed into the store, pretending like nothing was amiss. The slight grin on her lips said otherwise.

"Jacob!"

Ralph Hudson hailed Jacob from his office door Thursday morning and half jogged across the factory floor to where Jacob stood.

"Mr. Hudson." Jacob nodded a greeting.

Hudson allowed a partial smile to bend his lips. He paused a moment, then inhaled. "Before we get down to business, how are William and Annabelle and their family?"

Jacob didn't mind the delay at all, especially considering the subject matter. "Keeping themselves occupied as always." He grinned. "Theodore is top of his class at the boys' academy and Millie is already showing signs of being just as tenderhearted as her mother and grandmother before her."

"How old is she now?"

He always had trouble remembering details like that. It seemed every time he turned around, they were celebrating another birthday. He had a hard enough time remembering his own age, let alone his niece's and nephew's. "Umm, ten. . . no, eleven, I believe." Yes, that was it. She was born just after the turn of the new century. "And Teddy is sixteen."

"Mmm. I've missed quite a lot since I moved here to Ford. And since Mr. Edison named your brother as chief financial adviser last year, I haven't seen much of him. Looks like I'll be getting the family updates from you now."

"Happy I am to give them, sir. You know that."

"Yes." Hudson withdrew a slip of paper from his coat pocket and held it between them, flicking it with the index finger of his other hand. "I received this message that you wanted to see me. Do you want to talk here or would you prefer a more private area?"

"Here is fine, sir." Jacob looked around. There didn't appear to be anyone interested in their conversation. Besides, they were at the Ford plant. It wasn't as if anyone would rush off to report what they'd heard to a rival company. He returned his gaze to Hudson, cringing a little. What he was about to ask wasn't easy. "I have a few questions about another car company, and with your connections, I thought you'd be the best one to ask."

Hudson had several other family members working in the automobile industry. He believed Ford ran the best operation in Detroit, but he also kept abreast of developments in other factories. That was why Jacob sought him out.

"What's on your mind?" Hudson asked.

"Well, sir, I don't want you to compromise anything by answering any of my questions. I'm not asking for any special favors."

Hudson held up his hand like a patrolman calling someone to halt. "Never mind that, my boy. I have no doubt your intentions are honorable." He flipped his hand palm up. "Now, what questions do you have for me?"

That went well. Now Jacob could breathe easy. "Well, sir, I have recently met a young lady whose family is being threatened by someone from one of our rival car companies regarding their farm and the land they own."

Wrinkles appeared on his supervisor's brow. "Threatened? How so?"

Jacob thought back to what Shannon had said on that ride to her farm. "I don't know all the details, but I believe they wish to purchase the land, possibly more than the one farm, and use it to build another factory. Perhaps they are attempting to increase production and allow for a greater sales volume."

"Yes, I had heard one of my cousins speaking of this a few weeks back." Hudson narrowed his eyes. "But I had no idea they were engaging in nefarious practices by which to obtain the land they sought."

"I don't want to cause any trouble, sir, but I did want to find out what you knew about it." Jacob thought of Shannon. If she knew he was making inquiries, she might ask him not to interfere. "I also don't wish to cause any problems for this certain family, sir. The eldest daughter is who told me, but I made up my mind to seek out more information on my own."

"Duly noted, my boy." Hudson grasped both lapels of his coat and squared his shoulders. "I was aware of the plans to expand and had even been included in a conversation where my cousin had shared some other ideas for increasing production. They own some undeveloped land north of the city, but nothing has been decided yet. From what I could ascertain, the board of advisers is still in the decision-making stage, weighing all options and determining the best course of action."

"So they aren't close to starting on this new plant, then?" This was excellent news. It meant there was still a chance to help Shannon and her family.

Hudson dipped his chin and regarded Jacob over his spectacles. "I can't say for certain one way or another, but I promise to find out what I can, on all accounts."

Jacob splayed his hands out. "That's all I can ask, sir."

"Mr. Hudson?"

The two men turned to see Hudson's assistant approach from the direction of the meeting rooms.

"Yes, Mr. Keyes? What can I do for you?"

"Mr. Ford wanted me to inform you that the production meeting is about to begin. You really should be making your way there, sir."

Hudson nodded. "Thank you, Mr. Keyes. Please inform Mr. Ford I will be there momentarily and that Mr. Berringer will also be accompanying me."

Jacob jerked his head at that. Him? In a meeting with the advisers and Mr. Ford himself? He'd heard about the meeting from talk around the plant. But he'd never imagined he'd be invited to attend.

"What do you say, my boy?" Hudson now addressed Jacob with a clap on the back. Mr. Keyes had already left. "I've always been impressed by your ingenuity when it comes to improvements around this plant. I believe you'll bring a lot to this meeting." He drew Jacob toward him, lowered his head, and continued in a conspiratorial whisper. "I hear tell there's going to be talk of modifying the assembly methods for streamlining operations and reducing the number of injuries. Perhaps you can share some insight from the time you spent working on the line prior to your promotion."

Smoother production? That sounded like a fantastic idea. "I'm honored you've asked me, sir. I'd be happy to join you."

"Excellent!" The supervisor draped an arm around Jacob's shoulder and redirected him toward the meeting. "I don't particularly care for these things." He winked. "At least with you there, you're sure to bring a good bit of fresh air to the mix."

Hudson looked like the proverbial cat that caught the canary. His smile beamed from ear to ear as he steered Jacob along with him. Hoping this meeting would be as interesting as it sounded, Jacob followed without resistance. But thoughts of what might happen afterward nagged at him. Should the men gathered settle on a viable solution, it could mean more automobiles in less time, more demand from buyers, and more factories to keep up with that demand.

That spelled nothing but trouble for Shannon and her family—and others like her. He'd been there, facing the possible loss of everything. And they had lost it all. Well, almost. Had it not been for his parents' steadfast faith, they never would have fared as well. For a time, his brother hadn't done well and had even stumbled in his faith. Jacob didn't want to see that happen to Shannon. He wasn't sure, but she seemed to have some measure of faith. A turn like this could be devastating.

Jacob prayed he wasn't walking into a meeting that would be the beginning of the end for Shannon's family. Because if it was, it would be the end for him and Shannon as well.

Chapter 6

Shannon waited as Johnny loaded the crates into the back of her wagon. She would rather be back home working on her latest quilt or helping Mama with some of the cleaning. But she had to admit, coming into the city offered its own level of excitement. When her sister accompanied her, the visits became even more fun. Still, there was a certain appeal to the everyday details of quilting and farming.

"Oh, Miss Delaney," Mr. Mulligan called from the front of the store after he hung up the telephone behind the counter. "I almost forgot. You have a nice payment coming to you for the sale of your quilts."

"You mean you've sold more than one in the past week?" She glanced over her shoulder to look at the corner where the owner had set up a display of her work. Only one quilt remained. She'd given him three last Saturday, and there had been three already there.

"Yes, a new customer came in a few days ago asking about them. She said she heard I had some for sale." Mr. Mulligan turned his back and bent down to retrieve his cash box then reappeared, setting the box on the counter between them. "When she saw them, she bought five and asked how often I get new samples."

Excitement made Shannon's heart skip a beat. She licked her lips and inhaled a sharp breath. "What did you tell her?"

He shrugged. "I told her I don't have a set schedule but that I would speak to you about it."

Shannon's thoughts took flight. Imagine. Someone with enough money to buy five quilts at once and interested in buying more. If she told her friends and they told their friends, she might be able to turn this into a viable business or moneymaking endeavor.

"Well, it does take some time to acquire the fabric squares and to assemble the quilts in an attractive array." She twirled a loose tendril of hair from her braid and made a few mental calculations on cost, time, and available supplies. "But if she was interested in more, I have other completed ones at home I could bring. After that, I'd have to spend a bit more time on them." She might even make better use of Mama's sewing machine.

Mr. Mulligan rooted in the cash box a moment and withdrew some bills clipped together. "Based on what Mrs. Mitchell paid for your quilts and the fact that she seemed rather adamant that I have some new ones for her the next time she visits, I'd like to carry a few more if you have them." Counting out the money in his hand and jotting down some figures in his record book, he then held out the cash to her.

Shannon stared for a moment before finally taking it from the grocer. She wasn't about to insult him by counting it again, but her mind whirled with how much could be there. Then the name Mr. Mulligan said came back to her.

"Mrs. Mitchell?"

Where had she heard that name before? It didn't belong to any of the families who farmed out her way. But something about it rang familiar.

The grocer nodded as he closed the cash box and bent to tuck it back under the counter. "Yes, she's Mr. Sorenson's mother-in-law. He's one of the men in charge over at the Highland Park plant."

"Oh, you mean with the Ford Motor Company."

"One and the same."

The one where Jacob worked. That's where she'd heard it. Jacob had mentioned her name the day they met. He'd taken her for a ride in that motorcar or something. But he couldn't have spoken to her about the quilts then. He hadn't even known about them yet. And she couldn't be sure if he'd been the one to say anything. So, no use trying to figure out how Mrs. Mitchell had learned of the quilts. She liked them and wanted others. That was all that mattered.

"If I bring in three more quilts next week, will that be enough until I can sew more?"

The grocer looked to the corner, then back at Shannon, running his fingers over his mustached upper lip. "That should do for now, yes. Of course, if Mrs. Mitchell tells her friends, you could have a bona fide business on your hands, little lady." He smiled, wrinkles forming around his twinkling brown eyes. "I'd be happy to sell them here for you for now. But if the demand increases, you might want to look for a bigger and better location."

Increased demand? A place of her own? The idea seemed almost preposterous and too far-fetched for her to fathom. She'd do good to rein in the excitement for now. Let what would happen take its own course. She'd take it one step at a time until then.

"Your wagon's all loaded, Miss Delaney."

Johnny cleaned his hands on his apron and stepped behind the counter to join Mr. Mulligan.

"Thank you, Johnny. As always, you do an excellent job, and I'm so happy to have your help."

"My pleasure, Miss Delaney."

Shannon smiled. No matter how many times she'd asked him to call her

Shannon, he wouldn't agree. He said she deserved more respect than that, which she found humorous because they were the same age. If they'd gone to school together, it would be a moot point. But he lived on the other side of the city, and they'd only met when he got the job nearly two years ago. So, the formal address it was.

"Mr. Mulligan, thank you again for allowing me space to display my quilts and for selling them. I will bring those three I promised next week."

With her head spinning yet again on the endless possibilities, Shannon fairly skipped to the front. She rushed through the open door at the same time a man was entering.

"Ooomph!" Shannon came to a dead stop when she collided with a broad chest.

"I'm sorry, miss," came a very familiar voice as he reached to steady her. "I didn't see you there. I—" He paused, and Shannon looked up into the soft hazel eyes of Jacob. "Oh, hello Miss Delaney. It appears we have run into each other yet again." Maintaining pressure on her arm, he added, "Are you all right?"

Shannon fought to catch her breath, both from the collision and from his proximity. "Yes, yes. I'm fine. Thank you." She brushed off her skirts, even though they weren't dirty. But it gave her something to do while she regained her composure.

"What had you in such a hurry?"

"Hurry? Me?" All right. She had to pull herself together. Otherwise she'd continue to sound like an addlepated twit. "No, I'm afraid my mind was on some great news I'd just received, and I might not have been paying attention."

"Great news?" He raised his eyebrows. "Want to share the details?"

She stepped to the side of the main entrance, and Jacob followed. "Remember the quilts I had for sale here?"

"Yes. I am still thinking about buying one or two for my mother and sister."

"Well, Mr. Mulligan told me five of my quilts sold in the past week. All to the same woman." Shannon's voice caught in her throat as her heartbeat increased. She bounced on her toes and clasped her hands together. "And she wants more. Can you believe it?"

Excitement lit up his eyes as he shared in her joy. "That is fantastic, Miss Delaney. I knew it was only a matter of time before someone spotted the quality and craftsmanship."

"But I've only sold one every few months. Never five all at once."

Jacob shrugged. "Like we said the other day, word spreads fast among people these days."

Shannon again visited the thought that he had somehow been involved in Mrs. Mitchell learning of her quilts. She decided to test the theory and see if it was true. "Yes, especially when administrators hear it from their supervisors and tell their mothers-in-law."

"That's one way, I sup—" He stopped midsentence and peered down at her, surprise written all over his face.

She pressed her lips together in a half grin and quirked one eyebrow. He grinned in response.

"How did you find out?"

At least he didn't deny it or try to make it appear as if he had no idea what she was talking about. "I put two and two together when Mr. Mulligan told me the name of the woman who made the purchase." She reached up and pressed her index finger to her lips. "Mrs. Mitchell sounded familiar to me, but I couldn't place it until I asked who she was. Mr. Mulligan told me, and I remembered you mentioning her name the day we met."

"Excellent memory, Miss Delaney." His eyes widened. "I am impressed. I only mentioned her name the one time, I believe."

She shrugged. "Little details like that tend to stand out in my mind, and I store them away in case they're needed later."

Jacob shoved his hands in his pockets and gave her an impish smile. "An obvious benefit for you, but a fact that worked to my detriment in this case. But hey, now you know. I'm guilty as charged."

Shannon couldn't help but smile. "I promise not to hold it against you. In fact, I'm pleased you thought enough of my work to tell someone else about it. I insist on repaying you in some way." She snapped her fingers. "Perhaps a custom quilt for your mother?"

Jacob appeared to consider her offer for a moment. "That could work." His eyes brightened, and a gleam shone from the center. "But I think I have an even better idea."

"Oh?" Whatever was on his mind, she had a feeling he hadn't just thought of it.

"Do you by any chance like baseball?"

"Baseball?"

"Yes, you know. Bats, balls, mitts, men running around the bases."

Shannon rolled her eyes. "I know what the game is, Mr. Berringer. My brothers, father, and many of our neighbors engage in the game during various picnics, especially once the harvest is complete."

"Well, how would you like to see a professional game?"

"As in watching in a real ballpark?" Her brothers would be green with envy if they found out. "When?"

"Is this afternoon too soon?"

"Today?" That was a lot faster than she'd expected.

"Yes. I have a pair of tickets to the first Tigers' game in the new ballpark."

"I heard they were remodeling. It's done already?" Her brothers told her it had been built just after she was born.

Jacob beamed like a little boy in a candy shop. "Yes. The wooden bleachers and grandstand are all gone. So are the ropes marking off parts of the outfield. It's all new steel and concrete, and the capacity is far greater." He looked ready to burst with excitement. "Everyone in the city is abuzz about it."

She'd love to go, but didn't know if she could. Gesturing outside to her wagon, Shannon frowned.

"I have my supplies to get home; then I'd have to return to the city after they're unloaded, not to mention notifying my family of where I'll be. I don't know that there's enough time. When does the game start?"

"Should probably get there as early as possible. I hear tell it's going to be a crowd that will fill the ballpark's capacity and maybe even more."

There was no way she'd have enough time to get home, unload the wagon, and get back. Even if her brothers helped. And if she had to ask them, they'd ask why she was in such a hurry. It didn't seem like there was a plausible solution to her dilemma.

"I could deliver your crates, Miss Delaney."

Johnny took a hesitant step toward Shannon and Jacob, looking almost apologetic.

"Sorry for eavesdropping, but I couldn't help but overhear."

Shannon waved off his apology. "That's all right, Johnny." She wouldn't be upset if he was willing to provide a solution for her. "What were you saying about my supplies?"

He wrung his hands in his apron as he replied, his voice soft. "If it's all right with you, I wouldn't mind driving them to your farm for you. That way you wouldn't have to go all the way home just to turn around and come back to the city in time for the game." He ducked his head. "And perhaps Miss Maribeth could direct me on where to put the crates once I'm there."

Shannon opened her mouth to agree but paused. For the first time since she'd met him, Johnny appeared embarrassed and a little hesitant, despite the hope she also saw in his expression. Could she have been wrong about him all this time? Had he really been interested in her sister instead? That would certainly explain a lot.

"Sounds like an excellent resolution, Miss Delaney," Jacob interjected. "Your crates would be delivered, and you could accompany me to the game."

Shannon was still dwelling on Johnny's probable interest in Maribeth. Did her sister even know? If not, Shannon would make sure she did soon.

"Yes, it does appear to be the answer to everything." She raised her eyebrows in Johnny's direction. "Are you certain you don't mind?"

Johnny brightened, relief replacing the embarrassment. "Not at all. I have to make a delivery for Mr. Mulligan out that way anyway. I could transfer everything to the other wagon, add the other order to what you have, and take care of both deliveries in one trip. Your team and wagon can stay here until you return to get them."

With a shrug and palms upward, Shannon smiled. "It seems as if everything is all arranged, then." Of course, when her family found out where she'd gone, they'd no doubt start storing up the questions for the moment she set foot inside the house again. At least Mama and Maribeth had already met Jacob. And Papa, Jeremiah, and Matthew knew of him from her reports on her weekly trips. She hoped they wouldn't be too upset to receive word from Johnny regarding her whereabouts. They'd met Johnny once or twice before as well. Perhaps his interest in Maribeth would supersede any concern for her.

The young man might not be outwardly bold in his assertions, but he was confident in what he wanted. Maribeth would do well to consider him. Shannon would have to speak with her sister tonight after the ball game. She turned to face Jacob again and dipped in a tiny curtsy.

"Mr. Berringer, I'd be delighted to accompany you to the game."

Jacob bowed slightly and touched the brim of his cap with a knowing grin. "Miss Delaney, it will be my pleasure to escort you."

❧

Shouts, children's cries, exclamations of delight, and cheering all joined the smells of popcorn, peanuts, newly cut grass, and fresh air. Shannon soaked up the atmosphere like a dry towel to water. The excitement surged in the air like the electric lamps buzzing on the streets of the city at night.

Jacob hadn't been kidding when he said it would be a full house. The Tigers against the Naps from Cleveland. Fans were packed elbow to elbow, straining their necks to see over the person in front of them. Shannon had to fight hard to keep up with Jacob as he meandered through the throngs and led them to their seats. After the third time of stopping so she could catch up, he reached back and grabbed her hand, holding tight.

She probably should have protested at the intimacy of the action, but she was too relieved to know she wouldn't get lost. Her long braid slapped against her back as Jacob pulled her behind him, making her steps erratic and uneven.

"Well, here we are," Jacob announced with a flourish, his arm sweeping wide as he grazed it over where they'd be sitting. "I hope you like them."

Shannon took a moment to catch her breath. She raised her hand to brush back flyaway strands of hair and to tuck a few back into her braid. Finally, she could get a good look at where they were. With widened eyes, she gasped.

PATTERNS AND PROGRESS

"Wow! We're almost behind home plate!" And it wasn't nearly as crowded here. She shifted her gaze to Jacob. "How did you manage this?"

Jacob squared his shoulders and beamed a broad smile, raising his voice above the din from the thousands of fans. "Let's just say I have a few tricks up my sleeve and a few connections that helped a lot." He squeezed her hand.

It was that moment she realized he hadn't let go. Looking down at their joined hands, Shannon felt her face warm. He must have noticed because he immediately moved to assist her into the row. As soon as she stood in front of her seat, Jacob released her hand and sidestepped to stand in front of his seat.

For several awkward moments, they didn't say anything. She wished she knew what he was thinking. Was it about her, or was he completely taken with the excitement of the game?

"So, what are these connections you have?" Shannon asked in an attempt to break the silence.

Jacob gave her a sideways glance and shrugged. "My father knows one of the previous owners of the Tigers, George Vanderbeck. He asked George to call in a favor with Mr. Frank Navin, the current owner and the man who ordered this reconstruction." Jacob stretched his neck and swayed to the left and right, then pointed. "That's George down there, right near the dugout and just off the field."

Shannon looked in the direction he pointed only a few rows below and to the right of them. Her sight settled on a man who bore a distinct air of importance. He couldn't be anyone but Mr. Vanderbeck. The way he watched the field as the players practiced before the game, the way he acknowledged others speaking to him without taking his eyes off the players, and the way he caressed the knob at the top of his walking stick as he sat. It all spoke of a man in tune with the ballpark and with a keen interest in everything taking place.

"I'm surprised to see him here," she said without thinking.

"Why?" Jacob turned to her. "He might not be the owner now, but that doesn't mean he's lost interest in the team."

"Yes, I suppose once you're a fan, you're always a fan."

"That's what they say."

He lapsed into silence again, but this time it was a comfortable one. And considering the raucous shouts from everyone all around her, not having to strain to hear Jacob suited her just fine. Shannon took the time to look around the renovated ballpark. Its newness fairly shouted from every nook and cranny. She hadn't ever been inside Bennett Park, although her brothers had told her about it. Something about the idea of wooden bleachers compared to the cold steel spoke of greater warmth to her. The thousands gathered here today didn't seem to mind, though.

People from all walks of life had set aside whatever they were doing in order to attend the first game of the season. Businessmen in tailored suits sat just a few seats away from farmers, factory workers, and merchants. Women who had seemingly spent extra time on their appearances accompanied their husbands or beaux, and everyone appeared thrilled to be present.

Shannon peeked out of the corner of her eye at Jacob. He sat with his full attention on the men out in the field. So much about him fascinated her, but at the same time gave her cause for concern. How had she so easily been persuaded to join him here this afternoon? He had asked, and she had almost immediately accepted. Even without Johnny's offer of assistance, she'd been making plans to find a way to make it all work. What was it about Jacob that had her forgetting herself?

The elevated voice of a peanut vendor interrupted her musings. He offered both peanuts and popcorn for sale.

"Would you like something?"

Jacob turned to her with raised eyebrows.

Before she could even think to ask, he'd offered. "Peanuts, please," she replied. "Thank you."

"Two peanuts, please," Jacob called after signaling the vendor. Once the exchange had taken place, he passed a paper bag of peanuts to her and settled back with his own.

"Did you know this new layout actually puts home plate where the left field corner used to be?"

Shannon looked below them toward first base. If that were the case, then the old home plate would've been about where the right field corner was now.

"Why did they do that?"

He shrugged. "I don't know. I just know that Navin bought the rest of this block that they hadn't owned before, tore down the wildcat bleachers and the old Bennett Park, and built this one right on top."

"Wildcat bleachers? What are those?"

"They were built on the rooftops of some houses that used to sit behind the left field fence." He chuckled and shook his head. "Can you believe it? People actually used their rooftops so they could see the games played here."

"I can see why. If my brothers lived that close to a ballpark, they'd likely do the same thing."

Jacob cocked his head in her direction. "They love the game that much?"

"They would play all day long if they could. But work on the farm comes first." Images of impromptu games in the middle of a field or in the yard in front of their farmhouse came to mind and made Shannon smile. "Still, that doesn't stop them from engaging in a game or two every chance they get."

A bemused expression appeared on Jacob's face. "What do you think they're going to do when they find out you came to this game without them?"

She grimaced. "I was actually avoiding the thought of that until I had to face the reality."

"My guess is they're going to be a bit jealous. If I had known, I would have done my best to get more tickets." He glanced around at the full stadium. "Then again, I'm not sure tickets were even needed here today. They probably could have gotten here without them."

"I won't tell them that, though. I'll be in enough trouble with them as it is."

"Well, tell them it was an unplanned celebratory invitation for the successful sale of your quilts. That's the truth after all." He snapped his fingers. "Then say I'll get tickets for them to another game."

Tickets for her brothers? "Both of them? You don't have to do that." Although it would mean they could come enjoy a day at the ballpark as well. See it firsthand for themselves.

"Sure I do. And I don't mind." He raised his hands in a helpless gesture. "What good is knowing someone important if you can't use it to give someone else what they want?"

What an excellent perspective to take. And here she thought he was nothing more than a selfish industrialist who only cared about the latest inventions and model cars. She had been so wrong in her assumptions and silently asked God for forgiveness.

The hint of tears came to her eyes, so she averted her gaze. "Thank you," she said softly, intending the gratitude for both God and Jacob. "They will be quite surprised, but love it."

He nodded, then sat forward in his seat. "Ah, here it comes. The first pitch!" Jacob didn't say anything further. He clenched his fists in his lap until his knuckles turned white. Every bit of him appeared tense and eager.

Shannon looked out toward the pitcher on the mound in the center of the field, around the bases and the field, then to home plate, where the batter and catcher both stood ready for the pitch. A surprising hush fell over the crowd as the pitcher pulled the ball to his chest, raised his leg and drew back his arm, then let the ball fly, zooming toward home plate.

No sooner had the ball left the pitcher's hand when a cacophony of noise erupted from all around the ballpark. Everyone still sitting jumped to their feet to join those who were already standing. It didn't matter that the batter didn't hit that first ball thrown. They were just excited to celebrate the start of the game.

"Oh look! There's Ty Cobb!" Jacob leaned close and pointed toward a batter swinging two bats in a semicircle at shoulder level around his body. "Sam Crawford and George Mullin are right there, too." He shook his head. "It doesn't matter how many games I attend. I'll never get tired of watching those men play ball."

Shannon had heard those names mentioned around the dinner table or at the games her family and neighbors played every now and then. She didn't know their statistics, but she had heard some of their stories.

"The Tigers are playing the Naps, right?"

"Yes, why?"

"Well, my brothers mentioned one of their players, Joe Jackson, many times, talking about how great a ballplayer he is."

"Shoeless Joe. He's one of the best." Jacob nodded toward the opposing team's dugout. "Playing today, too."

"Shoeless Joe?"

"Yes. Got the nickname during a mill game in South Carolina when he had a blister on his foot from his new cleats. He took them off and batted anyway."

"Without his shoes?" She could see why the name would be given to him.

Jacob laughed. "Great story, isn't it?"

Shannon chuckled and shook her head. This game was certainly more interesting at the professional level than she ever would've imagined. "He'll have something to tell his children and grandchildren someday."

"And he'll no doubt love telling it," Jacob agreed. "Cy Young retired last year, but he and Nap Lajoie are sure to be remembered, too. These men are making history."

There was no way Shannon could keep up with talk about player statistics or details, but she wanted to feel like she could contribute to the conversation. She searched for anything that would work.

"I really like the Tigers' uniforms and the letter they use for Detroit."

Jacob didn't bat an eye at the change in subject. He seemed to take it all in stride and accept what she felt were feeble attempts to sound intelligent.

"It used to be this boring square letter until about eight years ago when they decided to make it in the Old English style."

"Have you always loved baseball, or is it something you took an interest in later?"

"Since I was a little boy. Willie and I used to play catch a lot." Sadness washed over his face for a moment. "When the financial crisis hit, baseball was the only outlet we had to keep from getting too dejected about our circumstances. Even once Willie and my father found work again, they still made time to play."

"I can understand that." Finally, another connection they shared. "The games we play on the farm help us even when the harvest is slow or a hailstorm has ruined our crops, or even when we just need to get together and have some fun."

Jacob nodded, once again relaxed and in high spirits. "Exactly. There is something about the game that makes you forget about your problems for a while. Something that brings everyone together, no matter what the circumstances." He reached out and rested his hand on her arm, compelling her to look at him and holding her gaze with his own. "I'm really glad you could be here with me today," he said, his voice serious.

"Me, too," she managed around the lump in her throat.

All of a sudden, he removed his hand, a chill replacing the warmth on her arm. If he hadn't looked away, she could've gotten lost in the depths of his eyes. For a moment, she wished she had. Here they weren't at odds with each other over industry and progress. Here they weren't talking about motorcars or airplanes or manufacturing. They were just two friends enjoying a day at the ballpark. If only it could stay that way.

Chapter 7

"That was such an amazing game. So glad the Tigers won. Even if it was just by one run."

Jacob guided Shannon through the crowds, his hand at the small of her back. He'd almost lost her when they arrived at the ballpark earlier. He didn't intend to make the same mistake again. A part of him wished he could take her hand again, but by the way she'd reacted the first time, that might not be such a good idea.

"I enjoyed it a great deal," Shannon spoke up from beside him once they were outside of the stadium. "Thanks to all the games I've watched over the years, and even the few I've played, I was able to follow everything that happened."

He jerked his head to the right and stared. "You've played the game as well?"

"Well, yes. Not professionally, of course, but my brothers have let me hit a few balls at times." Her expression softened as a charming smile graced her lips. "Women, children, and men all play on the farm. It's a great way to bring families together and to keep children out of trouble or danger during the game."

"I can see how that would help." Jacob could just see younger children running around while the men and older boys played. "A baseball can really hurt as fast as they're thrown or hit."

"Where are we headed now?"

Jacob shook his head at the abrupt change in topic. He looked around and saw they were standing at the edge of the sidewalk outside the ballpark. If truth be told, he hadn't thought about anything for after the game.

"Um, I'm sure you need to get back home," he began, frantically formulating a plan in his mind as he spoke. Looking up at the sky, he continued, "The daylight won't last much longer, and I don't want you to arrive in the dark."

"I had wondered about that myself."

He looked down into her upturned face. There was a lot of innocence in her expression, but there was also a hint of uncertainty mixed with hopefulness. Jacob wasn't about to explore that last emotion. He could get himself into a lot of trouble. And that was the last thing he needed. No, he wanted to see more of Shannon. That began with getting her home safe and sound.

"Why don't we head back to Mulligan's?" He turned in that direction, silently praying his spontaneous plan would work. "I believe he has a horse I can borrow and tie to the back of your wagon so I can get back home."

"Oh, you don't have to do that," she protested.

"And leave you to venture all that way alone? My mother would tan my hide if she found out I hadn't escorted you safe and sound to your front door." Not to mention how much he wanted to prolong this day a bit more.

Shannon looked about to argue, but then she took a second or two to regard him and finally nodded. "Very well. I appreciate your kindness."

Perfect. His plan had worked. Grinning, he extended his elbow toward her. "Shall we?"

Shannon tucked her hand into the crook and stepped closer. It wasn't holding hands, but it was good enough. One of these times, he might even get her into an automobile. He just had to bide his time.

Once they reached Mulligan's, he secured the extra horse, and in a matter of minutes, they were on their way toward Shannon's farm. At first neither one of them spoke. Jacob watched her from the corner of his eye, taking note of the way she relaxed against the seat and seemed to be enjoying the ride. He felt so at ease with her, and the silence allowed him to maneuver the wagon along the city streets without distraction.

By the time they reached the city's edge, though, he was ready for some conversation.

"You know, I was thinking about our conversation earlier this week when you made the chance trip into the city on Wednesday."

Shannon sat up straighter and tilted her head as if trying to remember. "Do you mean when we discussed the horrible news of the *Titanic*?"

He hadn't meant to bring up such a sad topic, but it was necessary to lead to the other one he hoped to talk about. "Yes, but we covered that one rather thoroughly. What we didn't get around to was another article right below it."

"The one about Harriet Quimby?"

She'd seen that, too? He silently chastised himself. Of course she'd seen it. She likely read the entire newspaper from front to back.

"Yes, about her flying across the English Channel and being the first woman to do so."

Shannon nodded. "Johnny and I talked about how her story likely got missed by so many due to the tragic news of the *Titanic*." She sighed. "Such a shame."

"I agree. To accomplish something like that, she should be heralded in a much greater way."

"As I'm sure you know, I don't cotton to airplanes much. About the same as automobiles in my mind."

"Just another noisy contraption to you, no doubt," he said with a grin.

Surprisingly, she also grinned. "Precisely."

He had to wonder if she held fast to her stance on these machines for legitimate reasons or merely because she enjoyed the thrill of the argument. Knowing what he did about her, he suspected a little of both.

"Nevertheless," she continued, "I have no problem giving credit where it's due. And Ms. Quimby accomplished a great thing with her flight. To be the first woman as well is doubly amazing."

Jacob relaxed his hold on the reins a bit and let the horse take the lead. "Just goes to show you that women are every bit as enamored with progress, modern technology, and advancement as men."

"Only some women," she corrected. "And only some men. It isn't a unanimous appeal." Placing her hands primly in her lap, she faced forward, her lips set in a firm line. "There are a good number of both men and women I know who would much rather see things stay as they are. Simple, uncomplicated, and easy to manage."

"You mean without the hindrances of what you would call 'modern inventions'?"

"Yes. The natural order of things."

Jacob looked around them at the trees, sky, clouds, flowers, and weeds, along with the occasional horse or cow or pig. Simple? Uncomplicated? Everything about their world was complex. He didn't want to be too contrary, though. Not yet, anyway.

"But what if we in our simplistic state were called in some way to create something that might make it easier for the average person? Improvements are part of life, and I believe certain people are born at a certain time to achieve specific things."

Shannon angled her chin toward him and gave him a sideways glance. "I won't argue with you there."

"Think about where we'd be if it weren't for men like Thomas Edison or Benjamin Franklin or Orville and Wilbur Wright." He inwardly cringed at bringing up the Wright brothers and their airplane. That was a bit too close to the technology she abhorred.

Shifting on the seat, she pivoted her legs so her left was flush with the leather and tucked her right foot behind her other ankle. She looked ready to do battle, but in a polite and ladylike fashion the way she was poised.

"Those men have made contributions to our lives in one way or another. I agree."

He was right. Calm and collected. He alternated his gaze between watching the road in front of them and looking at her. Not a hint of ire could be seen on her face. An innocent bystander would think they were merely taking an early evening ride, not disagreeing on the merits or disadvantages of progress.

"However, for every advancement, it seems there is an equal setback. And at times, those setbacks prove to be far more detrimental than the improvement."

"Such as?"

Shannon extended her left hand toward him, palm up. "Well, take the locomotive, for example," she began before placing her hand back in her lap.

Jacob raised his eyebrows. "Going that far back, are we?"

The barest hint of a smile tugged at the corner of her mouth. But she resisted. "It's true that the train improved the speed at which goods could be delivered and made outlying areas far more accessible."

"People, too, don't forget."

"Yes, people, too. Traveling by train put more people in touch with each other and allowed families or friends who had been separated to visit once again." Giving him a direct glance, she continued. "But it also increased the frequency of robberies and accidents. A greater amount of valued goods could be carried on trains, making them a more appealing target. And the speed at which they moved increased the chances of derailing, not to mention explosions in the engine."

"Robberies were just as common with the stagecoach or wagon trains as they've been with the train. And people with money have been targeted, no matter where they were." He noticed she didn't mention the trolley system. Just another reminder of her more rural surroundings and perceptions compared to someone who lived in the city. "As for the speed of the trains, going slower wouldn't necessarily prevent accidents. Those are usually caused by faulty machinery or track."

She shook her index finger in one single downward motion, as if to indicate she'd caught him admitting something. "Exactly. Faulty machinery or careless engineers and builders."

"But that can happen with anything." Jacob didn't want to hit close to home with her, but she was being unreasonable. "Even with wagon wheels, harnesses for a horse, and plows."

"Yes, but if something goes wrong with those, it only hurts the person using it. It doesn't endanger a large number of people."

"It would if the wagon was driving through a busy city street and lost a wheel or if a horse broke loose and became a runaway."

"With trolley cars and your new automobiles becoming more commonplace here in the city, though, how often would that happen?"

Jacob clenched his teeth and took a deep breath then released it slowly. He didn't want her to see evidence of his frustration. He'd never met a more stubborn woman in all his life. Unless, of course, someone mentioned his sister-in-law. Now that would be quite a show—pairing Annabelle against Shannon. At least Annabelle wasn't resistant to change.

"The trolleys and motorcars haven't completely taken over transportation in Detroit." He splayed out his hands in a placating manner, holding the reins between his fingers. "I'll admit, the frequency of wagons on the city streets has decreased, but individual horses and the smaller horse-and-buggy pairings are still quite common."

"And you're saying accidents or runaways happen just as much as anything with a trolley or motorcar?"

The obstinate tilt of her chin and the way she pursed her lips were enough to incense even a saint with how unyielding she was being. Why did she refuse to listen to reason?

"I haven't taken an actual count. I leave that up to the authorities in the city. But I'd say it's close." Trying not to appear like a father scolding a child, Jacob softened his tone. "Remember, aside from malfunctions, accidents usually occur from careless behavior on one side or the other. Whether it's a horse or a motorcar, we all have a responsibility to be careful with whatever we're handling."

Shannon opened her mouth to reply then slowly closed it. Her shoulders slumped an inch or two, and a loud sigh escaped from her lips. Turning away from him, she propped her elbow on the side of the wagon and dropped her head against her hand. Her silence gave him hope. Maybe she was starting to come around to his way of thinking after all.

"You're right," she spoke again. "We do have a responsibility, but it's far easier to be careful with a horse and buggy than it is with a motorcar."

He rolled his eyes. Just when he thought he was seeing a reason to be optimistic, she doused it and deflated his confidence in his persuasive abilities. How in the world would he ever get through to her?

"Are you so against industry and progress because of its dangers, or is there something more at stake here?" Braving physical contact, Jacob shifted the reins to one hand and reached out to touch her shoulder with the other. She stiffened for a second then relaxed. "Because as we've discussed, dangers exist no matter where you are."

Shannon closed her eyes as a frown marred her beautiful face. "I just don't want to see the life of the farmer or the simplistic outlook we share to disappear. It seems that with every new invention and every step forward we make, more and more of the lifestyle I love is disappearing before my eyes."

Was he imagining it, or did he see a tear glisten at the corner of her eye? When she reached up and touched her fingertip to her eyelash, he knew the tear wasn't only in his mind. Finally, something other than her obstinate behavior. Not that he wanted to cause her distress or see her unhappy, but if he could get to the root of the problem, he might know better how to help.

With a little pressure on her shoulder, he silently encouraged her to raise her eyes to him. When she did, he had to resist the urge to pull her against his chest. Thankfully, his other hand still held the reins. Otherwise, he might not have been successful.

"You know, no matter what happens with technology, we're still always going to need the farmers and farmland." He gave her a tentative smile. "It would be difficult to live without beef, milk, eggs, and vegetables. We'd starve in no time."

A soft smile appeared on her lips, and the sheen in her eyes diminished as she blinked a few times.

"There. That's better." Jacob moved his finger to brush against her smooth cheek just an inch or two from her mouth. "You're so much prettier when you smile."

He half expected her to pull away, and when she didn't, his eyes fell to her lips. How easy it would be to lean toward her and give her a quick kiss, taste the sweetness he was sure would be there. But not today.

"Thank you," she said in a half whisper, effectively breaking him from the trance.

He raised his gaze to take in the rest of her face. The look she gave him said he might've gotten away with a peck, but he didn't want to be too bold and possibly ruin his chances entirely where their relationship was concerned.

Forcing his attention back on the road and removing his hand from her shoulder, he saw her farmhouse in the near distance. Good. He needed something to distract him and take his mind off Shannon. At least in regard to the temptation of her mouth.

"We're almost there." Not that he needed to announce that. She knew where she lived. His brain felt like mush, though. Stating the obvious was the best he could do at the moment.

"Mr. Berringer, I know the topic of conversation we had during this ride wasn't the best, but I appreciate you at least hearing my point of view and not laughing."

Laugh? At her? For what? She hadn't said anything funny. Jacob shook his head. He had to focus. Now, what had she said about laughing? He didn't know. The only thing he recalled was her thanking him.

"You're welcome, Miss Delaney." At least that was a safe reply as he gathered his thoughts. "We might not always agree, but I promise to always respect your opinion." Mischief surfaced, and he felt his confidence returning. "Even if it's wrong."

That did it. Shannon pulled back, putting a few extra inches between them, and stared. "I beg your pardon!"

Keeping his eyes on the road ahead as he guided the horse and wagon closer to the farmhouse, Jacob shrugged, an impish grin on his lips. "No begging necessary. I'm just speaking the truth."

She crossed her arms in a huff and jutted her chin into the air. "Well, that's certainly a matter of opinion."

"That's my point."

"What is?"

"That it's all opinions. And I'll respect them, even if I disagree."

Shannon let out a gruff sigh that sounded more like a groan. "You said that already."

"I know I did."

"Then what are we arguing about?"

"Your guess is as good as mine." He chuckled. "Sometimes I wonder if you disagree just for the fun of it."

"Fun? Is that what you call this?"

He pulled up on the reins as they reached her house then turned in the seat to face her. "You mean you aren't enjoying our conversation? I find it very entertaining."

The look she gave him in response told him she thought he was daft. Like he must have lost his marbles. For several moments, she sat without saying a word. Could he have been wrong? He didn't think anything had been unbearable. And she had engaged in the banter just as much, if not more, than he.

"I suppose there could have been worse topics," she finally said, interrupting his musings. "Or worse companions for the drive."

Something in her tone made Jacob study her face a bit closer. And then he saw it. That miniscule twitch of her lips. Her shoulders also shook once, just barely. It was enough for him to know she was teasing him, though. Good. They were back on amiable terms again.

"Miss Delaney, I must say you are proving to be an excellent opponent in issues of touché." He looped the reins around the brake and hopped down from the wagon, rushing to her side. "Now, do allow me to escort you to your door." Extending his hand up to her, he waited for her to accept his assistance.

With a twinkle in her eye and a charming smile, she placed her hand in his and stepped down to stand in front of him. Again, he wished their relationship were different than what it was. At this close proximity, how could he wish for anything else?

"Thank you, Mr. Berringer, for driving me home and again for the enjoyable afternoon. I know I will be asked to recount the game in full detail to my brothers, but your promise of getting them to another game will make any jealousy they might feel a little easier to handle."

"Miss Delaney, it was my pleasure." They walked together to the foot of the steps and ascended to the porch. "Perhaps one day soon, I'll convince you to take a ride with me in a motorcar."

Shannon's eyes widened, and her eyebrows rose. "I wouldn't get too hopeful if I were you, Mr. Berringer."

"Sometimes hope is all we have," he countered, waggling his eyebrows.

She giggled then covered her mouth. Sobering a few seconds later, she looked toward the front door and windows of her home. Movement behind the curtains a few feet away caught her attention. Jacob saw the shadowy outline, too. He should have expected that someone would be waiting for Shannon's return. Would they come out and greet him or allow her some privacy?

"I should probably be getting inside," she said, interrupting his musings and drawing his attention back to her face. "If I tarry too long out here, you might end up being interrogated as well." She grinned. "I'm sure there'll be no end to the questions once you've left."

"I'm surprised your entire family hasn't made an appearance as your personal welcome wagon."

As if his statement had been heard through the closed window, the front door opened and a man Jacob could only assume was Mr. Delaney stepped onto the porch. His hand remained on the screen door though as he maintained a stance halfway between inside and out. Jacob tried to read the man's expression, but the shadows from the fading sun partially concealed his face. From what Jacob could see, though, Mr. Delaney didn't seem upset in any way.

Remembering his manners, Jacob took a step forward and extended his hand toward the older man. "Jacob Berringer, sir."

Shannon's father moved from behind the door and gave Jacob a firm hand-shake. "Jonathan Delaney."

From his vantage point, Jacob could finally see Mr. Delaney's face. And it showed complete trust. Not a hint of disapproval. "It's a pleasure, sir."

"Thank you for escorting my daughter home safe and sound, Mr. Berringer. Her mother and I appreciate you being aware of proprieties."

"I wouldn't have it any other way, sir."

After a quick glance at Shannon before looking again at Jacob, Mr. Delaney cleared his throat. "Well, I'll leave the two of you to finish saying your good-byes. Shannon, you won't be long, will you?"

The man didn't even look her way, but he didn't have to. The tone of his voice said it all.

"No, Papa. I'll be inside momentarily."

"Very good."

With that, Mr. Delaney disappeared. A moment later, the shadow behind the curtains returned.

Jacob couldn't help but grin at the predictable way the scene played out. "You realize you'll be stepping into an inquisition as soon as I leave, don't you?"

Shannon smiled. "Yes, but it's nothing I didn't expect."

Taking her hand in his and bowing over it, he replied, "Then I will say good night." Raising his head just enough to make eye contact with her, he continued, "Until we meet again, Miss Delaney." He placed a kiss on her knuckles and straightened, then touched two fingers to his cap. "I'm sure it will be soon."

With a wink, he spun around and headed for the buggy, his head held high. As he took the reins in his hand once more and called the horse into motion, he allowed himself one final glance at Shannon. She raised a hand in farewell, which he returned. Her sweet face lingered in his mind's eye long after he'd left her farm.

Yes, they'd definitely see each other again.

Chapter 8

"Shannon, would you come and help me with the dishes, dear?" Mama called from the kitchen after everyone had risen from the supper table. Jeremiah and Matthew had both joined Father outside to finish the evening chores. Maribeth headed to her room to complete her studies.

"Coming, Mother," Shannon called. She gave a final swipe to the table with the rag in her hand and made her way to the kitchen.

"Come grab a clean towel, dear." Mother issued her instructions without even turning around to see that Shannon had entered. "I'll wash, and you can dry."

Mama grabbed the first plate and scraped off the extra food then plunged her hands into the basin, giving the dish a good scrub. Shannon took it from her when it was clean and rubbed the towel over it in a circular motion.

It had been almost a month since Jacob had taken her to the baseball game and driven her home. She'd still seen him at Mulligan's Grocery each week she went into the city, but nothing much had happened to take their friendship any further. They chatted like they had before, bantered a bit, and even had a tiff or two about motorcars and airplanes. It lacked the spark of that afternoon and evening, though. Had she done something wrong? Something to dissuade him in some way?

"So, how are you coming with your latest quilt pattern?"

Mama's voice interrupted her pensive state.

"Hmm?"

"Shannon, dear," Mama said as she handed over another plate. "Would you like to tell me what's been bothering you lately?"

"Bothering me?"

"Yes. You haven't been acting like yourself for the past few weeks. You've been unusually quiet at meals, going off by yourself during the day, and when someone asks you a question, they sometimes have to repeat it a second time before you hear it."

Shannon finished drying the plate in her hand and shuffled to put it away in the cabinet on her right. Had she been that bad? If so, had everyone noticed? No one had said anything to her about it. Until now, that is.

"I'm sorry, Mother." She sighed. "I honestly didn't think my behavior had changed that much."

She turned back toward the sink and saw Mama regarding her with a bemused expression on her face.

"No change? Unless someone else has come and taken the place of my daughter, there is a definite difference."

Shannon gave her mother a sheepish grin. "I have been out of sorts a bit."

Mama shook off another plate and handed it to Shannon with a knowing look. "For starters, how about you tell me his name? Although I'm fairly certain I already know. We'll work through everything else from there."

"His name?"

"It's no use pretending with me, dear. I haven't raised four children without being observant."

Mama had a point. Shannon should've known she couldn't keep something like this hidden. Truth be told, she hadn't really been aware of her actions much these past few weeks.

"Jacob Berringer," she finally said. "Ever since the baseball game a few weeks ago, I've been feeling something's different."

"Different good or different bad?"

"I'm not sure." Shannon took the next plate from her mother and methodically dried it. "Our conversations have been pleasant enough, but I still feel something's not quite right. Especially when the topic is motorcars."

"Hmm." Mama grew quiet for a minute as they continued to wash and dry. "Have you ever spoken of your initial meeting with Mr. Berringer?" she finally said. "Let him know that you don't still blame him or find him solely at fault for your run-in?"

She took a glass from her mother. "What difference does it make? That accident happened nearly two months ago."

"The difference is honesty, my dear," Mama replied, settling in to scrub the utensils. "And if there is any hope of a relationship with this gentleman, whether it be friendship or something more, you need to start on the right foot." She handed Shannon six forks. "That begins with being truthful."

Shannon hated how her mother could still make her feel like a little girl. At twenty she should be beyond the need for discipline and verbal reprimands, but obviously she wasn't.

"You're right, Mother. I'll tell him the next time I see him."

"Good. I promise you'll feel much better once that's behind you." She shook off the spoons and handed them to Shannon. "Now, what else is bothering you? Because I know it's something more than just the reason for a chance meeting with a stranger."

Shannon hesitated. Mama was being very direct tonight. She must have reached her limit in how long she'd let her daughter drift without being questioned.

With a sigh, Shannon put away the forks and spoons and took the mixing utensils next, wrapping them in her damp towel. "Well, you already know about the motorcar."

"Yes."

"My meeting with Mr. Berringer was only the start of the arguments we've gotten into regarding automobiles, new inventions, technology, and a lot of other related topics."

"Knowing what I do of you, my dear, I can easily assume the center of your discussions is probably somehow related to progress."

As her mother swished her hand in the water to check for any remaining dishes, Shannon put the rest of what she'd dried away and wiped up the small pools of water that had gathered on the countertop.

"Yes, and I'm afraid we don't see eye to eye on many things at all."

Satisfied that the basin was indeed empty, Mama drained it in the sink and rinsed out the soap.

Shannon leaned against the counter. There was a certain level of comfort in the mundane, everyday tasks of running their farm. Everything in her world could be falling apart or unbalanced, yet she could come home to routine and somehow nothing seemed so bad.

"Why don't we move our little tête-à-tête into the living room?" Mama suggested after stowing the basin.

Yes, the living room was perfect. Shannon could pick up her quilting pieces and work on her latest pattern. She'd provided a new one every two weeks to Mr. Mulligan, and they continued to sell at the store on a regular basis.

Shannon walked across the wooden floorboards, avoiding the spots that creaked. For years she'd made a game of it, trying to step as silently as possible. Stepping past the sofa, she settled into one of the wingback chairs in front of the fireplace. The early start of a quilt top was draped across the back of her chair, so she reached down beside her for her supplies and pulled several pieces of fabric to her lap. Maybe she'd be able to set up the frame tonight for the top and use the sewing machine to begin assembling.

"It looks like your pattern is coming together rather nicely," her mother noted with a nod. A moment later, the clacking of her knitting needles accompanied the pop and swoosh of Shannon's sewing.

"Yes, I'm sure Mr. Mulligan will sell this one easily."

"You have done quite well with this new business. I'm pleased with your dedication."

Shannon tucked the needle through the fabric and back up in one smooth motion. "I've always loved creating beautiful quilts, Mother. You know that."

"I do, but the fact that you have found a way to bless others with your gift speaks highly of you. Your father and I are happy you're able to profit from something you love."

"And I'm thankful God has provided the open door." She chuckled. "I'm also glad I didn't miss it when the opportunity presented itself." She flattened the material in her lap and looked up at her mother. "Mr. Berringer has even told some of his associates about my quilts."

"Oh?"

Shannon nodded. "Remember the woman who purchased five of them from Mr. Mulligan? She's related to a man who works with Mr. Berringer."

"This young man must think very highly of your work." Mama grinned. "He has excellent taste."

"I'm surprised he went to such lengths to talk about the quilts, though." Even a month after learning what he'd done, Shannon was still amazed. "He had nothing to gain from bringing about a sale for both me and Mr. Mulligan."

"Perhaps," Mama mused, regarding Shannon over the top of the afghan she was creating. "But regardless of his reasons, his actions have helped you out a great deal."

"And that's exactly why I'm having such a problem." Among other things she wasn't ready to mention to her mother yet.

"You're having trouble accepting his act of goodwill?"

"No, no. It's not that." How could she put this so that it made sense? Shannon hadn't even managed to make sense of it in her own mind. Staring at the piece she attached to the quilt, she tried to sound somewhat coherent. "I guess I'm finding it difficult to reconcile the generosity of Mr. Berringer with the irritating way he continues to press me to accept automobiles." She groaned. "He can be so insufferable!" she said, jamming the needle through the fabric, then jerking her finger away when the point pierced her skin. "Ouch!"

"You should be more careful, dear. Perhaps discussing this should wait until you don't have a sharp object in your hand."

Shannon gave her mother a wry glance as she sucked on her finger. "No, I just need to not take out my frustrations on an innocent piece of fabric."

Mama pursed her lips and returned her attention to her knitting. "So tell me, is it really the idea of motorcars that is causing such a quandary, or is it this young man?"

Shannon wasn't ready to answer the question, so she sidestepped a bit. "I only worry what it will mean for our family and our farm if some of the outcomes of the inventions he supports really do come to pass."

"Our farm has been here for several generations, my dear. There has been a great deal of change and progress during those years, and our family has still managed to survive."

"But it seems as if things are moving so fast these days." Shannon smoothed out her fabric. "So much faster than it ever has before."

"That's only because the changes are so different from everything we've known," her mother pointed out as she looped her needles and tied off another end to a row. "And remember, not all evidence of technology is a bad thing. It's brought us a great deal of benefit to this farm. Just think where we'd be without a pump inside the house for our water or without my sewing machine to quickly mend or make clothes. And I have a feeling it won't be long before your father decides to have a telephone installed, not to mention electric lights."

Shannon had to agree. Each advancement didn't mean something bad would happen. "I'm just afraid we'll lose a part of ourselves by giving in. How long can we hold out against the inevitable?"

Mama gave Shannon a stern glance. "Don't start borrowing trouble that doesn't yet exist." Her expression softened. "We haven't spent all our lives working hard just to have a few new inventions destroy everything we've established."

"I know. But that doesn't mean the thoughts aren't there."

"No, it doesn't," Mama agreed. "We just have to remember to grab tight to our faith and do our best with what we've been given." She raised one eyebrow. "Now, let's get back to this young man who seems to be at the center of your current problems. You've already told me about his solid faith. Is there perhaps more to what draws you to him?"

"Why is it that you have to ask the difficult questions?"

She smiled, love and patience shining in her eyes. "It comes with being a mother, my dear."

A role she mastered quit well. Shannon again regarded her own quilt stitches and thought for a moment. What really was at the center of her problems?

"I suppose it could be a little of both." She resumed the methodical looping motion as she spoke. "On the one hand, we obviously disagree about the benefits all these inventions bring into our lives. On the other, he has demonstrated such courteous and generous behavior, not to mention his easygoing manner when discussing God, that I sometimes feel as if I'm encountering two entirely different people. In a way, it's fascinating yet aggravating."

"And you are finding it difficult to reason one with the other because you believe anyone who is in favor of progress can't possibly possess the qualities you've described as being present in Mr. Berringer."

Her mother summarized it so succinctly. Shannon wished she'd been able to do that. It would have saved her hours of mental anguish during the past few weeks.

She lowered her hands to her lap. "Mama, I am amazed. You've done it again. And the way you put it makes me realize how unfair I've been to Mr. Berringer."

Mama merely smiled in her knowing way, as if confident she'd have all the answers. "So, we have the problem identified. Now you need to determine what you're going to do about it."

Shannon sighed, the puff from her breath making a few flyaway strands of hair dance then settle again in a frame around her face. "That won't be easy."

"It never is, dear."

Mama spoke with a wisdom borne from years of experience. Shannon had shared many conversations like this with her, and each time her mother shared details from the dilemmas she'd faced, their bond grew stronger. One day down the road, Shannon would be the one imparting wisdom to her children. She hoped she'd be as good at it as her mother.

"As you sit and wonder," Mama continued, "might I suggest that you start with prayer? It is, after all, the one place you can go where you know your requests will always be heard and answered."

Remorse crept in as Shannon realized she'd neglected to talk to God about all this. "You know, Mama, I've been so preoccupied with my frustrations, I've somewhat pushed my faith off to the side."

"Trying to come up with the best retort during your conversations with Mr. Berringer as well, I'm sure."

Shannon blushed. She'd been caught again. One of these days, she'd learn she couldn't hide from God—or Mama.

"Thank you, Mama." She made sure to make direct eye contact. "It feels good to have this out in the open. I will spend a great deal of time this evening with my heavenly Father." An impish spark lit inside, and she grinned. "Maybe one day soon, I'll talk with my father here as well."

"Talk with me about what?" Papa poked his head around the wall from the kitchen. "Is this something I should be concerned about?"

"Jonathan!" Mother's face lit up when she beheld her husband. "I didn't hear you come inside." She pursed her lips and gave him a mock glare. "Shame on you for sneaking up on us and eavesdropping."

Papa held out his hands. "I wasn't eavesdropping at all." He jerked his thumb over his shoulder. "I only just entered through the back door and heard Shannon mention speaking to her father."

"Well, your daughter and I were discussing her newest quilting business and some other topics related to it."

"Uh-huh. And I'm sure somewhere in there, mention of a certain gentleman was made." He winked. "Just be sure to tell me when I need to send Jeremiah and Matthew out on the hunt."

"Papa!" Shannon's face grew very warm.

"Jonathan, behave yourself," Mother added.

"I always do, Rachel." The twinkle in his eyes and broad smile beneath his mustache said otherwise.

The front door swung open and banged against the wooden block on the floor.

"Matthew James!" Mother scolded.

The younger of Shannon's two older brothers immediately ducked his head in shame. "Sorry, Ma."

Shannon giggled quietly. A grown man who stood an inch over six feet with the build borne of honest hard work could be reduced to a little boy with two words.

"Apology accepted." Mama placed her knitting in her lap. "Now, why don't you tell us what has you so worked up that you've forgotten basic manners when entering a house?"

Matthew waved a piece of paper in the air. "The mail courier just delivered this. I was sure Father would want to see it right away."

Papa walked toward Matthew and took the paper from him, giving it a momentary perusal. All of a sudden, his face darkened and a frown seemed to turn the edges of his mustache downward.

"What is it, Jonathan?" Mother was the first to ask.

He held up the paper, glancing first at Matthew and Shannon, then settling his gaze on his wife. "Another letter from the car company asking us when we'll reach a decision regarding their offer."

"They just sent the amended offer last week." Mother clenched her hands around her partially completed afghan. "How many times are they going to accost us with their discourteous methods?"

"I'm going into the city first thing Monday morning and see if I can't straighten this out." Papa stepped toward the sofa and placed both hands on its back, crinkling the paper against the upholstery. "I realize they own the land to the west of us and want to move on this, but they don't have any leverage over us, and I will not be bullied."

Mother pursed her lips. "Just be sure and watch your temper, Jonathan."

A low groan emitted from Papa's throat, and he spoke through clenched teeth, "I will."

"I can't stand it when people in the city think they can take advantage of us farmers." Matthew pummeled his fist into his hand. "It gets under my skin the way they see us as nothing but dirt farmers with no brains and no common sense."

"Not all of them are that way, Matthew." Shannon felt the need to speak up on Jacob's behalf even if she didn't mention him specifically. "Some actually realize the benefits farms like ours bring to them, like food and clothing."

"I do have to admit I find the motorcar fascinating." Matthew groaned. "If only this company wasn't sullying my views on the ones that make them."

"Don't be so quick to judge them all by the actions of the one, Matthew," Papa cautioned. "As your sister pointed out, there are more good seeds among the bunch than bad. You just have to weed through the patches to find the ones worth harvesting."

"I guess the city *does* give us a few things we can't get out here among the farms." Matthew snapped his fingers. "That reminds me." He pointed at Shannon. "Remember when that Mr. Berringer you mentioned offered to get Jeremiah and me tickets to a ball game at Navin Field?"

The abrupt change in subject jarred Shannon, but she nodded anyway. "Yes."

"Well, the Tigers are out of town, so it wouldn't be possible today. But it's a good thing they're not here."

"Why?" What could've happened that would make Matthew not want to be at a professional baseball game? It had to be something serious.

"The players went on strike."

"What?" Shannon and her parents all exclaimed the word at the same time.

"Matthew's right," Jeremiah added from where he stood framed in the front doorway. "We got to chatting with the courier when he was here just now. He told us everyone in the city was talking about it."

"What happened?" Shannon wanted all the details. It might give her something to discuss with Jacob the next time she saw him. Perhaps it would even help ease her into the other subjects she had to broach.

Matthew's eagerness made it seem like a little of that boy in him still existed. "We told you about Ty Cobb taking a swing at that heckler in New York three days ago and punching him."

Shannon shook her head. "I still can't believe he'd do that. But yes. You told us. He was suspended, right?"

Jeremiah stepped fully into the house and latched the screen door behind him. "Right. The other men on his team didn't like it, so they went on strike. And today the managers had to put together a team of sandlot players for the game."

Papa moved to the fireplace and took his pipe from the mantel. He struck a match and lit the pipe then took a few puffs.

Shannon put her attention back on her brothers. "Sandlot players?" That seemed like an odd name for professional ballplayers.

"Substitute players," Matthew supplied. "It means they're amateurs. Replacements."

So not professional at all.

"Aren't they in Philadelphia?" Father asked, touching the tip of his pipe against his mouth.

Jeremiah looked across the living room. "Yes. And from what the courier told us, someone phoned in from Philadelphia with the score." He grimaced. "It wasn't good."

"What was it?" Why did her brothers insist on dragging out a story so much and making everyone anxious with anticipation? She looked at her parents. All right, so maybe only she was anxious.

Matthew looked right at her. "The Tigers lost to the Athletics in a final score of twenty-four to two."

Ouch. Shannon wasn't an expert, but even she knew a score like that wasn't typical for this game.

"Whoa." Papa whistled long and low. "I bet Frank Navin and the managers weren't happy with that one. I wouldn't be surprised if this spurs a word from the president of the American League. Incidents like this don't look good for the sport."

"Not a bit," Jeremiah confirmed, then looked at Shannon, waggling his index finger. "So when your friend, Mr. Berringer, gets us tickets, make sure the game is played by the real Tigers."

"Yes," Matthew echoed, leveling a playfully threatening look in her direction. "We appreciate him doing that for us, but we don't want to go see some sandlot players where the skilled ones should be."

Shannon shrugged. "I can't make any promises, but I'll do my best."

Jeremiah gave Matthew a sideways glance and moved to stand next to him. The two of them nodded at each other then looked at Shannon with smirks on their lips. A second later, they both crossed their arms across their broad chests. It was her oldest brother who spoke.

"Just tell this Berringer fella that he doesn't want to disappoint us. We've wrestled with plows and workhorses. A city-bred chap will be like child's play."

Shannon bit her lower lip to keep from laughing. If they only knew. Jacob was every bit as defined as they, and his build had come from honest work, too. It was just in an automobile factory instead of on the farm. She could tell them, but it would spoil their fun.

"I'll be sure to make that clear," she said instead.

"All right, boys." Papa pushed away from the mantel. "Let's go get cleaned up. Then maybe we can have ourselves a rousing game of checkers before turning in for the night."

"Yes!" Matthew exclaimed.

Jeremiah punched Matthew in the arm then rubbed his knuckles against Matthew's head. "I'm looking forward to a rematch."

Matthew ducked away from Jeremiah and scoffed. "I'll only beat you again. Wait and see."

Their banter continued as they disappeared into the kitchen. Papa and

Mama shared a private look between them, as if to say they wondered if their boys would ever grow up. Once the men had left, Shannon again resumed her quilting. She glanced up at Mama once to see her smile and return to her knitting. In tandem, they both reached to their sides and turned up the oil lamps next to them.

That talk of baseball and the tickets Jacob had promised made Shannon wonder when that gift would be given. At least her family seemed to accept Jacob as her friend. . .for now. She could only imagine what would happen if they became something more. There'd be no end to the teasing then.

Chapter 9

Hey, Berringer!" Mr. Hudson hailed Jacob as he approached.

"Mr. Hudson. What can I do for you?"

"One of the guys in parts removal had a death in the family. You know your way around that department. Could you lend a hand for a little bit until we can get another worker to fill the spot?"

Jacob assessed his current department. They could get by on their own until he could return. "Sure thing."

He'd agreed immediately, but returning to that department wasn't exactly high on his list of preferred tasks. At least it was only temporary.

Jacob let out a deep sigh as he hauled scrap iron away from the south end of the machine shop. The rest of the usable pieces were sorted and boxed and prepared for their journey to the assembling department. How well he remembered the daily monotony of this work. Thankfully, he hadn't been there long. Parts of his work were exciting and energizing. Other parts, such as disposing of scrap, he could do without.

Shannon no doubt felt the same way about some aspects of farming. Like mucking out stalls in the barn or harvesting crops as the sun beat down upon her back. At least she had her quilting and the weekly trips into town to purchase supplies. From what he knew of her, she dutifully performed whatever task was asked of her, even when it wasn't a favorite thing to do.

Much like hauling scrap. Jacob hefted a bin of leftover iron pieces and headed for the disposal area. One piece fell to the shop floor, so he propped the bin on his left thigh as he bent to retrieve the lone chunk. Tossing that bit back in with the rest of the scrap, he stood and had to shift the bin to get it balanced again.

"Aaarrrgh!"

The bin went crashing against the concrete floor, clanging and clamoring in a roar that rivaled some of the massive machines on the other side of the shop. Jacob looked at his right hand almost in shock. He grabbed his towel from his back pocket and pressed it against the gash to stop the flow of blood.

"Jacob! What happened? Are you all right?"

Bryce skirted around several bins and rushed to Jacob's side. Jacob had almost forgotten this was Bryce's department. His friend took one look at the bloodstains on the towel, and his eyes widened.

"Someone get a medic over here. Quick!" Bryce helped Jacob to the nearest bench, then knelt in front of him. "We'll get you taken care of as soon as possible, buddy. I promise."

Jacob groaned low in his throat and clenched his teeth against the pain. He silently criticized himself for being careless around the scrap. One wavering move, not paying attention to the pieces he'd sorted, and a jagged piece of iron had sliced right through the fleshy part below his thumb and across his wrist.

"How did you manage this, old buddy?"

Jacob swallowed and squeezed his eyes shut then opened them again. "Being stupid is how," he grunted. Thinking about Shannon and not keeping his mind on his work was a more truthful answer, but Bryce didn't need to know that.

"Hey! Did I hear Jacob got hurt?" Kendall rushed down the main aisle and dropped to his knees beside Bryce and Jacob. "How bad is it?"

"I'm not sure," Bryce answered. "But from the blood on the towel, I'd say it's a deep one."

Jacob groaned. "It's a gash from my thumb a few inches up my arm. A jagged piece of iron sliced right through the skin. I'd show you, but it was bleeding a lot."

Kendall waved away the offer. "No, no. I'll take your word for it." He shifted his gaze to Jacob's face. "At least you're a supervisor now, so you don't have to be taken off the floor for an injury like this."

"True, but that doesn't mean I won't still feel the effects." Jacob nodded his chin toward his hand pressed against his chest where Bryce held the towel tight. "It *is* my right hand. Have to wait and see what the doctor says." He moved his eyes to the left and right, searching for the man Bryce had called.

"Well, maybe you'll get lucky and it won't be so bad," Bryce suggested. "I sure wish I was a supervisor, or even working in the assembly and testing division. But I haven't been given the chance to move yet."

"Yes," Kendall echoed. "I'd love to get moved, too."

"But if that happened, you might be farther away from my department, and I wouldn't have you two around to heckle me." Jacob mustered as much of a grin as he could.

Kendall waved off his pseudoprotest. "Ah, don't worry about it. We'd still find you."

"Or you could capitalize on your supervisory position," Bryce countered, waggling his eyebrows, "and use your influence to get us moved as well."

Leave it to Bryce to be the comedian of their trio. The man never could take many things seriously. Except his work, of course, and even in that he always found a way to make light of things. Today Jacob appreciated it. Took his mind off the pain.

"Please clear a space, gentlemen." The medic approached and went right to work. He pulled out fresh bandages and a bottle of alcohol. "Let's take a look at what we have here."

Jacob winced as the man pulled the towel away from his hand. When the fresh air hit the wound, he snapped his jaw shut and tensed the muscles in his right arm. Maybe it was worse than he'd thought.

"Hmm," the medic murmured. "It's a deep cut. That's for sure." He carefully examined the wound. "But I've seen worse. . .especially here at the plant."

Jacob had no doubt about that. Some of these machines could maim a man if he wasn't careful. Thankfully, he had only been hauling scrap. If he'd been at his station, the consequences could've been far more serious.

"You were lucky, son," the medic continued. "You could've severed an artery or even lost a finger."

Jacob couldn't argue with that. He silently thanked God for His protection. The edges on some of those pieces could easily cut through flesh and muscle and even bone. He was fortunate the iron had cut him where it had.

"This is definitely going to need stitches," the medic stated with authority. "Let's get you to the infirmary."

"We're coming with you," Bryce said as he and Kendall lifted Jacob to his feet and stood on either side of him.

The medic glanced at all three and shrugged. "As long as you don't get in the way."

Kendall muttered near Jacob's left ear, "We were both due to take a break anyway. Might as well use it to make sure you're all right."

"Thanks," was all Jacob could muster.

As soon they had Jacob settled on the table, the medic signaled an assistant then held Jacob's attention in a direct gaze. "I won't lie to you, son. This is going to hurt. But I have some chloroform available if you need it."

Jacob nodded. "Do what you have to do, Doc."

"We'll hang right here with you, pal, until it's all done," Kendall vowed.

Bryce waggled his eyebrows again. "And maybe if you think of that gal farmer, it'll help keep your mind off the pain."

"Are we ready?" the medic interrupted, his face stern and focused.

Jacob took a deep breath and let it out slowly. This was going to hurt, but he could handle it. "Ready."

The medic held a thick, clean bit of bandage to Jacob's mouth. "You might want to bite down on this, son." He looked to Kendall and Bryce. "And if you two could make sure his arms remain immobile, I'd appreciate it."

"You got it, Doc," Kendall replied.

Jacob clamped his teeth on the gauze as Kendall and Bryce got into position to hold him still. The medic laid out a cloth and extended Jacob's arm to have room to work. After dousing the wound with a liberal amount of alcohol, the medic took up his needle and thread and commenced with the suturing.

As he drifted just on the edge of consciousness, Jacob took Bryce's suggestion and again thought of the one person who could make him smile. Shannon. He brought her beautiful face to mind and dwelled on her delicate features. Her bright eyes and smooth skin. Her enticing lips that had tempted him more than once, and her long hair always secured in that single braid down her back. What would it look like flowing free? He could imagine himself there to tuck the loose tendrils behind her ears or even to run his fingers through the soft strands.

"All right, we're all done."

The medic's voice penetrated Jacob's foggy mind. Why did he have to interrupt such a pleasant thought? Wait a minute. Done already? That was fast. Jacob opened his eyes and looked down at his hand, bandaged and resting on his chest.

"Wow, Doc," he croaked through dry lips. That gauze he'd had in his mouth must've soaked up all the moisture. He licked his lips and moved his tongue around. "I hardly felt anything. You're good."

The medic laughed. "Either me or the alcohol I poured over your hand."

Or it could've been the nice distraction Shannon provided in his thoughts. And now for the tough question.

Jacob held up his hand. "What does this injury mean for me and work, Doc?"

As he put away his equipment and cleaned up the area a bit, the medic pressed his mouth into a thin line. "Well, I would say that depends on your manager, but I am going to recommend that you not be called upon for any machine work for about two weeks. And you'll need to have someone else perform any repairs in your place as you supervise. I'll come and check on your stitches then and determine if the wound is healed enough for you to return to full duty." He clicked one of the glass cabinets closed and reached to help Jacob off the table. "In the meantime, I'll give you some extra bandages, and I want you to clean that area two to three times a week."

Jacob nodded. "I appreciate it, Doc."

"Next time try to be a bit more careful around these leftover bits and pieces, all right? And take extra care around these monstrosities they call machines." He winked. "I'm sure Mr. Ford would like to keep his employees safe and not dismembered."

"I will." Jacob reached out his left hand. "Thanks again."

The medic engaged Jacob in an awkward handshake then nodded toward the main floor. "You're free to go."

"All right, buddy," Bryce spoke as soon as they had left the infirmary. "Let's get you up to the Employee Claims Department so we can have this incident reported and on file."

"I'm surprised a supervisor hasn't arrived yet to investigate," Kendall mused, his brow furrowed as he looked up and down the nearest aisle.

"They're probably still in that manufacturing meeting, remember?" Jacob reminded them. "Mr. Hudson told us about it the other day."

Bryce took Jacob by the arm and started walking them both toward the nearest door to the outside. "Well, maybe by the time we get to the Administration Building, they'll have finished their meeting, and we can speak directly with Mr. Hudson." He glanced back over his shoulder. "You coming, Kendall?"

"I have to get back to my station."

"Well, we *should* probably get the mess cleaned up back in scraps first." Bryce nodded toward that area.

"Guys," Jacob spoke up. "I can make it to the offices by myself. I don't need any assistance."

Bryce gave him a look of disbelief. "Are you sure? You've lost a bit of blood. We don't want you getting woozy and passing out on your way there."

"I'll be fine." Jacob made a shooing motion with his left hand. "You two go back to work and relieve the guys who replaced you during your break. These machines might appear to run themselves, but they still need us to feed them their blocks of iron."

"Jacob's right, Bryce," Kendall agreed. "We shouldn't abandon our posts. If something gets thrown out of whack, it could mean big trouble for the next stage in the procedure."

"All right." Bryce didn't seem happy about it, but he nodded anyway. "Just make sure you come tell us immediately when you get back. We want to hear what they've decided for you."

"I will." Jacob touched one finger to his forehead and saluted them. "I'll see you two later."

Tucking his arm close to his chest, Jacob headed out the south side doors and made his way to the Administration Building. No matter how many times he saw it, the massive number of windows never ceased to amaze him. Perfectly lit and ventilated, the engineering that went into that building and the entire factory, in fact, was an example of the most modern methods available. What would Shannon think of a place like this? It wasn't the noisy and chaotic existence of the factory floor. No, this building was everything the other buildings weren't—pristine and splendid with plush carpeting and scattered Oriental rugs. In fact, the foyer reminded him of the Grand Hotel on Mackinac Island. His family spent one or two weeks there every year. And no motorcars were permitted. Shannon would feel right at home.

Wait a minute. Why was he imagining Shannon on that island? One second he was wondering what she would think of the Administration Building, and the next he was picturing her on vacation with him at Mackinac. He had to get back to the present.

No, Shannon would never want to set foot near this factory. Not even the area where the business is conducted. He'd do good to put any thought of that out of his head and focus on his purpose for being there. He'd have time to think of Shannon later.

❧

"Good morning, Miss Delaney."

Jacob appeared at her side, with gentle eyes and a crooked grin.

"Good morning, Mr. Berringer." She gave him a knowing smile. "And what brings you to the store today?" As if she even had to ask.

He ran his finger around the glass jar on the counter that held a wide assortment of gum balls. "Oh, I was sent to the delicatessen to pick up some sandwiches for a handful of other supervisors over at the plant. And this is the best one in the city." He tipped his head toward the street. "Saw your wagon out front and thought I'd stop in to say hello."

Shannon regarded him for a moment and quirked her mouth. His explanation sounded feasible and so much better than saying Mr. Mulligan had called him again. True, she often came at the same time each week, but today it appeared he had another reason for being there.

"Can I help you with the last of your supplies?" Jacob offered before she had a chance to say anything.

"Umm, yes. Thank you."

She paid Mr. Mulligan for her purchases and followed Jacob outside. He seemed to favor his right hand as he awkwardly held her crate of supplies. And he slid the box onto the wagon bed instead of hefting it over the side before climbing up to make sure everything was secure. He placed his left hand on the side and vaulted to the ground. Shannon caught a flash of white as he landed and gasped when she saw what it was.

"What happened to your hand?" Without thinking, she immediately reached out and took it in both of hers.

"Oh, I cut it cleaning up scrap metal at work a few days ago." He shrugged like it wasn't a big deal. "The gash was pretty deep, but the medic stitched me up, and I'll be as good as new in a couple of weeks."

Stitches! Shannon could only imagine how painful that must have been. "Are you still able to work?"

"Well, as a supervisor I don't get involved as much with the machines. And for the next few weeks, I have an assistant by my side to take care of any manual work." Jacob flicked his fingers against hers and grinned. "Are you going to let me have my hand back, or should I look into asking for another? A new one might not hurt as much."

"Oh! I'm sorry." Shannon immediately let go and blushed. She couldn't believe she'd held on that long. Such an intimate gesture right there in the middle of the street.

"Hey." Jacob tipped up her chin with his finger. "Don't worry about it. I certainly didn't mind."

Flustered, Shannon searched her mind for something else to say that would get them on a different topic. Anything.

"So, umm, your role as a supervisor." She did her best to appear unaffected. "Have you been one long?"

Jacob leaned back against the wagon and folded his arms across his chest. "A few months. I've been making my way up the ladder since I started a few years ago. Mr. Hudson used to seek me out for my take on a few decisions the board of directors made during the years. Eventually, someone saw my potential and promoted me." He raised his bandaged hand. "Even this injury hasn't dissuaded them from considering me for something more."

"Did you say Mr. Hudson? As in Hudson Motor Car Company?" That was another factory in the city, which likely competed with Ford in production.

"Yes." He nodded. "But it's not what you're thinking," he rushed to add. "Mr. Hudson is related to the ones who run the other automobile company, but he isn't a direct relative."

Shannon raised her eyebrows. "A relative, yet he chose to work for Mr. Ford? That was a bit bold on his part, wouldn't you think?"

He shrugged. "Depends on how he feels about the other members of his family. He told me he isn't in line to inherit anything, so he felt his skills were best used elsewhere." Jacob leaned forward then looked to the left and right before returning his gaze to Shannon. "Between you and me, he also said he wasn't as impressed with their plant. He'd rather work for Ford."

"What makes Ford so different? They're still a factory that makes automobiles."

"Yes, but they maintain a high level of quality and excellence in their product as well as their service. Mr. Ford prides himself on that fact."

Jacob's loyalty certainly wasn't in question. She still didn't trust the company, though. "I'm sure he can't oversee every aspect of his company to make sure everyone follows those standards."

"No, but he has hired a staff of supervisors, managers, and board members who assist him." He crossed one ankle over the other, seemingly unfazed by her doubts. "Each man in charge is a valued member of Mr. Ford's team, and he trusts them implicitly. I haven't met them all, but I have met some, and I'm impressed."

Shannon took a couple steps toward the front of her wagon and ran her hand over the brake lever. Then she rested her arm along the side of the wagon.

"But that's just your experience, and you're only one man. Surely there are others who don't feel the way you do." Shannon didn't want to insult where he worked, but the reality couldn't be as good as Jacob described it to be.

"I'm sure there are others who aren't happy with the conditions or their supervisor or even their job and position in the company. But overall, Ford has the highest pay scale and the best working conditions of any other company here in Detroit. That's saying a lot."

Shannon had never been inside the Ford plant, or any plant for that matter, but she'd heard of the conditions in factories. She pointed to Jacob's hand. "You got hurt, though. Bad enough to require stitches. That doesn't sound very safe to me."

Jacob held up his hand again. "This? It didn't happen because of unsafe working conditions. It happened because I was careless and not paying attention to what I was doing. And it didn't even happen on a machine."

"Still, the larger the machinery or the more these factories attempt to increase their output, the higher the chances are for more serious injuries."

"You're absolutely right. However, what you're forgetting is there are just as many dangers, if not more, on a farm just like the one your family owns."

Shannon shook her head, elevating her chin just slightly. "No. That's not possible. You're mistaken." Her farm was far safer than being amongst machines ten times her size that punched through steel like melted butter.

"Am I?" He raised his eyebrows and challenged her with the look he gave her. "You own a plow with very sharp edges to till the ground. What would happen if one of your brothers or your father were to get caught somehow beneath that equipment? They'd be just as injured as I am right now. Or worse."

That would never happen. But even as she thought it, she knew it was a possibility.

"And I noticed the table saw with the hydraulic method to keep it constantly moving. What happens if his hand slips or he gets too close to the blades? He could lose a finger or even an arm."

Shannon had watched Father operate the saw and even assisted him from time to time. The way Jacob described it was right.

"What about you and your mother?"

Shannon knitted her brows. "We don't involve ourselves with large machinery."

"Maybe not large. But do you own a sewing machine, perhaps?"

"Of course. What woman doesn't these days?"

Jacob shrugged. "That needle moves awfully fast when the machine is running.

It could do some serious damage to a finger or hand if you lost control while pushing the material through."

She'd never thought of it that way. He made some excellent points. "How is it that you know so much about the everyday tools we have on our farm and in our home?"

"I'm involved in manufacturing a great deal. Not only at the Ford plant where I work but also in my reading and watching the developments elsewhere." Jacob made a loose gesture toward the people milling about nearby or walking to and fro on the sidewalks around them. "I also talk to a lot of people and pay attention to their stories."

Shannon was impressed. He was well informed, and he managed to put things in a perspective that made sense to her. "It's no wonder you were promoted to a supervisory position. If you've proven yourself at work the way you have with me, the men in charge at Ford would be daft not to see your worth."

A slow smile spread across Jacob's face and reached all the way to his twinkling hazel eyes. Shannon felt the heat rush to her cheeks at the compliment she'd just given him. Maybe she shouldn't have been so forward. It might be too soon for her to be that honest with him. Then again, Mother had told her it was best to begin with honesty.

"Miss Delaney," Jacob began as he unfolded his arms and placed his bandaged hand on his chest then dipped his head in her direction. "Thank you very much for those words. It means a lot to me to hear you say them."

He appeared so solemn she almost laughed. It wouldn't be the right time or place, though, so she swallowed and held back the chuckle.

"You're quite welcome," she replied. The rest of her conversation with her mother repeated itself in her mind, and she continued. "I also owe you an apology."

"An apology? For what?"

Shannon wet her lips. This should be much easier. But it wasn't. The lump in her throat made it feel like she'd swallowed a piece of meat that refused to go down. She had to get this out, though. With a deep breath, she just plunged forward.

"Remember the day we met on the road?"

He grinned. "How could I forget? One of the luckiest days of my life."

She'd address that remark later. If only he wasn't so charming. "Well, as you no doubt recall, I wasn't exactly kind to you."

"As I recall," he said with a smirk, "you had some rather choice words to say to me and all but accused me of being a reckless driver."

Shannon winced. "Yes, about that." Why hadn't Mother told her it would be this difficult? She'd done as she'd promised and gone straight to God first. Now she really needed His help.

"Something you want to say?" He straightened and released what sounded like a mock gasp. "Don't tell me you want to confess to causing the whole near accident."

"Actually, not the whole thing, but I am partly to blame." There, she'd said it. Or at least started it.

Jacob folded his arms across his chest again, looking very interested in what she had to say. "Go on."

Shannon shifted from her left to her right foot and back again. She reached down and clutched a bit of her skirts in her fists and worried the material with her fingers. With another deep breath, she just blurted out the rest of her confession.

"I'm afraid my mind wasn't on my driving either as I approached that intersection. So it wasn't all your fault that we both were nearly run off the road."

Finally. She'd managed to get it out. A great feeling of relief washed over her. Like a heavy burden had been lifted. There was just one problem. Jacob remained silent. He didn't respond in any way, save the pensive manner in which he studied her. Quiet unrest settled into the pit of her stomach. What was he thinking? Wasn't he happy she'd admitted some guilt? Why wasn't he speaking? She couldn't stand it any longer.

"Don't you have anything to say?"

He opened his mouth to answer then shut it. A few seconds later, he opened it again. "I, uh, I'm not sure what to say. This seems so unexpected after this much time has passed. It's been almost three months." Jacob reached up and scratched his head with his left hand. "Why now? What prompted this?"

She had hoped he would simply accept the apology and be done with it. Why did he have to ask the reason?

Looking down at the ground, she stubbed the tip of her boot against the dirt. "Well, I'd like to think that we have a good friendship, and well, that means we should be completely honest." Shannon raised her head and looked him straight in the eyes. "I wasn't honest about our meeting, and God convicted me about it, so I wanted to clean the slate."

This time his response came much faster. "I see." Pushing away from the wagon, Jacob took a step closer, the expression on his face softening as he drew near. "Miss Delaney, once again you surprise me."

"So you're not angry?"

"Angry? Me?" He flattened his hand against his chest. "Not at all. In fact, I'm glad you think so much of our friendship to be honest." He leaned his hip against the wagon, much like how Shannon had been poised. "I tell you what. Since we're being honest and you've asked so many questions about the Ford factory, how about the next time I see you I bring you a booklet they have available to all customers? You can read about the company, the new plant, the machines, the employees, and everything you ever wanted to know about Ford. Might help you understand a bit more about where I work and why I love it so much."

A booklet? She couldn't believe they had such a thing. "I would like that."

If Jacob wanted her to learn more about his work, maybe he also wanted their friendship to grow. That thought alone warmed her cheeks. She almost leaned forward and placed a kiss on his cheek, but mindful of their public location, she refrained. It wouldn't be proper. Of course, if they were alone. . .no, that would mean there was something more to their relationship. And there wasn't. Not yet, anyway. Although the afternoon and evening of the baseball game made her think there might be. But what about how he'd been acting since then? All right, she really needed to shift away from that train of thought.

"Consider it done, then," Jacob said with finality. "I'll pick up a booklet first thing Monday morning and have it ready for next week."

"Thank you." At least he hadn't divined any of her thoughts.

"My pleasure, Miss Delaney." He reached for her left hand with his and bowed over it. "It's the least I can do for a friend," he said as he placed a light kiss on the back of it. "I should get myself over to the delicatessen before the men back at the plant wonder what's keeping me."

The warmth returned to her cheeks at the look in his eyes and the way he had said "friend." Maybe there really could be more to their friendship. She certainly hoped so.

Chapter 10

Shannon laid out her quilt top across the table in the corner of the living room. The pattern was coming along nicely. She had the top left corner completed and most of the top right. Now she needed to work on the center pieces.

"That's shaping up to be a beautiful quilt, dear," Mama said as she stepped off the stairs and entered the room. "It might be one of your best yet."

Tilting her head to the left and right, Shannon observed her work with a more critical eye. It wasn't nearly finished yet, but the arrangement of the lattice design, tulips, and crocheted flowers stood out in bold array. She supposed Mama was right. Then again, every quilt she made was her pride and joy while she was working on it. Once completed, she always had trouble parting with it and leaving it for sale at Mulligan's.

"One of these days," Shannon mused, "I will create one that I want to keep exclusively for myself. One with a value beyond worth that I could never sell."

"Do you mean like your great-grandmother's quilt that sits on your bed upstairs?"

Shannon nodded. "Just like that."

The starburst pattern had been modified with replicas of smaller flowers Shannon had picked along the walk from the small town of Clifford to where her great-grandmother had lived. The buds surrounding the center starburst made the quilt personal and unique, telling a story in its lovingly crafted design.

She loved the two or three summers she'd spent as a little girl with her great-grandmother. The memories of baking, learning how to quilt, and hearing stories from the sweet lady's life came flooding back. If she could do nothing else, she'd at least preserve her great-grandmother's love of quilting.

Heavy boots sounded on the porch outside. They stamped a few times on the wooden boards before the front door swung open and admitted her eldest brother, Jeremiah. The grim expression he wore couldn't be anything but bad news.

"What is it, Jeremiah?" Mama asked before Shannon could say anything.

"It's Digby. I fear he's gone lame." Jeremiah sighed and ran his hand through his hair, making the thick waves stand up on end. "His knee is swollen to twice its size, and it's not looking good." He turned on his heel and headed for the kitchen.

"Oh no. Not Digby," Shannon called to his retreating back. Regret made her brow furrow. That horse had been in their family for more than fifteen years. He'd been hooked to the plow for almost as many. He and Tiller were two of the best horses she'd ever known. Braedon served her quite well and was still her favorite, but everyone in her family loved Digby and Tiller.

The sound of the pump being primed floated into the room where she sat. The splash of water against the basin and intermittent water dropping into the pool meant her brother was rinsing away the dirt and grime from his hands and arms. He'd no doubt spent a good deal of time working with Digby and determining the seriousness of the horse's injury.

"I'm afraid to say for sure," Jeremiah continued, returning to the room and holding a towel as he dried his hands. "We'll watch him overnight and see if the swelling goes down. If not, we'll have to switch and put Crimson on the plow. Maybe Digby can use a little break. Crimson could benefit from additional time."

"Or we can bring in that tractor I told you about," Matthew spoke through the screen door before coming inside and letting it slam behind him. "It would do twice the work in half the time. Or close to it, anyway."

"A tractor?" Shannon couldn't believe she was hearing her brother say such a thing. "Do you mean one of those gasoline-powered machines that make all that noise and emit puffs of smoke from their pipes?"

Matthew rolled his eyes. "I mean one of those efficient inventions to help farmers achieve greater success and be more productive in their efforts. You're not out there every day like we are. Otherwise you might feel differently." He walked over and flicked Shannon's braid. "Not all machines are bad, little sister. You might just have to accept the fact that we've entered a new century. And a new century brings progress. Progress brings better equipment, and that in turn gives us a better chance to produce a higher profit."

"Yes, Shannon," Maribeth's voice sounded from the stairs. "You spend so much time with your quilts and your old-fashioned methods that you've missed out on some pretty great discoveries that have become quite popular with a lot of people."

"And what are you doing down here, young lady?" Mama reprimanded. "Aren't you supposed to be upstairs getting a head start on your advanced studies? You won't finish a year early like you wanted if you dally."

Maribeth gave Mama a helpless gesture, her palms up and her elbows bent. "I saw Jeremiah leading a limping Digby into the barn from my window, and I wanted to come find out what happened." She pranced over to the sofa and plopped onto one of the cushions, dropping her elbows to her knees and resting her chin in her hands. "Besides, this is infinitely more interesting than history and literature."

Mama gave Maribeth a look that said she'd allow it for now. But the break from her studies wouldn't last long.

"Matthew's got a point," Jeremiah chimed in again, bringing the conversation back to the previous topic. "I'm not too sure how I feel about these tractors, but I'm definitely willing to take a look and give it a try." He hooked his fingers around his suspenders. "Besides, with Digby possibly lame, we'll need another solution fast. It's worth at least trying it. We can always go back to horses if it doesn't work out."

Mama regarded her two sons in a contemplative manner. She pursed her lips and tilted her head to the side. "I don't suppose it would hurt much to try it out."

Papa stomped his boots on the porch before entering through the front door. "I see they managed to convince the women of the house that we should bring this new equipment out to the farm and give it a try. See if it's worth what so many are saying about it."

Shannon looked at her father then went back and forth between her two brothers. Papa must not have been too far behind them and had been listening at the door without making his presence known.

"Well, they've convinced Mama and Maribeth," Shannon corrected. "But they haven't convinced me."

"That's still two out of three," Matthew taunted. "And that means a majority. You're outnumbered, little sister."

Shannon stuck out her tongue at Matthew, who did the same in return, accompanied by a goofy face.

"All right, children." Mama sighed and shook her head. "Let's try to act our ages, shall we?"

Maribeth bounced on the sofa, her face alight with joy. "Does this mean we're going to see this tractor in action right here on our farm?" She clapped, appearing less like a young lady of sixteen and more like a girl of nine or ten. "This is so exciting!"

"We don't have the tractor yet, Maribeth," Papa pointed out. "We are only talking about the possibility at the moment."

"But who do we know that could provide one to us?" Mama asked next. "I haven't heard of anyone among our neighbors who has one yet, and the farms that do are farther to the west of us."

Matthew held up both hands as if to halt any further conversation. "I have it all taken care of."

"You do?" Jeremiah gave Matthew a questioning look. "When did you have any time to do anything about this? We've only just started discussing it today."

"Actually, I've been in contact with a sales representative from Hart-Parr Gasoline Engine Company in Charles City, Iowa, for a few weeks now." Matthew at least had the good sense to appear apologetic. "We got a brochure in the mail at the start of the planting season, and I decided to investigate on my own."

"What made you believe you had the right to do something like that, young man?" Papa crossed his arms and leaned against the door frame. "And why didn't you mention this outside when we were having our discussion?"

"Well, for one," Matthew began in a respectful tone, "I'm not a kid anymore. And since I'll either be running this farm or one of my own eventually, I figured it was high time I started looking into ways to increase output. So I went ahead and contacted the salesman when I heard he was coming through Detroit."

"Does he have a tractor ready for us?" Jeremiah had already seemed to be in favor of the idea, and now his eyes took on a bright hue.

Matthew kept his gaze on Father. "Well, if we had a telephone, I could call him." The way he spoke made it sound like he was giving a hint they needed a phone installed. He moved his head to look at Jeremiah. "But since we don't, I have only to make one trip into the city where he has a temporary office and speak with him. I believe he said he could arrange to have a tractor delivered within the week."

Silence fell upon Shannon's entire family. She sat in the chair next to where her quilt was laid out and regarded each of her parents and siblings, one at a time. Maribeth was obviously excited. Her beaming smile from ear to ear and wide eyes gave that away. Mama seemed a little hesitant, but her curiosity had definitely been piqued. Matthew's enthusiasm didn't require any analysis, and Jeremiah didn't seem too far behind him. Finally, she came to Papa. He didn't make decisions like this without giving them a great deal of thought. Shannon was surprised when he spoke again so quickly.

"Very well," he began, his voice layered with a mixture of firm control and anticipation. "We'll go into town tomorrow and speak with the salesman."

"But, Father," Matthew started to protest, but Papa held up a hand.

"Let me finish, please," he added in a tone that brooked no argument.

"Sorry. Go ahead."

"I was going to say that we'll go, but you will be the one to go inside and speak with the man. I will wait in the wagon."

That answer seemed to satisfy Matthew, who only nodded. Jeremiah took a step forward, drawing attention toward him. "I'll stay here with Digby and see if I can't help get his leg to heal or at least figure out just how bad it is."

Papa nodded. "That sounds good, son. We should be back by lunchtime, and we'll know then what our next course of action is."

So they were really going through with it. For the first time ever, her father and brothers were going to bring a gasoline-powered machine onto their farm. They were going to interrupt the peaceful ambiance with that noisy contraption. It made sense from a strictly farming perspective. What farmer wouldn't want to increase production and decrease the time it took to get it done? But did they have to sacrifice everything she'd come to love in order to do it?

Realizing she would have no further say in this conversation or decision, Shannon turned her attention once more to her quilt. At least this was one thing she *could* control. She glanced up and caught Mama's eye. A silent look said Mama knew how she was feeling and echoed her concerns. Her mother pressed her palms together and looked heavenward. With nothing more than an almost imperceptible nod, she silently told Shannon to do the same.

Prayer and quilting. *Two* things she could control. The rest she'd have to leave to God. Surely He'd give them a sign if this wasn't the right thing to do. And if not, well, she prayed the lesson learned wouldn't be a hard one to handle.

❧

"Your family is really going to be testing out a brand-new tractor on the farm?"

Jacob tossed two sacks of flour and one of sugar into the back of Shannon's wagon as she prepared to return home. She noticed the bandage was off his hand, and only a long red line marked the area of the gash. It looked to be healing nicely.

Another Saturday, another trip to the city, and another bit of time shared with Jacob. He always offered his assistance, and she enjoyed his company. Talking with him brightened her day. Today, though, she had more important things on her mind.

Like this tractor waiting back in the fields at home.

She'd spent the past four days in prayer as they waited for the tractor to arrive. Digby had shown some improvement but nowhere near enough to be put back on the plow. At least they wouldn't have to put him down, but they couldn't utilize him either. And her father had opted not to put another horse in Digby's place. Now the tractor sat in the field, and they'd be testing it that afternoon.

Shannon nodded. "This afternoon, yes. I'm not sure I want to be there, but a part of me is curious. I'll admit to that."

"Why don't you want to be there?" Jacob tested the back gate to be sure it was secure then dusted off his hands and joined Shannon at the side of the wagon.

"I'm just afraid something is going to go wrong."

"Who says something has to go wrong? Everything could go right."

She grumbled. "With new machinery? That's not likely." Despite her distrust of this tractor, she couldn't keep the worry from creeping into her voice.

Jacob obviously noticed it, too. He stepped closer and reached out with his left hand to tuck a stray tendril behind her ear. "Hey," he said softly. "You trust God, right?"

"Of course," she replied without hesitation, her breath catching in her throat at his gentle touch.

"Then trust Him to do His job in protecting anyone in your family who will be dealing with the tractor." He moved his hand to lightly graze her chin in an upward motion. "And if something does happen, trust that God will be there in the aftermath to see things through."

How could Shannon possibly be upset with sound reasoning like that? Jacob definitely had a point. She trusted God in so many other aspects of her life. She had to fully trust Him in this instance as well. Of course, Jacob's compelling eyes and tender smile helped, too. She had to swallow several times before finding her voice.

"You're right, of course." Shannon propped her arm on the side of the wagon and leaned her head on her hand, letting out an exasperated sigh. "I just wish it wasn't so difficult to trust when things don't seem to be going the way I'd like them to go."

Jacob gave her a knowing look. "That's the true test of faith. Trusting when things *aren't* going right. Otherwise you can't say much for your faith."

"Yes, I know." She'd heard it all before, but coming from him, the reminder didn't seem so irritating. Plus, the fact that he shared her faith meant that much more.

"When will the testing take place?"

"Around one o'clock." Shannon looked up at the blue sky, devoid of clouds, then consulted her pocket watch. "Which means I should be getting back to the farm. The midday meal will be served shortly, and the men will be getting to work immediately after that."

"May I come out to watch?"

"Pardon me?" Had he just asked if he could come to her farm?

Jacob extended his hands out as if advising someone to slow down. "I apologize if I'm being forward by asking, but I don't often get to see that type of equipment fired up."

Shannon hesitated. If she agreed, she'd be involving him even more in her family's affairs. They hadn't declared anything with their friendship, but her family would all know something existed between them if he came. What other explanation could she give?

"I know what you're thinking." He lifted his left hand between them, palm facing her. "How about this? Let's say I come strictly as an observer. I do work for Ford, and they have experimented with automobile plows in recent years. Where did this tractor come from?"

"Umm, a company in Iowa, I believe." She tried to remember what her brother had told them, but the details wouldn't come to mind.

Jacob nodded as if he knew the exact company. "The Hart-Parr Gasoline Engine Company, no doubt. This is perfect."

"What is?" She wasn't following his logic at all.

"Well, I could be there to study the new equipment. I could take notes about the structure and successes or failures for research on machine development. I'm always working on automobiles, but a tractor would be fascinating to study."

The reason seemed plausible enough. As much as Shannon wanted a definitive line drawn to their relationship, she wasn't certain she was ready to take that step right now.

"I'll even come out in my own buggy after lunch. That way you'll have a chance to return home first."

He had thought of everything. At least everything that came to her mind. If she denied him his request now, it would be cruel. Jacob looked so excited at the prospect of seeing this tractor, she couldn't turn him down. Besides, one more visit to the farm might help her family get to know Jacob better and he them.

"Very well." She reached for the reins and loosed them from the brake. "Do you remember how to get to the farm?"

"Head north out of the city and go almost northwest for about four miles. When I see the old abandoned barn, I turn left and your farm is at the end of the road."

She was impressed. He'd only been there twice before, yet he recalled each and every detail of the drive out. An excellent memory, a considerate nature, and a charming personality.

Shannon smiled. "Yes, that's exactly right." She placed her foot on the running board only to have Jacob right there at her side, offering his hand to help her into the wagon. Glancing down at him and into his twinkling hazel eyes, she almost lost her balance. "Shall we say around one, then?" she managed, despite the catch in her throat.

"One it is," he replied, still holding on to her hand. After a quick squeeze, he released it and stepped back.

"I'll see you then, Mr. Berringer."

He tipped his cap and winked. "I look forward to it, Miss Delaney," he said with a grin.

If she didn't get away from him soon, she might be tempted to join him again on the sidewalk and act out some of the daring thoughts in her mind. Jacob was far too attractive in so many ways for his own good. Or perhaps it was for her good. Shannon couldn't say for sure. She only knew she needed to leave. Now.

Without a further word, she settled into her seat on the bench and slapped the reins. The typical jerk of the wagon pressed her against the back of the seat, but she regained her perch and expertly guided the team north out of the city. Jacob's handsome face remained in her mind during the entire ride home. It was a good thing she'd be seeing him in just a couple of hours. She didn't know if she would last another full week.

❧

A charged feeling electrified the room as Shannon and Maribeth finished the dishes from the midday meal. Matthew was barely able to contain his excitement, and Jeremiah had picked up on the anticipation as well. In fact, her two brothers probably would have been jumping up and down if they weren't both full-grown adults.

"Come on, you two," Matthew called from his position by the front door, his hand resting on the knob. "You don't have to get every single drop of water off every dish. Some of it will dry on its own."

"Just a couple more minutes," Shannon replied. "We have to dump the scraps; then we'll be ready."

"Well, hurry up, then," Jeremiah said. "We're wasting time just standing here."

"Go on outside and wait for us." Maribeth grabbed the pail and headed for the back door. "We'll be right there."

"All right." Matthew turned toward the living room. "Father, are you coming?"

"Of course. I wouldn't miss this even if you hog-tied me to the fence post outside." His heavy boots clumped across the wooden floor. "Let's go."

The deep voices of her brothers and father jumbled together but grew quieter as they stepped outside onto the porch and headed for the front yard. Shannon took a last look at the kitchen to be sure everything was put away then accompanied Maribeth out the back door. As soon as her sister had emptied the pail, Shannon reached for it only to have Maribeth hold it out of reach.

"Don't worry about taking it back inside. We've kept Papa, Jeremiah, and Matthew waiting long enough," Maribeth stated with a keen wisdom. "The pail will be just fine right here, and it will still be there when we get back." She grabbed on to Shannon's arm and pulled. "Let's go."

As they rounded the side of the farmhouse, the *clip-clop* of horses' hooves drew everyone's attention to the road leading to their house.

Jacob!

Shannon recognized his shadowy form right away. An unbidden smile formed on her lips as she watched his buggy draw ever closer.

"I wonder who that could be," Maribeth mused, reminding Shannon her sister stood right there and might notice any reaction, no matter how small.

Shannon schooled her expression into one of calm indifference. But inside, her heart beat an erratic rhythm, and her stomach fluttered like a garden full of butterflies taking flight from their now-pollinated flowers.

Jacob drove the buggy into the front yard and came to a stop just a few feet away from her father and brothers. Shannon wanted to rush over there and greet him, but that would give away her excitement. Instead, she calmly walked with Maribeth to join the men. Mama stepped out onto the porch and descended the front steps but remained there.

"Good afternoon, Mr. Delaney," Jacob greeted before anyone else could say anything.

"Good afternoon, Mr. Berringer," Father greeted. "Shannon mentioned that you would be joining us this afternoon."

Jacob hopped down from the buggy and approached, his hand extended. "Yes, I hope you don't mind."

Papa took the hand and gave it a firm shake before letting go. "Not at all. In fact," he said with a glance at Shannon, "I'd have been surprised if you weren't in attendance."

"Papa," Shannon spoke lowly, grateful for the overhead sun and hoping it hid her flushed cheeks.

Everyone immediately turned their eyes to Shannon. It was a good thing she wasn't looking at Jacob at that moment. Papa had all but stated outright that he expected Jacob to be involved in their family's affairs. The expressions on the faces of her brothers and father said so much more. In fact, they almost appeared amused.

Shannon stepped forward to be even with the human wall the men in her family presented. "As I mentioned earlier, Mr. Berringer works for the Ford Motor Company and he is here to do some research."

"Research?" The bemused expression disappeared, replaced by a confused one. "What kind?"

"Sir," Jacob interjected, "if I may. As I told Miss Delaney this morning, I would like to document various details about the tractor itself, how it runs, its performance, and anything else related to it that might be worthwhile. I work around motorcars all week long. It would be nice to get a different perspective of a similar machine."

Shannon could have hugged Jacob in that moment. He appeared in every way to be completely detached from her and remained wholly businesslike in his mannerisms and speech. He didn't even look at her once. Under other circumstances, she might have been upset or wondered if something was wrong. At the moment, though, it was just what he needed to do in order to validate his objective. . .and give her time to figure out just what she wanted where their relationship was concerned. It seemed her family had already made up her mind for her, but she wanted to be sure.

Papa seemed to approve. "I don't see why not. In fact, I applaud you for wanting to branch out and learn more. By all means, come join us." He gestured with an inviting wave of his hand, telling Jacob to follow them. "Mr. Bennett is already at the fields and waiting for us by the tractor. We shouldn't make him stand there too long."

Jeremiah and Matthew hesitated a moment and gave Jacob a questioning glance. Jacob didn't look away or cower at all. He held their gazes until they decided to follow Papa toward the main field. As Jacob passed Shannon, though, he gave her a quick wink.

Maribeth nudged her in the ribs. "What was that all about?" she asked as soon as the men were out of earshot.

"What was what about?" Shannon feigned ignorance.

"That wink from Mr. Berringer." Maribeth planted her fists on her hips. "You know you can't deny it."

Shannon turned to look at her sister. The determination in her eyes and the firm set of her jaw said she wouldn't budge until she had her answer.

"And don't tell me it was nothing, because I know better." She grinned. "I've ridden a full wagon ride with the two of you, remember? It's time to confess. Is there more than just friendship between you two?"

Shannon gazed at Jacob's retreating back. There were many times she hoped for more and many times he indicated he might want the same. But right now, she couldn't say for certain.

"Maribeth, you've already said we have kept the men waiting long enough. Why don't we go to the field, and I'll answer your question later?"

Her sister huffed, her breath blowing the bangs on her forehead away from her face. "Well, all right." She pouted. "But only if you promise to tell me every single, teensy-weensy detail later. You can't leave anything out."

Shannon laughed. "Very well. I promise." She gave her sister a shove in the direction of the fields. "Let's go."

As she trailed behind Maribeth, Shannon caught sight of Mama moving away from the front steps and coming to join them. She could tell her mother had been listening to every word and observing the entire scene. She didn't have to say a word. She only had to raise one eyebrow as a slight grin tugged at the corners of her lips. Shannon looked away and back again twice before the two of them almost burst into giggles. She covered her mouth to prevent Maribeth from hearing. That conversation later would come soon enough. No need to make things worse by giving her sister more ammunition now.

Besides, they had a tractor to see.

Chapter 11

"M atthew, don't get too overanxious," Mr. Delaney said.

Shannon's brother walked toward the tractor with an eager gait and called back over his shoulder, "Mr. Bennett went over the operation and instructions this morning. And he cleared me to operate this on my own."

"Yes, I know," said Mr. Delaney. "But you still need to take it easy. You've never handled one of those machines before, so you need to be careful."

"Yes," the salesman added. "You've already purchased this model, and I'd prefer you be able to keep it, not suffer from damaged equipment right from the start."

Mr. Bennett seemed to prefer to remain in the background, only available for questions that might be asked. He'd presented all the important details. Now he stepped back to allow the Delaney family to test the machine.

Everyone had taken a close look at the tractor the minute they arrived at the field. Well, all of the men had, anyway. Shannon, her sister, and her mother remained clustered together a safe distance from the machine, content not to be that involved.

Jacob enjoyed looking over the various components piece by piece. So much resembled the engine of a Ford motorcar, but he also took note of the many differences.

All of Shannon's family stood off to the side of the partially plowed field, waiting and watching. Jacob had purposely chosen a place on the other side of the man he now knew as Jeremiah after a brief introduction. He needed to maintain his professional appearance, and to do that he needed to be away from Shannon. Less distraction that way.

Matthew hooked the plow onto the back of the tractor and jumped up onto the ledge behind the engine and carburetor, where he took hold of the steering wheel. He looked so proud and confident standing there, and his eager face was almost comical. Jacob knew exactly how he felt. He'd been there once, too, with the new prototypes of Model Ts at the Ford plant.

"I'll be all right, Father. Don't worry." Matthew reached down to start the engine. "Besides, Mr. Bennett also provided me with a booklet that has all his instructions in writing. He also told me I can enroll in a training course they've just recently developed to help get the most out of this newest addition to our farm."

Jacob had heard of that course. He leaned slightly toward Jeremiah. "Sounds like an excellent way to instruct new tractor owners on all the safety measures surrounding their newly acquired purchase."

Shannon's brother nodded. "I agree. Matthew told me about it earlier this week after he'd already made arrangements to have this tractor delivered. It also seems a perfect way to explain the various parts and what they do, plus how to best put it to use."

"Indeed it is, gentlemen," Mr. Bennett interjected. "That is the very reason we have created the course and revised the instruction booklet."

"Ford had similar pamphlets on the operation and components of their motorcars," Jacob added. "Sending them home with each new owner has helped reduce the number of questions that come back to the Follow-up Department in the form of correspondence."

The chugging of the tractor interrupted any further verbal exchange. All attention was again focused on the tractor and Matthew.

"Slow and steady, son," Papa advised. "Remember, we've never plowed this section of land before. We don't need to take any unnecessary risks right away."

"All right." Matthew waved at everyone. "Here goes," he called as he shifted the transmission.

The tractor appeared to lurch like the motion of a motorcar when it got started. Matthew held tightly to the steering wheel as he rode forward away from his family and Jacob.

Everything seemed to be going quite well. The tractor pulled the plow with ease, and the blades of the plow cut into the dirt without a hitch. Matthew had gone about sixty or seventy feet when he turned to look over his shoulder at everyone.

"I'm going to finish out the row," he shouted.

"Matthew, wait!" Mr. Delaney hollered. "There's a rock!"

There was no way Matthew could have heard his father over the noise of the engine. Jacob heard the collective gasps from the Delaney family and scanned the ground in front of the tractor.

All of a sudden, the tractor jumped as it struck the rock. Matthew lost his grip on the wheel and flailed his arms before falling forward against the engine area. He grabbed for the wheel again only to miss and get knocked off the back with another bump of the tractor. But he didn't fall straight to the ground. Instead, he hung off the back with one arm extended and his legs bouncing against the dirt between the tractor and the plow.

"Someone help!" Matthew called, his voice panicked.

"Dear God, be with us!" Mr. Delaney prayed aloud as he ran toward his son.

"It looks like he's caught somehow!" Jeremiah added, darting alongside.

Jacob took off in a sprint across the field. The immediate swish of skirts and additional footfalls sounded behind him, but he never broke his stride. His focus was the Delaney men. They might not have much experience with gasoline-powered equipment or machines, but he did. If they needed his help, he wanted to be there.

He actually outdistanced the two men and reached the tractor first. Jacob hesitated only a moment to get his footing before grabbing hold of the left side and vaulting himself to the platform. He went straight for the crankcase and shut off the engine. The tractor stopped and Matthew banged against the rear wheel.

Mr. Delaney and Jeremiah hopped over the plow and flanked Matthew on either side. Jacob looked just to the left of the radiator where Matthew's sleeve had gotten caught on one of the bolts and his hand tangled in one of the hoses. Reaching down to free the fabric, he stopped when Matthew let out a pain-filled cry.

"Ahh! My wrist. My hand," he bellowed. "I think they might be broken. And it burns!"

Jacob looked around. Matthew's hand must have touched or rubbed against the carburetor long enough to get burned. That metal got hot very quickly, so Jacob wasn't surprised.

"Here, let's at least get you on your feet," Mr. Delaney said as he and Jeremiah lifted Matthew so he could stand behind the tractor and put his weight on his feet. "Now we'll see how badly you're hurt."

Jacob quickly loosed the sleeve of Matthew's shirt while his attention was diverted but grabbed his arm to keep it immobile. "All right, someone needs to hold his arm while I remove the hoses and untangle them from his hand."

"I've got it," Mr. Delaney stated. "Are you sure you know what you're doing?"

"I've been working on automobiles for several years now, Mr. Delaney," Jacob replied with authority. "I've seen my fair share of accidents and injuries. The components are arranged a little differently, but the basic framework is the same. Just thank God Matthew wasn't hurt worse."

He could've gotten upset at Shannon's father questioning his skills, but it was only natural. Jacob was almost a stranger, and this man wanted to see his children kept safe. He couldn't be faulted for that.

With the utmost care, Jacob disconnected one of the hoses and slowly removed it from around Matthew's wrist. After bringing the hose under Matthew's hand, he connected it again. There. Shannon's brother was free.

"Matthew, I'm going to hold your arm while you bring it back close to you."

Jeremiah yanked his bandanna off and held it out. "We can put his arm in this and make a temporary sling. Help keep it from moving. It's not all that big, but it will work for now."

"Perfect." Jacob scooted along the platform on his knees, closer to Matthew as the man drew his arm toward his body. "I'm sure I don't have to tell you not to jostle it," he said with a grin.

Matthew answered with a combination of a grimace and a smile. In no time at all, they had the bandanna around Matthew's arm and knotted behind his neck. His hand hung limp right at the edge of the material.

"Is everything all right?" Mrs. Delaney asked from only a few steps away.

Jacob hadn't even noticed them in all the activity, but at least they had only hovered nearby. They might have been in the way otherwise.

"The tractor did indeed run over this rather large rock here," Mr. Bennett spoke from the front of the tractor where he appeared to be examining the equipment.

In all the commotion, Jacob hadn't even thought about the salesman. He doubted anyone else had, either. They were all too focused on Matthew.

"The tractor doesn't appear to have sustained any damage," Mr. Bennett continued, looking at the men gathered with a mixture of both concern and reassurance on his face. "Will Mr. Delaney be all right?"

"Matthew will be fine," Mr. Delaney replied, answering both his wife and the salesman, his attention never wavering from his son.

"We should probably get him into the house and call the doctor," Jacob suggested.

"We don't have a telephone," Jeremiah replied, regret tingeing his voice.

"We had discussed it, but we never had one installed." Mr. Delaney looked guilty, as if not having one were somehow his fault. But that was ridiculous. No one could've known something like this would happen.

"Then I'll ride out for him myself." Jacob walked alongside the Delaney men as they all headed toward the three ladies waiting to hear what happened. Then another thought entered his mind. "Do any of your neighbors have a telephone? It might be faster if I can get to one of the farms and call from there."

"The Schooners do," Jeremiah answered. "They had one put in a few weeks ago."

"Great. I'll ride there and call the doctor."

Mr. Delaney nodded. "We'll get Matthew inside and up to his bedroom where he can rest."

Matthew took a deep breath and expelled it. "Is the tractor all right? Is anything broken?"

"It looked all right to me," Jacob replied. "And Mr. Bennett said there was no damage."

"I would think you'd be more concerned about your hand than a piece of machinery," Mr. Delaney scolded.

"But we paid a good chunk of money in order to have that tractor delivered here. If anything were to go wrong with it, we'd be out all that cash."

"Money can be replaced," Mr. Delaney stated with a hint of frustration in his voice. "You can't be."

Matthew hung his head. "I'm sorry, Father. I shouldn't have been so careless."

"Let's get back to the house, shall we?" Jeremiah suggested, nodding toward the three ladies standing nearby. "Ma, Shannon, and Maribeth are worried enough as it is. We shouldn't waste much more time. Let them have a chance to fuss over Matthew a bit."

"Oh great. Just what I need." Matthew grimaced. "Three women fretting and getting into a tizzy over me."

"Some men would love to trade places with you, little brother," Jeremiah teased. "You might want to enjoy it while it lasts."

"Good point." He grinned. "Let's get moving. Why are we still hanging around the tractor?"

As soon as they reached the women, Mrs. Delaney took control. She examined her son and directed her husband and Jeremiah to take Matthew inside. Just before she followed the men, she turned to face Jacob.

"Thank you, Mr. Berringer, for your help." She wiped her hands on the white apron tied across her front. "It's certainly not the first broken bone Matthew has had. But it might have been far worse if you hadn't been here." Turning to go, she paused and glanced over her shoulder. "Send the doctor upstairs as soon as he arrives."

He nodded. "I'll do that. And you're welcome."

"Come along, Maribeth," Mrs. Delaney called as she walked away.

Maribeth hesitated, glancing between Shannon and Jacob. When the young lady looked back at her sister, they shared a bit of silent communication. Maribeth gave one quick nod with her head and bounded off, her skirts flying behind her.

"What you did for my brother is greatly appreciated." Shannon spoke first, drawing Jacob's attention back to her. "But just like I feared, something *did* go wrong."

"Now, Miss Delaney, as I've said before, accidents happen all the time. You can't shy away from every form of advancement simply because you're afraid something might happen or someone might get hurt." He spread his arms wide. "Where is your faith if you live that way?"

Shannon bristled. "My faith is fine, Mr. Berringer. It's inventions like that tractor that are the problem, not my beliefs. If Matthew hadn't convinced my parents that bringing that machine here was a good idea, none of this ever would have happened."

Jacob wanted to stay there and prove her wrong, but he had a doctor to fetch. Maybe there would be time later to speak with her. For now, he had to leave.

"Miss Delaney, as much as I would love to continue talking about this, I told your parents I'd ride for the doctor."

Guilt flashed across her face. "Yes, Matthew needs him here as soon as possible," she agreed. "I'm sorry for causing any further delay."

"When I return, Miss Delaney, we'll discuss your misguided assumptions yet again," he said with a grin and a tip of his cap.

She opened her mouth to reply, but he did an about-face and headed for his buggy, not giving her a chance to say anything. A smile found its way to his lips as he took the reins in hand and set the horse in motion. Maybe when he returned, she would be in a better mood.

❧

An hour and a half later, the doctor arrived with Jacob leading the way. Jacob must have waited at the crossroads for the doctor instead of returning to the farm. Perhaps to give her family some time alone without him present? Shannon didn't know. She stood on the front porch watching the buggy and motorcar approach. When they stopped, the two men jumped out and headed for the porch.

Dr. Lodge! How had Jacob known to call the man who always made house calls for them? She didn't recall anyone mentioning their doctor's name. Maybe their neighbor told him. No matter. Matthew would just be glad to see someone familiar instead of a stranger treating him. It had been some time since he'd needed to come to the farm. She should have guessed he'd own one of those automobiles. It only made sense, considering the distances he traveled on his rounds.

"Good afternoon, Dr. Lodge," Shannon greeted, stepping onto the porch and holding the screen door open with a smile. "My brother is upstairs. I'm sure you know the way."

"Miss Delaney." The doctor removed his hat and tucked it under his arm as he clasped his medical bag with his other hand. "Yes, I remember. Thank you." With that, he disappeared inside.

Shannon let the door close with a *click*. From the corner of her eye, she watched Jacob's movements. He walked toward the east side of the porch. She turned to see him more fully. From all appearances, he looked quite relaxed, with his left ankle crossed over his right and his elbows resting on the railing. But he didn't say anything.

Did he expect her to start a conversation? She wasn't sure she could. She'd spent the entire time he'd been gone going over the accident and trying to come to terms with it. Jacob had said accidents could happen anywhere. And he was right. But that didn't mean they couldn't take certain strides to avoid them as much as possible. There was no sense being foolish and inviting accidents to occur when they might be prevented.

The silence continued, and Shannon grew uncomfortable. She chanced a look at Jacob only to find him with his eyes closed and his mouth moving.

335

Prayer. Now why hadn't she thought of that?

Before Jacob left for the doctor, he had challenged her in her faith. She had been insulted that he'd question her about it, but when it mattered most, she had failed to tap into that faith. Now he was doing the very thing she should have done right from the start. Once again, she tried to take it upon herself instead of seeking God's help. When would she learn she could never handle it alone?

Jacob certainly seemed to understand that concept, yet when the circumstances tried her the most, it eluded her. She glanced again at Jacob. There was a time a few years ago when prayer was the first thing she did, no matter what. Then she made the transition from child to adult and somehow decided she had to solve everything. It had caused her nothing but grief. Just looking at Jacob and his relaxed state made her wish she could have that peace again.

Jacob opened his eyes at that moment and caught her staring. A flush warmed her cheeks, and she averted her eyes. She glanced toward the porch roof and thought of Matthew. Any injury could cause a minor setback in their farming schedule, but a broken bone would be substantial.

"I'm sure your brother will be just fine, Shannon," Jacob finally spoke.

Shannon spun around and stared. Did he realize he'd just called her by her first name? She supposed she should be upset, but it actually sounded nice. The calm reflected on his face was either peace following his prayer or confidence in his decision to drop the formalities between them. Then again, it could be a little of both.

"Yes, I'm sure he will be, too." She attempted a miniscule smile. "As my mother said before, it's not the first broken bone he's had. And it likely won't be the last. Although we hope once he settles with a family, the injuries will diminish. He's always been the riskiest one of us."

"Then it makes sense why you were upset to learn he'd arranged to test out the new farm equipment."

Wait a minute. Was he agreeing with her? Before, he encouraged the idea of trying something new. Now he seemed to be recanting and instead sympathizing with her.

"I just had a feeling something bad would happen." She didn't want to make it sound like she wished the accident on Matthew, so she decided to explain. "Matthew has always been a bit impulsive, and unfortunately he's also plunged ahead at times without being fully informed."

Jacob pointed toward the fields. "Like today, you mean. When he mentioned the booklet he had but rushed ahead to put the tractor in high gear without being fully prepared for the jolt or the rock it hit."

"Exactly." Shannon walked past Jacob toward the far end of the porch and looked out toward the other fields with crops in various stages of growth. She leaned against the corner post and wrapped her right arm around its girth. "Had he planned ahead, he would have gone over the land to make sure it was ready for the plow and either removed the rocks himself or had Jeremiah or Father do it. Regardless, in his excitement, he was negligent, and it cost him."

"So it's really not the tractor at all that's the issue today," Jacob observed.

Shannon looked over her shoulder at him. "What do you mean?"

He pushed away from the railing and walked toward her, resuming a similar pose on her left. "Your anger and frustration is really directed at Matthew, and the tractor provided a ready excuse."

There he went again, trying to tell her what she was thinking and attempting to dissuade her from her aversion to progress.

"I don't believe it's the machines you detest," he continued before she could protest. "It's the reckless behavior of the few and the consequences of their actions that have you wanting the world to stop right where it is now." He folded his arms across his chest. "Because if nothing changed, you would feel safe and protected in the comfort of the familiar. You'd have no need to alter your habits in any way, and you could keep on doing the same things you've always done." He gave her a smug look. "Am I right?"

As much as she hated to admit it, he was. It infuriated her how often he seemed to hit the nail right on the head where she was concerned. She looked away again. "Yes, you're right," she mumbled.

"But Shannon, careless people will still be careless even if nothing new gets invented and there are no new temptations to get their minds whirling with ideas." Jacob unfolded his right arm and turned it toward her, palm up. "You said it yourself just a few minutes ago. Matthew has always been a bit of a risk taker. Do you honestly believe that will change even if he spends the rest of his life right here on this farm?"

Matthew? Give up being a thrill seeker? A small giggle escaped her lips. "Not likely."

"There, that's better. You're much prettier when you smile."

Shannon blushed again. The man could go from serious to flirtatious in no time at all. It was that innate charm at work again. He probably used it to help ease the blow of the truth behind the words he spoke. And it worked, too. She had a lot of trouble staying upset with him when he presented such an appealing persona.

"Mr. Berringer—"

"Call me Jacob. . .please," he interrupted, placing his right hand on his chest. "I'd like to think you and I are beyond calling each other by our last names. At least I hope you're comfortable with it."

His earnest gaze was nearly her undoing. He fairly pleaded with his hazel eyes, and Shannon felt a part of her melt at the sight. But was she ready for the intimacy that came from using his first name? She wouldn't know unless she tried.

"Very well. . .Jacob."

It wasn't as hard as she thought it might be. And in all honesty, it sounded just right. Now, where was she before he distracted her from her train of thought? Oh, right. The apology.

"I owe you an apology for getting too angry with you earlier, before you left to bring the doctor."

"There's no need—"

"Please," she cut him off. "Let me finish."

He silently nodded and encouraged her to continue.

"As I said, I need to apologize for my behavior. You are correct in saying my anger stems more from people's behaviors than it does from technology and progress." Shannon thought of the handful of new inventions Mother had pointed out to her several weeks ago. She had no problem with them. "While there are some aspects of technology and industry that I don't like, I can't deny that I do enjoy the conveniences that other aspects provide."

"Like a sewing machine and a pump that brings water into the house, no doubt," he said with confidence.

"Yes, to name a few." All right, it was time to be fully honest again. "But as I'm sure you're aware, my temper gets the better of me, and I end up making things out to be far worse than they really are."

"You? Have a temper?" A slow smile spread across his face. "I hadn't noticed."

"Now you're just being kind." Shannon looked away again.

She heard him shift then felt his fingers on her chin, gently turning her to face him and holding her gaze with his.

"Look, you are who you are," he began softly. "And there are some parts of you that aren't going to change. At least not easily, anyway. It's what you do with who you are that makes the difference. Someone like you?" He moved his hand to brush his fingers down her cheek. "Well, you're like a motorcar waiting to be put in gear so you can show what you're made of."

Shannon felt the sting of tears burn her eyes at his words. She blinked several times to clear them away, but she couldn't break the hold his gaze had on her. He started to lean toward her. When he licked his lips, she realized he wanted to kiss her. She also recognized the desire she had for his kiss. Her eyelids fluttered closed, and she held her breath in anticipation.

The screen door opened, its *creak* on the hinges and spring startling her and Jacob apart. The spell was broken.

"Dr. Lodge," Shannon croaked, then cleared her throat. "How is Matthew?"

"Miss Delaney," the doctor began, seemingly oblivious to what he'd interrupted. "Your brother will be just fine. I've put his wrist in a temporary brace and will be back later this evening to replace that with a cast. It might make farming a bit more difficult." He winked. "But perhaps it will gain him sympathy with the young ladies."

"Th–thank you, Dr. Lodge," Shannon managed to say around a surprisingly dry throat. "As always, you've come to Matthew's rescue."

Dr. Lodge raised his medical bag and gave it two solid pats. "All part of my job. Good thing I love what I do." Replacing his hat on his head, he dipped his chin. "Mr. Berringer, it was a pleasure to meet you. Miss Delaney, I'll see you again shortly."

As quickly as he'd appeared on the porch, he was gone, the chug of the engine leading his motorcar away from them and down the road.

Shannon watched him for several long moments, unsure of how to broach what had almost happened between her and Jacob. Thankfully, she didn't have to. He cleared his throat and drew her attention again.

"Well, I suppose I should be getting back home. I have to make a stop on my way, and I'd rather not enter the city in the dark, even if the gas lamps are lit."

She tried not to look disappointed, but she was. He appeared to feel the same. When she didn't say anything, Jacob reached for her hands.

"Will I see you next Saturday?"

The hope in his expression made it impossible to deny him. "Yes, of course," she replied.

"Good." He gave her hands a squeeze. "Until next week, then, Shannon."

In a move that surprised her, Jacob leaned forward and placed a soft kiss on her cheek. When he pulled back to look at her once more, his eyes had darkened, and she could see he wanted more. But he maintained control and instead backed away from her, only dropping her hands when the distance he placed between them forced him to let go.

"Have a good evening."

"You, too, Jacob," she echoed.

She followed his movements all the way back across the porch, down to his buggy, and even as he began his turn to drive away. He looked up at the porch and raised his free hand in farewell. Shannon responded in kind, already wishing for next Saturday to be here.

All of a sudden, the summer looked rather bright.

Chapter 12

J acob stood with Bryce and Kendall off to the side of the factory workers gathered for their monthly meeting. He had to admit, after his months of supervising, he was much more aware of the employees, the condition of the factory, and even areas where improvements could be made.

"Let me assure you, gentlemen," Mr. Hudson stated in a voice that calmed the rumblings among the crowd. "We here at Ford are doing everything we can to maintain our high standards of excellence in both production and employee satisfaction. We remain the highest-paying factory here in Detroit, and the cost of our automobiles cannot be beat."

Jacob could attest to that. He'd seen the prices on the other companies' motorcars, and he'd heard about the wages some of those employees received. Once again, he thanked God he worked for a company like Ford. It would be exciting to see where his employment took him.

"We also are forever improving our assembling processes and making other factories take notice." He looked at Jacob before continuing. "There are even some companies who are rethinking their expansion ideas in favor of revamping their factories to be more productive."

Was he referring to the company that had made the offer to the Delaney family? If so, that could mean great things for Shannon and her family. She hadn't mentioned the letters or any further requests for her family's land. Then again, they had been rather busy with Matthew's injury and still finding a way to continue farming with his temporary restrictions.

"And as a means of keeping all of you informed," Mr. Hudson went on, "the board of directors is in the process of exploring other options for wages and work hours. We're all hoping to regulate the workday, provide a more reliable wage, and improve conditions all around. But that's still a ways away." Mr. Hudson pulled out his pocket watch, flipped it open, and looked at it, then snapped it shut and returned it to his pocket. "If there are no other questions, I'm calling this meeting to a close in time for all of you to start your shifts."

Mumbles and a chorus of conversations sounded from the assembled workers as they dispersed to their stations. Jacob kept his eye on Mr. Hudson as the crowd thinned.

"You still have to speak to Mr. Hudson?" Kendall asked, placing a hand on Jacob's shoulder.

"Yes. He asked me to stay after the meeting, and he never said why."

"All right. We'll see you on the floor."

Jacob looked at Kendall and Bryce and nodded. "I probably won't be long."

His two friends left, and Jacob waited for a signal from Mr. Hudson to approach. He wanted to give the man a moment to shift gears. Mr. Hudson tucked his note cards into the inner pocket of his suit jacket then glanced up and caught Jacob's eye. With a beckoning wave, Mr. Hudson invited him to draw near.

"I see you remembered, Mr. Berringer."

It had only been a week since Mr. Hudson asked him. Did his manager really think he'd forget? "Of course, sir. Your request intrigued me."

Mr. Hudson pressed his lips into a thin line, looking distracted. "Good, good."

"Sir, is something the matter?"

"What?" He patted his pockets and checked both inside and out. "I seem to have misplaced a letter. . .oh wait, here it is." He withdrew a sealed envelope and handed it to Jacob with approval in his eyes. "This is for you, my boy. A copy of the same letter I gave to Mr. Ford and the board of directors to promote you onto the Research and Development team."

Jacob took the letter and held it in his hand as he stared at his name written neatly on the front. "A promotion, sir?" was all he could manage through his tight throat.

"I'd say you've earned it. You've gone above and beyond your duties here at the factory, and your ideas have been well received by everyone in management." Mr. Hudson clapped Jacob on the back. "You've got yourself a keen mind, son. And we don't want to see it go to waste."

Finally, Jacob made direct eye contact with Mr. Hudson. "Thank you, sir. I can't wait to tell Bryce and Kendall and my family."

"Ah yes. Those two friends of yours are under our scope as well. You keep some fine company, and I'm sure we'll be finding ways to help them as well before long."

"I agree." Jacob couldn't have asked for two better friends. He held up the envelope Mr. Hudson had given him. "They'll be happy to hear about this, sir."

Mr. Hudson draped an arm around Jacob's shoulder and leaned close. "Funny how things work out and I moved to Ford, only to become your manager." He shook his head. "I remember talking to your brother a number of years ago, right after he'd been hired by Edison. Your brother had secured a good job and was in a quandary over a certain young lady."

Annabelle. Jacob remembered the agony his sister-in-law put Willie through, but it was all for the best. She helped him be a better man.

"I'll tell you something similar to what I told him," Mr. Hudson continued. "I don't know for sure, but I'd bet my britches that the Miss Delaney you mentioned at dinner last week is quite important, too. With your upcoming promotion as well as the wage you'll be receiving, you're in an excellent position to make solid plans for the future." He held up a finger and wagged it in front of Jacob's face. "Don't be a fool. Act now."

Shannon's face immediately came to mind, and Jacob grinned. "You can count on it, sir."

"Excellent." Mr. Hudson steered Jacob toward the double doors leading to the main part of the machine shop. "Are we still set for dinner Thursday night? I believe your parents mentioned we'd be discussing the upcoming state fair in just a few weeks."

"As far as I know, the dinner is still planned."

"Wonderful." Mr. Hudson patted his stomach. "I look forward to the delicious meal I'm sure your mother will be preparing."

"Annabelle and William will be there as well."

"The more, the merrier."

They entered the machine shop, and several workers looked their way. Mr. Hudson became all business again as he turned to Jacob and extended his hand. Jacob clasped it in a firm handshake.

"Mr. Berringer, thank you again for all your hard work. We look forward to the good things in store."

Jacob gave a single nod. "It's my pleasure, sir."

They parted ways, and Jacob headed toward his station. He could hardly wait to tell Bryce and Kendall. Then he'd have to start making plans to tell Shannon. But it couldn't be anything plain or simple. He'd have to make it extra special. With the fair just a few weeks away, that might prove to be the perfect time and place.

ॐ

"I'm sure my bull will take first prize at the fair," Matthew boasted as he came through the back door, followed by Jeremiah.

Shannon looked up at her two brothers. Dr. Lodge had been by last week to cut the top portion of Matthew's cast off from the elbow almost to the wrist. He said the bones were healing nicely and if all went well the cast could be off in time for the fair. She thanked God again that his injury hadn't been worse. Of course, Jacob had a great deal to do with that, too. Her family owed him a lot.

"And what about my boar?" Jeremiah countered. "I've been grooming him and feeding him just right all year. It'd be great if we came home with two blue ribbons."

"Don't forget Mama's jellies and pies," Shannon added. She stood at the kitchen table where Mama was overseeing her mixing of the ingredients for a fresh cherry pie.

Jeremiah stuck his finger in the bowl with the filling for Mama's peach cobbler. "How could we forget?" He shoved his finger into his mouth as Mama grabbed a spoon. "Delicious!" he said with a grin.

Mama swatted his arm with the wooden spoon. "You go on and get out of this kitchen this instant. You know better than to stick your hands in what we're making before it's ready."

Matthew trailed behind Jeremiah and did the same thing, only Shannon's bowl became his target. She anticipated his move and yanked the bowl out of the way before her brother could reach it. Cast or no cast, he wasn't going to get away with anything.

"Hey!" The indignation on his face almost made Shannon laugh. "You used to let me sneak tastes all the time. What gives?"

"You heard Mama. Out of the kitchen." Shannon continued to hold the bowl away from him. "You'll have your chance to taste it when it's done. And not before."

"Boy, you're almost as bad as Ma now."

Shannon beamed. "Thank you. I consider that quite a compliment."

"Uh-oh," Jeremiah remarked from the doorway. "Looks like we've got two mothers now." He gave Matthew a look of warning. "Better listen to her, Matthew, or you might find your backside bruised along with your ego."

Matthew grumbled under his breath as he headed for the living room behind Jeremiah. Shannon giggled and shared a silent glance with her mother, who shook her head and rolled her eyes. Her brothers might be men, but they still acted like boys.

"Shannon, dear, would you do me a favor and call Maribeth in from the garden? I'd like to get her involved in this as well. She can work on the preserves."

"Of course." Shannon wiped her hands on her apron and poked her head out the back door. "Maribeth!"

"Yes?" came the somewhat muffled reply.

"Mama wants you to come inside and help with the pies and jellies and preserves."

"I'll be right there!"

Shannon returned to the kitchen and resumed her position by the table. "She's on her way." She took her spoon again and began mixing. "You know, I'm impressed with Maribeth for continuing her studies through the summer. She'll finish and graduate in early December, a full year and a half before I did."

"Yes, she's quite determined. Definitely takes after me," Mama added with a wink. "Your father would've rather gone fishing during the summer months than pick up a schoolbook."

"Where are your mother and sisters?" Papa's excited voice sounded from the living room.

Shannon and her mother exchanged curious glances as they tuned their ears toward the doorway.

"They're in the kitchen," came Jeremiah's reply.

"Rachel, Shannon, Maribeth! Come here. I've got excellent news for everyone!"

"What's all the commotion?" Maribeth asked from the doorway. "First Shannon tells me to come to the kitchen, and now you want us in the living room. What's going on?"

"Yes, Jonathan," Mama echoed. "Don't keep us in suspense. What news?"

Papa waited until everyone had gathered in the main room before continuing. He raised his arm to display a white envelope. "I hold in my hand a letter from the motor company."

Another letter? How in the world could that be good news? Every other time they'd sent something, it had been to make yet another offer in hopes of persuading them to sell. Papa's face reflected such joy, though. It was hard not to find his enthusiasm contagious. Shannon's heart leaped at the possibilities of what he might say. Had the company changed their mind?

"Jonathan, please."

Papa took a deep breath. "Seems they've rethought their original plans to build a second plant and are instead going to renovate their existing one. They've retracted their offer!" he said in a rush. "We won't be hearing from them again."

"Praise be to God!" Mama whispered as she raised her face and looked heavenward.

"All right!"

"That's great."

"Fantastic."

Everyone in her family rejoiced. Papa took three large steps and swung Mama around in his arms then set her on her feet. Maribeth came over and put her arm around Shannon's waist, and her brothers clapped each other on the back.

"I'm feeling quite well now," Papa announced, then looked down at Mama. "How about some of that venison in the ice house for dinner tonight?"

"Ma and Shannon are baking some delicious pies. Let's add those as well," Matthew suggested.

"Sounds good to me," Jeremiah sounded off with his stamp of approval.

Mama laughed, face flushed and partially out of breath but obviously happy. "That settles it, then." She looked at her husband. "Jonathan, you get the meat ready. Shannon and Maribeth, let's get started. We have a lot of work to do."

❧

Later that evening after supper, Shannon stepped out onto the porch for some fresh air. The feeling of relief remained throughout the afternoon and supper, and it continued as the men challenged each other to a few games of checkers. Maribeth even got involved in the fun.

Shannon could have stayed inside and cheered for her favorites, but she wanted a little time alone instead. Taking a seat on the swinging bench, she used her toe to kick it into motion, tucking her leg beneath her and letting the other one dangle. The crickets chirped, a handful of birds tweeted, and a soft breeze blew through the trees, rustling the leaves in a symphony of evening sounds. Dusk was her favorite time of day to reflect and just enjoy nature's melodies.

They didn't have to be bothered with any further communication from the car company, Matthew's arm was almost healed, the state fair was just a few weeks away, and before long it would be harvesting season. So why did she still feel a little melancholy?

She knew why. Jacob.

Ever since the day of Matthew's accident, they had grown closer and deepened their friendship. He had even hinted at the possibility of something more. What was holding him back?

The rumble of a motorcar broke the peaceful moment. Shannon looked down the road to see a shiny black model racing toward their house. Why was the person in such a hurry? She squinted in an attempt to make out the driver. As if her thoughts had conjured him into appearing before her eyes, she identified Jacob behind the wheel.

As always happened when she saw him, her chest tightened, and she inhaled sharply. Not able to sit and wait for him to stop, Shannon jumped up from the swing and nearly tumbled down the front steps. Jacob pulled into the yard and barely managed to stop the car before hopping out and rushing toward her.

He took her hands in his and smiled. "Shannon, I have some great news for you!"

"So do I!" She gave his hands a squeeze. "But you first."

"I just received a phone call from Mr. Hudson, my supervisor at work, and he told me the other car company has decided not to build that second factory out this way."

She nodded, excitement again bubbling up inside her. "Yes, Papa received a letter this afternoon from the company retracting their offer."

"Oh, so you know already." He looked a little dejected. "And I borrowed my father's car, then rushed all the way over here to tell you."

Shannon couldn't bear to see him even the slightest bit upset, so she gave him a wide smile. "But I'm glad you did."

"You are? Good. Because there was something else I wanted to discuss with you." He looked toward the house and quirked his mouth as he tipped his head in that direction. "Is there somewhere we can go where we won't be watched?"

Shannon turned her head just enough to see the front windows where the sheer curtains swayed and a few shadowy figures stood. Of course. Her family would have heard the motorcar too and come to investigate. They must have seen Jacob arrive but they must have decided to stay inside. Shannon made a mental note to thank them later.

"We could go into the barn," she suggested. "It's not as comfortable as the porch would be, but it's private."

"Perfect." He held on to just one hand and started pulling her toward the barn. "Let's go."

She stood firm and tugged her hand free. "Let me go inside and tell them where we're going first."

"All right."

She rushed up the front steps and opened the door just enough to poke her head inside. Ignoring the knowing grins, she kept a straight face. "Jacob and I are going to the barn. I'll be back shortly." And with that, she closed the door. Let them watch at the window if they wanted.

She joined Jacob again and walked with him toward the barn. Once inside, she took a seat on a crude bench near Papa's work area. There was just enough room for two on it, and she waited to see if Jacob would join her. When he did, her heartbeat increased and her breath came in short spurts. He turned his knees toward her and reached for her hands once more.

"I was going to tell you this a few weeks ago, but I wanted to wait until it was official."

Again, Shannon's mind raced with possibilities.

"After an employee meeting, Mr. Hudson pulled me aside and handed me a letter of recommendation that he'd sent to Mr. Ford and the directors."

"A recommendation?"

"For a promotion to the Research and Development team!"

Shannon pulled her hands free and covered her mouth. "Oh, Jacob. That's wonderful!" She lowered her hands to her lap. "You said you were waiting for it to become official. Does that mean you've received the promotion?"

Jacob grinned from ear to ear. "I have. And along with the news about the other car company, I knew I had to come and tell you right away."

"I'm so glad you did."

She leaned forward and gave him a quick hug, but his arms around her back prolonged the hug . When he released her and leaned back, she caught a glimpse of the restrained ardor in his eyes. He swallowed and took a deep breath as if to gain control of his emotions.

"I won't keep you much longer, and I certainly don't need your father or brothers coming out here to check up on you." He winked. "I bet that cast on your brother's hand would pack a mighty wallop."

Shannon giggled at the image that popped into her mind of her brothers intimidating Jacob. She was sure he could hold his own, but it would still make a comical sight.

"So, now that the best news is out," Jacob continued and cleared his throat, "you know the state fair will be here in a matter of weeks."

"Yes." She had hoped he'd come to ask her.

"I'd like to escort you there myself, if you would accompany me."

Shannon wanted to shout her acceptance, but she didn't want to appear too eager. Instead, she forced herself to offer a slow smile as she attempted to keep a tight rein on her breathing. "Of course, Jacob. I'd love to go with you."

"You would?" He looked like a little boy in a candy shop. A second later, he schooled his expression and appeared more mature. "I mean, that's great. I'll make sure you have a grand time."

A spark of boldness lit inside of Shannon. "If I'm with you, I know it will be grand."

Jacob leaned forward and placed a chaste kiss on her lips then backed away. She freed one of her hands and touched her lips with her fingers. As if he suddenly realized what he'd just done, consternation flashed across his face. Shannon couldn't believe he'd just kissed her. And from the looks of things, neither could he.

What should she do? Should she be upset with him for not asking? Should she reassure him? Or maybe she should throw all caution to the wind and return the kiss.

"Shannon, I'm sorry. I didn't mean. . .that is. . .I hadn't planned. . ."

She flipped her hand and put a stop to his rambling. He closed his mouth and waited, regarding her with tenderness in his eyes. Unable to speak around the lump in her throat, Shannon merely offered him a hesitant smile, hoping it would let him know she didn't mind.

It took a moment before his face showed he understood her silent communication. He recaptured her hands and this time brought them both to his lips. Gazing at her over the tops of her knuckles, he grinned.

"I should probably excuse myself and get back to my car. If I don't leave soon, I might be tempted to kiss you again." Standing, he drew Shannon up with him. "And that *would* bring your brothers after me, looking to skin me alive."

Finally able to find her voice, Shannon laughed. "I'm sure you could outrun them in your motorcar. They'd have to saddle the horses first."

Jacob chuckled. "Well, that gives me a slight advantage." He grew serious again. "Still, I'd rather not test my luck at this point. I need to stay on their good side."

Before Shannon could ask him what he meant by that remark, he took her hand and led her toward the large opening left by the two doors. After peeking out toward the house, he breathed a sigh of relief.

"Good, it appears as if they lost interest. Or they're hiding somewhere in the yard and will jump out when we least expect it."

Shannon gave his back a little shove with her free hand. "I'm sure they went back to their game of checkers. You have nothing to worry about. It's me who will receive the interrogation the moment I go back inside."

Jacob glanced over his shoulder and grimaced a little. "Yeah. I guess you would." He turned to look at the house then back at her. He swallowed and said hesitantly, "I could go with you, if you'd like."

She glanced toward the house and considered all that he was offering. "Are you certain you're ready for that?" Shannon wanted him to say yes with every fiber of her being.

"No time like the present. Besides, I should probably speak to your father and make my courting you official."

"Courting?" Were they? Everything about their relationship pointed to it. Shannon had just hesitated to put a name to it until Jacob made the first move. Now that he had, everything seemed to fall into place.

He shrugged, assuming that endearing boyish smile. "Well, yeah." She could almost see him scuffing his toe against the dirt. "Unless you don't want me to court you."

Not want him to court her? Was he daft? "Oh no. I'd like it more than anything in the world."

He breathed a sigh of relief. "Good." With another glance toward the house, he stepped outside of the barn and pulled her along with him. Stopping halfway between his motorcar and the porch, he turned toward her. "Before we go inside, I wanted to say I'm glad you were on the porch when I drove up. I'm ready to face your family now, but I don't know that I would have been before." He brushed a kiss across her knuckles.

"I'm glad I was there, too. It made the moment we shared that much more special."

"I couldn't have said it better myself." Jacob tucked her hand into the crook of his arm and led her to the front door. "Ready?"

"Ready as I'll ever be, Mr. Berringer," Shannon replied with a smile.

Together they stepped inside to face the other five most important people in her life.

Chapter 13

"Oh, everything is just wonderful!"

Shannon spun in a circle, holding tight to the ice cream cone Jacob had bought her lest it fall to the ground. She didn't want to lose even a tiny drop of the sweet treat. It had been ages since she'd enjoyed such a delight.

"I'm glad to see you're having such a good time, Shannon."

"I am, Jacob. I truly am." Tucking her arm through his, she resumed licking her cone. "I've been to the fairs before, but I can't remember when I've enjoyed one this much."

"I'd like to think I have something to do with that, but I don't want to assume anything."

The smile was evident in his voice, but Shannon turned to get a glimpse of it anyway. She wasn't disappointed. Accompanied with the tenderness in his eyes, it nearly made her melt in a puddle right then and there.

"The company does have a lot to do with it, but that only improves the day we've had."

"Yes, your family has done quite well in the competitions so far." He took a lick of his own ice cream cone and gestured, cone in hand, toward the livestock tents. "Just as they boasted they would, Matthew and Jeremiah both will be going home with blue ribbons." He chuckled. "And your father. I can't believe he entered—and won—the pitchfork and hay challenge."

"Pa always did have a competitive streak in him." She bit into her cone and swallowed, then giggled. "Of course, it helped that he and my brothers used to race to see who could pile the most hay the highest and the quickest. When they were done, they would jump into their piles, then roll down to the barn floor." Shannon shook her head. "Mother used to accuse them of acting like little boys, and they readily agreed."

"I have no doubt about that." Jacob finished his cone, pulled out his handkerchief to wipe his hand, and tucked the cloth back into his pocket. "Still, I wouldn't want to be on the other end of that pitchfork if your father was wielding it."

"If you behave yourself, you never will," she teased.

"I'll do my best." He gave her arm a squeeze. "Let's talk about your accomplishments today. I was impressed to see you win second in the pies competition."

"So was I." Finishing her cone, she started to lick her fingertips, when Jacob presented his handkerchief for her to use. "Thank you," she said and returned it to him a moment later. "As I was saying, I couldn't have been more surprised."

Jacob looked at her with a puzzled expression. "Why? I tasted some later. It was delicious."

Shannon shrugged. "Well, it was the first time I'd ever entered a pie. I would always do the jams and jellies. They're by far my best item."

"Maybe you've discovered a new skill at pie baking." He patted his stomach. "I know I wouldn't mind being a taste tester for you."

His antics made her laugh. She felt so comfortable with him, and he had such patience with her, even when she was being stubborn.

"I'm sure you wouldn't. But I still bow to my mother's superior baking skills. After all, she taught me everything I know."

"And it shows. She gets to add two more blue ribbons to that collection you said she's gathered over the years."

"Yes. She does have quite a few." Perhaps one day Shannon would be able to say the same. For now she was happy with her second-place ribbon. It was a start.

"You'll get there, too," Jacob assured her as if he'd read her mind.

Instead of answering, Shannon merely tucked her hand farther against Jacob's side. A comfortable silence lapsed between them. As they walked throughout the fairgrounds, meandering past the main stage and vendors hawking the appeal of their booths, they came to a few tents Shannon didn't remember seeing earlier.

"Where are we going?"

"You'll see," Jacob replied mysteriously.

So he knew—and it seemed he'd planned it. Curious, Shannon tried to peek through the gaps in the tent curtains, but she couldn't make out enough to determine what was inside. Then they rounded the corner, and the flaps at the back of the tent were pulled back to display everything in the showcase.

Shannon stopped dead in her tracks.

A wide array of quilts in so many different colors, patterns, and sizes hung on frames and were on display for all to see. Fairgoers walked up and down the makeshift aisles, inspecting the quilts and speaking to each other in low tones. Her eyes zeroed in on one of her own creations she'd given to Mr. Mulligan to sell. She turned to Jacob.

"You knew about this and didn't tell me?"

He gave her a sheepish grin. "Guilty as charged."

Shannon couldn't decide if she was upset that he'd gone behind her back or excited at the idea of so many more people seeing her work. More likely the latter.

"I know I should have asked you, but I thought a surprise would be better."

How could she fault him for that? "Are these for sale?"

He nodded. "They will be once the competition is over."

"My quilts." Shannon bit down on her lower lip. "In a competition with so many other skilled seamstresses."

Jacob wrapped his arm around her waist and pulled her close. "You're every bit as good as they, if not better. And it's time others knew it."

"Come on," she suddenly said. "Let's go look at something else."

He looked at her with eyebrows drawn. "You don't want to stay and wait for the results?"

She shook her head. "I wouldn't be able to bear it if I was standing right there when my quilt didn't win. We can come back and find out later."

"All right. If you wish."

They continued past a few more tents, and Shannon paused when she heard a man speaking loudly about some of the latest farming equipment. Curiosity made her take a step toward the opening in the tent.

"Don't tell me you're actually interested in machinery now." His tone belied his disbelief.

"Well, it couldn't hurt to learn more, could it?"

Ever since Matthew's accident and the way Jacob had jumped right in to save him, she'd begun to trust Jacob more and more. He obviously had her best interests at heart, so she couldn't help but give him the benefit of the doubt. She cautiously took a step closer and turned her ears toward one of the men discussing the safety and risks of the latest tractor. For several minutes, she paid attention to his presentation. Once it was done, she stood in silence and contemplated what she'd just heard.

"Makes sense, doesn't it?" Jacob said, interrupting her thoughts. "Your brother was a bit overeager in his desire to test out the new equipment. But just like any new machine, he should have taken more time to familiarize himself with it first. That way when the tractor hit the rock, he might have been better prepared to compensate."

"Yes, I know that now," she admitted. "But I doubt I would have been ready to hear that several weeks ago when it happened." She smiled up at him. "I have you to thank for that."

"Why don't we go sit on the bench over there and finish this conversation?"

"All right."

She sensed he had more to say and didn't want to be conspicuous while doing it. The bench provided enough privacy. When Jacob didn't say anything to start, she decided to take the lead.

"You know, I admit I have struggled with a few close-minded beliefs."

Jacob merely quirked one eyebrow at her and grinned.

"While I'm not willing to fully embrace everything about the gas-powered machines," she began, trying hard not to be affected by Jacob's obvious anticipation of what she might say, "I am open to the potential."

Clasping her hands in his, Jacob beamed a smile that melted her heart. "And that's all anyone can expect. Even me." He paused and grew serious. "In fact, I'll be happy to stay right here by your side to help you come around to the endless possibilities that exist."

"I'd like that."

Looking down at their intertwined fingers, Shannon warmed at the thought of a long-term relationship with Jacob. She couldn't have found a better man who understood her, tolerated her, and matched her, wit for wit, in so many ways. It was perfect.

Again, seemingly in tune with her thoughts, Jacob freed one of his hands and tipped up her chin with his crooked index finger. She raised her eyes to meet his, her throat constricting at the tenderness she saw reflected in their depths.

"I kissed you once without your permission. This time I want to do it right. May I kiss you, Miss Delaney?"

Not trusting her own voice, Shannon merely nodded. As his face drew nearer, her eyelids fluttered closed and she waited for the soft touch of his lips on hers. When it finally happened, she lost all rigidity and fell against him.

Jacob was the first to pull away, but he didn't go far. Instead, he leaned his forehead against hers and grinned. Sweet and full of love is how Shannon would describe the kiss.

"From now on, I promise to get your permission before kissing you again."

Licking her lips and swallowing twice, Shannon found some semblance of her voice. "I think that sounds like an excellent idea," she half whispered.

With a kiss to her nose, Jacob shifted and placed his arm around her shoulders, drawing her close. Shannon snuggled into his embrace. They might have had a rocky start to their relationship, but they'd managed to smooth it out a bit as they went along. That was what she'd call progress. And with God's help, even when the pattern of their lives got a little tangled, they'd find the smooth spots again. She might not know what the future held, but one thing she knew for sure.

Jacob definitely factored into hers.

God had truly blessed them both.